Published by Luvbutton Press, Cambridge, England

a division of Luvbutton Ltd

1st "village" edition - October 2019

Illustrated by Dawn Larder

The cover picture is an early 20th century postcard of the Lorna Doone coach descending Porlock Hill, taken from an original photographic postcard by Alfred Vowles, photographer, Porlock, shown above. The cover version is hand coloured from the original by G.H. If you look carefully you can see the skid under the back wheel which stops the carriage running away down the hill.

Acknowledgements

Firstly, to “Mr Porlock” himself, Dennis Corner, who raked over his superb memory of the pre-war village to provide me with the accurate historical and geographical context for the setting of the book. I did my best to take notes of what he said, and his help was invaluable, but I am sure I will have made mistakes with some aspects of Porlock life over 100 years ago, and I apologise for any errors that you may spot. Here is Dennis sitting in Porlock library where he kindly allowed me to take a photo to put in the front of this book.

Also firstly, as I cannot separate the two, to my wonderful illustrator, Dawn Larder, who lovingly produced the drawings which you will see on the following pages, and which are so atmospheric and just the way I wanted them – my sincere thanks Dawn!

Spot-the-difference picture clues

This murder mystery is a mystery with a difference... a "spot-the-difference". Each pair of pictures gives you a clue to the story.

Many of the differences are easy to spot, some are less obvious, and others are quite tricky.

In all the pictures except one, the main clue is easy to pick out. The exception is in the picture of the car going up the hill where the clue is very small, but you can have fun trying to find it anyway and it won't spoil the story if you don't get it.

The number of differences to look for is printed with the pictures, and the answers are in the back of the book where the clues are highlighted.

Setting the Scene

The Hill

It is 1904 and we are in the age of horse power, but not motorised horsepower, for in 1904 the motor car is just a rudimentary cart on skinny wheels with a feeble engine.

We are at the foot of Porlock hill... Famed, feared even, across the whole of England...

Through reputation and popular exaggeration, Porlock hill is a precipice. In the minds of those who imagine it, to embark on a journey either up or down its rugged, wheel-scarred face would be at best foolhardy, at worst likely to end in injury or death. A visit to this part of North Somerset was often made as much in morbid fascination as it was from a desire to view the wondrous scenery. No trip would be complete without a glimpse of the monstrous hill, the first and steepest part of which winds 600 feet up the side of the cliff in just half a mile to the gorse and heather of the Exmoor moorland above. When the clatter of a carriage was heard, the spectators would gasp in expectation, each of them wondering how it could be dragged up the incline, even with the might of six sturdy horses at its head. Before the steepest part of the rise, all the gentlemen aboard were obliged to get out and walk.

If the load was particularly heavy that day, the coachman would suggest that ladies below the age of 40 might also like to disembark to save the poor horses the extra burden – this usually had the desired effect of emptying the carriage entirely of all women-folk except those who, through infirmity, were positively unable to climb to the top of the 1 in 4 gradient.

And then there was the descent...

Porlock - the Mystery of the Thirteen Steps

ONE

The "Lorna Doone"

"Hold on to your hats, ladies!... And don't forget those thighs! Keep 'em clenched tightly now... We're heading down!" Coachman Ned let slip a mischievous chuckle as he bellowed his advice.

"Aaahhhh!" shrieked Mrs Lillian Arnold, gripping her daughter's gloved hand for support. "Oh Clara... God help us!... Are we going to die?"

"No mother... Not if you stay calm."

Ta-raaan... Ta-ra-ra-raaaaaaaaaaaaah!" came the shrill blast from the guard's coach horn, startling the old lady, turning her face a shade of greenish white.

"I want to get off!" she moaned resignedly.

"Yes mother. Everyone on this coach wants you to get off, so they don't have to listen to the fuss you're making."

There was a clattering and grinding as the morning *Lorna Doone* coach commenced its descent of the treacherously steep drop down Porlock hill and into the village below.

Map of Porlock Hill circa 1900 showing the high part of the hill and the top quarry (bottom left), the tea rooms and bottom quarry (lower centre) and The Ship Inn (top right)

"Whoa... whoa..." Ned called out to his four brave nags at the head of the carriage. Smoke plumed and red sparks speared out from beneath the rear wheels of the coach, locked stationary in the metal skids which protested their rough and roasting passage down the cinder-strewn rutted roadway. "I hope none of you purr—chased a return ticket... This is a one-way trip to Armageddon!"

Wails of woe rose up from the unfamiliar travellers seated behind him who gripped onto anything they could grab, while the regulars ignored the coachman's teasing – they had heard it all too many times before. The first-timers felt the blood drain from their bodies and prayed. Mrs Arnold squeezed Clara's hand so hard the poor girl feared she would never recover its use.

"I want to get off!" wailed the anguished parent, while Clara grinned as she enjoyed the exciting ride, probably the most thrilling in all of England, especially when experienced from the open top of a four-in-hand coach.

Teddy and Jess at the head of the four pushed back as hard as they could, desperately fighting for some grip as their hooves tore into the friable red coloured shale surface of the steep road. Jasmine and Fred behind had the full weight bearing down upon them and were engaged in their own battle to stop the whole procession from running away.

And then... a terrible loud scraping *scraunchhhh* sound followed by a flurry of limbs scrabbling on the dust while the coach took a violent lurch to the right as they approached the first sharp bend. Poor Fred's front hoof had slipped and given way and instantly Ned roared "Steady now... Steady..." as he encouraged his steeds while the passengers all shrieked.

Herbie, one of the boys from the village, threw himself flat onto the floor and grabbed a seat leg. Poor Mrs Arnold, seeing the lad's theatrical move, at once knew she was going to die, and promptly threw herself down on top of him, squealing and bemoaning her fate to the heavens, fellow passengers and the flying birds above, as her skirts and bloomers blew like sails in the wind whipped up by the toppling carriage.

"Clara! I love you!" she screamed, as if for the last time, for such did it feel. "I shall soon see the Lord and tell him never to travel on this contraption! It is not a fit conveyance for any person, god, or deity!"

Herbie groaned from beneath Mrs Arnold's epic apparel – his favourite trick of dropping to the floor in mock fear so as to scare the newcomers on the journey had backfired – he had not expected one of his victims to leap on top of him, especially not one so amply attired to suffocate him!

As for poor Fred, there were several untoward things that could happen during the descent of Porlock hill by a coach and four, and the gravest of all was a "horse over". The poor beast would lose its footing and collapse, not only leaving the entire weight for the other three to try and hold, but also unbalancing the cavalcade to such an extent that the carriage slewed around, dragging more animals down whilst sliding sideways, often itself toppling, only coming to rest against a hedge or bush at the roadside.

"Whoa... whoa..." Ned called out again as the weight behind became ever more unstoppable, trying to fling them down the hill into oblivion while Fred stumbled, flailing fetlocks flurrying to find a footing on the loose powdery surface. But the horses hardly needed telling to "whoa" – they knew they were in a fight for their lives now. The passengers who could see what was happening at the front looked on in shock and terror, unable to draw breath, fearing being pitched headlong into the bush and scrub by the side of the road... or worse, directly onto the hard-packed shale surface of the roadway itself. Fred whinnied loudly, and all who heard it could sense the fear in that sound, for no one knew better than he the mortal danger they were in. As on all such occasions of unfolding peril, time seemed to slow to a crawl and every lunge and sway and shimmy from the horse's body was taking minutes from the lives of the onlookers, until suddenly, beyond a miracle, all was calm as the gallant horse sorted out his feet and placed himself firmly and defiantly on top of all four of them, his hooves steady now, in full contact with and firmly planted upon the steep and unforgiving surface of the track.

"Freddy my boy!" driver Ned called out in praise of his stout-hearted horse. If he was relieved at the pleasant outcome, his voice betrayed no sign of such a feeling. But inside he surely must have felt just a little rattled at the prospect of landing himself and his entrusted fellow travellers in a heap on the roadside.

"Hooray for Freddy!" cried out one of the mightily relieved members of the upper deck fellowship, bonded together now by shared adversity and survival. "Three cheers for Freddy! Hip Hip..."

Hooray! came the merry shout from all, even from the lips of Mrs Arnold, still in her tumbled down position as she began an attempt to raise herself and her weight from poor Herbie, crushed beneath her, flat as a banana skin.

"Hip Hip..." *Hooray!*

"Hip Hip..." *Hooray!*

"Help me up Clara, help me up," she ordered.

"Yes," came a faint voice from beneath a seat. "Please help her up Clara, for my sake... your mother is no light woman."

"Come mother." Clara held out her hand.

"What did he say?" queried her mother in an offended tone. "Did that young man just say what I thought he said?"

"Probably mother, although your hearing is a little faded nowadays. But I shouldn't take offence. It was a choice between him, or a conversation with the Lord which you had already pre-planned – I distinctly heard!"

"Yes. And when I do finally meet him I still intend to raise the subject. This is not a fit conveyance for any living soul." She turned to the object on the floor beneath her. "And as for you young man, you should exhibit more kindly manners to a lady who is your older and wiser..."

"...And heavier," continued Herbie, completing her list of attributes with an unrepentant flourish.

Ned gave a gentle "Cummon" and they set off slowly to complete the rest of the trip, the horses doing their job and holding a good wide line to the left of the road on the sharp right hairpin before last and steepest part of the descent, finishing with the final sharp bend to the left after which the slope lessened for the run down to The Ship Inn at the bottom, with its welcoming stables for the horses and refreshments for the travellers.

As they arrived, the guard blew a merry peel on his coach-horn as Ned pulled on the reins to call the ensemble to a halt.

"Get me down Clara. I need something from the hostelry to calm my nerves."

"You shouldn't have ridden on top, mother. I told you to take a seat inside the coach."

"Oh. And you think I was going to let you ride outside on your own do you? A young girl on her own... What kind of mother do you think I am?"

"Overly protective I would say. I would have been perfectly fine on top by myself... I wanted to see the view which Harriet had told me about, and which was indeed spectacular."

"Well I don't know how you can say that. It was most taxing and quite the worst journey I have ever undertaken. I never saw any of this *view* you mention, and certainly nothing which could make me wish to repeat such a dreadful experience."

"You didn't see the view, mother, because you spent most of the trip on the floor on top of poor..." Clara looked at the lad, realising she didn't know his name.

"Herbie, Miss."

"Poor Herbie here. Look at him... He is quite dishevelled from your antics. You should know better at your age."

"Oh it's quite all right, Miss. I was very glad to be of assistance to your mother... She really thought that she was going to die you know." Herbie played the gallant young saviour, not wishing to let on that he had done it on purpose to frighten the old lady.

Mrs Arnold looked at the boy.

"Yes. Thank you young man. I *did* think I was going to die – and little comfort did I get from my own daughter." She looked sternly at her offspring. "Come Clara... Get me down and lead me inside this Inn where I can take advantage of a tonic – I am in much need of revivement."

Clara sniggered. "Come then mother... take my hand... but be careful not to squeeze so hard this time. I think it is my poor little hand that is in most need of "revivement", as you so quaintly put it!"

"Brandy! I need brandy!"

"Yes mother. Brandy. How is it that I can never remember that brandy is the thing you most often need?" Clara teased her mother unashamedly as she escorted her flustered parent through the entrance to the old coaching inn.

Ned dismounted and walked to the rear of the coach. He urged his horses to nudge the carriage back a couple of feet so he could pull the skids out from under the wheels by tugging on the chains which held them in place... they were still smoking gently from the descent, the iron-work much too hot to touch. The blacksmiths in Minehead and Porlock were kept busy renewing these vital pieces of equipment which acted as the brakes for the carriage, each skid surviving only ten or fifteen trips down Porlock hill before being in need of fettling. He then went back up front to take a look at Freddy and see that he was all right. He patted his horse affectionately on the side of the neck, then checked out the leg that had given way, running his hands either side up and down the knee and squeezing the fetlock, which the horse didn't seem to mind.

"Dung!" Ned uttered loudly to no one in particular. "I reckon you slipped on a pile of dung back there on the hill, din't you boy?... You wait till I see that Francis – he's a-sposed to make sure it's a-cleared up afore a coach comes down!" And with that he patted the horse one more time and popped inside The Ship for a pint.

TWO

The "Red Deer"

Waiting patiently outside The Ship Inn was the *Red Deer* coach ready to ascend on its tortuous journey to Lynmouth and Lynton, four-in-hand but with a pair of "trace horses" hitched on in front to provide the extra power for the heave up onto the moor.

The "four" were in the charge of the coachman who held their reins along with his long whip in the right hand, hence the driver was also often referred to simply as "the whip". The leading pair, the extra muscle for the start of the journey, were detached at Whitstones, two miles along the road and eleven hundred feet up, high on the moor. They were then led gently back down for a feed and a rest before their next exertion. To carry out this task, one of the pair had a boy sitting atop its back, whose job it was to drive the two steeds ably up the rise, thence to return with them after their work was done. Of course, boys selected for this task were greatly honoured, and there was competition for the privilege; but the overriding factor in who was chosen was the lad's weight – a skinny boy would hardly be noticed by the horse beneath him, so the beast's full strength could be applied to the slog to the top. The boy employed on this day was Will Cooksley, fourteen years old, yet looking eleven or twelve at most. His grandfather William had also worked on the coaches, as had his father too.

With a gay *tarantara!....* from the guard's coach-horn, Tom the driver signalled he was ready for the off. Will gave a slight dig of his heels and the six-horsed procession drew easily away on the gentle slope outside The Ship, with full power from six fresh horses clip-clopping against the hard-packed shale of the road.

The real climb started at the sharp right turn in front of the tea rooms where all who were gathered for refreshment had eyes only for the excitement and sounds of six sturdy beasts taking on the challenge of the hill, the coach slowly trundling behind, followed by the trailing trudge of its human cargo making their own difficult progress up the 1 in 4 slope, the children easily keeping pace right next to the carriage, while the adults plodded behind, thinly spread out according to their vigour and infirmity.

Will, seated on his grandstand perch at the front of the procession, gently encouraged Pug and Delia, while with every step the sound of the giant breaths from the four behind him grew louder like a Great Western steam engine starting away up the grade from Stogumber station. Every so often a hoof would slip and there was a clatter as the horse regained its footing, always managing to do so it seemed, for experience in a horse counted for everything, and each was shod and maintained by the farrier with meticulous care.

"Cerrrmmm on... Cerrrmmm on..." came the encouraging cry from coachman Tom, barely audible to Will above the noise and rumble of the coach-wheels on the road and the hissing snorting beasts behind.

The long left-hand bend to the next hairpin was the hardest part of the climb. Then, there came the fearsome hairpin itself... The guard gave a cheery blast on the coach horn, making sure that any other vehicle descending unseen from above would be warned of their approach. The hairpin was always taken on the right side of the road, for the left was both sharper and steeper, and likely to topple the coach; it was therefore marked out with large stones placed several feet into the road to prevent any incursion too near the inside of the bend. Then came the long turn to the right which, while not as steep, demanded continuing effort from the tiring animals who were becoming more and more exhausted by this point, and up onto the moor where the gradient eased enough for the horses to rest briefly, foaming at the mouth and snorting like bellows, while the passengers climbed back on board.

The road to Whitstones was still another mile and a half of steady ascent, and by the time it was reached the animals were out of breath, their muzzles coated in lather foam from their panting, aerated spittle which hung in strings from their eyelashes, blown up their faces on the westerly headwind which, more often than not, whisked across the moor straight from the Atlantic ocean. Will dismounted. His first job was to clean up the mess – he kept a short length of iron from the hoop of a barrel hidden in the gorse. Using this, he scraped the thick froth from the panting horses' faces and mouths until they were presentable once more, then dried them off with a rag. He then helped the coachman undo the chains attaching the pilot horses' harness to the other four, then hitched the gear clear of the ground in readiness for their journey back down to The Ship.

The moor in early morning on a Spring day such as this was benign, almost affable. It was hard to imagine the Autumn evenings when the mist in patches obscured the gorse only inches in front of you, when it swirled around the ghostly stumpy trees, contorted in gnarly shapes according to the wind and weather prevailing in each of their growth seasons, until each uniquely writhen form presented a history of that sapling's struggle to thrive in this harsh landscape. In the dusk, the stunted forests looked like galleries of misshapen beings, bearing down, waiting to cackle madly, scaring boy and horse alike.

But today was not like that. The sky was clear, the heat from the early sun making the view of Wales appear to shimmer across the Bristol Channel from the north, seeming almost close enough to touch and yet, in truth, ten miles distant. The early frost was melted except in the most sheltered spots in shadow of trees and shrubs. It was without a care that Will set off with his charges, back the way he had come, his pockets stuffed with the coins offered by the passengers as a customary tip "for the lad", the expression of their gratitude for guiding them safely up the hill. What could go wrong on a lovely day like this?

The Glimpse of White

Pug and Delia ambled around the gentle left hand bend which seems to go on forever where the hill steepens somewhat, just above the hairpin. On the left of the road was the wooded Cunnigar Plantation, thick with trees, but on the right the ground had been cleared to a scrubby coarse-grassed field, divided at right angles to the road by a low dry-stone wall which marked out a field, making it suitable for rough grazing. A flash of white caught Will's attention, huddled against the wall ten feet from the road, but hidden in the gully next to it and almost obscured by the low bushes. Just a sheep sheltering, thought Will, snug against the wall while gathering the rays from the freshly risen sun. But he had misgivings which made him continue to look at the object – it was just too white, too white for a sheep's fleece which is normally a dirty cream, a yellowy tinged tint, whereas this glimpse of white was pure, daylight white.

Will dismounted from his horse. The vision was just a sheet, he thought... That's what he hoped anyway... He waded into the thicker vegetation which separated the field from the road. The sheet was still mostly concealed until, there in front of him, presented the most dreadful picture he had seen in his life. Tresses of long dark hair spilled from the far end of what was now not a sheet, but a pure white dress, one small shiny shoe still attached and hanging on its foot beneath the hem, the other out of sight or missing. He stood still while feeling a surge of nausea flood from his stomach to his head, but without being actually sick. Then, dreading what he might find, he knelt beside the calm and resting figure, praying for a breath, a flicker, a touch of warmth on the skin. Her hands were in front of her face, towards the wall, her arms bent at the elbows flat to her chest, her shawl fallen slightly from her neck and down her back. The shawl... he thought it looked familiar. With the back of his hand Will touched the tiny part of her left cheek not covered by her brown locks. It was not warm. Even though he had expected this might be so, the realisation that she was cold made him shudder. He immediately tried to think positively: maybe she had just been lying there too long and the frost's early chill had not subsided from her exposed flesh? He tentatively slipped his hand up her left sleeve to determine if the arm was also cold. It was. He pressed her wrist. There was no pulse that he could detect. Her hair had fallen forward somewhat over her face, exposing her left ear in which a tiny jewelled earring glittered in the gathering sunlight. It looked brand new. The next thing, which he knew he had to do, was also the worst thing he would ever have to do. He didn't want to see what she looked like. He didn't want to gaze into a face that stared only at the ice upon the rough cast of a wall for a mirror. He didn't want to know who this girl was, yet unfortunately from her dress and shape and hair, he already knew. And that made his task much worse. He pulled the hair up over the ear, revealing the nose and mouth and upper cheek and eyes, then felt his head collapse involuntarily onto her left shoulder while he wept. Piteously wept, until his tears were almost run dry.

"Florrie... My dear Florrie... Why?" he felt himself saying, although whether the words were actually uttered, or they merely rushed around his head straight to his inner ear without trembling the outside air, no one, not even he, could ever know.

With painful effort he lifted his head and looked down upon her, a simple girl from the village, seventeen years old, a May Queen, and now in this month of May she was no more. Her eyes stared, as if from the depth of a lifeless pool. He could only think how he felt, and at that moment he could only feel in verse...

There was no doubt that she was beautiful
Her skin as white as the white dress she wore
Her hair emblazoned bright against her shawl
Her waist tiny beneath her pinafore

I took her hand... smooth skin... oh I was lost...
The feel of where her nails sprung from the tips
of fingers slender, grasping at the frost
sent shivers through me... then I touched her lips...

What was the last thing that between them passed?
What did those eyes behold that stare unclosed?
How did a cheek so soft end on the grass?
What brought her to this spot, her last repose?

This deed was done by hand or drug or knife.

He kissed her cold cheek and felt sick with himself, sick for doing so, sick that he could not retract that kiss even though no one else would ever know; but *he* would know, know until the time he came to join her, whenever that might come... And what would most likely be his dying thought?

A kiss is not a kiss without a life...

He closed her eyes with his fingertips – *erghhhh* how he shuddered as he felt her so-dainty lids, impossibly fragile and soft – then covered her face once more with her hair, and without more ado leapt to his horses and spurred them down the steep drop thence to the bottom of the hill and onward to The Ship Inn.

"Fetch Doctor Kingslake!" he shouted as he approached to anyone who might be in earshot. "Fetch Doctor Kingslake and Constable Greedy!"

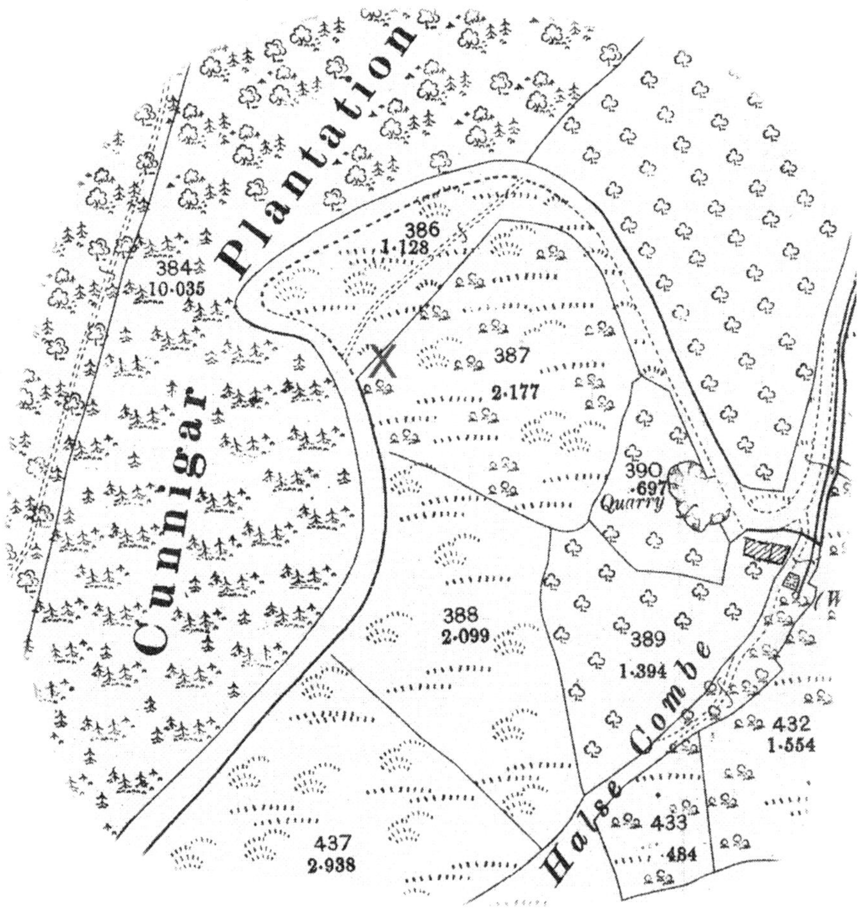

X marks the spot where Will found Florrie, next to the wall

The Doctor is Summoned

Doctor Kingslake was a bumbling fellow, dressed all in tweeds and plus-fours. He arrived at The Ship in his pony and trap with his black bag stowed safely by his side.

“Right young William, I’ve been told you’ve discovered a casualty on the hillside – please lead on and show me where he lies.”

“Yes, right away doctor... Where *she* lies...” Will mounted Delia who was now unharnessed from Pug and saddled ready for the journey back up the hill. They trotted along the first slight slope and then, on reaching the sharp rise, Will threw the doctor a rope which he hitched to one of the shafts of his trap so that Delia might help his pony pull him and his cart up the steeper part of the ascent. Half way up they passed Constable Greedy making his way to the scene on foot.

“Good day doctor.” Greedy touched the peak of his helmet in deference as he spoke, and the doctor similarly acknowledged the policeman with a tip of his hat. They rounded the hairpin and a little further on Will steered Delia to the left side of the road, pulling her up in the little passing place by the start of the footpath which leads across the hill back to the village, cutting off the detour which the road makes around the sharp corner. He hitched his horse to a tree while the doctor carefully applied the brakes on his cart and stepped down, carrying his bag.

“She’s just by the side of the wall here sir,” said Will as he retraced his steps through the scrub to where he had found Florrie twenty minutes earlier. The doctor followed, knelt beside the body and opened his bag to reach for his stethoscope.

“Is this just as you found her?” he asked.

“Yes sir,” Will replied. “I only moved her hair slightly so I could feel if her cheek was cold, and then lifted her hand to check for a pulse.”

“I take it you didn’t find one?”

“No sir.”

The doctor listened for a heartbeat. “No... There is none now. I’m afraid she has left us.”

Will felt the tears welling up again. “Do you know how she died, doctor Kingslake?”

At that moment Greedy arrived on the scene. “What’s the news then doctor?”

“Not good, Greedy, not good. I’m afraid she is quite dead.”

The constable paused before he spoke again. “And is it young Florrie Nichols?”

“Yes it is...” The doctor stood up, bowed and doffed his hat, holding it to his chest in his right hand. The others present did the same.

“Right,” spoke the doctor, breaking the bleak silence, “Help me get her up on my cart. I must take her back to the surgery and thence to the mortuary.”

Greedy then spoke. “Does she have any obvious injuries doctor?”

“All I can see thus far without disturbing her clothing in any way is that there is no blood anywhere around the body, or bled onto her dress – it would be easy to see as she is wearing white. But there is a contusion on the side of her head, as if she has fallen and hit it on something hard.”

“Like a wall, for example?” Greedy was interested to know.

“Yes possibly. But it could also have been caused by a blow from some other source. We cannot know until I have examined her properly, *post mortem*. Of course, the contusion may not have been the cause of death at all.”

The task of lifting her body and carrying it to the doctor’s pony-cart was a miserable one. Will hated the feel of her soft garments upon his hands, especially as they could not disguise the cold and stiffened body which they enclothed. The horses shied their faces away as the body passed by them, recognising death and not wanting to embrace it. Once installed on the rear of the doctor’s cart, Kingslake took a sheet from the stowage compartment and wrapped Florrie from head to toe so no part of her body nor hair was on view. Will detached Delia from the doctor’s pony, then watched as Kingslake beckoned Greedy up on to the driving seat whence they turned and set off back down the hill into the village. Will decided to go back to where Florrie had lain. It was an uncomfortable choice to make, but when he had first found Florrie, and when he had held Florrie’s lower legs when carrying her, he had noticed that she was only wearing one shoe, and he felt he must search for the missing one. He looked around for it, even probing through the undergrowth. It was not there. Will climbed back onto Delia and the three of them set off down the mournful road on their return journey to The Ship.

The Constable Would Like a Word

"I'd like a word, young Will." Greedy sounded stern. "Come with me to the police house – I need to take a statement from you."

They walked from The Ship, down and around the corner into the High Street. The Castle Hotel soon came into view on their right, and just past it, on the opposite side of the road was Doctor Kingslake's house and surgery where Florrie now lay, his pony and cart stationed outside. Onward past St Dubricius' Church and then around the left hand bend with the bakers on the corner, it was then a right turn into Lowerbourne, just opposite the Wesleyan chapel. The police house was set back from the main road, at the entrance to Lowerbourne Terrace, behind a row of shops and cottages.

The constable unlocked the door and ushered Will into the reception room. Will took careful note of the severe and unfamiliar surroundings, and all the objects that were there contained.

"Right." Greedy extracted his notebook slowly from his pocket, licked his pencil, then stared down at the lad from over his desk. Will felt most uncomfortable. "Mmmmm. When did you first notice the body?"

"When I was riding back from Whitstones sir. There was an unusual flash of white by the low wall separating the fields on the steepest part of the hill. I thought at first maybe a sheep had taken shelter, but her dress was much whiter than any sheep."

What things do you see in the picture?

Write six things down here – there are clues to help you.

1. ______________________________ (A room where you lock up a prisoner)

2. ______________________________ (Something you wear)

3. ______________________________ (Something you use)

4. ______________________________ (An animal)

5. ______________________________ (A light)

6. ______________________________ (A pair of ...)

The first letters spell out a clue to the story.

"Mmmmm. Could you say if it was already there when you drove up the hill earlier with the *Red Deer*?"

Will felt sickened when Greedy referred to her, Florrie, as "it". How could *she* suddenly become an "it"?

"I couldn't say, sir, because I didn't see her – she would have been hidden from view behind the wall on our way up – but I strongly believe she was there at that time as she was quite cold when I found her on the way down."

"Mmmmm." Greedy purred as he wrote slowly in his book. "Did you disturb the body at all after you found it?"

Will winced.

"I felt her cheek with the back of my hand – she was cold. I pressed my hand to her wrist – there was no pulse that I could feel. I slipped my hand up her arm beneath her sleeve to see if there was any warmth there – there was none. I then pulled her hair away from her face and realised that it was Florrie." He stared at Greedy, searching for compassion in the harsh features of a world-worn policeman. He knew he couldn't tell the PC that he had kissed her. He felt bad... he was withholding evidence, but there was no way he could confess to that. He regretted having done it even more now. "I felt sick then, so I covered her face once more and headed straight down to The Ship to get help and call the doctor. And yourself of course."

"Mmmmm." Greedy wrote for a long time, taking care to get down all the details that Will had described.

"Well lad," he eventually spoke after licking his pencil several times. "I will probably have to call you back after getting Doctor Kingslake's report when he's examined the body. I just need to know one more thing for now... Do you think she could have fallen from the *Lorna Doone* coach on its descent and hit her head fatally as she landed?"

Will thought about it for a few seconds.

"I don't think that is likely Mr Greedy. How could she fall without someone seeing? Or hearing her scream as she tumbled?"

"Mmmmm." Greedy repeated his favourite response. "I heard that one of the horses lost its footing on the way down and the carriage swayed to the right side. You found the body on the right side, did you not? She could have fallen during all the panic that was happening on board without anyone noticing."

"I don't think that is likely Mr Greedy, for we on the *Red Deer* set off immediately after the *Lorna Doone* arrived at The Ship. Surely, if what you are saying is what actually occurred, Florrie would still have been warm when I found her, don't you think?"

Greedy puzzled over the evidence in his head.

"Mmmmm," he said after a while, "You could be right – I shall ask the doctor for his opinion. Unfortunately, if what you say is true, that makes this a very bad matter... very bad indeed. I was rather hoping that it was an accident. You realise young Will, this means..." Greedy stared him down from a great height... "that you are now a suspect!"

Will gulped.

The Puzzle – 1

Will left the police house and was immediately aware of a new strange oppressive atmosphere that had overtaken the village. There were people in huddles outside doorways, discussing in low murmurs what might or might not have happened, shock and excitement seeping out from them like a low suffocating fog clinging to the ground. As Will walked along he became mindful that in every group he passed the murmuring stopped, and the many eyes within each group became one and stared at him. It was unnerving. It was as if they had heard Greedy's last pronouncement. Will couldn't help wondering: *do they all think it was me who did this terrible thing?* Thankfully, as he entered the main street he spotted his sister Harriet who seemed to be agitatedly looking out for him.

"Will, Will," she called as she hurriedly crossed the road. "I was just up at The Ship meeting Clara, my pen-friend from London. They were all gossiping in there about you. About what happened... They said you had been led off by the village bobby, so I came straight here to find you... What did you see? What did Greedy say?"

"Oh Hattie! Will heard himself wailing like a child as he embraced his sister, with his head on her shoulder he talked straight into her ear. "Oh Hattie, I found her, I found Florrie... And she was cold... Gone... Gone with the angels..."

"Oh goodness Will – how terrible. For you I mean, as well as her."

Will lifted his head and looked into Harriet's eyes.

"You knew her, Hattie – why would she have been on the hill? Was she on the *Lorna Doone*? Could she have fallen without anyone noticing? That's what Greedy asked... I don't think she could have. I don't think she did fall. I think it must have been..."

"Sssshh," she quickly consoled him... "Let's get out of here: everyone is staring at us."

"At me you mean... They're all wondering if I did it." He paused for a second. "They all *know* I did it..."

"Sssshh I said... Don't think such thoughts... It will only make things worse. Let's go to my shop and you can tell me exactly what you saw and then we can try and work things out."

Harriet looked around, noting all the people and feeling the weight of their unblinking gaze. She took Will's hand and they set off at a fast walk, passing the dairy and the bank, then speeding hell for leather until reaching the safety of Burgess's bakery next to the church. They burst through the door, startling old Mrs Huish on the way. Mr Burgess stopped serving his one customer and looked over the top of his half-moon spectacles to see what caused the commotion. "Ah Harriet... Why are you back so soon? You only just left... I thought you were meeting your pen-friend up at The Ship... What brings you here in such a fluster? I do hope your friend is all right!"

"Sorry Mr Burgess," Harriet greeted him urgently. "Yes I went to The Ship... Clara is perfectly fine, but I need to talk to Will in private. Please may we go through to the back for a minute? Everyone outside is staring at us."

Mr Burgess looked concerned. "Of course my dear. Off you go. You'd better take the rest of the day off, judging by that look on your face."

"Thank you Mr Burgess... that is most kind." Harriet pulled Will around the gap at the end of the counter where the till was and dragged him into the hot steaming sweet smells which flooded the room behind; this was the bakehouse where all the delicious bread and cakes were made. "Oh poor Florrie... What did Greedy ask you, Will? What did you tell him?"

"I just told him how I found her. He kept talking about her as "the body" and "it" rather than using her name. It was awful."

"He's a policeman. He sees a lot of death. They get immune to it. What does he think happened to her?"

"I don't know, but he didn't do a very good job... Look what I picked up at the spot where I found her after they had taken her away, poor soul."

"Will! You shouldn't have taken things from the scene! It's evidence. You need to take it to Mr Greedy!"

"I shall... In time... Don't fret Hattie."

Will carefully extracted a clean white handkerchief from his trouser pocket, neatly tied to make a little purse. He then loosened the knot.

"Hold up your pinafore Hattie so I can show you what I've found – we mustn't let any of them fall onto the floor or they may get lost amongst all the flour and sawdust."

Harriet lifted up her apron and held it out in front of her to make a soft white table onto which Will tipped the objects he had found from his hanky.

"We have a ha'penny," Will announced, pushing the coin nearer his sister so she could see.

"Yes – but it looks very old and dirty – that could have been lying there for years."

"Quite so..." Will continued, "And there is a snail shell..."

Harriet looked at him quizzically and with a certain disgust, as sisters often do when a brother produces something grotesque from his pocket.

"I'm not interested in a scruffy old empty snail shell... and I really don't want it on my clean pinafore – mother will give me a hiding if it gets dirty... Or, I may just tell her you did it – and then you know what will happen to you!"

Will flinched. "Please don't, Hattie."

"Father's belt!" she teased. Then, seeing his face aghast, she relented. "Oh I won't, silly..." Harriet paused and looked at some of the other things Will had brought along. "What is this silver charm? It is set with a beautiful blue stone; it's very pretty. Surely this must be much more important."

"Ah... Maybe... Or maybe not... Any one of these objects could be important, indeed any one of them could be the *most* important – even the poor empty snail shell. Sherlock Holmes always says never dismiss any evidence, no matter how trivial it might seem at the time, for it could later turn out to explain the whole riddle."

"Oh you silly... Sherlock Holmes isn't real! He's just a made-up character in a story!"

Will looked hurt. "Not real? How could you say that Harriet. He is more real to millions of people in the whole world than... than... than even God!"

Harriet looked shocked. "You wash your mouth out young Will, or I shall tell mother what you've just said!"

"But I'm right, Hattie. Sherlock Holmes solves crimes, finds the culprits and brings them to justice. When does God ever do that?"

"God saves us from our sins and gives us everlasting life..."

"Well he didn't save dear Florrie did he? Did he?" Will's eyes filled up at the thought.

"My goodness Will, you're crying... I thought you were just a typical heartless boy... I haven't seen you cry since you were five years old.

What is it Will? "This is different isn't it..." A look of recognition suddenly flashed across Harriet's face. She asked her next question slowly... "Were you carrying a torch for her?"

Will looked up at his sister through freshly running tears. "A torch?"

"Oh for goodness sake – were you in love with Florrie? *Carrying a torch* – that's what it means: a place in your heart all lit up for her and no one else... Did you have a crush on her?"

"Oh!..." Will was shocked and embarrassed, as he rightly would be, having been put on the spot by his sister about such a personal matter. "I don't know... She was..." He paused to find the right word, while Harriet waited, harbouring a mixture of surprise and amusement. "...Perfection."

"Gracious! That's strong Will... How weird it is to hear you talking like this. It's not how my little brother talks! It's not how any boy talks!"

"No, I suppose it's not. But honestly Hattie, I've never seen anyone, any *thing*, so beautiful, not a flower or a butterfly or a rainbow." He lowered his head and stared at the artefacts in Hattie's pinafore. "And now I never will see her, ever again." And the boy sobbed, washing the dirt from the ha'penny lying on Harriet's dress with the droplets of sadness which ran down his face then fell from his cheeks like dainty rain.

"In love, at your age. Really, I can't believe it..."

"But I wasn't in love, Hattie... or at least I didn't think I was... not until I found her... you know... found her... there... by the side of that wall, on that hill... and there she lay... so beautiful she could have been going to her own wedding... but instead... instead..."

He fell to his knees sobbing. Then, looking up at Harriet, he picked up the silver charm and pressed it to his chest, sobbing some more, before uttering, "It's so unfair Hattie... So unfair... Who could have done this?"

"You don't think it was an accident? The village are all saying she fell off the carriage. That's where she was found... On the bend, next to the road."

"I don't know... I just don't know... No one does – but I must find the truth, just like Sherlock Holmes would do. Will you help me Hattie? Will you be my Dr Watson for me? Please?"

She stared at him, disbelieving. “I haven’t got a revolver!” She then smiled and relented. “All right, I’ll try my best. But don’t you go talking about God like that again – it upsets me – and if mother or father hears you talking like that you’ll get a leathering you’ll not forget – just remember that!”

“Thank you Hattie, thank you.” Will wiped his eyes on his shirt cuff, then put his hand into his other pocket. “There’s something else I haven’t shown you...”

Hattie looked at the object and was immediately revolted.

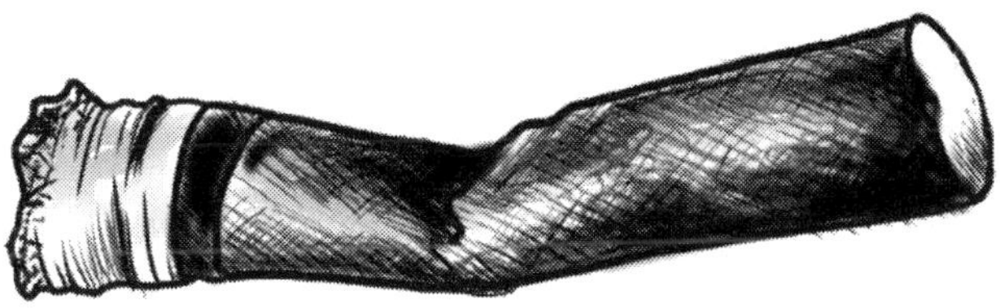

“Yeuk – that’s horrid – an old cigarette end – throw it away... And it stinks – you’re not putting that on my clothes or I really will get the belt from mother... I thought you were going to show me something else, the thing that is obviously missing... Maybe the police found it and took it with them.”

“Found what?”

“Her stuffed bear of course... Jack... She always carried it with her everywhere – you must have noticed surely? Florrie and her bear were inseparable!”

“Oh yes – now you say I do remember that she carried a small brown toy bear tucked in the pocket of her pinafore.”

“Yes – and I thought you were going to say you found it, but it looks like it was taken away. Was it with her when you found her? You must have noticed had it been there, surely?”

“I didn’t see it – I’m sure it wasn’t there. Unless it was hidden underneath her clothes.” Will thought for a second “You think Greedy may have taken it away then? I didn’t see him do so, and remember I was there first.”

“Precisely... It was either taken by the police... Or... By someone else! Someone nosy, like you for example.”

Will was offended. "I did not go rifling through her things while she was lying there Hattie, that would be a terrible thing to do!"

By the police then... Or..." Harriet paused, not bearing to think about what she was about to say. "Or, by someone who did her harm."

"My gosh!" Will pondered what his sister had just said. "We'll have to ask Constable Greedy if he or the doctor found the bear... Of course," he continued, sounding slightly relieved, "It could have been carried off by an animal – a dog or a fox or a badger or even a buzzard might easily have taken it."

"That doesn't sound likely to me."

"So Hattie, to proceed with our investigation we need to find out who she knew... who were her friends, her enemies, who she spent time with, and what she did with her life. Those are the most important things when solving a case. Finding someone with a motive to do her harm. And for that purpose, you yourself are the first and best witness... You must know quite a lot about her, she's only a year older than you are."

"Well, she works as a housemaid at Ashley Combe House. The owner is Lord Ralph King-Milbanke[1], grandson of Lord Byron the poet, but he's very old and hasn't been there for years, so it's rented out to Sir Cosmo Drake-Harrington. Florrie says he's very strict with the staff, but it's mainly the more senior ones who get the tongue-lashing from him. She has more trouble with his son, Rufus."

"In what way?"

"Put it like this – if Rufus walks into a room where Florrie is alone, she has to make an excuse and run for it, for if he catches up with her he pleads undying love, whilst making unwelcome advances directly upon her person!"

"Crikey!"

"Indeed, she finds it most uncomfortable. On one occasion he had her pinned down across the sideboard in a very compromising manner and her honour was only saved by the arrival of Frederick the groom who had heard the commotion and came upon the scene in the nick of time.

" 'Let her be, Rufus!' he commanded, 'Or I shall inform your father!'

" 'But I love the girl, Frederick... I mean her no harm, for she is the sweetest thing in the whole Shire of Somerset, I am sure of it!'

" 'She is a poor maidservant and you are misusing her gravely I fear, and if you continue like this I shall take my whip to you, and I care no heed whether you are the master's son or no... You shall not besmirch this girl and then discard her like one of your... playthings!'

"Apparently Rufus glared at his accuser, who after all was only a minion compared to himself, the master's son; but knowing that the groom had the very favourable ear of his father, he was aware of whose side Sir Cosmo would take in the matter and he therefore left the room without further protest. The groom asked Florrie if she was all right and suggested that she should take a couple of hours off to calm herself, whilst he would inform the housekeeper and the butler not only of his decision to give her leave, but also of what had occurred, although to be frank I think it was pretty common knowledge amongst the staff."

"You know all this in such detail, Hattie. How is that?"

"After the incident I have described, the poor thing ran to the village and I happened to be the first person of her age and acquaintance whom she bumped into. Shaking she was while I consoled her. It had been close, very close."

"But she still went back there?"

"Well yes... What choice did she have? A poor family needs all the bread it can get and what with her mother being a widow she couldn't just leave without another job to go to. But as it happened, the young master was a lot more courteous around her after that, knowing that the other staff were watching out for Florrie and that he was only one false step away from the horse-whip. Also, when he did talk to Florrie, usually to express his true and undying love, then she, in an attempt at forestalling his fervent attentions, informed him that she was to be married."

"And was that true?"

"I really don't know... I imagine it was just a ploy to distract Rufus and get him to turn his attentions elsewhere."

"Ah, but if he was that enraptured by the beautiful maid, her saying such a thing might have the opposite effect and rouse his temper?"

"Yes. That could be right."

"Poor Florrie. Well... We already have our suspect then, do we not? The young master Rufus appears to fit the bill."

"Ah, but remember what you told me just now about trivial evidence being important? The opposite also holds true: we mustn't jump to too obvious conclusions and assume we know the truth without considering all other possibilities."

"Well, let us do just that then... Who else did she associate with, or was close to?"

"She loved to arrange the flowers in the church. I know that she was so proud of how beautiful they looked, and then especially, come a Sunday, when the rector and the congregation admired them so. Of course, she didn't set out the displays all on her own."

"I thought it was all the old ladies of the village who did it?"

"They grow and pick the flowers and bring them along, and they do some of the arrangements, but the ones which are bigger or higher up require someone more youthful – so Florrie and John do those."

"John's the rector's son... yes?"

"Yes. They spend a lot of time together. In fact, I am pretty sure they are very close."

"Ooooh – do you you mean...?"

"No, I don't mean like that. But I think they confided in one another, as one does when one spends a lot of time with someone... Oh the poor boy... He must be devastated by her loss... *Her* loss, *his* loss, *every one of us's* loss..." Harriet filled with tears and Will put his arm around her. "This is so terrible, Will. I don't think I can ever forget her kind and pretty..." At that, before she could finish her sentence, she broke into proper sobs.

"We must find who did this, Hattie, for our sakes as well as hers."

"And her mother's..."

PAAAAARP...

PAAAAARP... PAAAAARP... BANG!

PAAAAARP... BUP BUP BANG!

"What on Earth is that!"

Harriet rushed out into the front of the shop closely followed by her brother. The few customers inside were cowering by the counter, too scared to go to the window. The two youngsters got to the glazed door and opened it just in time to see and hear the commotion outside as a lot of children and dogs rushed past on the High Street, cheering and shouting and barking in excitement.

“It’s The Scamps!” cried Will. “It’s The Scamps, and they’ve found a motor car!”

SEVEN

The Scamps

“My goodness!” Harriet looked out of the doorway while Will rushed past her. “Who could it be with a... motor car?”

Herbie, at seven one of the older Scamps*, looked across and shouted to Will and Hattie, “It’s Sir George... Sir George[2]...! He’s going to drive his motor car up the hill! Come on – we’re going to give him a push! SCAMPS TO THE RESCUE!”

By this time Will was already running along next to the procession, all laughing and screaming in fun while the bearded and well-dressed driver was grinning all over his face, encouraging them on.

“We shall tackle the hill!” he boomed in his deep northern accent. “Come on everyone, let’s see if this old girl will make it. She’s French you know, so a bit temperamental, which means she’ll need a bit of help!”

At which the car back-fired once more with an almighty BANG and Sir George gave two extra loud toots on the brightly polished brass bulb-horn, shattering the peace of the little village and shaking its sombre mood.

At the rear, toddling along as fast as he could, little Arthur, three, was directly behind the exhaust and, far from being scared of the bangs, seemed to be trying to catch up with them as the dense blue smoke swirled around his head.

“I... I... I’ve *weeeeeed* myself!” he screamed in his shrill little voice, rejoicing in the moment, not caring who heard.

---

*In the back of this book you will find an “Aide Memoire” which you can refer to, giving the names of all The Scamps and their ages.

And off the gathering proceeded, past The Castle Hotel…

…and onward to where the road took a sweep to the left before reaching The Ship Inn at foot of the hill proper.

"How do you make it go, Mister?" Dougie who was five wanted to know.

"I pull this lever here as far as it will go," chuckled Sir George, "Then I adjust this one until the engine sounds its best. And of course we must have the old girl, or should I say, *mischievous Mademoiselle*, in low gear."

"What's a gear, Sir George?" asked Charlie, who was six and one of the middle Scamps.

"It's some cog or other that makes the engine turn the wheels round, like the trains on my railway[3]. But they are steam. This new sort of engine runs on motor spirit."

"Oooooh – has it got a ghost inside. Is that what makes it go?" Dougie looked on in awe, thinking what a marvellous thing that would be: to have your own ghost pushing you along. "Does it go fast?"

"Hahaha!" Sir George guffawed at the thought. "The ghost which propels this machine is a little on the sluggish side I fear…" Right; we shall pull in at The Ship and check there are no coaches due to come down, for we don't want to meet anything on the way. Then we shall engage low gear as I said and 'Tally Ho!' we shall blast our way to the top and onward to Lynmouth. There's a thruppenny bit[4] in it for every one of you who shall assist me in this endeavour – the first motor carriage to surmount Porlock Hill!"

And off they went. The car's engine rattled away, intermittently banging and popping as if in joy and expectation of the challenge to come. Sir George pushed the lever to engage the clutch, then fiddled the throttle to give revs to the spluttering inanimate beast whilst shouting, "Come on everyone, push... push like the devil! During the wait at the inn, little Arthur had been standing in the very middle of the back of the car's bodywork, making sure he kept his place and was in the very best position for the adventure. To ensure no one would try and steal him away from his prime spot, he continued to shout shrilly, "I... I... I've *weeeeeed* myself!" Charlie who was six and much taller, stood behind Arthur and, pressing just below the folded down hood which stuck out above the little chap's head like an umbrella, urged him to exert his greatest strengths by saying "Come on then Arthur – push your hardest – I'll look after you." The exhaust pipe banged and spluttered, sending its clouds of blue smoke billowing beside them into the clean still Spring air.

Around the first steep bend the ensemble went, with all the children shouting and whooping gleefully as the miracle of modern technology and invention scrabbled for grip with its narrow hard rubber tyres on the flaky red surface of the roadway. The dogs all barked and scampered around, wondering at the fuss but enjoying it immensely. Whenever they got in the way, Sir George would perform a hearty squeeze on the bulb of his car horn and the loud PARP would scare most of them away, while the children would shout "Scamper!!!" at Betsy's dog Scamper, who was the naughtiest, just like The Scamps themselves.

In all, there were the six Scamps: Betsy 7, Herbie 7, Charlie 6, Dougie 5, Fanny 5, Arthur 3, plus Scamper the dog, plus Will and Harriet, although Harriet held to the side so as not to risk the wrath of her mother by dirtying her white pinafore. The car's engine banged more than it vrooomed as it struggled on the steep section above the bottom bend, and flames started to appear out of the exhaust. Suddenly a shout went up:

"Charlie's trousers are on fire!" "Charlie's trousers are on fire!"

"Quick – pee on him!" bellowed Betsy. Then noticed the younger girl Scamp hoisting up her dress. "No, not you Fanny – you'll wet your knickers!"

"I don't care!" Fanny shouted.

"Let Herbie and Dougie do it..." Betsy responded.

"Too late!" Fanny retorted in pleasure and defiance, "I've done it..."

"I... I... I've..."

"Yes!" they all shouted, "We know you have Arthur!"

And the little fellow beamed in delight and said, "I've done it too!"

"Aaaagghhhhh!" screamed Charlie, seeing the charred cloth with steam rising from its burnt remains and the painful singe on his leg.

"Keep pushing!" bellowed Sir George, unaware of the drama caused by his exhaust, "We're coming to the steepest part now!"

The hairpin loomed ahead, a right-angle plus another half of that again to the left. The flames were still popping red and yellow flashes from the back of the motor car, and steam had started rising in plumes from the front.

"Look," squealed Dougie as he saw the white vapour billowing upwards in a mysterious shape, "I think the ghost wants to get out!"

"Don't worry, keep going!" Sir George seemed happy to flog his motorised pride and joy to bursting point, knowing he could always afford to buy another one. They pushed and heaved, so hard that Arthur missed his footing and fell, but Charlie scooped him up with one hand and placed him back in position, where he carried on shoving as hard as his little legs were able, grimacing and grinning away to himself in equal measure.

"Come on everyone – nearly there!" the giant northern voice rang out again.

B'BOOOM came two of the biggest flashes yet from the exhaust and the rattle from the front changed note to that of a pound of nails shaking in a tin. Bright orange sparks leapt behind them, while Charlie, careful to keep his singed trouser leg, now wet and extinguished, away from the exhaust, took his place further to the front, pushing by holding onto the top of the driver's door, at the same time tooting the horn with is spare hand, much to Sir George's amusement. PARP PARP. PARP PARP.

"Nearly there! Nearly there!" His voice could hardly be heard over the mechanical noise, backfires from the engine and shouts of excited children. Will thought maybe he should have offered Sir George a rope for a tow behind one of his horses, but knew in his heart that that would have been cheating, and besides, Pug and Delia would both have been terrified of the banging and crashing from the car, accompanying their painful progress up the cliff.

"Nearly there! Nearly there!"

"I... I..."

"Yes, we know you have Arthur!" they all shouted.

"I have too!" shouted Fanny.

"Yes, I know you have!" shouted Charlie.

Then WHOOOOSH... Something shot into the air from the front of the motor car and everyone was shrouded in steam like the thickest fog you ever saw, but scalding as the hottest Turkish bath.

There are 18 differences to spot in the two pictures of Sir George's car going up the hill on the following pages – (just count all the sparks and smoke as one difference). The clue to the story is very tiny, but it will not spoil the story if you cannot find it.

“There’s the ghost again!” shouted Dougie, with a tinge of fear in his voice. “I never realised how big and white ghosts were, just like in the picture books but BIGGER.” Then, in a low voice, “I can see its eyes – wooooooohhhhhhhh...”

“No matter,” cried Sir George, “We’re nearly there, we’re nearly there... BANG!... HISS!... CLONK!... We’re there!” Sir George pushed on his lever and all the banging and fireworks suddenly stopped, as if the life had been extinguished from his mechanical horse. Just the plume of steam hanging above them gave any visible sign of how hard the little French motor car had worked in getting this far. “We shall stop here now and fill her up – just a drop of water will do the trick – but first we need to find the lid that goes on the radiator.”

“There it is,” Fanny shrieked excitedly and went to pick it up.”

“N-o-o-o-o! don’t touch it!” boomed Sir George. “It’s very hot! We need to pour some cold water on it first to cool it down.”

“I’ll do it!” squealed Fanny.

“No, don’t do that again!” they all shouted.

How complicated these new-fangled contraptions are, thought Will. Just some oats and peas and barley and a good night’s sleep – and we three can get a whole coach-load to the top of this hill... But on the other hand, I can see this is a much more exciting way to travel.

Sir George pulled hard on a giant lever on the outside of the car.

“What does that one do, Mr?” asked Herbie.

“That’s the brake, my lad. It is supposed to stop the motor car from running away on the hill. But just in case it doesn’t, I have these wooden chocks to put under the wheels – perhaps you could do that for me?”

Herbie’s face lit up as he grinned in delight. “I’ll do it sir, definitely sir, thank you sir – just like you do on a hand-cart?”

“Yes, just like that. What is your name?”

“Herbie, sir.”

“Very good – carry on then Herbie.” Sir George watched while Herbie shoved the blocks in place good and hard behind the back tyres. “Now guard her like your life depends on it young lad, while I top up the water.”

Sir George heaved a large jerrycan from behind his driver’s seat, undid the lid and poured some over the radiator cap which was lying where it had fallen by the side of the road next to Fanny who watched intently.

"You can pick it up now," enthused Sir George, while he then went to the front of his brand new 1904 Renault motor car and opened a flap to get at the engine. The radiator was on the side sticking out of the flap when it was closed, but the filler was inside amongst all the plumbing and moving parts. Having filled her up, he replaced the cap which Fanny handed to him and chuckled in satisfaction. Will looked on. He couldn't help thinking of Florrie whom he had found just hours before at a spot very near to where they were now stopped. He decided he just had to tell Sir George and ask for his help.

"Excuse me sir."

"Yes, what is it young man?" Sir George expected a question about his motor car, so what came next was rather a shock.

"I found one of the girls from our village this morning. Here. Near this very spot, just by the wall down there behind us. And... she was... dead."

"Good Lord!" Sir George looked most shocked. "That is a terrible thing... I am most sorry... I didn't know, or I certainly should not have allowed all this noise and carry on so close to the poor girl's resting place. Do you know what happened?"

"That is the thing, sir. We at first thought she must have fallen from the *Lorna Doone*, for her only obvious injury was a bump on her head."

"Yes, that is quite feasible. Descending the hill is always a precarious affair and the coaches sway quite unbelievably – I have seen them myself."

"But I don't think she did die like that. If she had then she would still have been warm when I found her, for the *Lorna Doone* had only just descended."

"Mmm, yes quite so... So what do you think happened then?

"I don't know sir, and that is why I wanted to talk to you; because you know all about Sherlock Holmes, because you put him in your magazine, and I have read all his cases... And I intend to find out what happened to Florrie."

"Florrie... That was her name? Ah yes, Sherlock Holmes... He would certainly be the person to sort out who or what was responsible. Unfortunately, I do not have his ear, even though, as you rightly say, he appears in my magazine. But I can ask Sir Arthur[5], who is a very good friend of his, if he could have a word. Do you have any clues so far which I could pass on?"

"There is one big clue which we have – my sister knew Florrie quite well and she pointed it out."

"Are you able to tell me about it?"

"Florrie always carried a little stuffed bear with her, wherever she went."

"And?"

"The bear is missing."

"I see. Well I suppose if she fell it could have fallen somewhere away from her. But of course you, being a student of Sherlock Holmes, will already have searched for that."

"I just did sir, while we were waiting here for your motor car to cool down. I can find no trace of it."

"So in that case, my advice would be, if you find the bear, you solve the mystery! I am sure that is what Holmes would say." Sir George paused. "This teddy bear..."

"Teddy bear sir?" Will had never heard the expression before.

"Yes, that is what toy bears are popularly called now – apparently the name comes from Theodore Roosevelt, the American president – his nickname is Teddy and he refused to kill a bear, so they named the bear Teddy. And the name has spread as far as London and beyond. Now all the shops in the city have teddy bears for sale – they are quite the rage."

"I shall find Florrie's teddy bear then, sir. That is what I shall do."

"Yes. I shall consult Sir Arthur for you, but I think you are on the right lines leading to the solution of this terrible tragedy." Then, "Ahaaaa!" Sir George let out a big bellow of inspiration... He held out his big hand for Will to shake; he had obviously thought of something he found amusing. "And what is your name lad?"

"Will Cooksley, sir."

"Will Cooksley... Mmmmm... I have just thought of a good name for you in your quest to solve the mystery of what happened to poor Florrie." He looked down at Will's face with a twinkle in his eye. "How about... *Porlock Holmes*? That would be a very fine name for a young detective, don't you think?"

"Oh yes sir, Porlock Holmes. I shall definitely take that title willingly, especially as it came from you sir." Will looked downcast for a second, displaying second thoughts... "Only..." He looked up at Sir George again. "My sister will laugh at me and tease me."

"Hahaha... of course she will, Will, hahaha. She is your sister, and that is what sisters do..."

"Yes, that is certainly true sir."

"One more thing before I go, young Master Porlock: did you know that Sherlock Holmes is currently appearing on stage? In theatres all around the country no less?"

"No sir. Cor! I should love to meet him! My sister says he's not real! Can you believe that? You wait till I tell her he is real, and that you said so."

"Haha, well that's not quite what I said. But anyway, when you have solved this case, which I am sure you will do, I shall take you to the theatre wherever he is appearing and we shall see him together, and Doctor Watson too."

"Ohh – thank you sir, thank you!"

"And on stage you will see there is also a young lad who is playing the part of Billy the pageboy – his name is Charlie Chaplin... He is about the same age as you I would say. You should keep an ear out for his name, Will, he is quite a talent."

"Oh yes, I shall sir."

"However," Sir George continued, but in a more subdued tone, "There is one thing that I find positively irksome. On stage, Holmes' pipe is the wrong shape. Sidney[6] always pictured him with a straight pipe in *The Strand* magazine. In the theatre he has one of these curving droopy things." And Sir George reached into his motor car and produced a beautiful polished tobacco pipe made from a briar formed into a most curvaceous sweep. Sir George held it up for Will's inspection. "It doesn't look right for Holmes to me... I believe they call it a 'full-bent'. What do you think Will?"

"I think it's much nicer than our clay pipes that the men smoke in the village, sir. And some of the women too!"

"Really? Then you shall have it... Here you are... Now you will look like the real Porlock Holmes!" He laughed at what he had just said. "Well, obviously, because you *are* the real Porlock Holmes! Hahaha!" He presented the pipe to Will then glanced around at the assembled company who were all waiting on his word. “Come on then everyone. We shall start the engine and with one final push we shall breast the summit!”

A loud cheer rang out, the dogs all barked and yelped, while Sir George got back into the driving seat and rearranged his knobs and levers.

“Swing the starting handle young Porlock Holmes, then when she fires, it’s chocks away Master Herbie if you please!”

And off they all went, embarking on the last part of the climb up onto the moor, the steepest section now way behind them, as the children pushed and shoved Sir George in his pursuit of the first ever ascent of Porlock Hill in a motor carriage.

“Out of the way, Scamper!” they all shouted as the dogs sensed victory and rushed in frenzied circles around the car, banging and popping its way to Lynmouth where Sir George would have it put on one of the trucks[7] on his Cliff Railway which would haul it up to Lynton and his home on Hollerday Hill.

The Lagoon

They soon reached the point where the hill eases off, just around the bend near the quarry, opposite the point where the path of the Lime Way* rejoins the main road. Sir George stopped the motor car again and handed all the children their promised thruppences to spend, most likely on sweets in one of the village shops.

"Thank you everyone!" he bellowed. "We are kings..." He looked around at the smiling faces, noting the presence of the girls, before continuing, "...and queens, of the castle, every one of us. Please may I beg of you just one more push to get me going, then I shall bid you all farewell and much good luck, whatever the future holds."

Arthur, still in position at the rear, heaved on the car as best as his little body could, while its wheels kicked up stones and threw them high into the air as Sir George set off on the last leg of his journey. When he gathered speed, there came a sudden loud crunch as he clanged the cogs into the high gear which meant the car could go even faster, onward and upward to where the splendid bright yellow blooms of the moorland gorse awaited him with a perfect picture of loveliness.

"Another thing, young Will!" Sir George shouted over his shoulder as the car gathered speed. "I have something for you!" He reached down onto passenger seat and picked up what looked like a sheaf of papers. "Take this! It is a copy of this month's magazine, wherein is presented the latest Sherlock Holmes tale: *The Adventure of the Six Napoleons.*"

Will chased after the spluttering vehicle. Running with his full might, he had just about caught up when Sir George tossed the journal over his shoulder and into the air, and Will gleefully swept it up in his arms with a cry of, "Thank you sir, thank you!" echoing on the faint breeze as the 1904 Renault motor car left its usual trail of blue smoke in its noisy wake.

---

*The Lime Way is a footpath which runs to the top of the hill, starting a little way above The Ship and ending opposite the quarry on the top bend.

The children all waved until he disappeared, then skipped happily back the way they had come, eager to spend their bounty.

"Look," shouted Charlie, "I've got treasure. Yo ho ho me hearties!" and he imitated a pirate with a parrot on his shoulder.

"There's pirates down next to the lagoon," Fanny trilled. "I saw their ship this morning – it's definitely pirates – I drew a picture."

"Pirates! Really? Real pirates? – Yeeeeeeeee!" Charlie cheered.

Betsy sounded dubious. "Oh don't be so daft – there aren't any pirates any more – they're only in the story books. We've heard of smugglers, but they're not pirates."

"Are!"

"Aren't!"

"Are!"

"Aren't!"

"Oh shut up you two!" Herbie wanted to believe there were pirates in Porlock Bay. "Let's have a look at your drawing Fanny."

They all crowded round to examine the picture. Will and Harriet were especially interested to note what they saw.

"You see? I did this picture early on when the sun just got up."

"But I can see the bay from here." Betsy pointed out to sea. "There's no ship there now."

"No, it's gone now," said Fanny matter-of-factly. "They can't hang around because they're pirates! They'll get spotted by the coast guard."

"Ohhh what a swiz!" complained Herbie bitterly.

There are 18 differences to spot in the two pictures of the lagoon on the following pages.

"Did you see which way they went?" Will asked, obviously keen to find out in his new role as Porlock Holmes.

"Back around Gore Point."

"That's towards Ashley Combe!" That is most interesting is it not Hattie... I mean, 'Watson'?"

Harriet gave him one of her sisterly glares.

"Let's get into town and spend our thruppences," whooped Dougie. "I'm getting a penn'orth of bullseyes and a giant gobstopper!"

"Yeeeeaaaaaahhhhhhh!" went up the cheer.

"Sh... Sh... Sherbet dab for me," chortled Arthur... a "J... J... Giant sherbet dab!" and The Scamps rushed off down the hill with Scamper and his friends by their sides, whooping and woofing.

Will and Harriet followed slowly along behind, Will chewing on his Sherlock Holmes pipe.

"Let's have another proper look for Florrie's bear while we're here," Harriet suggested. "If she fell from the carriage it could be a long way away from where you found her."

"Yes, let's," said Will. "But you mind you don't rip your stockings on the thorns, or, as you are always saying, mother will be very angry."

"Don't worry, I'll just tell her you made me do it!"

"Oh Hattie! You are such a......"

The Puzzle – 2

“For goodness sake take that pipe out of your mouth – you look ridiculous!”

Will was sitting in the parlour chair at Tinkers Cottage, the Cooksleys’ home in Sparkhayes Lane.

“My dear Watson, I do not look ridiculous, I look thoughtful; as should a distinguished detective quietly engaged in his deductions... And Watson, please do me the kindness of calling me by my professional name, which is Holmes.”

“Oh really, this is just too ridiculous. I know I agreed to be your Watson, but I really didn’t think I was going to have to take a part in some juvenile play-act!”

“A play-act? My dear fellow, Sherlock Holmes himself is at this very moment appearing on stage in theatres all around the country, with Dr Watson too! Sir George told me that. I shall soon be meeting them... I am hopeful that we may discuss my deductions together.”

“Aaaaaggghhhhh! I keep telling you, dolt-head... There is *no* real Sherlock Holmes, or Watson, or anyone else... They are made-up stories, in a magazine!”

“Yes, in Sir George’s magazine. So Sir George knows that they are *real* stories about the *real* detective Sherlock Holmes, as told by his great friend Dr Watson.”

“Very well. I shall not argue any longer. But one day you will learn.” Harriet decided to guide her brother’s thoughts back to the matter in hand. “What have you ‘deduced’ then, so far? Has the wonder-detective worked out what happened to poor Florrie?”

Will jumped up from his chair. “Aha! I was hoping you were going to ask me that!” Let us examine the evidence we have so far: what do we have Watson?”

Harriet thought for a moment. “A silver charm, a dirty old ha’penny, and a missing bear.”

"Ah yes... the teddy bear... that will be most important."

"*Teddy* bear? Why so? His name is Jack!"

"Yes, his name is Jack, and Jack is a teddy bear... Sir George told me. It's the new name for a stuffed bear... all stuffed bears in fact."

Harriet looked sceptical.

"Well I don't think that name will last – it sounds rather silly to me – Jack Teddy Bear?"

"Sir George spends a lot of time in London and his magazines have all the latest gossip, so he knows all the most fashionable words for things, and I believe him. You never know, it may happen that one day a stuffed bear is simply called a 'teddy'."

"Mmm, we'll see."

"So, my dear Watson, what else do we have for evidence then?"

Harriet looked at him and wrinkled up her nose. "An dirty old snail shell – but that could have come from anywhere. And an even dirtier cigarette end – yeuk!"

"Quite so – the snail shell could have come from anywhere. And Sherlock Holmes has solved many cases by analysing cigarettes and cigars for the types of tobacco they contained – he has written several monographs on the subject."

"And what pray is a *monograph*?"

"Errr..." Will looked slightly shocked. "Ahh... I'm afraid I don't know the answer to that Hattie. Perhaps it is like school work. Where you study something. And then you have to write about it."

"I studied needlework, but I never wrote about it."

"I think if you did, it would be how you sew something. Whereas a monograph would more likely describe the needles than the needlework – such as different types and where they came from and when. Then, if you found a needle at the scene of a crime, you would note its singular attributes, find them in the monograph, and that would aid you in your deduction."

"*Singular* attributes – what sort of language is that?"

"Oh really Hattie... Dr Watson always uses the word 'singular' when talking about all of Sherlock Holmes' cases – it means they are very unusual."

"How can you have an unusual needle? They all look pretty much the same to me."

"Oh, I don't know... I was just using needles as an example. Anyway, what other singular things have we noticed about this case? I think you are missing one Watson."

Harriet thought for a moment as she went through all the details in her head, counting them out on her fingers. "Toy bear, silver charm, ha'penny, snail shell, cigarette... I can't think..."

"What else was missing from the scene?" Will was enjoying himself, playing the detective.

"Ah yes, I remember... the shoe! Florrie was only wearing one shoe!"

"Correct Watson! And I have already made some deductions based on that fact."

Harriet stared at her brother. "You're getting very pompous Will... You should be careful, or your friends will start to disown you..." She paused before twisting the knife. "If you have any friends, that is... So... What are these deductions you have made?"

"Later Hattie. I just need to prove them first. Holmes never divulges his secrets until the end."

"Oh goodness Will! This is so frustrating... I don't think I can play any more with you acting like this!"

"Very well, but you could try deducing for yourself. It is quite obvious really. Why should Florrie have lost a shoe?"

"Because it fell off of course."

"Quite so. And why would it fall off?"

Harriet pondered for a second. Because she was... running!" Harriet now sounded excited. "Yes... she was running... running away from something..."

"Or more likely some *one*..."

"Yes, so we should go and find her shoe then?"

Will looked at his sister, masterfully, as if in control of the whole adventure. "Exactly Watson. We shall search the hill!"

Harriet stared at him, but he didn't move. "Well come on then! Let's go!"

"First, there is something else we must look into. It concerns what you said earlier, about her situation at Ashley Combe, about her 'difficulties' with the young master Rufus. Ashley Combe may very well hold the key to this whole mystery."

Harriet looked worried. "But we can't go poking about in Ashley Combe – we are old enough now to be brought before the magistrates for trespass, or even poaching... you could be locked up and then you would lose your job piloting the coaches... and mother couldn't deal with the shame... and... Please don't go there Will..."

"It is true that we would be in danger. But remember we used to play in the disused tunnels that riddle the grounds like a warren when we were children? All we used to get was a telling off from old Groucher the gamekeeper and told to scarper."

"Yes, but not now we wouldn't – he might set the law onto us, and Greedy already suspects you of... of..." And Harriet started to sob again.

"Dear Harriet, don't be upset. I have a plan! *We* shall not search the tunnels and grounds of Ashley Combe ourselves. We shall get The Scamps to do it!"

"But what if they get caught?"

"Oh, I'm sure they won't... they play there all the time... they know exactly how to avoid old Groucher. In fact, I imagine they know where he is at any particular moment better than he does himself!"

"How can that be? They make such a noise wherever they go."

"True, but when the situation demands, they can be as stealthy as... as... Sherlock Holmes himself!"

Harriet rolled her eyes. "Oh don't start all that Sherlock Holmes stuff again – it really is getting tedious now.

Will grinned, but with difficulty as he was sucking on his pipe.

The Tunnels

“Come on Arthur. Stop throwing pebbles. You know that Will has sent us on a mission don’t you... isn’t that exciting?” Betsy encouraged the little man, kneeling down and holding his shoulders while she spoke, in the hope that he might pay attention. “We have to walk along the beach for a bit, round Gore Point, then climb up the steps and through the tunnels.”

“Woof!” barked Scamper impatiently, wanting to get going, jumping up and down and scattering gritty sand all over them.

“Scamper, stop that!” Betsy admonished the irritatingly energetic dog.

“Roooofffff!” shouted Scamper gruffly, standing on his hind legs and looking eager.

“I... I... I’ve got sand in my eye!” Arthur chuckled cheerfully, as if sand in his eye was actually quite fun.

“Let’s go – *roooooaaaaaarrrrrrrr*!” roared Dougie pretending to be a lion, and the others all joined in, trotting, running and leaping over the pebbles on the shingly beach of Porlock Weir, a tiny hamlet by the sea about a mile and a half west of Porlock village.

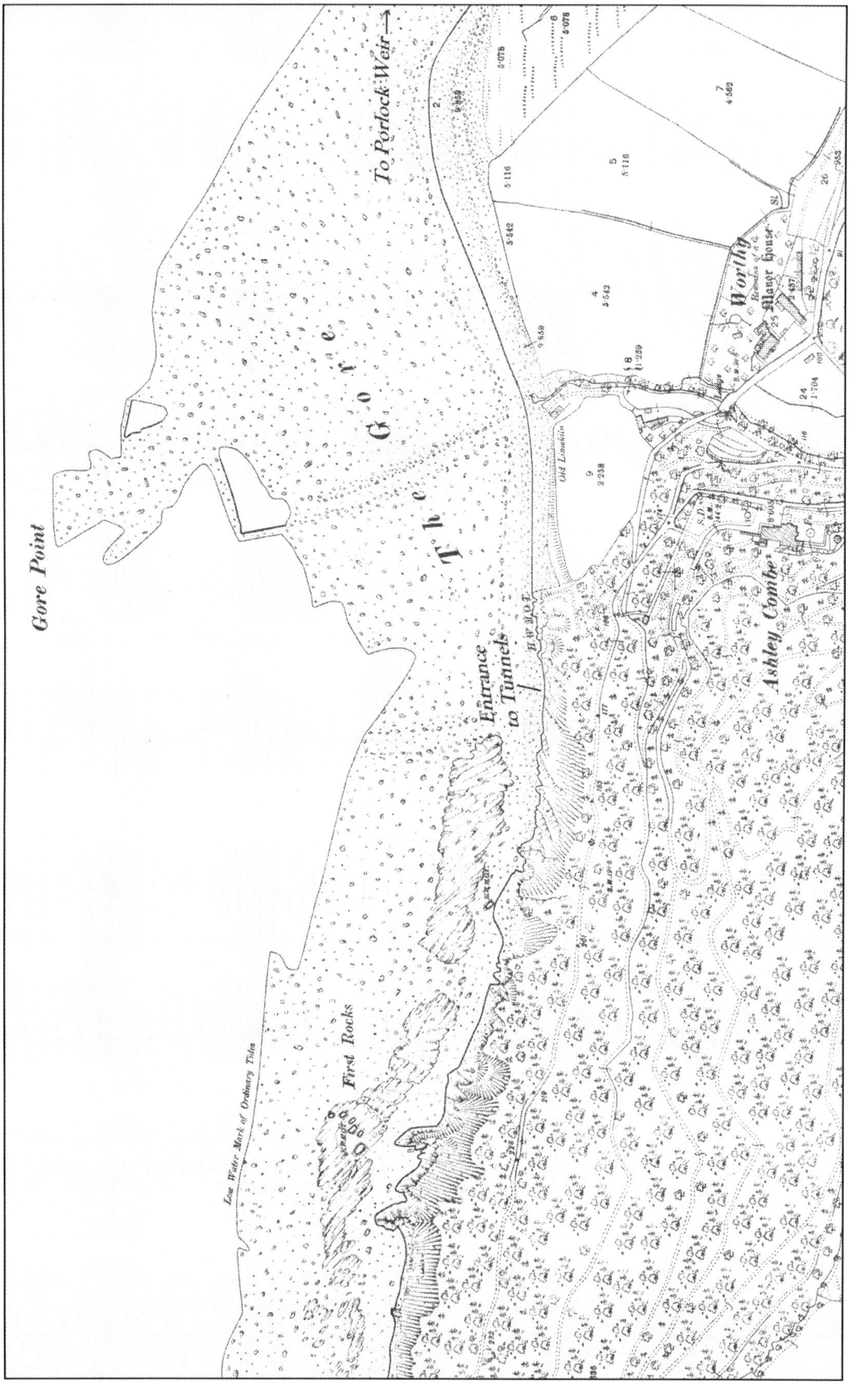
To Porlock Weir →
The Gore
Gore Point
Entrance to Tunnels
First Rocks
Low Water Mark of Ordinary Tides
Worthy
Manor House
Old Limekiln
Ashley Combe

They soon rounded the headland. The steps up to Ashley Combe from the beach were now in sight. These were the steps installed for the Countess of Lovelace, Ada King[8], so that she might privately visit the beach without being seen. They led up to a maze of tunnels, and all the secrets which they might contain. The Scamps had almost reached the steps when Arthur became agitated.

"I.. I... I see smoke!" he shrieked is his wee little high voice.

"Where?" Betsy asked urgently.

"O... O... Over there... on the rocks!" said the tiny chap excitedly.

"Quick! let's go and have a look!" And Herbie rushed off without waiting for the others. They hurried after him, heading towards First Rocks, the ones which guard Porlock Bay, where over the years many a ship had run aground in a storm, and the locals had rushed down to gather whatever plunder washed ashore from the stranded helpless vessel. Of course, nothing like that went on now in these civilised times at the beginning of the new twentieth century.

There are 20 differences to spot in the two pictures of the First Rocks on the following page.

"Right, come on, we've seen what's been going on here. Let's get back to the steps and up into the tunnels. And remember, keep quiet in there – we must look out for the miserable old Groucher and his even miserabler dog." Betsy ordered her companions along, because she was good at being bossy, and also the eldest.

"Rufffff!" went Scamper at the thought of Groucher's miserable dog. He owed him a few tattered bloody ears from their past encounters.

"I… I… I've…"

"Yes, we know you have Arthur!" shouted all the others as they crunched and scrunched across the loose stones, back the way they had come, to the foot of the steps that led up to the entrance to the tunnels and thence to the spooky old house with its terraces and hanging gardens and balconies.

Betsy hopped up the bottom two steps then turned round to address the others.

"Listen, we've got to speak quietly. I'll have my lantern lit and turned down low. If we hear anything we'll have to blow it out, then wait till the danger passes, or else we'll have to run back out again. Arthur can be at the front with me so he doesn't get lost. And he's got very good eyes for seeing in the dark, haven't you Arthur?"

The little boy beamed. "I… I… I've got a carrot!"

"Yes, and they make you see in the dark don't they Arthur... Now, follow me, and Scamper? Where is he? She turned round to look at the tunnel entrance behind her. Ah, there you are boy... You can sound the advance now."

"Arrorrrrr!" Scamper sounded the advance, but very quietly – (for a dog)."

"Good boy. Right, Scamper... if I make a 'ck...ck...ck...' sound then that means danger and you need to sound the retreat. And when you do that, you must go ahead of us and keep Groucher's miserable dog back until we are out of the tunnels, or in a safe hiding place."

"Arrerrrrkk." Scamper sounded less sure. He owed Groucher's miserable dog a scabbed leg and a broken tail as well as the chewed ear. What were the chances?

"Forward then. Come with me Arthur. And remember: keep quiet."

They climbed the steps and into the dark semi-circular maw which was the mouth of the tunnel. The darkness inside was absolute, and the lantern's faint glow didn't show much detail as they walked and stumbled. But generations of Porlock's children had come this way and, guided by their elders, the younger ones knew their way around all the different twists and turns, even in the almost pitch blackness. Every now and again, a skylight appeared, covered by a grating, which allowed in a few rays of light, although much of it was obscured by leaves which had fallen over the iron grid. The tiny light from the lantern cast huge shadows which moved fast back and forth over the walls as the flame flickered, like giant creatures. Scamper let out a little worried whine, and was immediately greeted by a chorus of 'sssshhhhhhhh' from the children which was much louder than the sound the dog himself had made.

They pressed on, enjoying the feeling of mild terror in the pits of their stomachs. There came a tiny little whisper from the front.

"I... I... I've..."

"Ssshhh Arthur, we know you have," the other Scamps whispered loudly from behind.

"N... N... No... I've seen a... b... b... b... bottle."

And the little fellow walked ahead a few paces while Betsy followed, holding the lantern up for him to see more clearly. In a very dark corner, beside a very dark rock, Arthur leant down and picked up what was indeed a bottle. "He-he-he," he chuckled whisperingly, and handed it to Herbie who was now right next to him. He then reached down and picked up another bottle and handed that to Charlie. Then another and handed that to Dougie.

“Where’s mine?” whispered Fanny.

“N... N... No more,” Arthur answered.

“Oh – poo-ey!” she grumbled in a sulk.

“It’s empty,” grumbled Charlie.

“Yes, they all are,” Betsy whispered, as if she knew all along.

“Mine isn’t!” chirped Charlie, much too noisily.

“Ssshhh!” they all hissed to quieten him down.

“Well open it then, go on.” Dougie was very keen to see what was inside.

“I can’t – it’s got a cork.”

“What does it say on the label then?”

“It’s too dark, I can’t see.”

“Come here and hold it in the light of the lantern,” Betsy beckoned Charlie over. “Try reading it now.”

Charlie peered. “Lee Cogg-Nack... Who is he?”

“Ooooh!” Herbie chimed, “Sir George has a cog on his motor car! Maybe it’s knack**** ”

“Sssshhhhh!” interrupted Betsy. “It’s French silly: *Le Cognac*. It means brandy. It’s medicine. Our nanna takes it for her lumbago. It’s very expensive: she gets a quarter-bottle at Christmas and it has to last her all year. But it’s usually gone by February.”

“Yuk – I’ve sniffed my bottle and you’re right – it does smell like medicine... nasty medicine... yeuggghhhhhh...” And Dougie wrinkled up his nose then screwed up his whole face to make his point.

“I... I... I like it,” giggled Arthur, drinking the dregs from another empty bottle he had just found behind a small wooden casket on the dark damp floor.

“Heh!” shrieked Fanny. “That’s *my* bottle! I didn’t get one! And now you’ve drunk it... Thief!”

“Ssshhh!” the others all went, trying to calm down the noise.

“No Arthur, you mustn’t drink that, it’ll make you sick!” said Betsy in her motherly manner. “Give it to me.”

"I... I... I..."

"You've drunk it!" Betsy held the bottle up to her lantern, then tipped it upside down to prove it. "Oh dear, what if he's ill?"

"Don't worry – there wasn't more than a sip left in it," Herbie reassured her. "Are you all right Arthur?"

"I... I... I can see... blood."

"Blood?" shrieked Betsy. Oh no! Where? Is it yours Arthur? Oh goodness, I shall be in so much trouble if Arthur gets hurt"

"I... I... can see blood over there..." And he pointed to some marks up the wall of the tunnel. "And there..." And he pointed to some more. "And there..." And he pointed down at the floor."

Betsy turned up the flame in her lamp so they could see more clearly, and there were revealed lots of red spots, like blood spatters, all around, and also more bottles, and other things scattered everywhere.

"Quick everyone, light your lanterns."

Herbie picked up one of the bottles. "Look," he pointed to the label, "Port Wine... That's what all these marks are. They are not blood, they are Port Wine. Someone's been having a party!"

Gosh! The pirates have had a party and made a lot of mess! There are lots of differences between the two pictures of the tunnels on the following page – if you just count the tankards and goblets and bottles being thrown on the floor as three differences then there are around 20 differences in total.

"Lots of people by the look of it." Betsy stared around, amazed at the scene. "Right, we'd better get going – this place is creepy.

"I... I... I like it," spoke Arthur, because he wasn't scared of anything much except sprouts. He reached into a crate a pulled out another bottle. He peered at the label and spelt out the letters... " *'r'*... *'u'*... *'m'*..."

"Rum?" said Herbie. "Whre does that come from?"

"Jamaica," said Betsy knowledgably.

"Jamaica... Wow..."

"It's just past Cornwall and keep sailing for a bit," said Betsy, which was roughly true.

Suddenly there was a noise up ahead, a scrabbling scurrying sort of noise. The Scamps froze, listening in terror.

"Put out your lanterns," hissed Betsy. "It may be old Groucher!"

"But it will be even more scary in the dark," complained Charlie.

"No matter, we must hide, behind these barrels. Quick. Come on Scamper."

They all found a place to duck down in the shadows then blew out their lanterns. The silence was as complete as the darkness. They peered ahead into nothing. It actually was quite scary, even for tough Scamps. Then two lights for eyes appeared from the blackness, close together, shining red, but from where? Must be light reflected from one of the gratings, thought Betsy, but she hardly had time to think as Scamper launched from behind his packing case and shot at the two red eyes which quickly disappeared. There was a flurry of scuffing paws and gnashing teeth then Scamper was back. He dropped something next to Betsy's foot with a thud.

"It's... It's... It's a mouse," Arthur announced.

"How do you know?" Herbie demanded, "It's pitch dark." But Betsy just screamed.

"Ssshhh" they all went."

"I don't like mice!"

"It's... It's... It's dead," Arthur stated matter-of-factly and held it up in front of Herbie's face.

Herbie still couldn't see so he held out his hand to touch it. "It's too big for a mouse, Arthur... It must be a rat.!

"Aaaaagggh!" Betsy screamed again. "I don't like rats!"

Arthur dropped the rat back down while Herbie lit his lantern, and in its glow there sat Scamper, looking very pleased with himself, his dead trophy lying on the floor just in front of him.

"Oh yeuuuk, that's revolting," Betsy was dismayed. "Please let's get out of here."

"No – we're exploring! We must find out what happened and report back to Will. He's relying on us."

Betsy didn't want Herbie taking over her self-appointed role as "leader", so she pulled herself together.

"Very well," she started to speak, but then there was another flurry of noise up ahead. This time two bigger eyes than before, farther apart, and bright green were picked out in the dim light of Herbie's lantern.

"Aaaahhhh!" squealed Betsy as Scamper shot off again past her and into the fray.

The Scamps looked on, not daring to speak in case their position was betrayed. It was sure to be old Groucher and his miserable dog, for dogs' eyes shine green in the dark.

Then there came a growling howling spitting seething teething noise of conflict and mayhem which seemed to last for minutes, louder and softer punctuated by the odd yelp and hiss and slavering roar.

"I... I... I think Scamper's winning," said Arthur confidently.

The others were too intent on listening to speak, not even to tell Arthur to be quiet. Then, they heard it...

"Arrerrrrkk! Arrerrrrkk!"

"Goodness! Scamper's sounding the retreat! What do we do?" Betsy was worried now, and a cold shiver ran down her spine into her stomach and legs.

"We retreat, I suppose," said Herbie.

"But we can't do that!" Charlie was appalled. "We can't just leave poor Scamper behind – what if he's hurt?"

"You're right," said Betsy, all of a sudden regaining her courage. "We must stay and help Scamper fight the evil foe... Sound the advance!"

"How do we do that? Only Scamper knows how to do that," said Herbie.

"We'll just have to do our best," said Betsy and she let out a shrill roar, somewhat like one imagines the rebel yell would have sounded in the American Civil War. But then, they heard something else to make their hearts miss a beat.

"What's going on? Are you fighting again? Come here and let's have a look at you." Then a pause. "What a mess: scabbed leg, chewed ear. And a broken tail as well! Who did this to you?"

As the children crouched down in terror, Charlie whispered loudly what they all knew already. "It's old Groucher! What shall we do?"

"It's that 'orrible dog belongs to those Scamps did this, I can see his handiwork. And that means those urchins are here somewhere. Come on Mugger, back into the tunnel and we'll flush 'em out!"

"Sounds like they're coming after us! What shall we do?" Charlie asked the same question again.

For some reason, they all looked at Arthur. He grinned and pointed to the barrels.

"No good Arthur," said Dougie, rocking one of the barrels. "We can't hide in them... they're full."

At that moment, out of the darkness ahead, Scamper leapt into view, slightly reddened on the white patches of his fur, but looking healthy enough.

"Arrrrooooooooorrrrrrr!" Scamper howled, "Arrrrooooooooorrrrrrr!"

"That's the advance," Betsy was surprised. "Scamper, we need to get out... Sound the retreat..."

"Arrrrooooooooorrrrrrr!" Scamper howled again. And he then jumped up at one of the barrels, toppling it over, whence it started to roll along the tunnel floor. "Arrrrooooooooorrrrrrr!" he let out another urgent cry.

"What's he doing? Betsy was confused by the dog's behaviour.

"The barrels," said Fanny calmly. "He wants us to roll the barrels along the tunnel so that they bump into old Groucher and his miserable dog."

"Yes, come on," shouted Charlie, seizing on the plan. "Quickly!"

They tipped four barrels on their sides so they covered the whole width of the tunnel then, as the footsteps approached from the darkness, they pushed and pushed until all the barrels were rolling, faster and faster, gathering speed.

"Arrerrrrkk," Scamper sounded the retreat just as the rumbling thunder made by the barrels turned into a cacophony of crashes and groans and whimpers.

The Scamps piled back the way they had come, not knowing the outcome.

"I hope we haven't killed old Groucher," Herbie spoke in a worried tone. "We'll be had up for murder."

"He's too miserable to die," Charlie mused cheerfully.

"Charlie!" scolded Betsy, "That's a mean thing to say! Wash your mouth out!"

"I think Charlie's right," said Fanny in her usual unsympathetic tone. "I hate him. It's his fault his dog is so miserable. If he was a nice person then he wouldn't have a miserable dog, would he?"

"Fanny's right," Dougie joined in. "I think his dog would be a nice dog if he didn't have to live with old Groucher."

Scamper looked shocked. "Errroooooooo!" he yelped and gave Dougie a stare.

"Come on," Herbie urged them. "We have to go and search the grounds now – Will asked us to find out if there are any clues around the house, and as Groucher's out of action for a bit, now is our chance."

"But to do that, we've got to go back to where old Groucher is, and I don't want to do that." said Betsy, always being the sensible one.

"No, remember the gratings which let the light in the roof? We'll just climb through one of those, right here in fact." Herbie pointed upwards at the little patch of light struggling its way through the leaf litter into the gloom beneath. "Right, Charlie you get on my shoulders and push the grating out of the way. Then climb up and I'll pass Arthur up to you. Then Fanny, then Dougie, then I'll push Betsy up – she can stand on my hands while I shove, and then I'll find a rock to stand on and pass Scamper up to you then I myself will follow - you can help by pulling me."

Herbie knelt down while Charlie climbed on his shoulders, then stood up and Charlie easily reached the grating as the tunnel roof was not very high. The boys both spluttered and groaned as a load of leaves and dirt and spiders and worms landed on them and went down the back of their shirts as Charlie pushed the grating over onto its side. Then he grabbed the edges of the square hole now revealed and was out and in the open air in a flash. Herbie grabbed Arthur and held the little man up in his arms above his head while Charlie reached down.

"I... I... I've"

"For goodness sake PLEASE! Not now Arthur!" wailed Herbie. "Just wait one more minute little chap, just a few seconds more! And Charlie grabbed the boy and whisked him out through the open skylight, Arthur chuckling in delight as he flew up in the air like a rocket. One by one the others followed until only Herbie and Scamper were left on their own in the tunnel. Herbie had scout round with his lantern and found a pile of bricks lying to one side of the tunnel, probably left over from when they built it. He made a little pile of them beneath the patch of daylight shining in from overhead, then reached down and picked the dog up with both arms and unsteadily climbed on top of the stack of bricks. Scamper shivered, nervous that Herbie might drop him. Charlie reached down, grabbed his collar, then pulled hard until he could get his other hand under Scamper's front legs and whoosh, there he was up and into the safety of the great outdoors.

"Now we're going to need two of you to pull me up," shouted Herbie through the open ceiling. "Get Dougie will you?"

Then he saw Fanny's face and her arm lowered through the hole.

"No Fanny, I'm too heavy for you. Go and get Dougie!"

"Oh he's gone off somewhere. And anyway you're not too heavy. I'm just as strong as you boys, you just see!" she said confidently.

"But you're a girl!"

"Yes and girls are better than boys any day. I'm the same age as Dougie... I'll pull you up."

At that moment, Herbie suddenly didn't care who pulled him up out of the tunnel: the sound of distant but rapidly closing-in barking came from somewhere along the underground passageway. The awful reality presented itself to poor Herbie: Groucher's miserable dog was coming to get him.

"Quick quick, both of you give me your hands, please! Quick! The dog's after me! Quick! QUICK!"

Fanny and Charlie both laid on their stomachs and dangled their arms down the hole. Reaching as far as they could, they touched the tips of Herbie's fingers, but not enough to take hold of his hands.

They shuffled along the ground, ever nearer the edge with all the danger that presented, stretching their arms and wriggling their wrists, trying to feel if there was enough of anything to grab.

"Try and lock fingers... Curl them a bit... Just a bit more! I've nearly got you!" Charlie urged him on.

"H-e-e-e-e-l-p! Hurry! Or something else is going to get me!"

With a desperate lunge, Fanny just about managed to grab the outstretched hands of her friend below and pulled him up enough so Charlie could get a grip of Herbie's other hand. With all four of their own hands now locked around the older boy's, they heaved upwards with all their strength, hoping that they would not fall down the cavity and join Herbie in whatever terrible fate would befall him at the mouth and teeth of Groucher's miserable dog. Herbie felt himself rising slowly from the pile of bricks, much too slowly for his liking because at the same time he could also hear the dog's feet on the gravel-strewn floor of the passage below.

"Quick!" he shouted as up he went, "Quick! Please! Help!" and then, "Ohhhhhh! He's got me! Help! Ohhhhhh!"

Fanny and Charlie pulled even harder but now they had the weight of the miserable snarling dog as well, hanging onto Herbie's shoe.

"Shake him off! Shake him off! screeched Fanny. "I can't pull any harder!"

"I'm trying!" shouted Herbie.

"Kick him with your other foot!" Charlie suggested helpfully, "Hard as you can!"

"Oh h-e-e-e-e-e-l-l-l-l-p!" Herbie was struggling now like a drowning man when WHOOSH – he became lighter and shot through the opening and into the sun, just as Arthur had down a few minutes earlier.

"Got you!" screamed Charlie.

"I told you I could do it!" said Fanny, more calmly.

Herbie sat by the side of the vent, shaking from the experience of being almost torn in half by his friends pulling one way and the miserable cur pulling the other, whilst Groucher's horrid dog sniffed around down below, chewing on something, searching for blood.

"Oh no!" Herbie moaned. "What shall I do?"

“What, are you hurt?” Fanny sounded almost concerned. “Did it get you?”

“No, it’s worse than that... Much worse!... The dog’s got my shoe!” Herbie peered down the hole. “And it’s chewing it up” What am I going to tell my mother? She saved up for ages to buy me these shoes... I shall never be able to go home now! Oh what can I say to her! Father will take his belt to me and I’ll never be allowed out again!” And the poor lad started sobbing.

“What’s the matter?” asked Betsy, overhearing the drama and commotion.

“Herbie’s lost his shoe... Down there...” And Charlie pointed into the blackness below.

“And his mother will kill him if he goes home with only one shoe!” said Fanny gleefully, like children do when one of their friends is in trouble but they themselves are not. On hearing which, Herbie burst into a renewed chorus of blubbering.

“Well, in that case, we must get the shoe back,” said Betsy, as if it would be the easiest task in the world.

“But how will we do that?” Herbie blurted between sobs.

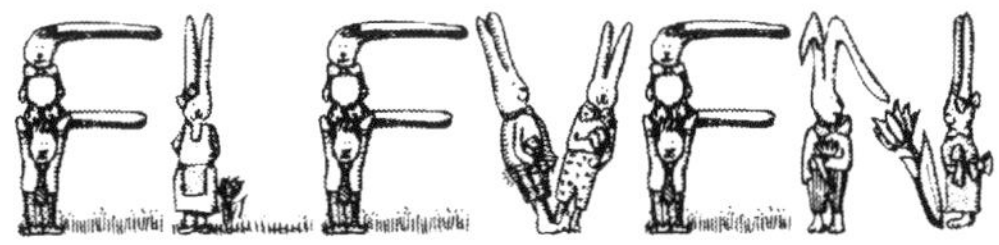

The Search for the Shoe – 1

She lay atop that hill, I cannot shift
the image of her white bright cheeks that glowed
as if a morning sunray gave a lift
that led me to her bed beside the road.

I cannot see her eyes without the gleam
of life within them, wide they were opened...
What had they seen? Had she thought it a dream?
An act within a play, and not the end?

I stayed until the glow began to fade,
so gently signalling finality.
I closed the lids: first right then left, I bade
her farewell – those two touches live with me.

I feel them now, treasure on fingertips...
I will find out who sealed her cold dead lips

Hattie and Will went up the hill, to fetch a......... well, hopefully a shoe... Florrie's missing shoe...

While The Scamps were investigating the tunnels at Ashley Combe, the pair set off along the road towards the foot of the hill.

"I must pop into The Ship and see Clara," said Harriet as they neared the inn. "Do you want to go on ahead?"

"No, I shall come with you," Will replied. "Clara was on the Lorna Doone coach coming down – she may have seen something."

"In that case, you will meet her mother too..." Harriet winced theatrically and pulled an agonised face expressing mock horror.

She walked up to the entrance and pushed on the old oaken door which creaked as it hinged open. Will knew he would be the centre of attention, but the sudden quelling of the babbling banter replaced by the complete hush which followed his entrance shook him to his bones... In one small fraction of a second, The Ship became eerie like a crypt. He could feel the temperature as it dropped like an ice-drip... He could smell the attention of the overly curious gathering and he could hear the silence of their mistrust... He could drink-in his own fear and he could taste the testy mood of the crowd...

Harriet spotted Clara, meekly sat in the shadow of her mother's formidable presence. The old lady's temperament, which prior to her unloved trip upon the morning Lorna Doone had been one of nervous foreboding, had now developed into a maelstrom of anger spinning within a boiling cauldron of disdain.

Will glanced nervously at Harriet. She nodded, indicating that these were indeed the pair whom they had come inside to see. He took a firm grip of his courage and strode boldly forward, approaching the table at which the two ladies were seated. Clara smiled broadly on seeing Harriet's return. Mrs Arnold lowered her glass from her lips and gave Will a withering glower of disapproval.

"So *you* are the young man we have been hearing about, are you?" Her tone was the mirror of her expression, and no more companionable than an adder-bite.

"Hattie, my dear Hattie!" Clara leapt from her seat and embraced her pen-pal, leaning over the small table to embrace her friend. "You must introduce me... I presume this is your brother Will who you told me about when we first met?"

"I am that," ventured Will, trying to sound brave.

Mrs Arnold could hold back no longer, her flow having been interrupted by the intervention of her daughter. "He's very *small* isn't he!" she observed, looking Will up and down, which she noted was not that far... Her next comment was aimed directly at the poor lad. "Do you often find young ladies in suspicious circumstances upon the hillside?"

Will gulped. "I never have before ma'am... and I hope never to again."

Mrs Arnold took stock, staring at her quarry for fully five seconds without making a sound. "Well for your sake I hope not," she finally announced. "It will not bode well for your career if this becomes a regular occurrence."

"No ma'am. And I intend to find out what happened to our dear Florrie. She was much loved by all in the village."

"All, it appears, except *one*!"

Will listened to Mrs Arnold's pronouncement, and gained a sneaking respect on hearing her deduction. He had not seen it in the way that she described before... He looked apprehensively at the imposing woman and noticed she seemed to have calmed somewhat.

"I see your glass is nearly empty ma'am... May I replenish it for you? A tonic, perhaps?"

"Ohhhhhh!" Suddenly her mood lightened, like the cheery sunshine after a storm. "Well yes young man, a tonic would be very welcome!"

"And that would be?" Will enquired, but before the old lady had time to reply Clara interjected "Brandy..." And Will thankfully escaped to the bar of the inn and ordered the lady a large measure of the spirit that would be her salvation, and his redemption.

"Such a nice young boy..." tittered Mrs Arnold to the two girls. "I don't know how you two could have been so hard upon him in your earlier discussion!"

"What!" exclaimed Clara, mystified.

"Well it's not his fault he's so small is it?" continued her mother... "It's the locality... I don't suppose they are fed properly around these parts."

"Oh mother, stop it now... You are being rude in front of my friend Harriet. There are lots of parts of London where the children are under-nourished. It's just that you refuse to see them!"

"Yes, I believe we have very healthy food here in the country Mrs Arnold. The land provides all that we need to be fit and strong... And most of the children are just that."

"Here you are Mrs Arnold..." Will returned and planted a large tumbler of brandy in front of her. He noted her eyes sparkle with delight at the sound as it landed, and the scent and size of the measure.

"I was just saying to the two girls here what a brave lad you must be, riding those horses up and down that hill all day. Some might call it foolhardy, but I shall say brave. And I am told that being short is a boon in your line of work?"

"Yes ma'am... practically a necessity. The horses don't even know I am there."

"Very good. Needless to say, I shan't be travelling that way again... Too much of strain on my poor nerves... But this tonic has made me realise that you perform a valuable function and I apologise for anything I may have said earlier. I can only excuse myself by stating that I was in a state of shock."

"That is quite all right, Mrs Arnold. You must enjoy yourself while you are in the country, despite all the hills."

Now that she was calm, he could venture to ask the question which had been burning inside him.

"Mrs Arnold... Miss Arnold... Did either of you see anything? Anything suspicious? Florrie must have been lying there by the side of the road and the wall when you came down on the coach."

Mrs Arnold stared at him and wrinkled up her nose in distaste.

"One of our horses lost its footing on the hill," said Clara, eager to help. "We were too much concerned that he might fall and were watching for his wellbeing with our hearts in our mouths, much too distracted to notice anything around us. While my mother here of course was lying flat on the floor and so saw nothing whatsoever of our descent."

Harriet couldn't help herself and giggled, while Mrs Arnold looked pained at having her unpleasant memory of the trip rekindled.

"It was a most shocking journey. I only have young Herbie to thank for saving me from being dashed to pieces against the roadside. I shouldn't wonder if your Florrie didn't meet the same fate on an earlier trip!"

"There is no earlier coach ma'am, so she could not have fallen from any coach but yours, and that possibility has been eliminated... You say young Herbie saved you? He is one of The Scamps. He probably had you lying down on the coach floor as a trick... It is one of his favourites!"

Mrs Arnold turned pale, then made a sudden grab for her brandy and swallowed the whole lot down in one gulp. The three of them stared at her in shock, wondering what would happen next... They could all hear their own breaths against the deathly quiet of the situation. But the old lady simply stared, shocked, into space... her eyes unfocused...

"Another tonic Mrs Arnold?" ventured Will, deciding to break the spell before it broke for itself.

"Yes..." came the faint reply. "Another tonic..."

"Mother, you must be careful or you will not be able to travel on to Minehead and we shall miss our train!"

"One more tonic will see me right as rain Clara, and ready to tackle the highest mountains between here and Minehead, of which I am sure there are many."

Will repeated his trip to the bar to replenish Mrs Arnold's glass.

"What will you be doing now?" asked Clara of her newly acquainted friend.

"Oh Will says we have to go and search for a shoe. It's missing you see."

"Why, has he lost one?

"No, it is Florrie's. When Will found her she was only wearing one shoe... He has turned detective and is determined to seek out the missing one. He thinks it will provide a clue."

Clara's eyes sparkled with interest. "Oh this sounds like quite an adventure, although in the saddest of circumstances. I wish I could come and help you search for the shoe..."

"You can!" said Will, who just overheard the end of their conversation as he returned with Mrs Arnold's pick-me-up. "Six eyes will be better than four."

"Really? Can I? Oh how exciting! I shall be back in a short while mother... You stay here and enjoy your tonic."

"What?" The old lady sounded alarmed. "You're not thinking of going off alone with this young man are you? That won't do at all! I shan't hear of it!"

"I won't be alone mother... I'm with Harriet. I'm sure she will look after me."

"Yes of course I will. I shan't let my disreputable little brother lay a finger on her Mrs Arnold... I promise."

"But he finds dead young ladies on hillsides! Where is it that you will be going?"

"Up the hill," Will announced with a flourish. "That is the most likely place the shoe was lost."

"Ohhh! Oh my word... Oh dear! Well if you insist on going on this wild goose chase Clara I shall accompany you."

"Mother... NO!"

"Well I forbid you from going then!"

Clara pouted. “Very well... You can accompany me then. But you won’t get far will you? Not up the hill. You will hate every minute of it!”

“Yes, that is true, but you have left me no choice. I shall have to suffer because of you.”

At which the old lady stood up, swooned, and fell straight down again with a *splat*, back onto the sofa where they had been sitting. Her eyes were closed and her head lolled across the top of the cushion back.

Clara checked she was breathing and made her comfortable.

“We’re leaving her here then are we?” ventured Will.

“Yes,” said Clara, completely unruffled by the turn of events. “She needs to sleep off her tonics.”

They left The Ship Inn and climbed steadily, up and around the corner overlooked by the tea rooms where the hill steepens to its full extent. As they passed the small quarry just around the bend, Harriet paused.

“Dear Clara, let us pick a bunch of wild primroses, a posy to lay on the spot where Florrie was... was...” Harriet felt the tears welling up and could not continue with her sentence.

“Yes of course,” said Clara and put her arm around her for comfort.

As the two girls crouched down to pluck the stems, Harriet looked up above her to where the stone had been gouged from the hill’s flank, and then even higher above that at the massed foliage and trees which covered the hill’s bottom slopes.

“We’re never going to find a shoe in this lot,” she bemoaned soulfully through the remains of her tears. “We would have to be very lucky even to stumble across it – we could walk right next to it and still miss it in the undergrowth.”

“True,” said Will, “But I’m hoping we shall stumble upon something else that will provide us with the very piece of luck which you mention. Now, do you think Florrie was running *up* the hill when she lost her shoe? Or would it be more likely she was running *down*?”

Harriet thought for a moment about how it would feel, running up or down, and which was the more likely.

“I suppose running up would mean your foot was pressing hard against the heel part of the shoe, and as you raised your foot, your heel would possibly lift out of the shoe and slip backwards leaving the shoe behind... Actually, thinking about it, leaving the shoe in front, as your foot would be behind it. Coming down, the force would be forward onto your toes. That would leave a gap at the back of the shoe between it and the heel of the foot, so the shoe could still fall off whichever way she was going."

"Very helpful," Will spoke ironically. "So we shall just have to hope that the slice of luck I am hoping for does come our way! How about you and Clara start searching below the wall where she lay, and I'll search above?"

"Very well, but if the shoe is not lying close the edge of the road, I don't think we have much chance of spotting it. Unless..."

"What?"

"Unless we have a dog to help us."

"True yes, but for a dog to find it we should need her other shoe so he could get the scent, and that is at Doctor Kingslake's surgery. Let us try our best for now."

They trudged up the steepest part, beginning to puff a little as their legs demanded more sustenance from the heart and lungs Soon they were standing next to the wall where Will had found poor Florrie just a few hours before.

Clara let out a little gasp of emotion at the thought of what had befallen a girl practically the same age as her here in this dank forbidding nook beside a mossy wall. Will too shuddered and removed his cap.

"This is a stark place now, is it not Hattie? I find it sends me into shivers."

"Yes, poor dear Florrie. She has risen with the angels from this very spot, and left it more full of emptiness with her parting. An emptiness which I fear may draw us in if we should get too close. Keep watch over us Will while we place these pretty flowers at the spot where she lay."

"Yes, it is a changed place, and I shall have to pass it every day," Will mused, melancholically.

The girls took each other by the hand and stepped up onto the thickly grassed bank beside the road, then carefully edged downward into the chilling hollow that had been Florrie's resting place.

"I wonder Will, why are the police not here searching for themselves? Do you not find that strange?"

"I think Greedy has already made his mind up and has no need for clues."

"You mean... he still thinks it was an accident?"

"I think that is what he thinks... And I also think that if that is not what he thinks, then he thinks that *I* did it. After all, I found her, and that casts suspicion on me, does it not?"

"No, not at all! Someone had to find her."

"Yes, but he thinks I was the first."

"Well, weren't you?"

"No."

"No?"

"No. There were others present here. And it may be that she was alive at the time. But I deeply suspect that she was not."

"How do you know that?"

"Please Watson, I don't know the details yet, but I promise you will be the first to know my theories as soon as they are crystallised."

She looked at him disparagingly.

"You know, you're beginning to bore me. I think maybe you *are* turning into Sherlock Holmes."

"Ooooh – do you really think so?" Will reverted to being an excited boy for a second.

"Well, as I haven't actually heard any of your so-called 'theories' yet, I don't know for sure. But you certainly are of the correct overbearing disposition, or at least quickly becoming so!"

"Well thank you for your support Watson, and trusted comradeship..."

"It's fine. Any time. Shall we start searching now?"

"Yes, that would be splendid."

"Oh yes... Let us get started for I shall have to get back to mother soon." Clara felt the clock ticking away and wanted the chance of being the one to find the missing shoe. She started to hunt around the wall's edge, following along its length into the field.

Harriet set off back down the hill, walking along the verge, poking around amongst the grass and freshly shooting bracken with a stick, while Will did the same going up from where Florrie had lain. Within a few yards she found something brown and leathery, obviously discarded, lying under the foliage. She picked it up.

"I've found a shoe!" she shouted up at Will.

"Goodness! Already? Well done Watson! Let me see..."

"Don't bother yourself Will. It's just an old boot. Worn out. Probably a tramp's."

"Oh Hattie, I thought you had found it." Will tutted... "Really..." And voiced his disappointment.

"Don't worry. This whole hillside is probably littered with abandoned footwear. I shall soon find more!"

"You, my loving sister, are a tease!"

"Yes. And you, my ever-loving brother, are an easy target. Show a little more respect and I shall stop teasing you. I may be Doctor Watson to your Holmes, but I am not a dunderhead, and you shouldn't treat me like one, even though your alter-ego may have done so... but his Watson was a more tolerant and easygoing partner."

"Sorry Hattie. We are a team you know. I promise I'll tell you what I know as soon as I know it. Know it for certain that is."

"Will... we know almost nothing for certain in this life. The church teaches us that the next life will be better, and that is the simple hope we cling to."

"Yes Hattie. Sorry. We'll carry on looking. We owe it to poor Florrie..." He paused... "And Hattie?"

"Yes?"

"I do appreciate your help. I shall try and show my appreciation more."

"Good. Let's get on."

Harriet continued working her way down, turning every leaf and stem along the way. Meanwhile Will concentrated on the upper slope.

"Have you found any money?" he shouted down to his sister.

"A penny and two farthings so far. How about you?"

"Nothing as yet. You are obviously tapping a richer seam than I. If you find anything silver, be sure to tell me won't you?"

"Why, do you want to share it? I shall expect to have a half share of any that you find too."

"Quite so Watson. But just be sure to let me know."

"Look!" The shout came from the field.

Harriet stood up and saw her friend some distance away holding something aloft in her hand.

What is it, Clara?"

"It's a shoe!"

"Oh well done... Will!" Harriet shouted. "Clara has found a shoe!"

Clara laughed. "No, don't call your brother... This is a man's shoe... old and battered. It probably belonged to a tramp."

Harriet laughed and the two girls had a long fit of giggling during which they could hear Will's voice shouting, "What is it? What have you found?"

"Nothing!" shouted back Harriet. Just another old boot!"

"Oh... Never mind!" Will shouted back, and they all carried on looking.

"Are you all right over there Clara?" Harriet enquired of her friend. "Take care not to get mud or grass stains on your pretty dress – your mother will have something to say if you do."

"When does my mother ever *not* have something to say?" Clara shouted back across the emptiness of the slope.

"Yes that is true... she is a little scary. Are you not afraid of her? My mother scolds me terribly if I should get even slightly dirty. It's so unfair."

"Your mother is probably a quiet lady then. My mother shouts and screams a lot, but I am the one who tells her what to do and how to manage herself. It is funny, but she is the child in our relationship, the one who makes all the noise but gets into trouble most easily."

"Oh, you are lucky!"

"Yes that is true. Poor Harriet, you should know that it is the quiet mothers who are the most stubborn and pernickety."

"Yes, that is exactly what she is! And prissy! Too too prissy!"

"But of course you still love her."

"Of course... Just as you love your mother, just the same..."

And the two girls laughed together once more.

"Come on you two! Stop chattering and giggling and get on with looking!"

The faint muffled sound produced by an irritating brother floated down from the top of the hill and into Clara and Harriet's ears. The stooped down once more and continued their searching.

Twenty minutes passed without any sign of their goal, and they noticed a coolness had begun to chill the air. Where a minute or two ago there had been bright sunshine enabling easy spotting of anything unusual in the undergrowth, now a mist started to descend from the heavens, a low cloud, as can happen so quickly on the moor. Harriet was a long way back down the slope at the sharp hairpin bend, and still there was no sight of a shoe, and she began to feel nervous both for herself and her friend.

"Let's head back now, Will!" she called up to him.

"Just ten more minutes!" he bellowed loudly down to her, trying to make himself heard.

"No!" Harriet shouted back. We cannot be out in the mist when it comes down thicker, and especially not with Clara out on her own in the field. Clara! Clara! Come back to the road! While you can still see where you are treading!"

"You are right!" shouted Will in acknowledgement of his sister's caution. "I will go and find her and escort her back to us... But then I shall just spend another ten minutes – I feel we are near to finding what we seek."

Will turned to face the field to go and rescue Miss Arnold when... How could this be? Joy of joy! There it was... nestling in the dust and grit at the edge of the road, beneath where the grass hung slightly over the edge of the track, breaking the neat line where green leaf meets reddish orange shale.

"Hurraaahhhh!" he shrieked in triumph, loud enough for Harriet easily to hear.

"You've found it? You've found it?" she yelled excitedly, immediately running up the tortuous slope as fast as she could. In a minute she was nearly with him, but when he came into view, he wasn't holding up a shoe as she had expected... He was staring at a place near his feet.

Maybe he has left it on the ground so as not to disturb the evidence, she thought to herself.

But then, as she stood beside him and peered down, all there was was a tiny glint of silver, dulled by the mist but still visible, in the spot where Will was pointing.

"Sixpence!" he said with glee. "Look Hattie... A silver sixpence!"

"Oh Will, I thought you had found the shoe." Harriet sounded disappointed. "Still, that's thruppence for me then!" But I thought we were looking for Florrie's shoe – why so much excitement about a sixpence?"

"Aha my dear fellow. Fear not. This is the piece of luck that we were banking on. The piece of luck that I said might come our way. Indeed, this clue, this sixpenny clue, will lead us to the very shoe which we seek."

"Oh you're still talking in riddles. It's a sixpence. It's not a signpost."

"Ah, but maybe it is! If I am right, this sixpence shows us exactly the spot where Florrie lost her shoe."

Harriet looked quizzical. "I suppose there is no point in my asking what leads you to that deduction?"

"I would rather hold onto it for the moment Watson, but I promise I will tell you as soon as we get back home, especially if we have found the shoe!"

"Isn't that tampering with the evidence? Surely we should take it to Greedy?"

"We shall. But first we must find it. You strike out across the field, there where Clara is, up to about fifty yards away from the road I should say. Keep her with you so she doesn't get lost. I'll search the same distance a little further up."

The three of them battered about amongst the scrub and bracken... one minute... two minutes... five minutes... ten minutes passed... Harriet and Clara fumbled their way back to the road before they became stranded in the fog, then walked along a little higher until they were standing within easy earshot of Will, close to where he was still searching.

"It's not here is it," said Hattie, stating a fact rather than posing the question.

"It has to be," Will came back. "It must be. It's got to be!"

"It's really getting very misty now... We must get Clara back safely to The Ship. And we should go home. You know it's creepy up here when the mist comes in. All the tree shadows turn to ghouls."

"Oh how exciting!" said Clara. "We don't get ghouls in London fog; only choking smoke that clogs your lungs and stops you from breathing. It's called *smog*."

"Wait Watson... I've had an idea! Don't think about ghouls... I realise now that I've been stupid..."

"I could have told you that!"

"Just give me two minutes!"

"May I come with you?" Clara sounded so eager and couldn't bear to be left out that Will felt a kinship with her.

"Of course you can... Follow me."

"No! Will! What are you doing? You can't take my friend off into the wilderness. What might happen if...!

But the pair had already disappeared into the haze, and were last seen by Will's sister scrambling up a five foot bank on the opposite side of the road and into the woods.

They've gone off and left me, alone, on the moor, in this fog... What if they should be unable to find me when they return? What if they never return? Poor Harriet's thoughts became prompts for panic. She knew, she mustn't let herself lose control. She had to stay calm. The trees began to assume twisted bodies, like those of dead men writhing, even though that could not make sense. They were looking at her, but dead, like ghouls... Like ghoulish glaring glowering gargoyles...

"Will!" Harriet called, the tremble in her voice betraying her inner panic. "Clara! Will! Talk to me one of you! Let me know you're still here! Please..."

"Of course I am!" came the reply which, although shouted, was only faintly audible through the muffling effect of the millions of airborne water droplets that make up a fog.

"Keep talking to me Will. Please. I can't be alone for too long up here. I'm scared!"

"All right Hattie. I'll keep talking. Boy there's a lot of branches on the ground here, and last Autumn's leaf litter, but that doesn't matter, the shoe will be lying on..."

"TOP!" Clara screamed. "It's here! I can see it. A lady's shoe! Just where you thought it would be!"

"Yes! Oh well done Miss Clara... Hattie we've got it, Hattie, Hattie! we've found the shoe!"

"Well hurry up back here then and let me see. We really need to get back down."

In a flash Will was sliding down the mossy bank. He slithered to a halt then he turned to take the hand of his co-explorer to guide her gently back onto the road without ruining her clothes, although there were now several patches of dirt on the hem of her dress and her white cotton sleeves as evidence of her boyish exploits. Will rushed back to his sister, proffering the item of footwear, clean and shiny on the upper, with just a trace of the muddiness clinging to the sole, from where Florrie had last trod. Harriet looked at it for a few moments while feelings of loss welled up in her.

"Oh my gentle Lord, it's just so... *sad...*" and she began to weep.

"Yes... To think the last person to touch this shoe was none other than her pursuer."

"What was that?" A gruff voice bellowed out of the mist and the three youngsters shrieked in fear and shock. They turned in the direction of the voice and stood petrified as rock while the large figure of PC Greedy loomed out of the terrifying swirls and shadows.

"The last person to touch that shoe was her pursuer, eh? Well young Will... You appear to be the last person to be touching it. What do you have to say to that?"

"Er, well sir, I came up here sir, with my sister sir, and my sister's friend sir, specifically to search for the shoe sir, and with luck, we have found it sir. I thought it might be useful to you sir... In your investigation sir."

"Mmmmm." Greedy mulled over the facts, as he saw them.

"Mmmmm. Why do you think this *pursuer*, if indeed there was a pursuer, would have touched the shoe?"

"Because..." Will looked to Harriet for support. "I found it some distance from the road, and in a place where Florrie could not possibly have been walking herself. Therefore, someone must have thrown it there. And therefore, that someone must have wanted to dispose of it so that it would not be found. And therefore, that someone must have had something to hide, and the only something I can think of is that that someone was chasing Florrie, and in her panic as she ran her shoe came off."

"Mmmmm." One could not accuse Greedy of jumping to conclusions. "This is very interesting what you say... Mmmmm... If the shoe was in such an unlikely spot, how were you able to find it? Shouldn't I be suspicious that you knew where to look? How do I know that you didn't just come up here to retrieve it in case it was found, because *you* did not want it to be found, because *you* are the one with the guilty secret that you wish to hide?"

Will again looked at his sister before responding. "Yes Mr Greedy sir, that is a very good question. But my answer is that I would not have done anything to hurt poor Florrie, and I came up here to help with your investigation, to find out who could have done this terrible thing."

At this point Harriet spoke for the first time in the presence of the policeman.

"Clara and I have been here searching for more than an hour, sir. We have searched half of this hill and its surroundings I am sure, and in that time we found nothing until just before you arrived. If Will had known where the shoe lay, why would he not have found it straight away? And why would he have brought the two of us up here to help in the search? We would merely have been unwanted witnesses to his actions."

"Yes Mr Greedy, and actually Will didn't find the shoe... I did!" Clara announced with some pleasure. "I asked if I could accompany him to the last place we looked, and there it was!"

Greedy looked at them all, in silence. For a moment they thought he wasn't going to make his characteristic "hum" as his brain's cogwheels turned. But when he eventually spoke he didn't fail them...

"Mmmmm. As I said. Most interesting. One of the reasons I came up here was to find the shoe myself. It seems that you have performed that service for me."

Clara smiled delightedly, while Will's and Harriet's hearts skipped in relief at what seemed the likelihood that Greedy was about to believe them and that he would hopefully recognise their actions as helping, rather than interfering, with his investigation.

"Well done then to all of you!" He sounded almost cheerful, but the tone didn't last. He soon spoke sternly again. "I have received the doctor's post mortem results. I shall need to take you back to the station for questioning."

"Very well Mr Greedy," said Will, feeling slightly dejected at the prospect of another Greedy grilling.

"And you as well Miss." Greedy turned his gaze on Harriet "I shall be needing a word with both of you."

"What, with Hattie too? Why so? She only came up here because I asked her to!"

"No need to panic. All routine. I believe this young lady knew the deceased quite closely. It's perfectly normal to talk to everyone who was acquainted, as it were. I just need to take a statement from both of you and get everything down in writing."

"I'm happy to come along Mr Greedy, especially if it helps you find out what happened to Florrie."

"I hope that that is what we are all striving to do, my dear."

"What about me, Mr Greedy? Don't you want to take a statement from me?"

"Mmmmm. You are Miss Arnold I assume. You are the other reason that I am up on this cold misty hill. Your mother awoke in The Ship Inn and found you missing. She created a fuss and insisted the police were called. But then, she's an *insistent* woman, isn't she?" and Greedy chuckled to himself. "I shall be returning you straightway to her tender care." Greedy bent down slightly and whispered, "Between you and me, I don't envy you your reunion!"

"But I should love to give a statement... It would be... so exciting!"

"Mmmmm. Personally I can't think of anything that could be much more exciting than meeting your mother... Anyway, come now, all of you, especially you ladies... It will be much safer going back down the hill into the village in this fog with me accompanying you, don't you think so Miss Harriet?"

"Oh yes Mr Greedy! Thank you. I shall feel much less scared, in fact, not scared at all with you for company."

"Quite so. Come along both of you. And you too young Will. And be sure to bring that shoe with you."

They wandered back down the road, and as they gained the lower slopes the mist began to clear and the trees assumed their normal friendly exteriors, casting off the phantasmagorical images and apparitions conjured up by their mist-laden cousins higher up on the hill.

They shortly arrived at The Ship. Clara paused at the entrance, then turned to see her friend Harriet. They looked at one another in kindly harmony.

"Will you be coming inside to say goodbye to mother?"

"Hah!" grunted Greedy, changing his customary dithering opening expression to one of decisiveness. "I wouldn't if I were you!"

"Remember what I said," continued Clara. "She's all bluster."

"I'll go in," said Will. "I like her... I think we get on well."

Greedy eyed him with unconcealed disbelief and astonishment. Clara sniggered and pushed open the door. As she walked in she immediately became aware of a huddle around the sofa upon which her mother had been sprawled when they left only an hour or so ago.

"Oh my goodness! Is she all right?" Clara exclaimed as she hurried over, thinking that the huddle may have been performing an attempt at resuscitation of her drunken parent. As she rushed across, the throng parted and its members looked at her barnstorming arrival, and as the bodies cleared Clara could see her mother sitting holding court for her admirers, a glass in her hand and a big grin on her face.

"You should listen to this lady!" chirped one of the audience, who were all male. "She tells the most wonderful stories... You should hear what she says about her daughter hahaha!"

At which Mrs Arnold's eyes sort of focused on Clara and a kind of snooty recognition passed across her face, removing the smile and replacing it with a faint irritation.

"Well everyone... this is my daughter Clara! She's so very boring... She told me I wouldn't enjoy the coach ride from Lynton... But I *loved* it! Simply *loved* it darlings..."

Will and Harriet, who had caught up by now and could hear everything that had been said, could not stifle the giant grins and silent guffaws that engulfed their bodies, hoping beyond hope that Clara would not turn round and see them, which would have gone a long way to destroying such a slowly built and swiftly demolished friendship.

"What *are* you doing, mother?"

Will and Harriet noted that Clara had been right... she did sound like the sensible adult.

"I have been waiting for you... Luckily, these new friends of mine have been most commodious and exorbitant in their care of a poor old lady." She peered disparagingly. "Unlike her daughter!"

"Mother! You have drunk too much... You can't even use the right words..."

"Oh yes she can!" spoke one of the men who had been listening to Mrs Arnold's stories. "Her use of words is nigh on malnutritious! We've been stood here a'laughing for nigh on an hour now, and we're nigh on full of spirit, as much as your dear mother haha!"

At this moment Clara turned, in hope of receiving the support of her friends. Harriet anticipated with a swift straightfaced frown, while Will instantly converted his smirk into a look of shocked bewilderment.

"She's all bluster," he ventured.

"Yes," retorted Clara. "It is all bluster, and now I'm taking her home, or at least to the next port of call on our journey."

"Oh, before you do that, where is that jolly policeman who was here earlier... He went off to find you I believe... Do you know what became of him?"

"Yes mother, he's outside, too scared to come in."

"Scared? Of what? What can a policeman be scared of? They see the most horrible sights."

"You, mother." Clara spoke the two words slowly, relishing the comparison.

"Me? Oh don't be silly... Tell him to come in... I want to give him a kiss..."

The members of the huddle all laughed.

"That'll certainly make the difference."

"I'll go and tell him," offered Will, and rushed off before anyone could stop him.

"Yes yes... good boy... I want to kiss the policeman to thank him for finding my beautiful daughter and returning her safely to me. Now Clara, do tell everyone... what have you been up to on your adventure?"

"Well mother, I walked up the hill, I got lost in the fog, I was attacked by a wolf but luckily I managed to fight it off, and then there was this pack of hounds baying for my blood but the wolf came back and killed all of them, and then just as I thought I was safe, a huntsman came along, lifted me up onto the saddle of his horse and carried me away to a castle where I was locked up in a dungeon in chains until, by a stroke of good fortune, Harriet here climbed down on a rope through the skylight, tied the rope around my waist, and Will, who was outside, pulled me up, wrenching the chains from their mounts, flinging me into daylight where we all escaped back down the hill on the huntsman's horse and returned here to the safety of The Ship Inn where my mother was engaged in telling made-up stories to a group of strangers."

Mrs Arnold considered her daughter's tale for a number of confused seconds, then pronounced, "I think you have left out the part where the prince offers you his hand in marriage."

At that moment Will arrived back with Greedy in tow.

"Errrrrrrr... You wish to see me madam?" Greedy sounded like he was about to face his executioner.

"Mrs Arnold squinted her eyes in his vague direction, before recognition set in and a beaming smile crossed her face.

"Yes constable... I want to thank you for the safe return of my ungrateful daughter Clara."

"My pleasure madam. I'm happy to have been of service. Now if you'll excuse me I have to interrogate these two... I mean *interview* these two suspects... I mean *witnesses*."

Harriet and Will exchanged uneasy glances. Greedy took hold of their arms and marched them towards the exit, leaving Mrs Arnold protesting loudly her desire to embrace the wonderful policeman.

TWELVE

The Search for the Shoe – 2

“Don’t cry Herbie... We’ll get it back.” Betsy put her arm around him, even though tough Scamps don’t like that sort of thing.

“We can’t go back into the tunnel,” said Fanny helpfully, “Because Groucher’s miserable dog is down there. So we need to find something to lower into the hole, hook onto the shoe and pull it out.”

“That will only work if the shoe is in sight under the hole,” Dougie observed. “We need to find a way of getting rid of Groucher’s miserable dog, then find Herbie’s shoe.”

“It’s... It’s... It’s still there!” said Arthur, grinning.

“What is Arthur? The shoe? Or the miserable dog?”

“I’ve... I’ve... I’ve seen it.”

“Seen what Arthur?”

“The shoe.”

“Where? Let me see...” And Charlie rushed over to the hole and peered in. “I can’t see anything. How come Arthur can see things in the dark?”

“He just can,” said Fanny. “That’s why we bring him. He’s no use for anything else.”

“Don’t say that about Arthur!” Betsy scolded her. “Arthur is our... our... little talisman. Like Scamper. He goes everywhere we go or else it wouldn’t feel right.” And she looked at the little chap, happily munching on his carrot that his mum had packed for his adventures.

“I’ve... I’ve... I’ve *weeeeeed* myself!” he proclaimed proudly, chuckling in merriment.

“Yes Arthur. We know you have.” Betsy went over to him and gave him a hug. Even though tough Scamps don’t like that sort of thing, Arthur was small enough not to mind.

“What shall we do then?” asked Herbie plaintively between sniffles.

"I know," said Dougie, having a good idea, "We'll go up to the stables – they have fishing tackle there. We'll borrow a rod, and we'll fish down the hole for your shoe. How about that?"

"Yes, good idea Dougie, let's go." And Charlie started off up the tree-covered slope towards the big house. "Come on everyone!" So they all followed after him, Herbie hopping along on one foot.

"Watch out for old Groucher," advised Betsy cautiously. "We'll have to make a run for it if he spots us."

"I can't run!" wailed Herbie, hopping.

She looked back at him. "Oh Herbie, why don't you stay here, near your shoe. We'll be back in a jiffy."

Herbie looked dismayed. "But I don't want to wait here on my own... What if Groucher's miserable dog finds me? What will I do then."

"Well you'll just have to come with us then and stop moaning. Take your other shoe off and walk properly." And with that, in her school-ma'am sort of way, Betsy huffed, and pranced off up the hill after the others.

Herbie slowly shuffled along behind, trying to keep up but not really managing. They reached the stable yard and looked around. The groom was friendly, and if he was there he often let them come and stroke the horses, much to the annoyance of old Groucher. Scamper made little whining noises; he could see the horses poking their heads over their stable doors and wanted to take a closer look.

"Calm down Scamper, we don't want to get caught," Betsy tried to quieten him.

The place seemed to be without any human presence. They tiptoed across the yard, slid the bolt from the lock and opened the door of the tack room.

There are 15 differences to spot in the two pictures of the stable on the following page.

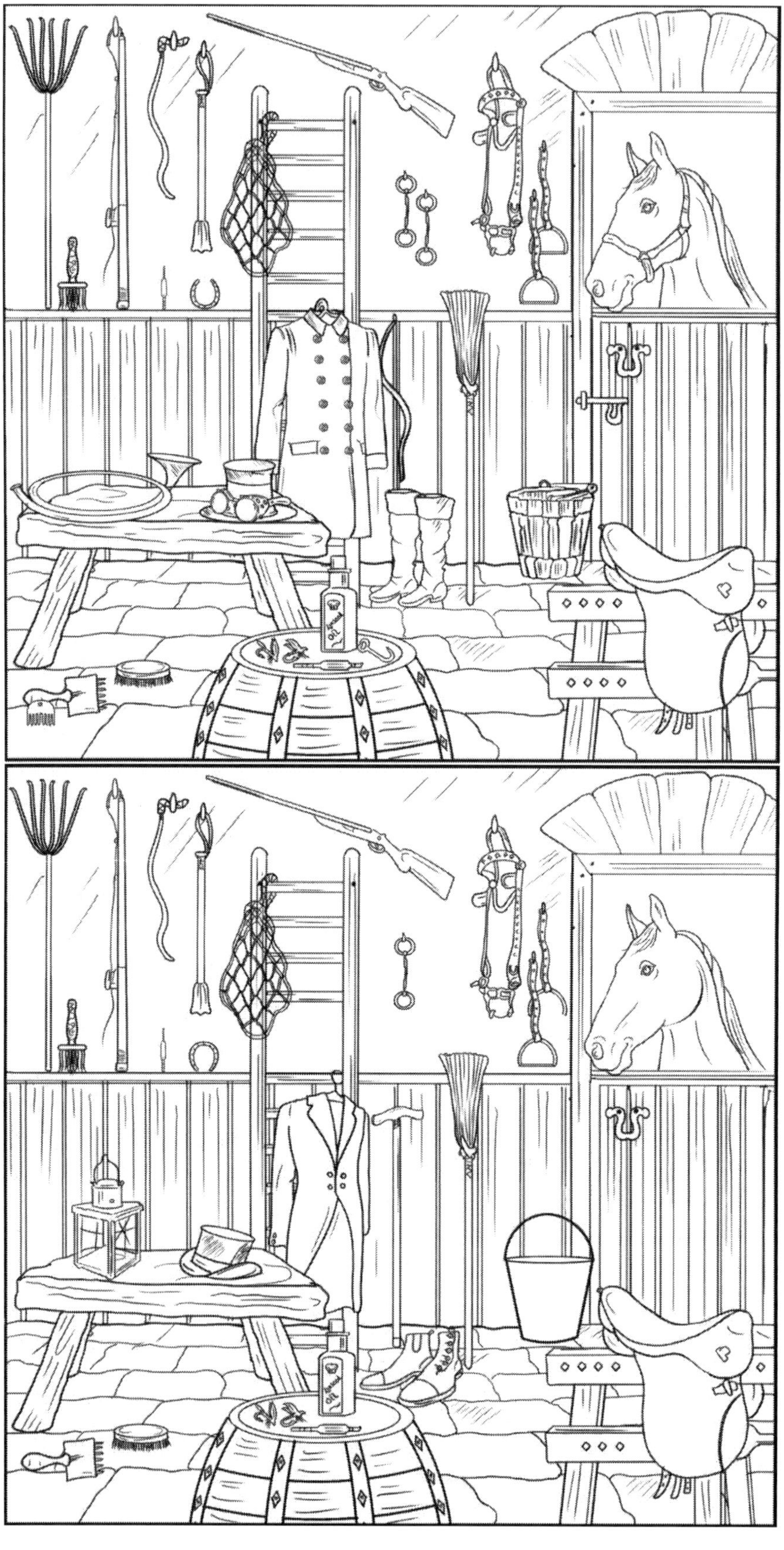

“The fishing gear’s over here,” Dougie whispered loudly. And he began to take one of the rods from the rack where it was stored.

“Wait Dougie,” said Charlie, “We don’t need the whole rod – that would be stealing, and if we get caught stealing, we could get put in Greedy’s lock-up, or even in the village stocks and get pelted with mouldy fruit and rotten eggs!”

“Carrots!” cried Arthur, triumphantly holding up his carrot for inspection.

“Yes, or even mouldy carrots,” Charlie continued. “All we need is some line and a hook. We can take that, put it in our pockets, and no one will notice we’ve got it.”

“Yes, right,” said Dougie. “It’ll be in one of these drawers here.” He rummaged about and selected a good length of gut and a nice big hook”

“You could catch a whale with that,” observed Fanny.

“Yes,” Dougie replied dismissively. “A whale, or a shoe. The same pretty much.”

“Come on, let’s get out of here now we’ve got what we need,” urged Betsy.

“Yes let’s!” Herbie had only just caught up but he willingly agreed and hobbled off back into the stable yard. Soon they were all back at the hole in the ground, the opening in the tunnel roof, the gateway to the shoe.

“I can’t see a thing down here,” moaned Herbie who was leaning with his head over the side. “My shoe is lost forever. Oh why should this happen to me? Why? Why? Why?”

“Stop wailing for goodness sake!” Betsy was losing her patience with him. “You’re not actually being any help at all, are you? Get out of the way and let us rescue your shoe for you!”

Herbie moved out of the way, still bemoaning his misfortune and contemplating the terrible consequences that were sure to come, while Betsy and Charlie stared into the dark abyss.

“Come here a minute Arthur and tell us if you can see anything.”

Arthur trotted up and stuck his head right down past the brick lining of the tunnel. Betsy took hold of his waist, just to make sure he didn’t fall in.

“It’s... It’s... It’s... DAAAARK...” said Arthur spookily, using his special spooky voice.

“Lower a lantern down on the whale hook,” said Fanny. “Then you’ll be able to see.”

“Fantastic!” Betsy greeted the idea. “I’ll light the lantern... Dougie? Can you bring the hook over here and we’ll pop the lantern down into the tunnel.”

Betsy lit a match and set the wick alight, then turned it up so the lantern shone nice and brightly.

“Charlie, hold my legs while I feed it down. You keep hold of the fishing line Dougie in case I lose it down the hole.”

The lantern reached the base of the cavern and lit up the surroundings. Three sets of eyes looked down from above at the rough floor and walls which were now faintly visible in the flickering light.

“It’s not there,” observed Betsy, her disappointment showing in her voice. Behind her she heard the sound of Herbie wailing even more pathetically as his faint hopes were dashed.

“We need someone to go down into the tunnel and get the shoe.” The Scamps all looked at each other, and all their faces were blank, except for Arthur’s, which was smiling happily. Then their heads turned all at the same time and they looked at Scamper.

“Arrrrroooooooffff!” The dog gave his answer, which roughly translated from doggy-language was: NOT LIKELY!

“Oh g-o-o-o on Scamper, please, just for us, just for Herbie...”

“Arroo...roo...rrrooooooooffff!” The dog was adamant. He was not going back down there, with the possibility of having to face another fight.

“Not even for a sausage?” Betsy kept some tiny pieces of chopped-up sausage in her pinafore for when Scamper needed encouraging to do something he wasn’t keen on. He looked up at her and wagged his tail.

“Here you are the boy.” Betsy held out the delicious morsel in her hand and Scamper swallowed it down without even tasting it.

“Now will you go and get Herbie’s shoe?” Betsy asked in her nicest voice.

"Arrooofff!" said Scamper, still refusing. He knew he could exact more sausage from his mistress before he agreed to go on the dangerous mission.

"Oh Scamper!" said Betsy, disappointed at the dog. She reached into her pinafore pocket again and took out some more pieces, then laid them on the ground, one just in front of Scamper, and then in a trail, each three feet from the previous one, right up to the hole-side. "Now, when I say, you can eat these treats and then go down the hole for us. Is that agreed Scamper?"

"Arrorrrrr!" Scamper sounded the advance, indicating he was ready.

"Sit then... Wait... Wait... Wait...... Go!"

Scamper leapt up and munched is way to the final piece of sausage which he gulped down on top of the others, then he sat and looked into the ominous cavity.

"Arrooofff!"

"Scamper...... That's not fair! You said you would go!" Betsy was frustrated now. She took out one more piece of doggy-delight and waved it in front of Scamper's nose. The nose twitched and locked on to the aroma. Betsy then slowly withdrew the sausage from Scamper's snout and dropped it down the hole. Scamper hopped to his feet and bent down, looking into the dimness for any sign of where it landed. Betsy waited for him to leap in... But no... He just sat down again by the side of the hole.

"Arrooofff!"

"Well I've run out now," she told the disobedient animal in a peevish tone, "So you won't get any more, and you'll go without dinner tonight! So there!"

But then...

"I... I... I... hear something!" As well as being able to see in the dark, Arthur had an ear for this sort of thing too.

"What is it Arthur?" they all whispered, and then went utterly silent while Arthur listened, his head hovering over the hole, his right ear facing downward, open and alert to any sound.

"Miss... Miss... Miss-orrible dog!" he exclaimed, and was so pleased he had got the description right (well almost) that he beamed with "small-boy has a go at a big-word" satisfaction.

"Has he got my shoe?" Herbie enquired hopefully.

"I don't know yet," said Charlie, with his head halfway down the hole and straining to see.

"Get out of the way and let me have a look!" commanded Betsy impatiently.

"No, why should I?" retorted Charlie. "I can see just as well as you any day."

"Yes but you're too short. I can get my head much further down, so long as you hold my ankles."

"All right then," Charlie replied with a chirp in his voice, "But I shall let you go, right on top of Groucher's miserable dog, and I'll dangle you there and he'll snap at your hair with his teeth! *Snap! Snap! Snap!*"

"Oh please stop it you two," pleaded the disconsolate Herbie. "I want my shoe back. I JUST WANT MY SHOE BACK!" His wailing made him sound like a rather small Scamp and not the biggest, which he actually was.

Betsy and Charlie both peered into the hole, trying to hear or see something in the dimly lit passage beneath them. Betsy shrieked as she felt something nudge her to one side, forcing its way between her body and Charlie's.

"Grief what's that?" groaned Charlie petulantly.

"Oh it's you Arthur!" Betsy sounded relieved as she saw the little man's face next to her, pushing through on all-fours. "You frightened me half to death – I thought that miserable dog had found a way up and was mauling me from behind!"

"Mauling your behind, don't you mean?" joked Charlie sarcastically.

Arthur, as happy as anything, pushed himself to the very edge of the hole and stuck his head down. Betsy grabbed his waist once again so he would not tumble. "What are you doing Arthur? Get back – it's dangerous! You might fall in!"

The little man was unperturbed. "M... M... Mugger!" he called sweetly into the echoing chamber down below. With that, there was a scraping of feet followed by the sound of rapidly approaching scampering footsteps. Scamper sensed something of interest was happening, as dogs do, and he too came to look down the hole, which was very crowded now.

"G... G... Go away Scamper," said Arthur, his little voice sounding firm despite its shrill tone. Scamper looked up, then down the hole again, then up again at Arthur, and gave a soft whimper of protest before walking away back to his favourite tree... not that any of them weren't his favourites.

Mugger appeared from the darkness with Herbie's shoe still gripped in his mouth like a prize trophy.

"He's here!" shouted Charlie.

"Has he got my shoe?" Herbie asked again, his life depending upon the answer.

"No, he's dropped it so he can eat Scamper's sausage."

"Wooooooaaaaagggghhhhh! wailed Herbie as if in the final throes of his short life on Earth.

"But he's picked it up again!" Charlie continued his running commentary. "He's giving it one last chew for luck."

"G... G... Good boy," Arthur cajoled, talking to the miserable dog in a nice way that the poor hound was probably not used to. Arthur lurched forward, dropping the top half of his body down the hole while stretching out his arm beneath him (well actually above him because he was upside down) but down the hole in any case.

"Oh my goodness!" exclaimed Betsy in horror, grabbing Arthur's legs to stop him disappearing altogether. "Charlie, you grab his legs too! Quick!"

Mugger growled softly as Arthur's hand came closer to his head. The closer it got, the louder he growled.

"Arthur, watch out! called Charlie. "He's ferocious you know... He'll have your hand off when he bites!"

"G... G... Good boy," Arthur repeated, putting the miserable dog at ease.

Arthur wiggled his fingers, managing to touch the toe of Herbie's shoe sticking out of Mugger's mouth. Mugger growled and gave the shoe a shake, as if in sport. Suddenly, Arthur dived his spare hand into the pocket of his shorts and took something out. He then reached down holding the thing he had taken and waved it above the dog's head.

"Aaaaaahhh!" Betsy bawled, dreading that she was about to lose her grip and dreading even more the thought of having to explain to Arthur's mother that he was lost for ever!

Arthur held his hand out nearer and nearer Mugger's nose, who snuffled the air around the object he was grasping. "G... G... Good boy," Arthur continued coaxing. Arthur raised his arm slightly, bit by bit, drawing his hand up, while the dog's nose followed it, smelling something sweet which might be tasty. "G... G... Good boy," Arthur continued to purr softly until, after a few seconds, the shoe was just about near enough for Arthur's to reach and grab it. With one swift movement he took hold of the shoe and simultaneously sprinkled white powder over the dog's nose and face and mouth!

Mugger started choking and sneezing, forcing him to relinquish his grip on the shoe which Arthur plucked to freedom! The dog gazed up at the lost shoe as it disappeared above him, and started growling and snapping at Arthur's hand. The little boy held out a tasty sweet liquorice stick just above the dog's nose, causing Mugger to forget all about the shoe. He snatched the tasty liquorice from Arthur's grasp, and ran happily away, licking his lips and wagging his tail, back into the seclusion of the tunnel where he could munch the magnificent delicacy in peace without anyone trying to steal it.

"U... U... Up!" Arthur called to the others as Betsy and Charlie hauled hard on the little man's ankles, gradually reining him in, like weighing a ship's anchor. Arthur gripped tightly onto the sodden dog-slimed shoe, like it was a beautiful treasure, fresh from the deep... which of course it was, to Herbie anyway. As The Scamps all cheered and rushed to present the despondent Herbie with his dishevelled shoe, Scamper hurried to the hole-side and poked his nose down to look at the miserable dog and gloat. But there was not a dog in sight, and all he could hear was the sound of munching... and how unfair was that? That Mugger had been rewarded for the theft of a shoe? Whereas he, a hero of the escapade, had received no such prize. He concluded life just wasn't fair for a dog...

The change in Herbie's face was magical. From one minute being beyond despair at what his parents would do to him, now here in his friends' hands was his salvation... Or was it?... His relief was brief. Herbie took the miserable specimen of footwear and looked at it with renewed hopelessness.

"It's all right," said Fanny, trying to be upbeat. "It's just got a bit of slobber on it. And a few teeth marks. And a bit of a rip. And the laces are broken. And the sole's hanging off. And the toe's squashed in. But you can say you got your foot caught in some rocks while you were climbing and when you pulled it out they scuffed your shoe and it ended up looking like that."

"I've got some polish at home," breezed Betsy. "We can give your shoe a good old polish and use the back of a spoon heated on the stove –

my father showed me – if you put lots of polish in the holes and then rub it in with a hot spoon then the holes disappear. That's what my dad did in the Army with his boots.

Herbie stared at the shoe, its upper forlornly floppy, its tongue punctuated with incisored commas and full-stops, the nails in the leather sole chewed and hanging from their mounts, the sole itself flapping like the mouth on a porpoise.

"She'll kill me," he finally stated, without emotion, resignedly accepting his fate.

Arthur felt sorry for Herbie and went over and hugged him. "Th... There... Th... There..." he said, comforting his biggest Scamp friend.

"Awww... Look at Arthur," Betsy was so proud of the little man.

"Arthur?" Charlie wanted to know something. "What was it you threw in the miserable dog's face that made him sneeze like that?"

Arthur's face lit up as he giggled with joy. "Sh... Sh... Sherbet dab!"

"That's genius!" said Charlie in awe. "I take my hat off to you Arthur!" And he doffed his cap to the little chap, before realising they had better get a move on.

"Come on... Quick! Let's get out of here!" he shouted, thus breaking the spell of footwear inspection. "This mist is coming in and we have to get back to tell Will what we have seen and found. And the tide's coming in too. We can't return by the beach or we may be cut off. We shall have to go back along the track, so we need to watch out for old Groucher... He's sure to be in a foul temper now, after all that has happened to him and his miserable dog."

"No matter," said Fanny in her usual dismissive manner, "He won't be able to see us in the mist... We shall melt away like shadows, like shades, like phantoms, like..."

"Oooooooo, ghosts!" enthused Dougie. "We shall creep up on old Groucher and scare the pants off him! Oooooooo..."

"Sssshh you two – you're making this place feel creepy." Betsy didn't mind ghosts for she was a Scamp, and Scamps aren't scared of phantoms, but with the mist rolling in and getting thicker all the time, the trees began to look spooky, and the tangly bushes began to resemble gnarled little people, and the holes in the ground leading to the tunnels began to feel like plug-holes, draining the life-force from the land above, and...

"Aaaaahhhh!" Betsy screamed and started to run, for she had scared herself, and you know what it's like when your brain thinks a beastly ghost beastie is chasing after you: you just can't turn round, daren't look back, for it's behind you and it's after you and it's faster than you and you just keep running... and running... and "Aaaaahhhh!" she wailed pitifully.

"Betsy! It's all right!" Charlie shouted after her... "Come on, we are with you!" but she was gone into the mist.

"She knows her way," said Fanny. "We'll just follow on down to the track and she'll be hiding in one of our usual hiding places."

And they all trogged along to where the main path was joined, and there, sure enough, under one of the brick bridges that cross over the top of the narrow trail, Betsy squatted with her back against the wall, panting to get her breath back, her face pallid and pale, as if she'd seen a ghost. Arthur went over to her and gave her a hug. She looked at the little chap, his face level with hers, his grin still planted on his lips. She attempted a smile, but it was only half-hearted and she joined in with his embrace, gaining comfort from his undiminishing cheerfulness.

"Are... Are... Are you afraid of the ghosty-whosty?" he whispered, his head gently nestled in her neck.

"Oh Arthur... No, that was just silly of me! I thought the trees were ghouls and the bushes were dead people and I scared myself!"

"I... I... I like ghouls!" chirruped Arthur, which he immediately switched into a high-pitch small-boy laugh, as close to a ghostly cackle as he could manage.

"But then..." Betsy held Arthur even tighter as she began to explain. "But then... I saw something even more scary. In fact really genuinely scary, because a ghost is just a ghost, whereas this was alive, an alive person in the mist, and the alive are much more scary than the dead..."

"Was it G-ruh... G-ruh.. G-rold G-roucher?" Arthur asked excitedly.

"That's what I was most scared of. But I realised straight away that the figure was too tall, too thin, too fast to be old Groucher."

"Oooooooo... G-rotten!"

Betsy gulped and shivered into Arthur's arms. "It... It... It came into view and I saw the face... It was bloodied... And it spoke..."

"Ooooooo... I... I... I'm scared!"

"Yes, it was terrifying Arthur, worse than any ghoul, a big gash across its forehead and it cried to me 'Get out of here or I'll loose the hounds!' and then it disappeared back into the mist, the way it had come..." She pushed Arthur away and held him in front of her and looked into his eyes. The others were all standing around by now, listening to her tale. "We must get out of here."

"Who was it?" asked Herbie, his voice all a-tremble.

Betsy looked up at him and slowly she spoke the words. "It was Master Rufus." She looked back down at the little chap, still valiantly comforting her. "Come on Arthur, take my hand and we'll walk back to the village. We need to tell Will what we've discovered."

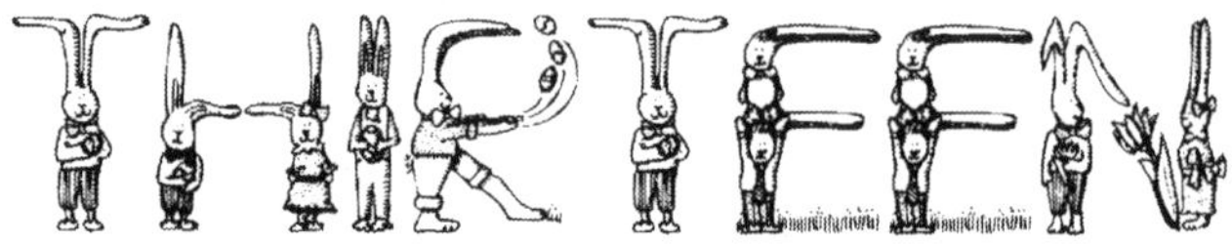

The PC Investigates

"Mmmmm." Greedy stood behind the desk in his police station house. He riffled through some papers which were held together with one of those toggles made of a piece of green string and two metal tubes, one at each end of the string, which go through a hole punched through all the sheets.

"Mmmmm," he mumbled again, as if clearing his head before starting what might possibly be something meaningful which was to follow.

"As I said earlier, I have here the doctor's post mortem results." Of course, Will and Harriet who were standing in front of him already knew this, as he had told them when they were back on the hill. "There are some interesting observations which he has made. Firstly let's start with the cause of death."

The pair glanced at each other, neither wishing to know the details, and yet at the same time fascinated, if that can be possible.

"There was only one wound to the body... And, thank the Lord, there was no other... *ahem...*" and Greedy cleared his throat to gain a pause before continuing, "in-ter-fer-ence," he spoke the word slowly and with due deference, leaving no doubt as to its sinister meaning, "with any other part of the young lady's anatomy." With that difficulty over, he relaxed, giving a visible sign of relief at having got past that most delicate part of the proceedings.

"Thank goodness," Harriet whispered, echoing Greedy's feelings.

"Quite so; a blessed relief to us all, and especially to the poor girl's mother... Which brings us to the injury which, as already mentioned by Doctor Kingslake when he first examined the deceased, is..." and Greedy proceeded to read from the notes in front of him, "a small confusion to the left side of the head, near the temple."

Harriet endeavoured to hide a snigger at Greedy's ponderous misreading of the doctor's notes. She knew she dare not look to her right at Will for fear they should both burst out in a fit of the giggles.

Greedy continued, “About the size of a farthing, but deep enough to have fractured a circle of bone and forced the loose piece into the brain cavity.”

“This con*t*usion,” said Will, emphasising the *t* in an attempt to make Greedy aware of his mispronunciation without wishing to humiliate him. “If that is the only injury then that must be the cause of death?”

Greedy skipped a few pages to the doctor’s summing up, licking his finger and turning the sheets until the relevant section was before him.

“The doctor says that it is *most likely* that the confusion was the cause of death, but he cannot rule out that it may simply have rendered the young lady unconscious, and she could then have died of the cold, which is, in medical language…” and he squinted closely at the page… “hippo-therm-ear.”

Again Harriet had to fight back a fit of mirth. She forced herself to stand rigid and stare fixedly at the posters on Greedy’s noticeboard on the wall behind him, not daring to allow herself to catch even a glimpse of the policeman’s face.

“Mmmmm.” Greedy flicked back to the beginning of the sheaf of papers once more, then thumbed to the next page. “Which brings me on to some interesting parts of this ’ere post mortem which apply to you two, which is why you are here.” He sounded stern, and Will and Harriet both felt a shudder travel down their spines – they hadn’t been expecting this – just *routine* the policeman had said. The PC fixed Harriet with his stare, which made her feel most uncomfortable, and in fear of what was coming next.

“The doctor examined the deceased’s clothes,” said Greedy keenly, in anticipation of getting to the heart of the matter. “And he was particularly interested in the shawl she was wearing…” Greedy paused and continued to stare at the poor girl in front of him. The drama was excruciating and Harriet just wished he would get on with it. “For, inside her shawl…” Greedy drawled, prolonging the moment and obviously enjoying himself, “was a name tag… And on that tag was… *your* name: Harriet Cooksley.” Pleased with himself, he took yet another pause before he continued by asking the crucial question… “How do you account for that, Miss Harriet?”

“I…” Her head was churning to think how this might have occurred, but nothing came to mind. Greedy could, *would*, read into this any number of possible reasons, none of which would be true, and none of which would help her in her struggle to determine her own innocence in the matter.

"I'm sorry... I can't account for it, sir. I do not know why she was wearing my shawl."

Greedy looked astonished – he had thought there would be a simple explanation, and even if there wasn't, he had assumed that Miss Harriet would just make up a simple explanation in order to placate him. What would he do now? He turned to Will. "Well... If Miss Harriet doesn't know how the shawl came to be on the deceased, maybe her brother does, for he is the only other person involved who could have passed the shawl on, could have taken it from his home and given it to Miss Florrie. Did you do that young Will? Is that what happened?"

Will answered quicker than his sister had done, for there was no need to think. "No sir! I most definitely did not. I would not take something of my sister's and give it to someone else without asking her first, would I Hattie?"

"No Will, of course you would not."

"Mmmmm." Greedy reverted to his familiar expression of confusion. "Mmmmm, this is most odd. I want to believe you, but I don't see how the deceased could be in possession of Miss Harriet's shawl without one of you two knowing about it. Did you notice it was missing Miss Harriet?"

"I have several, Mr Greedy, and I think that must be an old one that I have not worn for a long time. If it has a name tag in then it must be one I wore when I went to school, and I have not attended there this past year now, since I became fifteen."

"And where do you keep your shawls?"

"In a drawer in my bedroom. Only mother goes in there apart from me."

"Aha!" cried Will. "Mother! We need to ask mother, Mr Greedy. She will clear up this mystery. That is an old shawl and mother may have either given it away or sold it on."

"Mmmmm, that is a plausible explanation. I shall ask Mrs Cooksley when I next see her." The two youngsters watched, wondering if there were any other bombshells waiting to hit them. "Which brings me on to the next observation of the good doctor's. It says here that the deceased's left sleeve of her dress was wet, whereas the rest of her clothing on that side was almost dry. This could have been from a heavy dew before the frost, or after it melted, but that would logically have made all of her garment wet on that side, whereas it was only the sleeve. Moreover..." Greedy again strung out the moment to make his point more telling, "when the doctor squeezed the wet cloth between his fingers to gather some of the moisture on his skin, he then licked it... and it tasted salty..."

"She'd got it wet in the sea then?" Harriet posed the obvious question."

"Mmmmm, possibly." Greedy seemed unconvinced. "But the sea is a mile from where she was found, and in the opposite direction from where she would have started, assuming she started from her home."

"Maybe she got her sleeve dirty, and washed it in the sea?" Harriet continued her train of thought undeterred.

"Wouldn't she have used the village pump, like anyone else?" Greedy was picking holes in the seawater argument.

Will gulped, but he knew he had to tell the truth. He also knew that what he was about to say could be misconstrued, and in a way which had every chance of going badly for him.

"They were tears."

"What?" Greedy was taken aback.

"When I found her. I pulled back her hair and saw who it was." Will took a deep breath to try and hold back the new tears which were beginning to well inside him as he remembered the moment. "I cried, Mr Greedy... I cried... Tears... Lots of them... And my head was rested on Florrie's sleeve. And I cried until I had no tears left... And that is why Florrie's sleeve was wet, as the doctor described."

Harriet stared at her brother, mouth agape, wondering what would happen next. Behind his desk, Greedy became suddenly animated, discarding his customary lugubriousness and turning into the hunter in sight of its quarry, closing in on its prey.

"Aaahaaa!" he trumpeted. "You cried over her! You cried over the dead body of a girl! But why did you cry? Answer me that? Was it for pity, or remorse? Were they the tears of a perpetrator who had suddenly realised the consequences of his foul deed? Is that what they were, these tears of yours?"

Will had suspected that this would be Greedy's line of thought before he had spoken, but considered it best not to hide anything for fear of making it worse later.

"Please Mr Greedy. I have told you what I did, and I have told you truthfully, and now I shall tell you why I did it, Mr Greedy..."

Greedy's eyes flashed keenly, waiting for the boy to enlighten him, and hopefully admit his guilt."

"I cried because Florrie is... was... the most beautiful creature I have ever seen. And I cannot say any more than that." And Will's eyes filled again at the thought. Harriet hastily handed him a pretty hanky from her sleeve, while speaking to Greedy before he had time to digest what the boy had told him.

"Will carried a torch for her, Mr Greedy, for Florrie. He told me himself. It is quite natural that he was upset, and his tears were only those of love, not of malice, nor of remorse. He had nothing but admiration for Miss Florrie. He would never have done her harm, I know it."

Greedy struck again, not wishing to let his quarry escape. "But it could just as easily have been a lovers' tiff, a quarrel... or more than a quarrel... a squabble which led to a tussle which led to a scuffle which led to Miss Florrie being flung down against the wall, the wall on which she banged her head, the wall on which she received the confusion which pierced her skull and caused her vicious, violent and most wanton and untimely death!"

The pair stared at the policeman, unable to believe what they had just heard... Had Greedy learnt this speech off by heart? It sounded like something from the stage. Greedy stared at them, waiting for someone to respond.

"No, I didn't do any of that sir. I just loved her, that was all, from afar. She didn't even know, for I never told her."

"Yes Mr Greedy. She was much older than Will. She would have paid him no attention."

"And if I had done her harm, I wouldn't have been honest with you now, would I sir? I wouldn't have told you I cried over her dead body, would I sir? I would have agreed with my sister, that she washed her sleeve in the sea. I would have taken the chance of you accepting her explanation. But I didn't sir, because I just wanted to tell you the truth."

"Mmmmm." Poor Greedy turned back into his usual ponderous old self: his moment of glory seemed to have passed. He flicked some pages of the doctor's report, casually muttering as he picked out fragments, "Shawl, sleeve, new earrings, missing shoe... ah! And this!" Greedy's eyes flashed into life once more as he held up a rather crumpled piece of paper. "I don't know whether I should show you this." Greedy looked at each of the youngsters in turn, assessing their worthiness.

"Oh please Mr Greedy," Will enthused, "I would really love to help you with your investigation!"

Harriet gave her brother a glare and cleared her throat. Will noticed her theatrics and, on seeing her displeasure, immediately corrected his statement. "I mean... *we* would really love to help you with your investigation." He leaned towards her and whispered "Sorry Watson."

"What was that?" barked Greedy, looking up from the note that he was still clutching.

"Oh, it's just what I call her sometimes. We are a team you see. We hope to become proper detectives, and this is our first case."

"What?" The policeman seemed dumbfounded, but then a small grin wrinkled the corner of his mouth, raising the ends of his moustache, briefly cracking his stern features. "All right all right. Children's games I suppose. Talking of detectives, an Inspector is arriving tomorrow – I have a telegram from him here somewhere... yes... here it is... Inspector Les Word will be arriving at Minehead station tomorrow and catching the afternoon *Lorna Doone* coach, arriving in Porlock at ten minutes to the hour." Then Greedy looked up while he announced, "I'm sure he will want to have a word with you two."

Will groaned inwardly... not *more* questions...

"Please Mr Greedy, may we see the note? It may be important."

"Ah yes, the note." Greedy handed over the scrap of paper, but not to Will – he passed it to Harriet who took it with a thank you and grinned at her brother, a grin of satisfaction. Will felt slightly huffed.

“Well, what do you make of it young lady?” Greedy said after half a minute’s pause to give her time to examine it. Harriet didn’t answer, but held it out in her right hand so her brother could look at it too.

“The first two parts seem quite clear, do they not?” she said after a while. “Thirteen steps up, at sunset. But the circle of dots – what could they be... stars perhaps? What do you think it means Mr Greedy?”

“Same as you Miss. The circle’s got me stumped I do confess. What say you young William? Has the next great detective got a nose for this sort of thing? Maybe it was you who drew it?”

“No I didn’t draw it Mr Greedy.” Will prodded the little scrap of paper, carefully mouthing the number of dots pictured in the drawing as he went.

“Thirteen. But thirteen what? Thirteen in a circle. A...”

“Stone circle!” blurted out Harriet. “I’ve heard of it! Mother told me about it! There was a woman in the village, before we were born, mad as a March hare so it was said. Of course, the village called her a witch... Anyone strange in those days was labelled a witch... And this woman was stranger than most, always wailing, and droning on about a stone circle... A stone circle with thirteen stones! And she’d disappear for weeks, no one knew where to, and then reappear, calm for a few days before becoming anguished again and full of doom and despair, and then it was ‘the thirteen stones’ and how she must get to them and go and talk to the other witches. No one bothered checking up on her I think – the villagers were just relieved when she went off. Until one day some outsiders came and took her away in a cage on a cart. I thought it sad when mother told me her story. I don’t know what happened to her after that.”

“I do!” Greedy sprung to life. “Lord oh Lord I do!” He rushed to the notice board behind him and pointed to one of the posters which were pinned there. “ Greedy read out the details: ‘Important: Be Aware: The Last Patient In The Asylum Has Been Released. Native Of Porlock. Detained For Witchcraft 1888. Considered Harmless. This Day, Thursday The Twelfth Of May, 1904.’ Well who would have thought it, eh? What coincidence is that? Well done young lady!” And he fixed Harriet with a benevolent gaze.

“Well done Watson!” Will joined in with the congratulations, while Greedy became puzzled once more.

“What is all this ‘Watson’ rubbish?” he queried. “You mentioned it just now I believe, but I don’t understand.”

"Oh it's my daft little brother – he's been reading detective stories – Sherlock Holmes and Doctor Watson – he thinks they are real. He gets very upset when I tell him they are just made up."

"Ohhhhh. No Miss. I think your brother is right. I'm sure I have heard that they are real. They live in London you know: 221B Baker Street."

"Haaaa!" chirped Will in triumph.

Harriet could not believe what she was hearing. "Oh for goodness sake! They are detectives, and they are dreamt up to make a good story! Arthur Conan Doyle... He wrote the stories! They are his creation. They only exist in his head."

"Ah yes... Well... Maybe Miss... If you say so.. But this Detective Inspector is arriving tomorrow and he baint no Sherlock Holmes. What did I say his name was? 'Les Word'. And he'll want a word. Haha. With you two. Haha. Les Word will want a word... hahaha!" Greedy was pleased with his own joke.

Will smirked a little and then spoke up. "Are you sure that's his name Mr Greedy? In Sherlock Holmes, the Inspector is called 'Lestrade'..."

"Well it says here on this 'ere telegram 'Les Word' – you take a look at it yourself." He passed the Post Office Telegram to Will who squinted at it for a second and then laughed.

"It says his name is 'LESWORD'. Telegrams are printed all in capitals. What do you think Hattie?"

Harriet laughed. "Well we shall find out tomorrow one way or another. Have you finished with us now Mr Greedy? Only I have to go and clean my pinafore before mother sees it. I shall be sure to remember to ask her about the witch in the asylum, and the stones as well."

"Oh yes – and don't forget to ask her about your shawl as well, Miss. We must clear that up before the Inspector arrives. Inspector *Les Word.*" And Greedy let out a mighty roar of laughter, which was a most unusual occurrence, except for when he had been visiting the Royal Oak after he came off duty.

"Oh! Wait. I nearly forgot. We would like to ask you a question Mr Greedy."

"Fire away young lady."

"Did you by any chance find Miss Florrie's teddy bear?"

"I beg your pardon Miss, her what?"

"She always carried a toy bear with her, a stuffed brown bear, called Jack."

"I thought you said it was called Teddy?"

"Sorry, I should have explained. A teddy is just the type of bear... Sir George told us today that stuffed bears are all called teddy bears, after Teddy Roosevelt who is the President of America."

""Mmmmm. You've lost me now." The policeman shook his head. "She had no bear with her that I saw. And there is no bear mentioned in the doctor's report. Does that answer you question?"

"Yes sir, perfectly... Thank you." Harriet concluded.

"Right. Off you go then, and remember to ask your mother about the shawl and the lunatic woman."

"Yes Mr Greedy, thank you sir, we will," trilled Will and they left by the front door to find themselves the object of stares and mutterings once more from the little groups still dotted around the various porches, awnings and pathways of Porlock's cottages and shops.

Then the two of them heard a bit of a kerfuffle and a lot of shrieking and giggling getting louder all time as it was obviously headed towards them coming down the main street.

"There's only one thing makes that noise," observed Harriet.

"Actually seven things!" Will crowed as the hollering got louder and was accompanied by a yappy *woof woof* noise.

"THE SCAMPS!" they both cried in unison.

"I wonder if they have found out anything interesting for us?"

"Oh I don't doubt it Holmes, they nearly always do..."

Will stopped in his tracks and looked at his sister. "You called me Holmes! that's the first time you've done that!"

"So it is... Fancy that! But don't get too excited little brother, I shall probably never do it again."

"Never mind, my dear Watson. At least I've had the pleasure of hearing you say it."

"What's that noise about?" came a familiar gruff voice from behind them as Greedy emerged from his police house. "Is there a disturbance?"

"Only The Scamps," Will called back to him.

"Oh, those little monsters, eh? I shall be having a word with them."

"No no Mr Greedy, please don't. We sent them on an important mission... They may have vital information for us, about Florrie, about the case."

"Oh really? Well I'm not having them making all that racket in my police station. You can interview them yourselves and tell me what you find out that is of interest. Huummmph..." And with that parting signal of displeasure, he retreated back through his door to continue his paperwork and his cogitations.

Will and Harriet spied the noisy Scamps as they rounded the corner by St Dubricius' Church, whereupon the children rushed over and crowded round them, with Scamper bouncing on the edge of the scrum, trying to get in close under everybody's feet and yapping heartily.

"All of you, calm down, yes, yes, lovely to see you, yes, calm down, caaaaaalm please." Harriet tried to tame the throng as each Scamp demanded a hug in turn. Then she noticed that Herbie was not so cheerful as the others, being almost in tears.

"What is the matter Herbie?" she asked, feeling concern for the poor lad.

Herbie pointed to a dishevelled and pock-marked shoe which was flapping forlornly about on his foot.

"My mum will kill me!" he wailed, once again repeating his fears for his impending doom. Will looked at the ill-fitting object.

"Do not panic young Herbie! You were out on manoeuvres for me and my cohort Dr Watson here, and you suffered this injury, or rather your shoe suffered it, while carrying out your duties in a good cause." Will's hand slipped into his pocket and he scrabbled about amongst his tip money that he'd received early that morning up at Whitstones. "Take this half-a-crown and get yourself off to Mr Rawle the cobbler – give him your shoe and tell him it's urgent."

"Oh thank you, thank you!" Herbie couldn't believe his fortune.

"And while you're waiting for your shoe to be mended, I want you and the other Scamps to go to the bric-a-brac shop and see what you can find out there. I'll send the rest of your friends along when they've told me all that you learned at Ashley Combe and its tunnels."

"Oh yes, thank you Will. We shall find out everything you need to know! SCAMPS TO THE RESCUE!" he piped as he rushed off to the shoe-mender's and hoped-for salvation.

The Scamps began to tell of their adventure, and the pieces of the jigsaw that could now be dropped into place... Will and Harriet listened carefully to all the details, and of course the drama of the lost shoe and the miserable dog, which obviously, to Scamps, was the most exciting part.

“Right,” said Will as they concluded their thrilling tale, “Now please you Scamps, go straight to the Bric-a-Brac Emporium, see Mrs Agnes and have a good scout around for clues.... Watson? Can you go home and ask mother about the shawl and the stones?”

Harriet looked surprised. “Aren’t you coming home then?”

“I just need to investigate one more lead, one more piece of the puzzle – it shouldn’t take me long. I shall be home in an hour or so, please tell mother that I’ll be late – and then we’ll discuss what we know so far.”

Harriet tutted... “Honestly Will, you’re always up to something.”

“Sherlock Holmes is always ‘up to something’ as you put it... And when he isn’t, he is miserable.”

“We are all miserable little brother... Just thinking about Florrie makes us feel wretched and helpless.”

“Ah, there you have it in a nutshell my dear Watson... We are certainly miserable, but maybe not so helpless... By remaining intent on finding out what happened to poor Florrie, we can put aside some of our feelings of abject woe as we struggle to find the truth. The truth is out there... No one makes up the truth, it is there, it exists, and we are the ones to gather its mysteries and see what flows from that.”

“Will... You really do go on... I shall go and see mother, and mind you are back for tea!”

“And you mind you don’t let her catch sight of your pinafore... Or you shall get no tea, haha!” Will tittered as he wandered off in the direction of Doverhay. Harriet lifted the once-white apron from her skirt, looked at it and sighed.

The Cooksleys' Cottage

"Hattie... Is that you?"

"Yes mother." Harriet's voice was rushed, mirroring the sound of her hasty footsteps as she quickly trotted past her mother standing at the kitchen sink and made her way to the wash-house where stood the large copper, perched over the fire pit, cold and unlit."

Mrs Cooksley spun around as she realised her daughter was not stopping to chat. "What are you up to, my girl?" she demanded as she watched Harriet's back disappearing through the door.

"Nothing mother!" Harriet chirped back, airily. (Why is it that, when confronted by a parent or schoolteacher asking us "What are you up to?", we always reply "Nothing!". It so definitely means "Something!" And that means we shouldn't be doing it...)

"Haa-ree-ett!" The girl instantly knew she was in trouble. "Why are you in such a hurry?"

"I need to use the privy mother – I've been out a long time."

"Then if you are in such haste, why are you reaching up onto the shelf for the soap-flakes young lady?" Her mother stood in the doorway. "Come on, let me see that pinafore..."

"No mother, it's nothing, just a smudge... I'll wash it first and then I'll come back and show you... I promise."

"Goodness! It's like having a five-year-old. You're sixteen girl... You're a lady now... How do you always get yourself in such a mess? When you're wed, your husband will have something to say about it if you come home in the same state for him as you do for us! And I can imagine what he might do!"

"Yes mother... And that is precisely why I shall not be getting wed. I shall not be obliged to keep myself presentable for someone who will arrive home as dirty as he likes, and then expect *me* to wash all his clothes for him, like you do for father!"

"Really Harriet, your father goes to work every day at the tannery. It's a dirty job."

"Yes mother... He comes home bright orange and smelling of rotting corpses and expects *you* to wash his horrible things... And then you turn round and expect *me* to do it for you! Why don't you get him to do his own?"

"You're sixteen. You must help with the chores." She paused for greater impact before continuing on a sore subject. "Or else get wed and leave home."

Harriet took down the pack of Sunlight soap-flakes from the shelf and scattered some in a bowl. She then took the metal water jug from the draining board and poured some in, making a paste with the flakes, mashing them with her hands before dipping her pinafore into the mixture.

"I'll have this clean again in a jiffy mother. So you've no need to worry."

"Hmmmph..." Mrs Cooksley turned away in disapproval and made to flounce out of the door, back into her kitchen.

"Wait mother!" Harriet called. "I need to ask you something."

She hesitated, sensing that this was not a usual request. "Go on then.. What is it *lully girl*?"

Now Harriet knew her mother had forgiven her already, calling her by the affectionate name she had used for her since she was a baby.

"Mother... Have you taken one of my shawls? I can't find it... You know... The old one that I had in my drawer."

Mrs C thought for a few moments, then her eyes flashed recognition. "Oh yes... Dear Florrie took it..." And then, her facial expression changed of a sudden to one of shock and regret. "My goodness... Florrie... Poor dear Florrie... She borrowed it. She said she had left her own somewhere up at Ashley Combe... I said she could take your old one as you never wear it... I didn't think you would mind, Hattie. Oh poor Florrie, she must have been wearing your shawl when..."

"Yes mother, she was. Will and I were questioned by Mr Greedy. The doctor's report on poor Florrie noted that she was wearing a shawl with my name sewn in it. Mr Greedy wanted to know why that would be... and I couldn't tell him!"

"Oh Harriet, how awkward! Did he suspect you of having some part in this? I suppose he must have been very suspicious."

"Yes mother, he was. But as I had not lent Florrie my shawl, and no one else but you goes into my room, we soon worked out that it must have been you who gave it to her. So there's no need to worry. We'll tell Mr Greedy as soon as we see him again."

"Thank goodness."

"Which will be tomorrow by the way. He wants to see us again."

"Again? Why so? Surely it was an accident. Why would he need to see you again?"

"He wants to see both Will and me. There's a Detective Inspector arriving. He will want to hear all the circumstances, and as Will was the one who found poor Florrie, and as she was wearing my shawl, he obviously needs to see us first to tell him what we know. But it's just routine mother, there's no need to be anxious."

"Oh dear, my children being questioned by the police. What will the village be saying?"

"They be saying the first tittle-tattle that comes into their heads, just as they always do. And the gullible ones, which is most of them, will listen and turn it into a grand story, to be embellished and enlarged upon with each re-telling... But no matter... Best you just ignore them mother... Don't listen... Don't get involved... Say nothing."

"Oh what will your father say when he hears about all this? That his children are being interviewed by an *Inspector*, by some big detective from the city. Oh goodness..." Then Harriet's mother froze in fear at a sudden thought she just had. "We won't be in the newspaper will we? Please oh Lord, don't let our family be in the newspaper. Not like this!"

Harriet smiled. "I think you may just have to not look at any newspapers mother, just in case. Anyway, you never were one for reading a newspaper, so why should you start now?"

"Oh really Harriet... you don't understand. You're right that I don't pay much attention ordinarily. But if we're in it, our family, how can I *not* read it? I shall need to know what they are saying about us! Oh this is terrible... How could you have allowed such a thing Hattie?"

Harriet turned on her mother in disbelief. "Me! Allow such a thing! It was you who lent Florrie my shawl. I had no part in this! Don't try and make it my fault that the Cooksleys will be on the front page of the Somerset County Gazette!"

"Front page? Somerset County Gazette?" Harriet's mother screamed. "Aaaaaahhhhhhh!"

"Oh really mother, stop being so selfish! Imagine how much more terrible it must be for dear Florrie's mother. Would you rather it was me and Will on the front cover of the newspaper as a pair of witnesses? Or me dead in a ditch? Just put yourself in her position."

At which, Harriet's mother collapsed in a flood of tears. Harriet rushed over to her and took her head onto her shoulder, placing her arms around her mother's shoulders."

"I'm sorry mother, I shouldn't have said that. I'm sorry. Just forget I said it. Please."

"Oh what a terrible thought... I don't think I shall recover from it... Here lully girl... let me hold you tight... You are right though: this is so terrible for poor Mabel Nichols. How I wish there was something we could do to help her. Oh how I wish there was..." And she continued to sob wholeheartedly, hugging her daughter to her and never wishing to let go.

"There is, mother," comforted Harriet. "There is something we can do for Mrs Nichols... We can find out what happened to Florrie. The truth of what happened. Will is at this moment on a mission to do that. You know what Will is like once he decides to do something. He says the truth is out there and it is our duty to find it. And that means leaving no stone unturned. And talking of stones, I have to ask you another question mother, if you feel up to it?"

She looked up at her beautiful daughter and smiled in relief, the relief of seeing her own flesh and blood alive and well and holding her in her arms, counterpointed against the anguish that must be felt by poor Mabel, doubly injured first through widowhood and now this, her latest terrible loss.

"Mother," began Harriet, gently, "You know when I was small, you used to talk about the mad lady, the witch lady?"

Mrs Cooksley jumped as if startled at the thought. "Why yes... What could you wish to know about her all this time later? That was many years ago. They came and took her away you know."

"Yes mother, I know they did. And now, she is returned."

"What? Returned? Back here? In the village?"

"We don't actually know whether she is here in the village. But she is definitely freed. She is pronounced harmless. Let's admit, she probably always was harmless... All those stories of witches and witchcraft are usually just made up by village folk. Something to enjoy being shocked about, rather than based on fact are they not?"

"Yes well I never found her to be threatening, it's true. She groaned on about this and that and we never paid her much attention. Just the usual ramblings of a slightly demented soul I would have said. When was she released?"

"The day before yesterday."

"Glory be!"

"We need to talk to her. Will is very keen to do so, and so am I, truth be told."

"You shouldn't go out looking for her you know. After all this time, you never know what she may have become. Perhaps her madness will have overtaken her, stronger than ever."

"She's a harmless old lady, mother. You know that! Now where was it that you said she used to go to perform her strange rites?"

"To the stone circle of course. She was always chanting on about it. The thirteen stones arranged in a circle – they were her cathedral, a coven for one, a mysterious place all to herself. No one else dared to go there, to such a remote site, high on the moor."

"She will be there now then?"

"Yes. If she is at liberty, that is where she will be, there is no doubt." Harriet's mother seemed animated now, remembering how things were when she was first married with a young family, and how village life had changed through the twilight years of Queen Victoria's reign.

"So where is this place, mother? Can you remember? It is important that we find her. And can you remember her name?"

"Her name is Elizabeth, but of course we cruelly called her *Batty Betty*, especially when we were children. Names like that were freely given, and a source of much amusement – nobody saw anything wrong in it. As to the place, like I said, no one dared venture to see. But one of the coachmen then, Art his name, said he saw her once on the road to Exford, where it leaves the main road at Whitstones, the place where he was resting his horses for the rest of the journey. He called to her 'where are ye going at this late hour?' and the reply came 'to the stones, the thirteen stones, where solace and solitude lie, knotted together in harmony with the spirits of both high and low, heaven and hell!'. Sent shivers down him, she did; so he never forgot her words. He followed discreetly behind for a while, on foot; so none would hear his steps he kept to the heather, and in the deepening gloom of dusk, she suddenly disappeared to the right of the track, and that was as far as he dared go, for in any case he could see no more as the light deserted the place and the mist came down."

"Thank you mother – Will will be home shortly. I expect he will go dashing off to look for the stone circle as soon as he hears where it might be."

"We ought not tell him then, not until tomorrow. It is too late an hour to go off on a wild goose chase on the moors – the light will play tricks, and there are vagabonds a-plenty up on those hills."

"You can try to hold him back mother, but his impetuosity is part of his nature, especially now he has his teeth into solving this mystery."

"Are you sure there is a mystery to solve Hattie? As I said, it was probably an accident: the story I heard is that she fell from a carriage."

"Yes mother, you are probably right. The Inspector will give us his considered verdict tomorrow I am sure."

The Bric-a-Brac Emporium – 1

Mrs Agnes was at the back of her shop when she heard the shop bell ring, the door crashing open, and then a continuous *ring o ring o ringing* like the chime of a thousand clocks, as if a whole brigade of light infantry had charged into her establishment. She hurriedly put down the things she was sorting through and rushed to her counter to engage the onrushing crowd, be they friend or foe.

Her shop was indeed a shop full of curiosities, or should that be curios? There were bits of this and that, some tatty some neat, some old some not-so-old, and some really old: so old you couldn't imagine their ever being new, and more besides... There was pretty stuff and ugly stuff, their were clothes and there was furniture, there were trinkets, and there were mirrors and vases and cups and saucers and lamps and trousers and uniforms and hats and shoes and shoe-horns and... there was even a post horn which was very noisy when blown... Oh dear!

Paaaaaaarrrrrpppppp! Paaaaaaarr-parr-parr-paaaaaarrrrrpppp!

"What's that terrible noise?" Mrs Agnes heard the almost unbearably loud sound, so loud that the glass ornaments and glass beakers and glass candlesticks on her glass shelf rattled and shook and were, she felt sure, about to shatter all over her floor. She burst through the stock-room door like a scalded schoolteacher, scrawny and spectacled and mean.

"Oh no! It's The Scamps!" she bemoaned. "Why aren't you at school?"

"It's Saturday Mrs Agnes," said Betsy casually, as if nothing out of the ordinary was occurring, which it probably wasn't when it comes to Scamp culture.

"Oh dear," continued the flustered shopkeeper, knowing that she was outnumbered and bribery would be her only way around this sticky situation. "Please put down the..." *Paaaaaarrrrppppp!* "...post horn and I'll give you each a mint humbug – I have a tin here behind the counter."

“Mmmmmm... I like humbugs,” said Dougie. Come on Fanny – you can put the horn back on the shelf now where you found it.”

Paaaaaaarrrrpppppp!

She gave one final blast before handing it to Mrs Agnes who gratefully retrieved it and stowed it on the highest shelf she had, which was one almost touching the ceiling. Then she reached under the counter and brought out a decorated sweetie tin. She slid the snugly fitting lid upwards whereupon it opened with that tinny popping sound so beloved of children through the ages.

“Now, don’t snatch,” she ordered. “Wait your turn, and if you’re very good you can each have another one before you go home. You will be going home won’t you?”

“I... I... I’ve...”

“Yes, we know you have Arthur,” said Mrs Agnes. “And how old are you now?”

“Th... ree...” Arthur proudly answered, holding up four fingers.

“Yes, you’re three, which means you are now a very big boy and you really shouldn’t be doing the things that you do, quite so much.” Mrs Agnes checked herself from being too harsh on the little lad – after all he was very sweet and always polite... Unlike some of the other Scamps she thought. “Now, what did you all come in for?”

“We need to know if you have any clues that may help find out what happened to Florrie Nichols, Mrs Agnes. Will Cooksley sent us to search for clues,” Betsy explained.

“Yes,” continued Charlie, “We would like to have a look around if you don’t mind.”

Mrs Agnes inwardly groaned. “You can look, but you don’t have to touch anything do you? I know, it’s a terrible business, poor Florrie, but I would rather you didn’t pick things up that might get broken.”

“Of course we won’t,” said Fanny who, as we know, had already touched something belonging to Mrs Agnes without asking.

“Well take a quick look round then, and remember – if you’re very good you can all have another humbug.”

“Got any gobstoppers?” asked Dougie hopefully.

“You already got two giant ones this morning!” Charlie butted in, “Have you eaten them already?” he said enviously.

"Course I have!" replied Dougie, offended by Charlie's comment, which implied he might lack prowess in the art of gobstopper eating.

"Well in that case you must have a really big..."

"Yes yes!" cut in Mrs Agnes, hoping to avoid a squabble in her shop. She turned to look at Dougie directly. "No, I haven't got a gobstopper as you call it, but I do have a most extraordinarily giant humbug which I am sure would serve just as well."

"Ohhhh... Giant humbug heaven!" crooned Dougie while the others all stared at him nervously, fearful that they might be about to miss out here.

"Have you got more than one Mrs Agnes?" Charlie asked, hoping beyond hope that the bric-a-brac emporium might have an extensive giant humbug selection that they hitherto had not spotted.

There was a long pause, while six pairs of hopeful eyes gazed up at Mrs Agnes who now had total control over these scallywags, exactly as she had planned.

Just then, the front door of the shop opened, clanging the bell which jiggled on its spring, signalling the arrival of another customer. Herbie hopped in on one foot, but despite the awkward manner of his entrance, he was much more cheerful than before.

"Mr Rawle is mending my shoe!" he blurted excitedly. "He says it'll be ready in half an hour." He looked around him, and noticed the expectant expressions on the faces of his comrades. "What are you all staring at?" he asked, confused. The others realised the danger of the situation, which was that they might have to *share*, share a giant humbug with an extra mouth! This would call for strict diplomacy laced with skulduggery.

"Nothing," said Dougie jauntily.

"No, we're not staring," said Charlie nonchalantly. "We're just looking for clues."

"Exactly," said Betsy in hasty agreement.

"But we mustn't touch," said Fanny sternly.

"Rouuufffff!" said Scamper.

"And I... I... I've..."

"Yes, I know you have!" said Herbie testily, sensing he was being kept out of something. Seven pairs of eyes were now focused upon the half-shod Scamp, and apart from Mrs Agnes and Scamper, they all looked shifty. Realising that their stares were making it all too obvious they were engaged in a deception, they all turned away and started examining various nooks and crannies, some kneeling, some standing on tiptoe, and some craning their necks into unlikely places. It was a defiant show of busy-ness to distract their friend's attention from the delectable prize. Herbie stood there, puzzled.

There are 15 differences to spot in the two pictures of the shop on the following page.

Meanwhile, Mrs Agnes had disappeared into the back room once more. She really hoped she wouldn't hear any crashes or smashes, or paaarps or peeeps while her back was turned, but she thought she now had The Scamps tamed and in the palm of her hand. She went to a secret box which was in a secret cubby-hole in her stock room, in a secret part of the big old fireplace where she kept her secret valuables, *and* her giant humbugs, for they were for special occasions, and no one must know of their whereabouts. She took out a large waxed paper bag, its thick crinkly skin crackling beneath her fingers as she opened the neck and brought forth the biggest humbug that ever could possibly ever have been made, except of course for its brothers and sisters who Mrs Robbins at the sweet shop made specially for Mrs Agnes, and which no one else was to know about. She folded the neck of the bag until it was closed again and popped it back in its cubby-hole. Then, holding the humbug in the flat of her hand, she walked back through into the shop to witness the commotion which its arrival was sure to provoke. Herbie was standing there still, still looking baffled, until he spied the giant larger-than-life delight.

"A giant humbug!" he exclaimed, the others not having noticed or heard Mrs Agnes' return. "Oooooooooohhhhhhh..." Herbie continued in delirium, "I've never seen such a thing as that – is it for me?"

The other Scamps swung round to look as one, not only dismayed that the plot had been betrayed, but in terror that Herbie was about to claim the trophy for himself. At the same time, every Scamp in the room including Scamper was overwhelmed and in awe of such a confectionary masterpiece. Mrs Agnes grinned in delight at the impact made on the children by her showstopping, gobstopping, minty marvel.

"Is that for me?" asked Herbie once more, hoping Mrs Agnes would have heard about his terrible experience with the loss of his shoe and its virtual destruction, and would express her sympathy in the form of a comforting giant humbug.

"No it is not!" screamed Fanny."

"Even *your* mouth isn't big enough for that!" chipped in Charlie. "In fact, even Dougie's mouth isn't big enough for the awesome giantness of that majestic humbug."

"Hey *you...*" Dougie started to come after Charlie, but Mrs Agnes cleared her throat loudly and they all froze and looked at her... well actually at the giant humbug, transfixed by its stripeyness, mesmerised by its hugeness, in lust for its tastefulness.

“No one who is arguing or fighting will get any of this teeny tiny humbug will they now?” Mrs Agnes teased.

They looked amongst themselves and smirked nervously, not daring to put a foot wrong, but not knowing what was required of them.

“Who *will* get the humbug Mrs Agnes?” Fanny enquired timidly, hoping that a polite question would not disqualify her from receiving such a sublime sweetie.

“I... I... I like humbug!” said Arthur, cheerfully wrinkling up his cheeks as he spoke. “It... It... It’s very big as me!”

“The truth is,” continued Mrs Agnes, “That such a humbug as this is the prince of humbugs, the king and queen of humbugs, the emperor of humbugs all rolled into one, and as such can only go to the special person who most deserves its magical qualities.”

“Ooooh – does it really have magical qualities?” cooed Dougie.

“No, it just makes you feel magical when you’re eating it,” said Charlie, imagining how that would feel.

“M... M... Magic humbug!” Arthur’s face lit up at the thought.

“I think it’s magic,” Betsy chimed in, “It’s the most magic thing I’ve seen in my whole life, and that’s including Father Christmas!”

“That’s because you haven’t seen Father Christmas,” Herbie countered in a tone that meant Betsy was being stupid.

“Father Christmas was in the Post Office last Christmas Eve,” Fanny added without any emotion, “But it was really just Mr Arnold the postman dressed up. We sat on his knee and he gave us a present, but I got one which was meant for a boy – it was a wooden ship.”

“That’s because you act like a boy!” Charlie added spitefully.

“No it’s not!” retorted Fanny angrily, “Because Albert Perkins got a doll... So there!”

“Haha that was so funny!” said Dougie laughing as he recalled the moment when Albert’s sister told everyone what had happened, despite Albert threatening to hang her up in a tree by her hair if she did.

“Does anyone want this humbug or not?” Mrs Agnes was losing her patience as The Scamps had all started arguing amongst themselves once more. A sea of hands thrust into the air and shrieks of “I do Miss!” filled the shop. “Well then,” Agnes continued, “This humbug will go to whichever of you finds the most clues – that is why you are here isn't it?"

Immediately on announcing her intentions, the room burst into a flurry of hunting and rooting around, such that Mrs Agnes immediately regretted saying anything, as The Scamps forgot all about the DO NOT TOUCH rule and began to rummage through all the clothes and paraphernalia.

"Just don't touch the ornaments!" screamed Mrs Agnes above the din.

"Aha!" squealed Fanny, clutching a piece of paper... "Look what I found! It was in one of the pockets of that riding jacket."

"What does it say?"

Fanny examined the message which was written on the back of half a postcard torn in two.

"It doesn't say anything – it's just a lot of dots and crosses." Her face betrayed her disappointment. "It doesn't mean anything, does it? This isn't a clue at all."

"She's right," said Betsy after glancing at the note.

"Let me see." Mrs Agnes took the scrap of paper and then smiled broadly. "This is a lovers' code, used to send messages so no one else can read them, usually on a postcard. You make a grid and put all the letters of the alphabet onto it, then to make a message, you write just one square of the grid with a dot in the position of the letter you want to write, without writing the letter itself. Of course, you have to work out which layout the couple chose when they made up the code. If the position of the letters on the grid is jumbled up then the code is hard to break. But usually, the letters are written across the grid in alphabetical order A B C D etc. I have lots of postcards in my shop that have been written this way so it should be easy enough to work it out. I don't suppose it will give a clue as to what happened to poor Florrie though... but you never know."

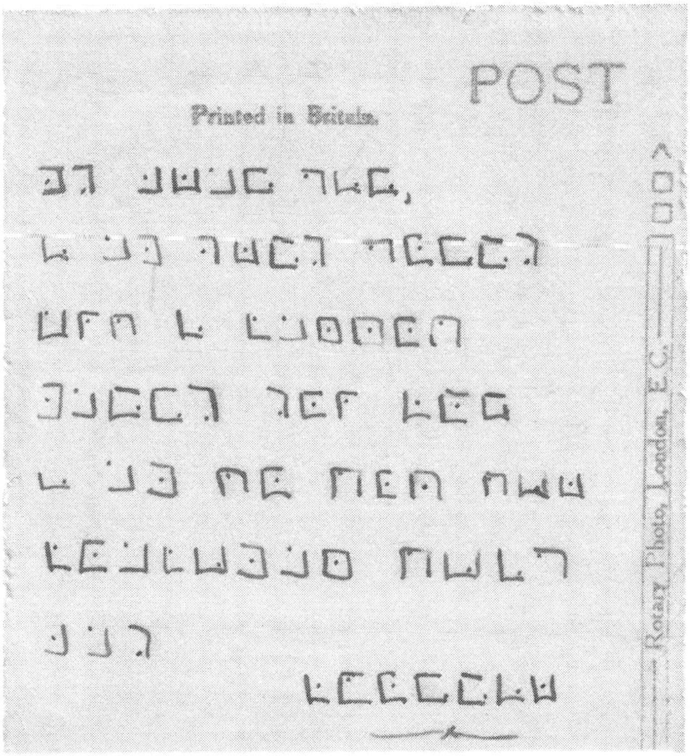

They all looked at the symbols on the paper. Mrs Agnes then continued, "You see that the dots go from the top left of each square to the bottom right, and there can be three different positions of the dot in each square, so a grid with nine squares will give you three possible letters for each square making twenty seven in all. Of course, there are only… how many letters in the alphabet?"

"Twenty six!" shouted out Betsy.

"Good, yes twenty six, so there are enough combinations of dots and squares for all the letters, plus one left over which isn't used. Do you see?"

"Cor! Is this how you send secret messages? Like when the army is about to attack?" asked Dougie keenly.

Mrs Agnes laughed. "Yes it is, but the army would use a more complicated one so the enemy couldn't decipher it. Anyway, if we try the simplest grid like this…" She took a scrap of paper from her counter top and pencilled a *noughts-and-crosses* grid on it. "Then we write all the letters on the grid, first across the top, then the next row, and then the next, until we run out of letters, we can see if the message makes sense.

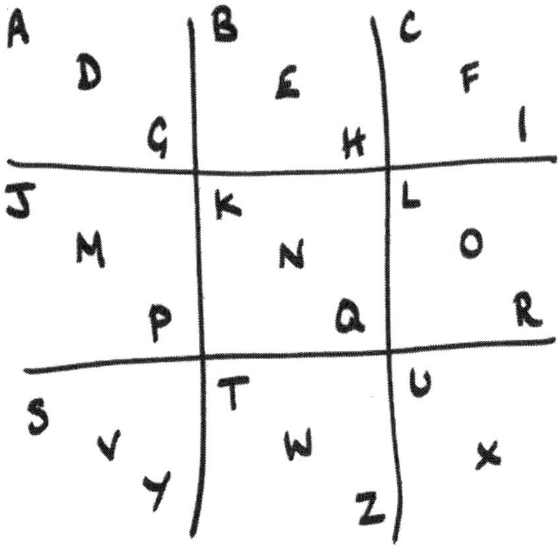

So  will be A, 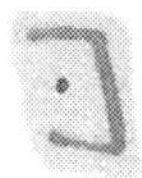 will be M, and N is special because it is the very centre dot on the very centre square, like this: . Now do you see how it works?

"Oh yes!" Betsy was fascinated now to see if she could work out the message for herself. "The first letter is M, then the next is…

"Y," said Fanny. "The first line is "MY DEAR SIR."

They all stared at the five year old child in wonderment. Betsy was aghast. "Fanny really, how do you know that?"

"I worked it out, silly."

Betsy looked horrified and snatched the piece of paper away.

"That's not fair! I want to do it myself without you spoiling it."

"Well go on then, Miss Clever Clogs…"

"Clever Clogs? You're the Miss Clever Clogs. And the Little Miss Smarty Pants as well! And the…"

"That's quite enough!" Mrs Agnes intervened to calm the girls down. "Why don't you all have a piece of blank paper which I shall give you, and you all share the piece of paper with the message, and write down what you think it says on your own piece of paper, and don't tell the others what the answer is? Yes?"

"Oh yes Mrs Agnes, thank you," said Herbie who had been quiet up to now, for he wasn't very good at puzzles. Betsy wasn't so sure, and glared at Fanny, fearing she wouldn't be able to resist telling them what the message said before they had all finished. Mrs Agnes sensed her discomfort.

"Don't worry young lady, I shall watch you all and make sure there's no hanky panky."

So Mrs Agnes handed out the paper scraps and pencils and watched while The Scamps puzzled and scribbled away. For a brief while, they all seemed to have forgotten about the giant humbug!

The Last Patient

Will returned from his brief excursion to Doverhay and met his sister back at Tinkers Cottage. She was in the wash-house scrubbing away at their father's filthy overalls. He had just got home from his shift at the tannery and who was now enjoying a bath in the tin tub in front of the open fire in the parlour.

"Look at my hands!" Harriet complained. "They're bright orange! I always look ridiculous after I've washed father's work clothes. I have to go out wearing gloves."

"Don't worry dear Hattie, one day I am sure that having orange skin will be the height of fashion[9]."

"Huuuhhh!" His sister grunted her displeasure. "Where have you been anyway?"

"To the Reading Room in Doverhay Manor."

"And why so? Did you discover anything interesting?"

"Yes, I believe I did. But I shall have to do a little more research. You know how it is when one finds complications."

She continued without looking up from the sink. "No, I do not really, for you never tell me anything."

"You sound peeved. I promise you I shall tell you all when I know it for myself... What did mother say? I presume you asked her about the shawl and the mad lady?"

"Yes I did. But I don't think it would be right for me to tell you what she said... Not until you tell me what *you* were doing... That would be tit-for-tat, would it not?"

"Oh Hattie!" Will let his exasperation bubble up, but then quickly realised that his sister was right. "Very well... I was examining a book about *molluscs* if you must know. Very interesting creatures, molluscs."

She looked at him with that look which says, *"Really?"*.

"That must have been interesting."

"Oh yes, it was... Most informative. I felt as if Sherlock Holmes was there with me, guiding me onward."

"So what were you really doing?"

Will was taken aback. "That's what I was doing... Don't you believe me Hattie?"

"No. I don't believe you. But never mind; I expect most girls have annoying idiots for brothers. If they have brothers that is. Girls that don't are the lucky ones."

"Hattie that is a cruel thing to say!"

She turned to him and smiled, this time a *"You better believe it..."* smile.

"Mother says that she lent Florrie my old shawl."

"Aha!" Will jumped with eagerness. "Just as we thought!"

"I'm glad you said *we*, otherwise I would have had to discontinue our conversation."

"My dear Watson, you know that we are equals in the art of deduction... well almost..."

"Almost? You mean that I am slightly better than you are, I assume? Yes, that makes sense."

She purred at the swiftness of the blow delivered by her put-down.

Will sighed. "Yes Hattie, do pray continue. What else did mother tell you?"

"She said that the lady who has just been released from the madhouse used to be seen about the village, and that she used to disappear at odd times, sometimes for days, even weeks. She spoke a lot about somewhere with thirteen stones. No one knew exactly where these were, but they all assumed that it was to the stones that she went, although whether these stones really existed or not – who could know?"

"This is most exciting Hattie! Did mother tell you where the stones were? Or did she not know?"

"No, she had no wish to know, and to find out would have meant following Batty Betty to her hideaway... that was what they called her by the way... mother felt it cruel but of course children use cruel words to describe people who are strange."

"And even not-so-strange, too," Will added, thinking of all the nicknames used for schoolmates and for teachers and even for policemen, behind their backs.

"And adults call people horrible things too, thus Batty Betty became the general term used for this poor lady, who was slightly deranged, and therefore labelled a witch."

"We need to talk to her. Are there any clues to her whereabouts now?"

"We know she is released, and there is every chance she will be at the thirteen stones, mother is convinced of it."

"But they could be anywhere."

"Not anywhere. One of the coachmen happened to see Betty wandering off along the Exford Road while he was resting the horses at Whitstones. He followed her briefly on foot until the mist and darkness came down and he lost her, somewhere in the hedgerow to the right of the road."

"I have travelled that road a hundred times, I know it like the..."

"Back of your hand... yes... But how well *do* you know the back of your hand little brother?" Harriet pondered her own, holding them out in front of her. "All I know is that mine are sadly orange."

Will paid no attention to his sister's melancholia. "Hattie! If the coachman followed her down that road on foot, it could not have been too far before she disappeared. I must search, right away."

"But it is late afternoon now... And the mist has descended on the moor: you won't be able to see a thing up there. Pray wait until the morning."

"I have to pilot the afternoon *Lorna Doone* to Whitstones just now in any case. I might as well ride one of the horses along the Exford Way while I am there." He paused, having thought of something which may just ease his task. "Besides, if she is as mad as people say, I shall not have to look for her... I shall hear her... I shall hear her through the mist!"

Harriet was unimpressed, but she knew that her stubborn brother, being up on the moor anyway for his work, would not hang back from seeking out the mystical stone circle.

"Very well. If you are determined on this course, and I can see that you are, then I shall come too."

“What?” Will was taken aback. “Hattie, I really don’t think you should!”

Harriet laughed, but in derision rather than mirth. “That’s what I just told *you*. And what notice did you take of me?... No notice at all, that’s what notice you took. So if you’re going then I am accompanying you... To look after you little brother... I have always been asked by mother to look after you, and I shall continue to do so, especially as I am now Dr Watson.” She knew this would rankle and enjoyed watching Will’s face betray his annoyance.

“Oh really Hattie! I shall be the one looking after you! The moor in a mist is no place for a girl!”

Harriet suspected this would be his response, even before he said it, but she held back her rage, knowing that she now held all the cards, and all of them were aces.

“Well my dear little brother,” she said, emphasising the word *little*. For one thing, I am probably near enough now a woman, rather than a girl, whereas you without doubt are still just a boy. So it is my responsibility, my duty even, to look after my little brother. For another thing, I think you will find, having read the Adventures of Sherlock Holmes, that Dr Watson accompanied him on almost all of his dangerous forays in seeking out clues to facilitate thc solutions to the mysteries upon which he was engaged. You did ask me to be your Dr Watson did you not? Or are you now taking back that request because the role is too dangerous for a mere girl?”

Will gulped and said nothing. There wasn’t much to say.

“I shall come with you to The Ship and I shall catch the *Lorna Doone* to Whitstones.”

“What if the coach is full?” Will continued to try and find a reason why she should not come.

“I have rarely seen it full, but if it is, then you know as well as I that driver Ned will let me ride next to him.”

Will’s attitude suddenly changed as he realised his sister was just as headstrong as he himself. He cracked a large grin and, taking his sister’s hand in both of his and squeezing it mate-ily, he extolled: “Watson, you are indeed a true friend and an undeviating dependable comrade – our endeavours shall not be in vain, for I declare I could not do without you!”

“Good, that’s settled then. I shall go with you... but if the mist is too thick I shall tell you so and you will turn back... you promise? I cannot leave you wandering off on your own on a fog-bound moor, for mother and father would never forgive me if you were to come to any harm. You must promise me that Will."

"Oh very well, but we shall have the horses – they can always find the way home, even wearing blinkers they could do it."

"Yes, that will be a comfort, but let us hope we have no need for them to do so! Come on then..."

Will looked surprised. "So, you are keen now all of a sudden?"

"I want to get going before it gets dark." Harriet went to the front door to leave, and just as she reached for the latch their came a dainty *knock knock* from outside which startled her. She pushed open the door, wondering who it could be, and there, standing outside on the little path leading up to Tinkers Cottage, was her friend Clara. Harriet flung her arms out and hugged her.

"Clara, I didn't know you were still here! I thought you had caught the early coach. I'm so sorry – I would have come and seen you off but Will kept dragging me around and we had to see Greedy the policeman."

Clara laughed. "Mother wasn't fit to ride earlier... she passed out again and so I let her sleep on. We caught the later coach to continue our journey on to Minehead where we shall catch our train. As we were passing by the end of your road, I asked the coachman 'where is Tinkers Cottage?', and he kindly stopped for me to say goodbye to you." She looked around at the tiny Cooksley home. "You do have a lovely home. It's so pretty here. Not like the smoke and bustle of London."

"Oh I'm sure London is pretty too – I would love to go there! It sounds so... exotic."

"Oh Harriet... you wait until you see. I don't think there could be anywhere less *exotic*."

"Well I'm sure it is... and I would like to come with you and see your home, but Will is making me tramp up that hill again."

"Why so? Is there another shoe gone missing?"

"No. This time we are on the trail of a witch."

"A witch? Oh gosh you do do exciting things. I would love to come with you again!" Clara was excited at the prospect, then looked downcast as she realised the reality. "But I can't... I have to see mother onto the train."

"Oh don't worry yourself, dear Clara. It's just one of Will's mad ideas. We won't really find a witch."

"I believe we shall," Will reassured them, talking from behind over Harriet's shoulder. Come... we must go or I shall miss my duty piloting the coach."

"Come Clara, we shall walk with you back to your coach. We can bid farewell to your mother."

"Yes, if she is awake. I left her inside the carriage, snoring."

They wandered down the lane and reached the main street where the *Lorna Doone* waited. Clara peered inside through the glass windows of the lower saloon.

"My goodness... where is she? She's not here?"

"No," said Will, laughing. "Look... Up there!"

Clara looked to where he was pointing and saw her mother sitting next to the driver. At that moment driver Tom handed Mrs Arnold a silver flask and she drank from it, then they both giggled in mirth, and, much to Clara's shock, they kissed.

"Oh goodness!" Clara cried out. "What shall I do?"

"Leave her," said Harriet. "She'll have a better journey if she has someone to talk to."

"She's not just talking though is she," Clara said in a tearful tone. "How shall I be able to cope with the embarrassment?"

"Oh don't worry," said Will hoping to calm the poor girl. "Tom always has an eye for a handsome woman. And your mother is, after all, a very handsome woman, wouldn't you say so Watson?"

"Indeed Holmes. Very handsome indeed!" She turned to her friend and embraced her. "Just get inside the coach dear Clara and pretend nothing is out of the ordinary. Then, you shall see that it won't be. Your mother is just enjoying herself! A sort of *holiday fling*."

Harriet kissed her friend's cheek. Clara smiled. "I'll try," she said. "I'll write to you soon." Then she turned and climbed into the carriage.

"Away boy!" Will cried up to Tom.

"Away away!" cried Tom in reply. "Sit tight there Lil! You can grab onto me if you think you're going to fall. I shan't a'mind!"

With a clatter of wheels and hooves, the carriage started to move, while above all the din there could be heard the sound of Mrs Lillian

Arnold, giggling like a schoolgirl at a funfair. Will and Harriet waved as they departed, then turned to make their way to the inn.

***

Things were busy at The Ship as the *Red Deer* was prepared for its departure for Lynmouth... The hubbub generated by the arrival of a coach was one of the highpoints of the day, and it was remarkable how many persons suddenly appeared on the scene, each with their own little jobs to do: feeding and checking the horses, making sure their harnesses were properly comfortable and secure for the long drag ahead of them, answering questions and directing passengers to the inn's facilities – much required during a break in a long journey, stowing and removal of luggage, ascertaining the weight of the load and therefore how many travellers needed to walk up the steepest section of the climb.

Will went into the inn yard and to the stables where Pug and Delia lived, next door neighbours to one another. He reached over Delia's stable door and she nuzzled him as he slid back the bolt to unlock it.

"Ah... Cooksley!" came a strident call. Will knew straight away who it was.

"Yes Wally?" he replied without turning round.

The guard of the *Lorna Doone* coach was in his mid twenties, and fancied that his station should command respect, especially from mere stable boys.

"My name is Walter and you'll call me by my correct name."

"I would rather not call you at all, so it is as well by me."

Walter was agitated by that remark, as Will knew he would be.

"I hope you will give us a smoother ride up than last time Cooksley. You almost pitched us into the stones on the second bend!"

"You know very well that my two pulled hard to the right to keep you out of trouble. Ned's driving was, how shall I say, loosened somewhat by his stopovers in the hospitable houses of Minehead. And the couple more he enjoyed in The Ship saw him as merry as a Lord!"

"You want to watch what you say! If word gets back to him that you are accusing a respected driver of drunkenness, then you will lose your employment."

"I'm not accusing anyone of anything... I am just telling you what happened. No one appreciates Ned's character and friendship more than I, and that is a fact."

"What if I should tell him what you just said?"

Will was getting fed up with the confrontation now, although with the bumptious Walter Collins he was used to it. "Tell him what you will. But he may think the less of you for mentioning it." Will waited for the guard's reaction and was rewarded with a look of indignation. "And I shouldn't think that telling tales about your fellows will be good for your advancement."

Walter kicked the straw-strewn surface of the yard with his boot. "Well be sure to give us a better haul up the rise this time young Cooksley, or you shall be the one risking your advancement... I shall see to that!"

And the petulant guard huffed off back through the archway to rejoin his waiting coach and passengers. Will watched him go, then harnessed up Delia and Pug and led them gently into the street where the four-in-hand was waiting, ready to have the pair hitched on in front. The truth was, and Will knew it well, that Pug and Delia were so experienced in their duties that if the coach did take a lurch to one side, the pair corrected it automatically with no need for the boy to direct them. Many was the time that they had saved a top-heavy carriage from pitching over by guiding the other horses and thereby keeping it to the correct side of the track. No horse likes to feel itself in danger and Will's two were as keen as any driver, guard or passenger to avoid the experience.

Will finished hitching the pair onto the others as Ned emerged from the door of the inn, a rosy glow on his cheeks, a broad smile on his face, indicating that his day had not gone so badly.

"Aha! Young Will! You shall carry us up while I take a read of the afternoon paper!"

Will laughed, and watched Walter glower as he listened to his master proclaiming his faith in the young horseman.

"Young Will Whortleboy!" Ned climbed up onto his seat and looked down fondly on the fourteen year old. "You are still the Whortleboy I hope, young Cooksley? Like your father, and your uncles, and their father before them?"

"No, not any more, Ned... We've a Whortlegirl now!"

Ned almost fell of his perch. “A Whortlegirl? Why that’s a turn up.” He looked down at Will’s sister who was waiting on the road beside the coach. “Is it young lady Harriet? Is she the Whortlegirl?” He turned to look at Will once more. “How did she whip all you lads then, eh? Quicker’n all o’ you was she?”

“No Ned, not me...” Harriet responded. “One of The Scamps she is... Fanny by name... Quicker and more thorough than all of us. Forty seven quarts in a day!”

Ned’s eyebrows almost reached the top of his head, so wide-eyed was he. “Forty seven quarts? That can’t be possible. She must of picked some the day before ’n hidden ’em somewhere!”

“No Ned, I watched her at work. She’s so low to the ground she barely needs to stoop, and her fingers work like sewing machine needles, busy ’neath the heather...”

“My Lord, that’ll never be beat I’ll wager.” Ned sighed. “Brings back memories o’ the only time I ever knew of a Whortlegirl afore. She was one o’ my aunts so she was, an’ she were keen of eye and fast o’ finger too just like your young lady. Aye, there was a lot o’ blushes among the young menfolk in the village when that ’appened – my own mother told me all about it, aunty Violet being ’er sister you see... Right...” Ned turned to examine his coach and cargo. “All aboard! Are you wanting a ride young lady?” He noticed Harriet still looking up at him and guessed she was waiting for the offer of a lift. “Up here an’ sit next to me then! Best seat in the place, when it’s not a-rainin’ that is. O’ course, it’s always a-rainin’!” And Ned chuckled loudly. Despite having to battle the folds of her pinafore dress, Harriet climbed nimbly up onto the seat, for she was used to clambering about in the same way as the boys. “Sound the horn Mr Wally! And tally-ho!” boomed Ned, signalling the getaway.

Will enjoyed seeing Walter looking even more pained as he planted the post horn to his lips and blew a rather less trilling fanfare than his usual *tarantara!...* Ned gave the call to his stout steeds with a gentle touch of the whip to his leading pair and Will turned his heels into Delia’s flanks whereupon the whole assemblage clattered away from the inn up the gentle first part of the rise. A couple of hundred yards on they passed the start of the Lime Way, along which farm labourers and packhorses used to carry the alkaline lime up on to the moor, there to neutralise the acid bogland in an attempt to make it suitable for the planting and growing of crops and pasture.

Three hundred yards more and the serious climb started with the rounding of the right hand hairpin at the foot of the hill. Pug and Delia began to draw breath like the steam engines on the Minehead branch line, their hooves digging ever deeper and slower into the loose surface which made the ascent all the more tricky. Another trumpet rang out from Walter's coach horn as they approached the sharp left bend, to warn any other road users of their presence. Now Will began to feel nervous, for just around the corner was the place where he had discovered dear Florrie, and he wondered if he would become nauseous on returning to her graveside, as it were, without being able to stop and pay his respects. On coming closer to the spot it was plain to see the beautiful splash of colour which had enriched the roadside where mourners and family had placed bunches of flowers in a great swathe to offer their respects and condolences, just as his beloved sister Harriet had done earlier in the day. As they reached the spot, Will was surprised by Ned calling "Whoaaa!", most unusually bringing the coach to a halt on one of the steepest parts of the climb, and he looked back towards the carriage to see what the problem was. He saw Ned take off his billycock hat and hold it to his breast, and so realised that the coachman had stopped the carriage so he could pay his respects to their dear departed Florrie. Will quickly took off his cap and did the same, bowing his head for a few seconds in contemplation as everyone on the coach fell silent. After a while, he looked up at Harriet sitting high above on the driver's seat, and she looked back at him, which made him feel all the sadness that had been hanging in his heart for the last hours, the thought that it could have been his dear Hattie, and how that made him feel, and how must Florrie's mother and brothers feel at this terrible time for them. He felt a tear breaking free from its tear duct and beginning to run down his cheek. He wiped it quickly away, turning his head away from his sister so that she might not notice, although why he did that he could not tell, except it was probably a natural "boys don't cry" response over which he had no control.

"Gee-up," encouraged Ned softly after the brief few minutes they had spent in quiet reflection, which was mightily shattered as the horses noisily dug in, starting the heavy load with difficulty once more, while the foot passengers, all male, who were following the coach, replaced their headwear and the fitter and stronger amongst them put their shoulders to the rear of the waggon and gave what assistance they could to get the procession going again. The wheels and springs of the carriage groaned as the horses struggled, barely managing to move at first, but the gradient lessened shortly after and soon the animals could pick up their normal speed. As they reached the top bend, Will saw Francis the road mender with his levelling implement, like a flat rake with no tines, standing back by the side of the road as they passed.

"Good evening Francis," he greeted as they continued up and beyond. Francis nodded his head in acknowledgement while he waited for the this, the last coach of the day to clear out of the way so he could carry out the vital work of levelling the shale where the horses had kicked it up, repairing the surface ready for the first coach in the morning.

On the flatter section the men clambered back on board and ten minutes later the hopeful travellers reached Whitstones where the usual ritual unfolded of detaching Will's pair and cleaning all the horses up while allowing them a brief rest before the final leg of the journey. Harriet hopped down, thanking Ned for his hospitality, while the kindly driver, smiling broadly, pulled a flask from his coat and took a healthy swig of whatever brew it contained, warming his cockles and keeping the chill evening moorland air at bay.

"You look after your sister, young Will!" Ned commanded from his perch. "Get her back down afore nightfall – this lonely moor is no place for a young lady to be out after dark! The shadows turn to grembles once the moon comes upon 'em, and if there baint no moon, then them's turns to gloombats!" He smiled at Harriet once more, touched his hat and ordered his steeds away, the clatter of the cart wheels on the granite chips giving a crunching accompaniment to Walter's next and more merry peel on his horn. They disappeared into the thickening mist in the space of a few seconds. Harriet shivered.

"I'm so glad we have the horses with us; they so bring me comfort..."

"I told you not to come, Hattie. You don't like it up here in the mist. You know you don't!"

"Yes, Hattie does not like it, that is true. But Dr Watson is practically fearless, and for that reason I shall be so too."

Will gently laughed, sympathetically for once. "Thank you Hattie... Or rather, thank you Dr Watson, for being here with me, setting out on this endeavour together, with you right by my side, and I by yours."

Will helped Harriet up on to the saddled Delia, and made sure his sister was comfortably ensconced, her feet in the stirrups and correctly adjusted, the rein on her lap. He himself then mounted Pug who was bridled but saddle-free, as any saving in weight was a bonus for the job the two horses had to do. Slowly, the pair set off along the

Exford road, maintaining a keen ear for any strange sounds that might crack the silence of the evening air, as it was impossible to see beyond the grass edge of the track. The noise of the horses' hooves was dampened by the fog, but unfortunately still made it difficult to pick out anything else, so they stopped every couple of minutes or so and strained for the slightest sound to reach their eardrums in that muffled cotton-wool world which gives the countryside such an eerie feeling when the cloud hangs so low that it makes all the body's senses operate as if under a blanket.

How far had they travelled along the narrow track? It was impossible to know, as it always seems further in the fog. Maybe a mile? More likely only a few hundred yards, but either way it was scary, with the contorted moorland trees, stunted and stooped and bent over like old men, looking every bit as spooky as one could possibly imagine. The deadness of the fuzzy air matched the deadness of the surroundings, like the smell of varnished coffins stacked in a morgue. Even the horses began to feel it, unused as they were to this extra trek, not part of their usual journey which they had tackled hundreds of times in all weathers. A figure, large, giant and shadowy lunged ahead of them, rattling the gorse as it brushed by. Harriet muffled a scream, while Will's stomach dropped to his knees before they both realised in was a red deer running across the road. This was the famous Exmoor red deer, whose title was adopted by the coaching firm of the same name, advertising the service's speed and natural oneness with the rugged landscape, just like the fine creature itself.

The two young detectives gathered their courage to continue, although every wafting plume and flitting spiral of mist tested their nerves. Did Holmes and Watson ever feel like this? Perhaps in the presence of dangerous criminals, but here there were no such real rapscallions... Just two minds playing tricks with shapes and sounds, with not a scoundrel nor a vagabond to be seen or heard.

The mist was thick. Now they could hardly see past the horses' noses.

"Will, I'm scared," Harriet spoke tentatively, trying not to sound too timid, even though she was."

"Me too!" Will gave the surprising reply. Harriet had felt sure her brother would tell her not to be so faint-hearted.

"What, really? You're scared too?"

"Of course Hattie... I mean *Watson*... I am probably more scared than you are dear fellow."

"But I thought Holmes was never scared?"

"Ah... Holmes' exterior demeanour is always to appear unruffled and in control, but who knows what he feels on the inside? Even Watson has doubts about Holmes' inner space, the space in which he lives from day to day. That is why Holmes needs morphia, and why Watson chides him for taking it, and advises him against doing so... Holmes needs the artificial comfort from the drug to calm his nerves I should imagine."

"Oh, I see. Well in that case, I'm not scared... I shall be the strong one. If Dr Watson is the calming guiding influence then that is what I shall be."

"My dear Watson, I couldn't have put it better myself!... HUSH! LISTEN!"

Harriet listened for a few seconds before whispering, "It's an owl."

"Listen a little more..."

They both tried to steady the horses to prevent them from puffing and clanking so they could hear any faint sounds through the fluffy fog. A tiny hullabaloo of wafer-thin hooting bounced off the damp cloud droplets clogging the air and settled on Will's and Harriet's straining eardrums.

"It could be an owl," admitted Will. Then, after a pause to listen again he continued, "But I don't think it is."

"It sounds a long way away."

"Everything sounds far in the fog... Even your own voice, Hattie, is reaching me as if it has passed through an eiderdown. Those sounds could be quite close... And, they are over to our right, which, if mother remembers correctly, is where the stone circle should be, is that not what she said?"

"She said the coachman saw Betty disappear to the right of the track."

"Precisely Watson! These things are never coincidence... We are on the right track, if you pardon the pun."

"I'm afraid I cannot. I am your sister and it would be wrong of me."

"No, you are Dr Watson, and your invaluable company is about to help solve one of the many little mysteries surrounding this case. It is all building into a picture, a jigsaw, which we can look at as a whole when finished and it will enable us to see what has happened here."

WHOOOOSSSHHH!

A tiny brown shape sliced the air, swooping across their path from right to left. It shot over the heads of the horses only inches above then vanished into nothingness as fast as it had arrived.

"See! It *was* an owl," Harriet said with justification. "The silent killer... This fog has brought it out early for its evening's hunting."

Will thought for a moment, still listening for any sounds of strangeness. "It could be a sign," he said at last. "The owl is an ominous creature, but not necessarily in a bad way. I noticed the direction it came from, from the right, and that is where we expect the stone circle to be, is it not? I suggest we look for a gap in the hedge that may have been trodden, for if there is such a circle, its path must be from the road, and it will have been used recently. And the owl has shown us the way."

"But what if we should become lost? This mist is very dense now." Harriet was rightly worried.

"We shall tie the horses to a stout branch on one of the bushes. If I call them they will fidget and scratch and whinny and we shall follow the course of their sound. But don't worry Watson, I am as nervous as you are!"

"Ned told you to look after me."

"Ssshhhh! There's another sound!"

It was faint, but not the same sound as an owl's wakening. In fact it sounded almost like a spoken word: *Dyu...... dyu...... eeeshhhsssssssss......*

"Someone's calling..." The hairs raised on the back of Harriet's neck. "Oh Will this is terrifying..."

"What is it saying?" said Will.

"It's something like *dew-ee-shus* I think."

"Quickly Watson, give me your hand... We need to get closer to the sound. I'll tie the horses while you go and see if there is a path through the hedgerow."

"Do I have to?"

"Yes Watson... It is most important that we find the stone circle."

"Oh very well, but I don't mind admitting I'm scared, and it's your fault if I get lost and die up here on the moor and then you'll have another dead girl who you were the first to discover and you'll have to tell mother and also Mr Greedy." She paused for breath. "And he will think that very suspicious indeed."

"Slow down, slow down Hattie... I shall be right behind you. I just have to sort out the horses and then I'll be with you. I'll talk to you the whole time you're looking if you like... Then you'll know I'm still here."

"Yes I would like that."

"Very well, now down you come."

Will helped Harriet down from her horse, then gathered the two nags together and tied their reins to a stumpy blackthorn.

Dyu...... eeeshhhsssssssss...... came the mysterious sound again.

"Oh Will! There it is again! Talk to me, quickly!"

"It's getting louder... It's her, I'll be bound... Betty... It must be. Have you found a place where we can get through yet?"

"Not quite, but I think I can see a lower bit where the hedgerow drops down just a bit further along, although this mist plays tricks with my eyes."

"Yes, but you have better eyesight than I, so I complete faith in you Watson."

"I've found it!" Harriet called.

"Wonderful, well done!" Will rushed to her side. "Come Hattie, I'll take your hand and you can lead me through the gap... And mind you don't snag your clothes... You know what mother will..."

"Yes, yes I know what mother will do."

The pair slipped through the hedge and onto the wild moor beyond. Will called out, "Betty! Are you there? Is that you Betty? Betty... Betty!" as they edged over the tussocks and coarse heather to where they thought the sound had first come. "Betty, is that you? Do not fear... We are just children, come to search for the stones. You know where the stones are, don't you? Don't you Betty? You are the guardian of the stones. You and you alone know the secrets of the..."

And at that moment a grey ragged figure loomed through the featureless mist, the mist that made all sharp points seem round and all roundness dull and stripped of detail.

"Aaaahh!" Harriet let an unintentional involuntary squeal slip from her lips as she beheld the haggard face, the whitened skin looped in curlicues around the cheeks and jaw like the folds of icing on an over-decorated cake. The pair looked on in awe at the apparition before them, at first in shock, but then in sorrow and sympathy as they took in the sight of a woman, released from the madhouse in only the rags she wore, and standing in this wild place like it was her home, her new home, or maybe her homecoming to the spot where she indeed felt most at home. And then, when the creature smiled, a warmth grew from her which seemed to thaw the chill from the youngsters' limbs and run up through their bodies to their hearts as the old lady looked upon them benignly and then softly spoke.

"You will not lock me up again..."

"N... no... of course not... We have come to find you to make sure that no harm comes to you..." Harriet spoke falteringly, not really knowing what to say, while Will was totally tongue-tied.

"No... You will not lock me up again... Eddie my gaoler has retired. Retired to live off my money for the rest of his days. For, you see, it was my own family which had me locked up! To escape the shame... And in a private madhouse, such as the one where I was sent to, the lock is only secured upon regular payment. And when my money was all spent in keeping me hidden away so as I couldn't besmirch the family name with my so-called witchery, the lock became a key, and I became free, and my gaoler is now embarked on his spree!"

But, that's awful," Harriet lamented. "Could you not get your money back from him? Maybe we could help?"

Through eyes that appeared to gaze in different directions, the old woman looked at her young supportress with fondness.

"No. Eddie was good to me. He deserves the money. He could have made life bad for me, but in truth his gaol had many doors, some of which were left ajar. And I have no use for the money. Not here. Not within these stones. The power of these stones stems from thousands of years ago, and you are now standing within their compass, their circle, their orbit, the orbit of the thirteen stones.

WHOOOOSSSHHH!

The small brown shape of their earlier recent encounter whipped between Will and Harriet where they stood, making them shudder through their bones in startlement as they had been lost and mesmerised listening to what Betty was telling them about this mystical place.

"Ah, Dubricius! You are back!"

Betty spoke to the owl as it landed on one of the thirteen stones, which was plainly its habitual and favoured perch.

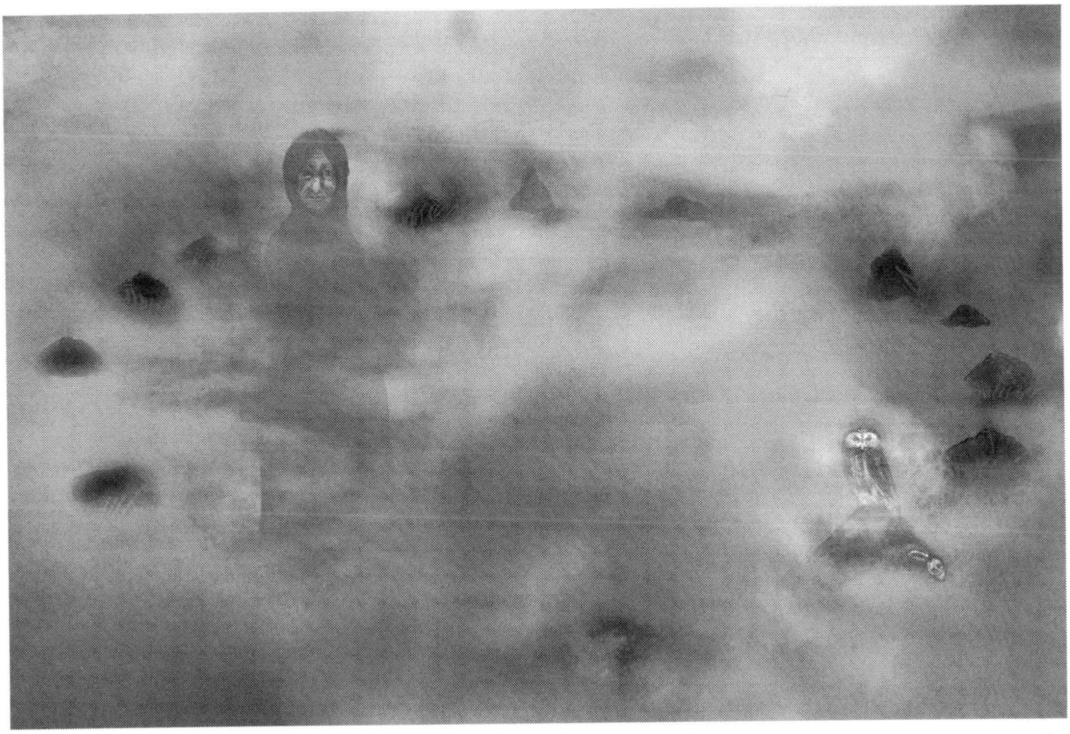

"*Dubricius*. So that's what you were calling... We couldn't make it out in the fog. You named the owl after the saint, the saint's name worn by our village church!" Harriet was happy at the thought of the owl having such a dignified name.

Betty laughed gently.

"You are almost right, my dear! But you know what I am going to tell you?" She looked at the owl and then back at Harriet. "So why don't you tell *me* first... tell me what I am about to tell *you*."

Harriet was puzzled, but then the same eery warm glow flooded through her body again and, on looking at the owl, she saw a glow flowing from the little bird to herself. And somehow she became aware... even though there was no explanation for it happening.

She felt silly for thinking what she was about to say, but knew that she had no choice but to say it, despite what her brother would now think. "You didn't name the bird *after* saint Dubricius, did you?"

The old woman smiled, the folds around her lips tightening slightly into gentle horizontal lines.

Harriet continued, "The bird... *is* Saint Dubricius."

The bird's wings shimmered and it let out a raucous hoot which startled them both once again. Will felt like the bones had been shaken out of his knees and that he was tumbling without actually falling anywhere.

"How on Earth did you know that, Watson?" he stammered.

Harriet looked at him, hoping he would not be too hard on her.

"Well Holmes..." Hattie decided to play along with the game, because if what she was about to explain had been part of a game then it would not seem too farfetched. "It was a simple deduction..."

"A deduction? But how could it be? There was no evidence for such a deduction as that, not that I could see anyway... Tell me your deduction!"

Harriet took a deep breath. "Did you not see the bird, after it landed here, after it settled? It turned into the image of a dragon... A Welsh dragon, with a red glow which grew around its body. Did you not see?"

"No Watson, I did *not* see... I think you are making this up!"

"No. She isn't making it up." Betty spoke softly to the boy. "The thirteen stones make the truth visible."

"But *I* did not see," countered Will, slightly miffed that he might be missing out on some supernatural sense that the others had and he didn't... or else, and worse, being the butt of some female joke at his expense. "And anyway, even if you could see a red glow, how does that show the owl to be the mortal form of the long-dead Saint Dubricius?"

"Like I said," Harriet continued with her explanation, "It became the image of a Welsh dragon, and Saint Dubricius was Welsh. You see? Elementary my dear Holmes!"

"No, I don't see." Will was frustrated. "This is just... witchcraft!"

Betty laughed deep and long before uttering, from somewhere amongst the tears and guffaws, "He's got it! Now I see your friend Holmes really *does* understand! There is hope for him to become a first rate detective yet!"

Will felt shamefaced. He wanted to believe, but felt cheated that he couldn't detect what the others had seen. And how did she know that he was practising to become a detective? Still, why waste time wondering about the why's and wherefore's when nightfall would soon be upon them. Time was ticking by and he had to get his sister safely home or there would be big trouble from his mother. And if mother was upset, then his father would be too, and that could be painful! He decided to get straight to the purpose of his mission:

"Betty, if the thirteen stones so ably present the truth, in all its beauty and horror, please can you tell us, what happened to Florrie?"

"Ah, Florrie. Sweet sweet Florrie... I talked to her just an hour ago."

"You did? What did she say?"

"She's in heaven now, with all the other witches."

"She was a witch?"

"*Learning* to be a witch. Just learning. We are all just learning. We are placed here to learn."

"Yes, but what did she say? Did she tell you how she died?"

"She told me about the three men."

"Three men?... That could be it!... Was it the three men who killed her?"

"The three men who wanted to *marry* her. She was... *is*... very pretty. She had three admirers."

"Who were they? Did she say? It's really important that you tell us who they are!"

"One was a rich man from a big house... One was a poor lad who rides a coach... One was a rogue, a brigand..."

Will's heart skipped a beat.

"Was one of them me? I mean, I ride a coach... sort of..."

Betty looked him up and down, studying as best she could through her boss eyes, a witch trying to make out which Will was which, the left or the right.

"No."

"No?"

"No."

"How do you know?"

"She was very specific. Man, not boy! She was very much bowled head-over-heels by his smart uniform and gay post horn."

"One of the guards! I'll bet it's that pompous Walter Collins – his father works in the stables." Will suddenly felt empty inside, hope replaced by...... nothing. He rested his head on his chest for a few long seconds before gathering the strength to express himself.

"In that case, she had four admirers... four *men* who wanted to marry her. For I would have married her, as boy or as man or as any other sort of being or even as beast I would have married her. And now all I have is that image, that last glimpse of her lifeless face stuck in my head forever and I will probably never marry anyone ever!"

Betty studied the boy weeping in front of her for a while before delivering her next words.

"If that is the case, that makes you a suspect."

"According to Greedy, I already am." Will blubbed through tears.

She pondered some more.

"But you *will* marry – I am sure of it – the stones tell me so."

Will felt easier with himself, as if some baked-in blockage had been freed and expelled from his wracked body.

"Thank you Betty... It is very kind of you to let me know that."

"It is the truth. However, for some reason, tomorrow you will be sternly tested, although I know not why. Now, be gone the pair of you, for the night is nigh, and you mustn't get caught up here, just like the coachman said."

"How did you know that's what the coachman said?"

Betty laughed. "Because that's what he always says. Now off you go – my supper will be arriving soon and I must prepare the spot where I shall eat it."

"Your supper?" Harriet was puzzled. "How will supper be arriving, in a wild place like this?"

"I told you. Eddie is very good to me. He's fed me every day for the last sixteen years. He sees no reason to stop now, for it would leave him without any purpose." She looked at them both in turn. "And we all need a purpose... A reason to live... However unlikely it may seem, I am Eddie's reason for living! Hahaha..." And Betty laughed wholeheartedly at the thought.

HOOOOOOT! St Dubricius trilled, as if affirming her statement.

"Well? What are you two waiting for? Be off with you! Oh... and don't be scared if you should meet Eddie on the way. You will know him, for he is much disfigured and presents an horrific first sight to those unaccustomed, but he is quite quite harmless I assure you even when he growls if you approach too closely. He has a chronic stoop, which means his head and eyes are permanently downcast. But as soon as he hears you, he will hide in the bushes until you are gone, for fear you may be footpads or vagabonds."

"Oh the poor thing, to be so fearful as that... How did he come to be thus tormented?" Harriet asked as she felt sorry for the creature, although she was also wondering just how horrific someone could look and was not looking forward to a possible encounter on their walk back to the horses.

"He is often baited and set upon by unkind souls for his appearance. But once here, with me, within these stones' embrace, he feels safe, just as I felt safe within his walls, despite their being my prison for all that time. I am the only person whom he will ever talk to, such is his shyness."

Will wasn't really listening but thinking back to what Betty had said about the imminent arrival of her supper. "What do you mean when you say that you must prepare the spot where you'll eat your supper? There's nothing here to eat it from, is there? No table, no chair, no anything..."

"Haha," Betty chuckled to herself again. "I must find the place where I should eat my meal. It changes by the day, the hour even."

"What?" Will was greatly puzzled.

"There is always a place where we should do anything at all. Which is to say, each thing that we do ought to be done in its own special place. Why, even when I was locked in my madhouse, I still knew where within those walls I should eat, wash, think, frown, cry... It is all mapped out for us, every one of us."

"Good Lord. How so?"

"I can only explain by example, for I fear you will not have the necessary sense." Betty looked at Harriet. "My dear. Are you cold?"

Harriet suddenly became nervous from the way Betty addressed her and from the feelings she was transmitting through her gaze which she could feel penetrating her clothing and embedding themselves in her flesh.

"Er, yes. Now you ask, I do feel unusually chilled." She looked tentatively towards Will, hoping his presence would comfort her through whatever was about to happen.

"Don't be scared my dear – it is easy – the map is laid plain before us. Walk around, anywhere, slowly, within these stones. When you find your place, you will feel suddenly warm. It is a quite unmistakeable feeling."

"You want me to walk around here and find somewhere that's warm? How can that ever be? We are on the desolate moor in the cold mist of an evening – where shall I find warmth up here?"

"You will find the place. Just walk my dear..."

Harriet stepped forward a few paces, and then to her right, feeling somewhat foolish, parading around aimlessly in front of a brother who would tease her mercilessly. Will just stood and watched, in fascination and in awe. Then, Harriet felt something strange happen. She stopped and looked around, all around, three hundred and sixty degrees around the whole area bounded by the thirteen stones. Betty looked on while the young lady she had instructed only moments earlier in how to find her special place, turned and walked quickly to a spot six yards in from one of the smaller stones behind where Betty stood, then grasped her shoulders with crossed arms and looked back at the other two.

"It is warm here," she said calmly.

"How did you know?" Betty asked, sounding gratified and intrigued.

"Yes, how did you know?" Will repeated, also eager to know.

"I saw the ground here glowed red, red as hot coals. So I simply walked to this spot. And now I am hot."

"Aha!" Betty shrieked and clapped her hands. "You are quicker to learn than could ever have been hoped!" She turned and addressed Will. "Your partner here has great perception. You should use that power in your quest for the truth about what happened to Florrie. Meanwhile, I shall eat my supper just where the young maid has trodden, for I too see the red flames, and they shall keep us both safe and warm, myself and my gaoler turned provider. Now. Off with you both – this is the last time I shall tell you... BE OFF WITH YOU, BOTH OF YOU, NOW!"

Harriet and Will took their final sight of the grizzled unfortunate woman before they turned away while her image swiftly disappeared into the mist. It was only forty yards or so to the road where Pug and Delia were tethered, but the fog made it seem so much further and Will was just about to clap his hands as a call to the animals to guide them when there, in front of them, just for the briefest of seconds appeared a hunchback figure which instantly leapt and flung itself into the broom-spiked undergrowth to their right while on the instant Harriet squealed a deathly squeal, unable to conceal her shock at seeing the form, even though Betty had warned them both.

"Eddie! Eddie!" Will called, hardly hearing himself above the outrageous thudding of his heart. "Eddie, please can we ask you something?"

"Grrrrrrr," came a bear-like growl from the undergrowth, and nothing stirred except the swirling grey water droplets of fog which eerily clung to the yellow flowers of the gorse, before cascading from the fronds in candle shapes like wraiths of fleeting stalactites. Will paused to look and see if Eddie was there, able to be seen, while Harriet cast her eyes down and away to avoid that possibility, just in case she should catch a sight.

"Please, let's go Will. I cannot bear it here. Please... I beg you..."

"Very well," he said, still peering hard into the bushes. Finally Will took his sister's hand then whistled, a plaintive sound in hope of rousing a response from the two horses. Instead there was another "Grrrrrrr" from somewhere low down but more distant now, quickly followed by a faint whinny from ahead which was their reward from the faithful beasts. They quickly made for the spot from where the sound came, diving between the knotted stumps for the haven of the lane and thence to where it led, their home. Will helped Harriet up into Delia's saddle, then unhitched the pair. Once he was mounted himself, they quickly trotted away from the eerie spot.

SEVENTEEN

The Puzzle – 3

I am now nearer to her, nearer now
to knowing why this date with fate she kept,
to knowing by what means, whose hand, and how
my sweetest Florrie by the roadside slept.

Am I in love? Drawn in by beauty so?
Am I policeman's enemy or friend?
Am I to set my heart free? Or guilty
of thus prolonging misery without end?

But I cannot, will not retreat from truth...
Her memory will rest with me blemished
if I deny my longing and the proof
that she died by cruel hand unkindly dished.

And here I vow to faithful witness be:
to her deliverance – my sweet Florrie.

"Gosh, that was strange... Quite the strangest thing. Don't you feel so? I hope the horses know where they're going."

"Don't worry Hattie, of course they do. It's only a few minutes to Whitstones and then the rest of the journey they've done a hundred times, more even... Mmmmm..." Will murmured to himself, as if arranging his thoughts. "It's a pity about Eddie."

"Yes. He seems a poor demented creature. I suppose working in the madhouse all those years has sent him scatty himself."

"Yes, I'm sure you're right, but I was thinking it is more of a pity that he won't talk to us, for he brings food up here for Betty at dusk, and to do that he must come up the hill, and therefore he may have been witness to what happened yesterday."

"He may well, but if that is so, what about Francis? He is also on the hill each evening. Maybe he saw something."

“Yes, that’s right... Well done Watson... We shall ask him, for he will be admirably more forthcoming than our friend the madhouse gaoler.”

“Oooohh,” Harriet shivered. “It is getting cold and I am a little unnerved in this solitary place with the darkness falling and mist swirling all around. I wish we could be nearer home and seeing the welcoming lights of The Ship at the foot of the slope, for then I should be warmed inside at the prospect of curling up in my nice warm bed.”

“You did a good job of being warmed in Betty’s stone circle... Did you really find that spot through witchery?”

“I don’t know. It certainly became appealing, as if something was guiding me to it. But of course I made more of it to please her. An extra little show to gain her respect. It never does any harm.”

“Indeed, one should always draw a witness in, make them feel comfortable, and important, as if they really matter. Which of course they do, especially in a case like this. So you’re not really a witch then? I must say I couldn’t see or feel anything special about the spot you chose. It must be a feminine thing.”

“Betty said we are all witches, did she not?”

“She actually said ‘we are all placed here to learn’. I assume she meant learn to be a witch. According to Betty, Florrie was a witch, or learning to be one.

“Yes. I imagine that’s what she says about all womankind – it’s because she likes to think she trains us in her ways – but of course she’s not really a witch herself – just likes to think she is – and perhaps that’s all there really is to being a witch anyway – just think it... and you are it... or should I say, *one*.”

“And what about all that rubbish with the owl turning into a dragon?”

“Oh, that was real. It was obviously Welsh. It hooted in a Welsh accent.”

“Really? I think you are teasing me. But never mind. I couldn’t ever have imagined that my Watson would turn out to be a witch, but so it seems... Witch Watson. It spins off the tongue and pleases the ears. Are you warmer now?”

“No, not really. But talking takes my mind off this place.”

“Do not fear Watson, for we are at Whitstones now. Witch Watson at Whitstones... That’s even better!”

"You're silly!"

"Watch Witch Watson at Whitstones Where Wild Winds Whistle."

"Now you really are being daft!" and she let out a little sprinkle of mirth, which rose as steam in the cold misty air.

"Right Watson." Will's voice sounded a more serious tone. "Let us discuss this case – that will take your mind off the cold and the desolation. What have you deduced so far?"

"Well... from the note which Mr Greedy showed us earlier I have deduced that Florrie was to climb some steps, maybe exactly thirteen steps, or maybe not, and that as the sun set and the moon rose she was to make her way to the thirteen stones. And the poor thing never got there – I am sure of that because Betty would have told us had she done so, which means she was waylaid somewhere and met her sad end on the hill, wearing my shawl."

"What else? Is there nothing else that strikes you?"

"I'm not sure... Let me think... I suppose there were all those bits and bobs you found where poor Florrie lay. Do any of those make sense?"

"Yes Watson, yes! Keep going... Come on... Think back to what we found. Together they add up to something. It was the ha'penny that first gave me the idea."

"What? That old thing? Just any old ha'penny that could have been there for years!"

"You said the word." Will looked at his sister and grinned.

"What word? Is this a riddle?"

"Of course... Everything is a riddle... You said 'old'... Let's move on to the next thing: the silver charm."

"Yes, I said that must be important... It had a blue stone set into it."

"Quite so. Exactly in fact. Remember that fact Watson. Next, your shawl she was wearing... Mother lent it to her so it was?"

Harriet's expression suddenly changed to one of understanding.

"Borrowed! I've got it... She was wearing new earrings, so that's the new. But surely she wouldn't have worn a grimy old ha'penny would she? How do you explain that?"

"As you correctly stated, the ha'penny had probably been there for years... But the fact that it was old led me to think of the rest: the new, borrowed and blue. I imagine she was wearing something old, but obviously I didn't undress her at the scene did I... It could have been anything she was wearing."

"Or!..."

"What is it Watson? You've thought of something haven't you! Tell me, what is it?"

"Florrie's bear! Jack!... It was all tattered and the fur was rubbed off in places... It must have been ancient!"

"Genius Watson! You know we really do make a magnificent team!"

"Thank you Holmes." Harriet felt comfortable now, her brain working overtime having warmed in some mysterious way the whole of the rest of her body.

"And Watson!... there is one more thing which clinches it. Remember when we were searching for the shoe? Remember, I said I knew that it was close by when I picked something up from the side of the road? Recite the rhyme, Watson."

"*Something old, something new, something borrowed, something blue, and a silver sixpence in her shoe.*"

"Yes! When I found the sixpence, I guessed that it had fallen from her shoe when her shoe came off. So, if someone had come back to dispose of the shoe by throwing it into the undergrowth, it couldn't be that far away."

Harriet looked amazed. "Well done Will, I mean Holmes! So Florrie was to be wed... But to whom? Do you know the answer to that one? Betty said she had three suitors, three men who wished to marry her."

"Four if you include myself."

"Oh yes – I forgot about your crush. But you never asked her to marry you did you, so you don't count."

"That's not fair of you Hattie... My love for Florrie is much more than a crush, so it definitely counts! But you are right – I never asked her for fear she would laugh and take pity on me as a silly boy."

"You are too young, Will – it is as well that you didn't ask. But now there must be three others, at least three others, who are also heartbroken now that they know they can never be united with Florrie until they themselves pass away. What of them? Was one of them her murderer?"

"We must not assume that the person who did her harm was one of the three, just as we mustn't rule them out. We also don't know if Betty was right about there being three – she probably just made it up to show that she was in contact with Florrie via the spirits."

"What she said made sense. The rich man – we know that Rufus was besotted with her. Then there was the poor man – you yourself knew of a coachman. Then the third: a brigand. The Scamps saw pirates in the bay, and Florrie met them too in the tunnels: you saw Fanny's picture... that is where she left her shawl, in the pirates' den, in the dark secluded cavern where they brought ashore their booty, safe from prying eyes and a visit from the customs men. A brigand!... A rogue!... A pirate!"

"Yes. I think you are right Watson! And, there is more evidence to confirm your deductions."

"Really? Pray what would that be?"

"Cast your mind to the other things I showed you this morning. Although you may not wish to be reminded of them, I assure you they are of the greatest importance."

Harriet screwed her face up in distaste. "Not the horrible cigar-end and rotting snail? I do not wish to re-imagine them if they are the things you mean."

"Quite so. I noted that the snail shell is unusual. If you study the picture of the snail shells on the shore at Porlock, you will see that the one I found beside Florrie bears no resemblance to any of those. When I returned form the village today, you asked me where I had been and I said I visited the reading room in Doverhay Manor. Fortunately, they had a work on the world's molluscs, picturing their shells. After trawling a large number of pages in my search, I found the sketch of the exact same shell which I had discovered next to dear Florrie in her resting place."

Will paused, to make the point more dramatic. Harriet looked at him, irritated by his antics.

"Yes... And?"

"And, my dear Watson, the creature whose shell that is, is found only in the Caribbean islands."

"So how could it have got here? Half way up Porlock hill?"

"Aha! I was hoping you would ask me that! You know what you said just now about pirates. Where do you think pirates come from?"

Harriet didn't seem impressed. "The ones round here come from Wales!"

Will looked disappointed. "Are you sure?"

"Well no. I'm not sure, but that's where father says they come from. He says they're a bunch of..."

"Yes, I know what he says. But I think *our* pirates, these pirates who brought all this brandy and rum and port wine, are much more exotic than that. Do you know where rum comes from?"

"From Jamaica."

"Precisely! Our pirates have come all the way from Jamaica carrying rum...... and shells! The book says that the shells of this particular snail are used on the Caribbean islands as good luck charms. I believe our amorous pirate left the shell near Florrie as a token, either of his loss, or of his regret. Or possibly both."

"You think the shell means the pirate was there with her, where she died?"

"I don't see how else a shell from the Caribbean could have got there, do you?"

"I suppose not. It seems most strange."

"But, I'm not saying he was there *when* she died. That would be leaping to a conclusion without being backed up by the facts. That, my dear Watson, is a different matter altogether."

"Mmmm. So was anyone else there at that spot? What about your disgusting cigar butt?"

"Yes, now that is most interesting – it is not the usual rough shag smoked by father and his fellow workers at the tannery, or anyone I have seen in The Ship. I haven't had time yet to call on the tobacconist and get an expert opinion on the exact type of tobacco and who would purchase it. I'm going to pay a visit to Mr Wiles when we get back in a few minutes. Talking of which... Look! We're at the top bend already! You see – the journey has passed in no time while we were engrossed in our thoughts and conversation. It has been most helpful. Remember, Sherlock Holmes himself said that 'Nothing clears up a case so much as stating the facts of it to another person'. Soon the welcoming lights of The Ship will come into view..."

"Oh I'm so glad."

"Yes and it is Saturday... The boys will be making merry and the music and singing shall be ringing out. You have a beautiful voice

Hattie – you should join in. They'll tip you tuppence if they have enough ale in them and an eye for a pretty girl... And that's a lot of tuppences!"

"Oh come Will, mother would never let me, and father might come through the door at any time!"

"Father? He'd be proud to hear his daughter singing for his friends. And he'd make sure they were free with the tuppences haha!"

"Maybe, but mother..."

"Yes, you're right... Mother wouldn't like it. She would think it would give a bad impression of our family."

"It's so unfair. You're younger than me and yet you're allowed to do whatever you like. Even The Scamps can do what they like, just because they are very young... When a girl becomes a lady, as mother says I am now, she's suddenly prevented from doing anything at all, at least without someone else watching them the whole time. My whole enjoyment of life has been carved away with a knife labelled *etiquette*, and not because of anything I've done, merely to please, or actually appease, other people's ridiculous expectations of how a young lady should behave... And if I insist on being different and choose to live that way, then they ostracise me and call me a witch, just as they did with Bettty!... Huuuuh!!!"

"It is most unfair Hattie. I shall make sure my daughters are brought up in freedom."

"That's easy enough to say, but I shall watch that you do! That is if you can find anyone who'll marry you!" And Harriet smirked gleefully, getting over her previous indignation with a pleasurable dig at her brother.

"I shall be a famous detective soon... Young ladies will beat a path to my door."

"That may be, but mother won't let them in! If she won't let me sing, she will definitely not allow you to cavort."

"Ah, but I shall have my own chambers. With my own housekeeper."

"Mrs Hudson."

"You know her?"

"I've read a few of the stories."

"She's a real person!"

"Oh, not that again... I told you – they're just stories... Characters... Fiction..."

"She makes Sherlock Holmes' dinner. She must be real, or else he would starve. So there!" And Will blew Harriet a raspberry.

"Very well, have it your way. And there's no need to be coarse. Look – there are the lights of The Ship now."

As they approached, a dark blob ballooned from out of the shadows in front of them, tottered, then turned into a lurching shambling figure before their eyes.

"Master Will..." it implored.

Harriet gagged in her throat, throttling a scream at the sight of the unknown thing in front of her horse. She pulled on the rein and dragged Delia back, but to be truthful Delia had already taken fright at the sight of the dark thing in front of her and had dug in her hooves, dropping back behind Pug who was not so concerned and cared little about anything. Will peered down. "My goodness, it's Francis! How long have you been out drinking? And just *what* have you been drinking – you can hardly stand!"

"Master Will, I can hardly stand because I can hardly bear myself, and that is in two senses in one."

"You're talking nonsense – tell me what it is that's the matter and I promise I will not judge."

"Last evening..."

He presented an image of misery and seemed unable to continue.

"Yes? You mean yesterday evening?"

"Last evening, the evening before this one, I was tamping the road."

"Yes, that is your job Francis. For goodness sake man, what happened?"

"It was dusk, the light was beginning to fade..."

"Yes?"

"Master Will..." He looked up at the boy, tears filled his eyes and his lined face was not only drunken but wretched. "I saw the girl."

"You did! What, Florrie? You saw Florrie? Did you see her alive? Or did you see her by the roadside?"

"Oh Master Will I saw her alive, very alive, beautifully alive... Alive and beautiful, in white, like she was going to her own wedding."

"Francis! Now, steady old fellow... Was she alone? It's very important."

"She was all alone. And it was that which worried me. So, I confess Master Will... I followed her. And now you're going to think I done her harm... But I didn't, I promise you... I followed her until I got scared and then turned back." Francis broke into sobs before composing himself again. "But I shouldn't o' turned back. Cos if I'd a-stayed, a-following behind, I may of saved her Master Will. I could of saved her! And now I have the guilt upon me, and last night I had dreams... An' I dreamed I followed her and killed her, and now I don't know if I did do that terrible thing or whether it were really a dream, but I know I turned back and that makes me a coward. Or a murderer... Or both!"

"Francis! Francis, now listen. You didn't hurt Florrie – I know that... And you must know that too... You haven't got a hurting bone inside of you so don't worry. But you must tell me what happened... How far did you follow her? And where? And what scared you so, that made you turn back?"

Francis gulped as he tried to contain his despair. "Master Will... I've drunk more than any man ever should to make these thoughts go away, but they just come back bigger and stronger... I followed her up the Lime Way, just above where you're standing now. I followed her until she were up to where the path splits off to Hawkcombe. And then I saw him..."

Francis stopped speaking as is something was choking him. Will was on the edge of his saddle, or what would have been the edge of his saddle if he had one. "Saw him... yes... saw who? Please... You've got to tell us."

"The pirate... The girl was climbing ahead of me, and she kept on climbing without a care, as if she hadn't a fear, and this nasty pirate caught sight of me and gave me such a look... a look of death and vengeance such as I've never seen afore... and I turned on my heels and ran back down the hill."

"Well that shows that you couldn't have killed Florrie then, doesn't it? You weren't even there, so you don't need to fear on that score. Have you told Greedy any of this?"

"No, no young Master Will, I have not for fear he would question me and I would say something I didn't oughta say and he would lock me up and I would see a-front of me a dangling noose all ready and prepared to embrace my wretched neck."

"Don't let that thought rattle around your head Francis – I think I am a more likely suspect than you. Greedy has already tried to get me to admit to it! You get yourself back into The Ship and console yourself with your soulmates – that is if you can walk that far!"

"But wait, there's more..."

"More?"

"I ran away back down the hill and when I reached the bottom o' the steps I saw the vicar coming up. In the darkness I only knew it was him because he was all dressed up in his garb like he was going to give a service, and I thought, this is strange, for what would he be doing out of an evening in such a place? And I were mighty confused. And he had with him a gentleman, tall, he was too."

"A gentleman? Did you recognise him? What was he wearing?"

"He wore a top hat, which made him look even taller, and a frock coat, and his face... Why, he had a powerful look with a fire in his eyes – even though it was dark I could see that, and that's what made me even more afeared and led me to drink, and into the state you find me in now, more's the pity."

"That is most interesting. But wait Francis... Before you go, do you know what time it was when you saw Florrie?"

"Sir, I don't possess of a timepiece as it would be a thing of more expense than I can muster, but like I told you, the light were just beginning to fade."

"And one last thing... "Did you happen to notice... and this is most important... whether Florrie had with her a little stuffed toy bear?"

Francis' eyes stared wide and his mouth fell agape. "Why yes, I think she did!"

"Thank you Francis. You have helped greatly."

"Oh thank *you* Master Will. You have put my mind at ease, and I thank you most assuredly. "Should I go a-telling Mr Greedy what I saw?"

"No, leave it to me. I'm seeing him again in the morning."

"Well rather you than me Master Will. I shall take my leave of you now and return to the warm of the fire."

"Yes, and I shall get these horses back in their stable and watered and fed for the night. Take good care of yourself Francis. And not too much more ale or the constable will be sweeping *you* up off the street!"

"Good health to you too Master Will... And to you Miss Harriet..."

Francis touched his cap and waved, almost falling over in the process, then staggered down the slope as best he could before falling through the door of the inn and back to the land of carousing and roistering that took place within its drunken and embracing walls.

"I do hope Francis will be all right," Harriet sounded concerned. "He looked in a bad way to me, in his cups, and you encouraged him to go back inside and drink more. I don't think you should have done that."

Will helped Harriet down from Delia and began to take off her saddle and bridle. "I know Hattie, but he would have done so anyway... I was just trying to comfort him and let him know it was not his fault what happened..." Will hung the saddle on its hook then continued with the unharnessing. "I just wish I knew whose fault it was!"

"Yes. That is what we are doing isn't it? The great detective and his assistant?"

"We are closer to solving the puzzle Watson but we are not yet there I fear. I am sure Mr Sherlock Holmes would have cracked it by now."

"But we have only been on the case for the best part of a day! Even he often took several times as much to solve a stubborn problem, did he not? We have tonight to sleep on it and then tomorrow I am sure all the pieces will fall into place."

"I hope you are right. It's true we have many clues, and among them many red herrings too I'll be bound. We need to sift through which of those are which and then – like a cloudy beer settling in the glass – the clear light will filter through, and the image on the other side will become apparent... the image in this case being... the unknown hand which fell upon the helpless maiden!"

"Oooooeeeerrrrr... You're making me shiver... You make it sound like the wildest horror story, and yet it is here in our little village where nothing ever happens."

"Nothing ever happens in anyone's little village, Watson. Until it *does*... That is the thing. Ask anyone who experiences an horrific crime on their doorstep and what do they say? 'This sort of thing never happens around here. This is such a quiet sleepy little place. It's the last place you would expect it!' And it's true... It is the last place... But that doesn't mean it won't happen there, does it? Because it *has*!"

"It changes the way people feel about a place, doesn't it... Do you think the village will ever forget?"

"Of course. The last people to remember what has happened here will be The Scamps, and when they are old, they will tell thcir grandchildren, but to them it will mean little or even nothing. Events get lost in the mists of time. They will be a few sheets of paper in a dusty folder in the police records office, and someone will chance on them one day, but it will be just another ordinary day, unlike this one. Come Watson, let us get into the village and see if it sleeps, or if the place is changed in some detectable way."

"Will?" Harriet's voice was unusually plaintive.

"Yes Hattie?"

"I know you won't want to...... But will you hold my hand?" Harriet felt embarrassed. "I mean, I know you are my brother, younger brother at that, and that you could get teased for holding your sister's hand while out walking. But, I just wondered if, on this day, that you might..."

"Hattie ssssshhhhh." Will looked into her large sad eyes and saw, perhaps for the first time, the beauty in his sister. He gently offered her his hand. She took it tentatively, wondering if it would be quite the correct thing to do.

"You don't know how much this means to me," she said. "I've never wanted to hold your hand before, and it feels like I shouldn't."

Will continued to look into her eyes, trying to be consoling, even though he knew he wasn't very good at it. "Nor I yours," he said. "Not since I was a tiny child anyway. But this day, I think you should..."

He offered his hand and felt her delicate touch nestle within its grasp. They walked from the stable out into the yard and thence through the archway which led onto the road.

"Will, Will, Hattie, Hattie, Wiiilllllllll!!! Woooof!" A crescendo of noise greeted them as they turned toward the village, and there assembled before them were six Scamps and a dog, five of them shrieking in unconcealed excitement, one woofing, and the final one aloofly licking on a giant humbug, which was almost the size of her face.

"Will, Will, Wiiillllllllll! We have a message!" "Yes a message!" shrieked another. "We have it here – it's a puzzle message but we know what it says!" "Yes – we know what it says – it's really important!" "Yes it must be really important because it's a code! It has no letters in it!" "No... no letters only funny pictures, little pictures which mean letters but aren't really letters. They're funny letters." "No they're not, stupid... They're code." Fanny stopped licking long enough to admonish one of her cohorts. "Oh – listen to Miss Smarty Pants. She's so smart... And she won't share either!" "That's right Miss Harriet. Fanny won't share! She got the giant humbug and won't share and so we hate her!" "Good!" said Fanny, sullenly. "Just because I was the one who worked out the code..." "You're just a Clever Clogs Smarty Pants and we hate you!" "Yes, hate you...! Hate you hate you hate you hate you...!"

"Enough!" screamed Harriet. "For goodness sake stop being so nasty to each other!"

The Scamps all looked a little shocked, apart from Fanny who carried on licking, while the others shuffled around.

"She sounds like a teacher," said Fanny, unconcerned. "Teachers all sound like that... Bossy."

Will laughed. "She called you bossy, Hattie! What are you going to say about that?"

"I just want them to be nice to each other, that's all."

"They're children... They're not nice..." Harriet gave Will a stern look. "But they are sometimes useful... Come on then young Scamps, show me the message you have found. And tell me where you found it."

"Wait!" Harriet ordered peremptorily. "Before they do that, I want them all to line up and shake hands with each other to show they're sorry."

"Now she really does sound like a teacher," commented Fanny from behind her humbug.

"And you," Harriet eyed the little girl as she spoke. "You can share that humbug... It's quite big enough for everyone to have a lick."

"Yeeeeuuuukk!" said Dougie. "I'm not licking it now she's licked it!"

"Yes, she wouldn't share and we hate her!" said Charlie vehemently.

"I... I... I'll have a lick!" said Arthur, grinning from ear to ear.

"No you won't!"

Arthur started crying.

"Now look what you've done!" Betsy exclaimed. "You've made Arthur cry. Arthur never cries!"

"Don't care!"

"That's not very nice now is it Fanny? Say sorry to Arthur."

Arthur looked up at Fanny and grinned once more.

Fanny looked down. "Shan't!" she said implacably.

Arthur continued to look up at his fellow Scamp while his grin became wider until, all of a sudden, he opened his arms and chortled, "I'm... I'm... I'm going to give her a kiss!"

"Raaahhhhh!" shrieked Fanny and leapt back to avoid Arthur's embrace, in doing so bumping into Herbie's chest and stomach which barred her way. Herbie took her shoulders and held her while Arthur proceeded to deliver his threat, as he had the stubborn pigheaded girl at his mercy.

"Mmm Mmm Mmm Mmm," mouthed Arthur, performing a mock kissing motion with his lips, inching them closer and closer to the protesting Fanny. She wanted to push him away, but that might endanger the giant humbug. What to do..? It didn't matter. Herbie had her tight in his grasp while Arthur sort of clambered a little to reach her neck, not being tall enough to gain access to Fanny's mouth, not that he would have especially wanted to anyway, and planted a wet smacker on her cheek as she flinched and turned her head away to the side to try and avoid him. But, on seeing that Fanny was now vulnerable, Scamper thought he would join in the fun too so he jumped up and licked Fanny's face, and now she didn't know which way to turn and could not fend off either of her persecutors without dropping the giant humbug.

The Scamps and Harriet and Will all yowled with laughter at Fanny's discomfiture as she flailed her arms around but didn't dare let go.

"Stop! Stop! Please! Yeuuukkkk!" wailed Fanny. "All right, you can have a lick Arthur. Stop it just please stop it. Yeu Yeu Yeuuukkkk!"

Arthur hopped back down, looked up and stuck out his tongue.

"Oh gross!" stropped Fanny, looking at the wriggly pink slimy vision before her. "Here... You can have it..." and she thrust the giant humbug into the grubby waiting hands of the little boy.

"I... I... I got it!" cooed Arthur, and his smile became even bigger, if that were at all possible, as he studied the glorious sweet. Then, before taking his first lick, he looked up at Fanny. "Do you want some?"

"Aaaaaggghhhhhh!" shouted Fanny in irritation and annoyance.

"Right...! That's it...! Enough...!" announced Harriet. I want us all to be friends again, and I want to see the last of any sour faces. Stand in a line please, to attention, then tell us what is in this important message that you have deciphered. And Fanny, take that miserable look off your face."

The Scamps shuffled into a line six abreast, looking along the row to check they were lined up straight. Scamper poked his head through the middle pair of Betsy and Herbie and sat down between them. The Scamps then clicked their shoes down in a military manner and puffed out their chests, like a little toy army waiting for inspection. Herbie presented the piece of paper with the cipher written on it. Harriet took it and frowned.

"Yes, it certainly makes no sense. What say you Holmes?"

Will inspected the note over his sister's shoulder.

"It must be a code, but what does it say? You Scamps know already don't you?"

"It's simple," said Fanny in her most condescending voice. "It says, *My dear sir, I am very sorry but I cannot marry you for I am to wed the coachman this day. Florrie.*"

Will and Harriet studied the note intently, attempting to work out how the characters corresponded to the message.

"You won't get it," said Betsy. "Not unless you know the trick. Mrs Agnes told us how to do it."

"I could have done it anyway," said Fanny boasting. "I got it straight away. Not like these dunderheads."

"You little..."

"Fibber!" shouted Dougie.

"Braggart!" screeched Herbie.

"Know-it-all-show-off!" squawked Betsy.

"Stop it, please!" Harriet tried to cool the situation.

"She couldn't have done it without the trick," said Charlie, speaking for the first time. "Mrs Agnes showed us the trick and then, it's true:

Fanny did it quicker than all the rest of us. She was the one who worked out the message first."

"Yes and that is why Mrs Agnes gave her the giant humbug," said Dougie mournfully.

"Yes, and then she didn't share!" Betsy was still sore.

"Yes Yes Yes! We've heard it all before now. I want you all to be NICE TO EACH OTHER!" Harriet at this point was running out of ideas. Will decided bribery was the only course. It was the one thing he knew always worked.

"Here..." He rummaged in his pocket. "Take a penny each of you and get some humbugs, normal size humbugs mind, from Mrs Robbins. And then please stop arguing! Oh, and where did you find the note?"

"It was in the pocket of a jacket we found in the shop – here is the picture Fanny drew so you can see for yourselves."

Will took the picture then handed out the pennies to coos of *yum* and *thank you.*

"And before you go, tomorrow I may need you again." They all snapped to attention once more to listen. "I have to meet PC Greedy and I have been warned, by someone who knows about these things..." He paused and winked at Harriet. "...That my meeting will probably go badly." He looked at the eager faces. "So this is what I shall need you to do if it does... My assistant here, Watson, will give you the nod if it should come to pass that the plan must be put into action!"

"Ohhh – we like a plan of action!" crowed Dougie.

"Raaaarrrrffffff!" agreed Scamper, taking a crafty slurp of Arthur's humbug while he wasn't looking.

"I... I... I'm ready for action!" grinned Arthur, saluting like they do in the picture books that he had seen.

"Good... Right... Squaaaaad... Ready!" Will shouted his orders. "Squad... Dismissed! Go on... off you go!"

The troop disbanded and scuttled noisily off into town leaving Will and Harriet alone on the dark hill.

"I'm sorry Hattie... You didn't have very long holding my hand." He offered it to her once more.

"It's all right. I feel better now... You don't have to."

Will smiled at her. "It's here if you want it. Go on. Take it."

Harriet smiled back and gently took hold of Will's fingers, and together they walked slowly home.

The Morning

Will awoke, threw on his clothes and dashed downstairs to the kitchen.

“Watson, Watson! Hurry! We have a lot to do this morning... Greedy will want to see me when the Inspector arrives and we must gather the rest of the clues before that happens!”

“Will? Is that you?”

“Oh – yes mother, good morning mother.”

“What is the meaning of all this Watson business?”

“Oh, er... yes mother, I thought you would want to know about that. Watson is Sherlock Holmes’ assistant and I am practising to be Porlock’s very own Sherlock Holmes, and Hattie is my Dr Watson. Isn’t that right Hattie?”

“It’s his new game, mother. He’s insisting that I play the part of Dr Watson.”

“How can Hattie be Dr Watson? She’s a girl?”

Harriet looked offended. “Why do you say that mother? Wouldn’t *you* have liked to be Dr Watson, with all the excitement and adventure that entails, rather than the dreary life you have now?”

“Dreary? That’s very harsh Harriet! I do my best to run a family and look after you two. It may be dreary to you, but it’s more important than running around pretending to be characters out of a book.”

“We’re not pretending... And they’re not characters...” Will sounded indignant.

“He thinks they’re real, mother. I’ve tried telling him but it’s no use. And I’m afraid you’ll have to get used to me being called Watson.”

“Yes. And you can be Mrs Hudson if you would like that?” Will chimed in.

Their mother looked around the room to see if he was addressing someone else before answering. “Who me? Me, Mrs Hudson? Why you cheeky young whippersnapper... what do you mean telling me I can be Mrs Hudson... Why, all she does is cook meals and clear up after them, and...”

“Yes mother. I think you just got it! You wouldn’t have to practise much for the part, would you?” Harriet smirked.

“But, but... Oh this is too much...” and she started to sob. “If my life is as dull as you say it is, maybe I should run away and leave you... leave you two to look after your father and do all his washing and feeding and...”

“I already do those mother and no... before you ask, I am not doing his bathing. He can have the tin tub in the front room all to himself.”

Harriet put her arm around her mother and looked at Will and grinned. See what you have done to our poor mother? She’s just realised her life is boring, and what’s more, it’s all our fault!”

“Yes... You’ve told me I’m boring... So maybe *I* should be Dr Watson and you can be Mrs Hudson, Harriet.”

“No thanks mother... I have enough chores already.”

“Come on Watson. I said we must hurry.”

“So... are you all right now mother? May I go now?”

She looked at her daughter as she wiped the moisture from her eyes. “Yes of course... Go on dear... I shall be here when you get back... I shall be here being Mrs Hudson... As always.”

“Fabulous!” Will exclaimed, and he rushed over and gave his mother a great big kiss on the cheek.

Harriet looked nonplussed. “You get away with everything young Will. Whereas I get away with nothing. It’s not fair being a girl!”

“No, which is why I asked you to be my Dr Watson. We are now squarely and irrevocably equals.”

“Yes... And don’t you forget it. Goodbye mother. We shall see you later in church. It will be so sad seeing Florrie’s flower arrangements on a Sunday without her being there.”

On hearing which, Mrs Cooksley started to cry again and held her pinafore up to her face to cover it.

“Bear up mother,” said Will. “We shall use our finest endeavours to discover who or what was the cause of her misfortune, you need have no fear about that. Holmes and Watson are on the case! The game is afoot!”

And the tearful lady heard the front door latch click shut behind her two young detectives.

"Where are we going this morning then Holmes?"

"Up the hill."

"Oh, not again! How many times have we got to go up and down that hill? This is getting tedious, and like I told you, I'm wearing the wrong clothes for all this gallivanting... I'm not dressed in plus-fours and thick woollen socks like Dr Watson you know!"

"No, and you haven't got a revolver either, so we must make sure we don't have the need to shoot someone during our mission. Come on!"

"Oh, must we go right to the top again? – it's hard on my feet."

"We are going up the Lime Way, the same path that Florrie trod on her final fateful trip."

"I'm not sure I want to do that."

"You'll be fine, you're with me. And it's vitally important, Watson. If I am right in my deductions, we shall discover something at the top of the Lime Way that will reveal a great deal of what happened up there on that dreadful evening. We must, for Florrie's sake, we must!"

"Very well. But I shall have misgivings all the way, I know I will, and if I should faint then you will have to carry me down."

"Hattie... I mean Watson... You are strong... Stronger than I... If you should faint then I promise you I shall have fainted long before, and you shall be the one carrying me down. Let us step forth boldly, for it is daylight and the birds are singing."

"I haven't walked this way in years. We used to play up here as children."

"Quite so. Now, the first thing to note is the start of the path. Look. What do you see?"

Harriet looked up, the narrow trail branching left off the road just on the first part of the hill, slightly above The Ship.

"I see the start of the path."

"Yes. And now let us begin to climb. And then tell me what you notice."

Harriet placed her foot on the first step, then abruptly became aware of what her brother was drivelling on about.

"The thirteen steps! I'd never counted them before. These are the thirteen steps on the note that Florrie carried with her when she died!"

"Yes Watson, yes! These are the thirteen steps... The thirteen steps to the thirteen stones! Now... Did Florrie write the note? Or did she receive it from her beau?"

"I imagine she received it. Otherwise it would have been in the possession of whomever she was going to marry."

"Quite so. Unless she was on her way to deliver it."

"No. If she was here at dusk then she was acting out the instructions on the note, so she must have been the recipient."

"Well done Watson. I think you have it exactly. So who did write it?"

"One of her suitors."

"Yes. If the note The Scamps found was written by Florrie – and it was signed by her so we must assume that it was – then she liked to communicate using code. But this note is not in a complex code – it is like a child's picture, very simply drawn, a very simple code. And which one of her suitors would use pictures rather than letters? Notice there are no words on this note at all, not even a single letter... Which of her suitors would never have been to school?"

"The pirate!"

"Yes! She was to marry the pirate. Francis saw the pirate on this very path. She carried his note with her, the note which led straight to her heart, and which led her to her hopes and dreams..."

"Gosh. Now you put it like that, I can feel it myself. I could fall in love like that too!"

"You'd better not tell mother!" Will chuckled, then quickly became sad on thinking what he had just said. "This note also led her to her demise, Watson. She was full of love and hope when she received it, and climbed the hill in delight and happiness... And then what happened? We must find out. Right. Here is where the path splits, this way to the right continues on to the top of the hill, and this way to the left goes to Hawkcombe. This is where Francis last saw Florrie, and where he saw the fierce-looking pirate who scared him so much that he turned back. We shall carry on up, as that leads us to the thirteen stones. From here on we must be on the lookout for the next piece of evidence, the next vital clue."

"Which is what?" Harriet thought for a second. "Oh no – we don't have to search this whole hill again do we? I shall snag my stockings and rip my pinafore to bits and if not that then at least get it all dirty and have to face mother again. What are we searching for this time?"

"I think, although I cannot be certain, that we are searching for a dishevelled pile of clothes... Pirate's clothes..."

"Pirate's clothes? Oh goodness, you don't mean that they... you know... the two of them... Florrie and the pirate... together?"

Will laughed heartily. "No, I don't think they did, Watson. Although you, being a doctor, surely should not be offended if they had!" And he continued to snigger, like a cheeky schoolboy, which until very recently he was.

"Oh don't tease me so! Remember I am your partner in this business, not your sister any more."

Will patted his sister on the shoulder affectionately. "I'm sorry," he said. "I am going to write something down, one word. Do you have a scrap of paper and something with which to write?"

Harriet delved into her pinafore pocket and drew out the note which The Scamps had found in the emporium, and a stub of pencil. Will scratched a short word onto the blank side of the note, folded it up and handed it back.

"When we find what we are looking for, I would like you to examine it, and then read the word I have written down."

"This gets more like a riddle with every passing hour. Do you really know what you're doing?"

"I think I do. But one can always be mistaken. Many are the blind alleys that have to be explored before the traveller enters the temple of light, but I think I am finally on the highway towards that revelatory place!"

"If you are on the highway, why am I having to tramp through a load of scrubby thorny bushes looking for a raggle taggle pile of discarded clothes?"

"My dear Watson, the highway is a highway of the mind. To reach wherever it leads, we must tramp through whatever is placed in front of us."

"Look!"

There are 20 differences to spot in the two pictures of the Lime Way path up the hill on the following page.

"What is it?"

"Behind the bushes there, I see a flash of red. It may be just some spring flowers, but it looks out of place."

Will leapt forward at a jolly gait. "Watson, where? Show me. Red is exactly what we are looking for."

Harriet took his hand and led him further along the path, further upwards and then around to the right where it became narrower and more densely foliated.

"There, behind those bushes..."

Will turned off the path and ducked under some low hanging twigs, catching his tunic on them while he reached down and parted the undergrowth. "Oh yes! Yes! Well done my dear fellow! There has obviously been an attempt at concealing their whereabouts... But to no avail... You did well to spot them, especially from such a distance and obscured among all these tussocks."

"So... are they the pirate's clothes then?"

"Yes, I do believe they are, and... look! Here is his pistol!"

"He carried a pistol! Gracious! Francis didn't mention that... No wonder he ran away!"

Will held up the gun. "He needn't have... It's a toy. Look! But the clothes are interesting, come and see!"

"What, underneath that bush? I can't go scrabbling about down there!"

"Oh very well... It is only the headdress – obviously the wearer didn't take all of the costume off or he would have been running around naked!" Will gathered up the piece of rag and reversed out of the scrub, ducking as he did so, then presented it for Harriet's inspection. "Look Watson... What do you see?"

"Oh no! Bloodstains... Whatever happened here?"

"You can look at the word I wrote on the note now."

Harriet scrambled for the piece of paper and unfolded it."

"BLOOD... You've written BLOOD."

"Yes. I suspected that there must have been a brawl up here, a fight, a contretemps of some description. I just wanted to test myself and make sure that you believed what I deduced and predicted, rather than hearing me say, 'I knew we would find bloodstained clothing' to which you would rightly have replied, 'You just made that up!'."

"Oh with such a distinguished Detective as Porlock Holmes at my side, there would be no reason to doubt his word, surely?"

"No... But it is better to have the evidence in your hand, don't you think?"

"I shall never doubt my little brother again," Harriet mused sarcastically. "What do we do now? Show them to Greedy?"

"Mmmm..." Will pondered. "This is a tricky decision. We should present the evidence to the investigating officer, and yet I fear Greedy will misconstrue it. And I haven't met this bigwig Inspector yet. I feel that we must first be sure of the origin of these garments... Where they came from... To that end, let us take them to the place where The Scamps found the other clothes and also the note."

"You mean Mrs Agnes' shop?"

"I think that would be best. I believe that it is from there that these clothes were purloined."

"Stolen? From Mrs Agnes' shop?"

"That is what I believe happened."

"But why?"

"That will become clear soon enough. Come along. Let us retrace our steps and go and see her now."

"All this to-ing and fro-ing. I shall need a new pair of shoes if these get worn out. As it is I shall be spending best part of half an hour cleaning them when we get home."

"Really Watson, I do think footwear should not be allowed to stand in the way of unravelling a mystery such as this!" And Will laughed with self-satisfied laughter. "Footwear! Stand! Do you get it? Hahaha!"

"Most amusing, yes. I shall be sure to ask Mr Rook at The Ship Inn for a *cut* of your wages to enable me to buy a pair of stout boots. I'm certain that Mrs Agnes will let me have some for a *snip*!"

"Come Watson, enough of this badinage – we have work to do before Greedy and his superior seek to pin the blame once more on Yours Truly."

NINETEEN

The Bric-a-Brac Emporium – 2

"Why yes... It was a most odd thing to have happened... I was out in the back of the shop, sorting out some things when I heard the entrance bell ring. I just at that moment had a large and rather unwieldy box in my hands and was stretching to reach the top shelf to stow it away. I didn't rush to the counter as most people come in to browse for a while and call me when they need assistance. I put the box in its place, then noticed some stray bits and bobs on the floor that someone might trip over in the gloom, so I put those away too, and then I heard the shop bell ring once more, so I assumed the customer had left. Of course it could have been another customer coming in, but it was late on a Friday and I didn't think that likely. When I did finally go through to the shop, I immediately noticed that there was now a very nice brass hunting horn placed on my counter. Well... Why would that be, I wondered? There were a number of explanations. I sometimes get people bring things in that they no longer want, but seldom anything as good as that, so more likely it was someone who wished me to sell it for them on their behalf, and take a share of the proceeds. But they had left no note with a name on nor any instructions as to what they wished me to do with it. The third possibility was that they had left it there in exchange for something else which caught their eye, although usually such a transaction would be carried out with me being present. Strange then, when I looked at my stock of clothing hanging on the pegs on the walls, I realised that I now had a coachman's outfit in a place where previously, I am quite certain, there hung a pirate's outfit just a few minutes before. Of course, I might have been upset had the pirate's costume been worth considerably more than the goods left in exchange, but in this case the relative values were definitely in my favour and so I was more than happy with the deal and thought nothing more of it until you arrived just now and presented me with part of the missing pirate costume. And the pistol! I had not even noticed that that was missing, not that it would have mattered for it is just a replica."

Mrs Agnes looked in turn at Will and Harriet, hoping for some explanation for these strange goings on.

“So what do you make of it? There must be some reason you brought these things back to me. Was it you who took them away in the first place?”

“No no... Not at all,” replied Will. “We just found the clothing along with the gun and we wanted to know if they came from your shop?”

“Well yes they did, and now you know. But I don’t know whether I should take them back as they were left in fair exchange.”

“Oh, we cannot give them back to you in any case, Mrs Agnes, for they are evidence. The police must see them before they are returned to your good self. There are blood stains on the pirate headdress, you see?”

“Oh dear! Yes, I can see that. What does that signify? I do hope whoever was wearing it is all right... Where did you find them?”

“More importantly Mrs Agnes, we would like to know exactly where you found *this*.”

Will turned to his sister.

“Watson... Please take the coded note and pass it to Mrs Agnes.”

Harriet took the note from her pinafore, unfolded it and handed it to the shopkeeper.

Mrs Agnes recognised it straight away. “This is the note that the children found. I showed them how to read the message – it’s in a lovers’ code you see. It’s what sweethearts use to hide the meaning from casual handlers, such as the postman.”

“Yes, The Scamps told us all about it,” continued Will. “And they also told us what it says. But what we would like to know is, which item of clothing did they find it in? And which pocket did it come from?”

“Believe it or not, it came from the coachman’s jacket that was left behind in my absence, the one I was telling you about! But I don’t know exactly which pocket it came from... The Scamps as you call them were creating rather a ruckus and hullabaloo at the time, blowing on the horn which they grabbed from my counter when they came in. I had to calm them with a giant humbug.”

Harriet laughed. “Oh Mrs Agnes, your giant humbug created more of a ruckus than you can ever have imagined! They were at each other’s throats when we met them yesterday evening! I used my best endeavours to pacify them, but in the end it was the littlest one Arthur who sorted it out.”

Mrs Agnes beamed. “Oh little Arthur. He is so adorable. Always with a smile on his face and a never-say-die attitude to life. Of course, we’re very proud of him… He is my great nephew you know.”

“Well you are rightly proud,” said Harriet.

“Yes, quite so Mrs Agnes. You have been very helpful, and thank you for your time. I have an appointment with another shopkeeper now, so we shall be on our way.” Will tipped his cap, turned to the door, opened it and waited for his sister to exit, while the bell clanged noisily on its spring. “Come Watson! We are now hot on the trail… I feel our efforts are nearing fruition. Only a couple more clues should suffice to see the grisly picture emerge in fullest form, clearly in its entirety!”

Harriet walked out of the doorway, giving Will an incredulous look as she passed. He followed her out into the street and onward to the next port of call.

The tobacconist

The smell was strong but inviting. It hit them both as the shop door clanged and the warmth and cloying aroma filled their senses. The overwhelming visual impression was of brown-ness, the claustrophobic brown panelled walls pressing in on all sides and making the brown haze more fuggy, more compressed. But the mingling of a hundred differing sweet smells tickled the nostrils and layered the mucus-coated passages at the back of the nose, such that the brown surroundings became merely a sideshow to the main olfactory event.

A small man with shabby jacket and round glasses with bottle-bottom lenses peered at them myopically from behind a very high and very brown counter top. Giant jars of various brown shredded leaves sat on shelves, some of the containers steeped in the dusts of time while others, presumably holding leaves of the more popular and cheaper varieties, were shiny in the extreme, their glass glinting even in the almost non-existent light, with their worn well-fingered lids polished through numerous removals and replacements under the brown tar-stained fingers of Mr Wiles, the owner of this establishment, noted not only for its tobacco, pipes and other smoking products, but also for the sale of walking sticks, umbrellas and an array of sportsman's equipment for hunting, shooting and fishing which was the lifeblood of the area.

"Aha" Young William!" Mr Wiles greeted as he peered over the top of his brown spectacles, which were seemingly glued to the centre of his nose. "And you have brought your beautiful sister along too... How lovely it is to see two glowing flushes of youth, even if my delight at your visit is tempered by such sad circumstances."

"Good day Mr Wiles. Please don't think that Harriet is here for no purpose, for she is my right-hand-man, as it were, in that we are a team... An investigating team of two detectives, enquiring into the mysterious death of our dear dear friend Florrie Nichols." Mr Wiles stared, motionless. "Which is why we are here, and also why we are pinning our hopes on your expertise that you may help us solve a part of the enigma."

"Well, I shall do my best. What is it that you need me to pronounce upon?"

Will took a rolled hanky from his pocket and placed it on the counter top, then unfurled it to reveal the moth-eaten dried out cigarette end which he had found at the scene of Florrie's demise.

Mr Wiles peered down through his lenses, studying for some time. He then reached for his drawer, opened it and took out a magnifying glass, then peered even more closely and intently at the putrid malodorous object which had been presented for his inspection. He then placed down his spyglass and raised the grubby dog-end to his nose, sniffing lightly along its length, to and fro like a dog with a particularly enticing sniff, and continued to do this for several seconds. He then took a brown stained handkerchief from his pocket and blew loudly into it to clear his nasal passages, then took a glass ashtray and proceeded to unwrap the cigarette paper, such as was left of it, and tipped the contents into the receptacle. Thus spread out, he examined the leaves minutely with his spyglass once more before picking some of them up and rolling them between his fingers to release the odour, such as one does when crushing the fragrant leaf of a lemon tree or mint bush to sniff its delights. Finally, he presented his astringent smelling fingers to his nose to complete the diagnosis.

Satisfied, he replaced all particles in the ashtray and gave his verdict.

"Very interesting, and, luckily for you, most unusual."

Will felt a twinge of excitement. He had hoped that the discarded cigarette end might be a clue, but that could only be the case if it had some feature to distinguish it from the run-of-the-mill.

"Balkan!" proclaimed the tobacconist triumphantly. "And, not only that, but from a particular grower in a particular part of the Balkans; Serbia in fact! A particular grower whom I happen to know, and who supplies me with the leaves which I blend with a smidgin of hickory, an essence of Slivovitz which is a plum brandy local to that area and, finally, to make it truly magnificent and traceable to my shop and my shop alone, a distillation of whortleberry juice freshly plucked from our own moors hereabouts!"

"Crikey!"

"Gosh!"

Will and Harriet exclaimed, both at the same time.

"You can know all that, from that horrid little stump?" questioned Harriet.

"Oh yes. Without doubt. I can detect all sorts of things from tobacco. It is a lifetime of study and familiarisation you see."

"Sherlock Holmes himself would be proud of you Mr Wiles!" blurted Will.

The proprietor raised his eyebrows giving himself an uncanny resemblance to an owl, especially enhanced by his owl-like spectacles.

"Sherlock Holmes? Why, he is an amateur. Since when has he been a distinguished purveyor of the finest blends of the world's most esoteric tobaccos for the last thirty and more years?"

"I am certain that Sherlock Holmes has written monographs on the subject," suggested Will. "I model myself upon him you know, and this person here is my partner Dr Watson!"

Mr Wiles laughed benignly. "Oh I see now, hahahaha..." and he clapped his hands together in front of him in acknowledgement. "I now see exactly where you are coming from. Forgive me. When you said your sister was here with you for good reason and that you were detectives, I thought you were youngsters playing a game. But now I know that you are aspiring to the heights by following in Holmes' and Watson's footsteps... Even though they are just amateurs, I shall always do my best to assist you in any way I can."

"Thank you Mr Wiles – that will be a great comfort and benefit to us and we value your help most certainly, especially in this case."

"Thank you young lady. Most kind of you to say."

"But Mr Wiles," Will sounded full of urgency. "We need to know the most important thing, the thing which you haven't told us... We need to know..."

"Ah yes!" Mr Wiles cut him off before he could reach the point of his question. "This is the tobacco that I blend especially for the occupant of Ashley Combe House."

"Yes!" cried Will. Oh thank you thank you Mr Wiles. That is one more vital link in our little chain of puzzles which join the events of this case ever more closely together."

"Yes, thank you Mr Wiles." Harriet turned to her brother. "Come Holmes, lead me to the next clue."

"Coming Watson. But first, I wonder if Mr Wiles would keep these pirate clothes safe for us – I don't think I should be carrying them around with me at the moment, for fear of incrimination."

"Yes, of course. No problem young William. They will be here under my counter when you need them."

"Thank you so much again, and good bye," Will aired cheerily as Harriet opened the brown door so they could take their leave.

Once they left the shop, the blandness of the air was almost as much of a shock as the overpowering smell of entering the richly aromatic room from which they had just emerged. However, another and perhaps bigger shock was about to befall them, for around the corner lurked the forbidding form of a dour and determined PC Greedy.

"Mmmmmm..." he opened ominously. I'd like a word with you two."

Will had known this was coming, but still it gave him a twinge of the collywobbles.

"Yes Mr Greedy?"

Greedy puffed himself up to deliver an important pronouncement.

"The Inspector has arrived. He is waiting for you at the police house. I would like you to accompany me there now."

Will shivered, while Harriet found herself clenching her hands without wanting to.

"Very well Mr Greedy. Have you told the Inspector about all the evidence we have so far uncovered?"

"I have informed him about the circumstances of the discovery of the body and about Miss Harriet's shawl. I have also given him the notes from Dr Kingslake's post mortem, I have shown him the note with the steps drawn upon it, and he has also seen the missing shoe."

"Good. In that case he should be able to solve this case in no time."

"He's held in the utmost high regard at Scotland Yard... I'm sure he will be on to the culprit in very short order." Greedy stared suspiciously at Will, making him feel even more uneasy. "Very very soon indeed I shouldn't wonder... Come along you two."

TWENTY ONE

The Inspector

Greedy ushered the pair into the reception area of his police house. The Inspector was leaning across Greedy's desk, poring through the post mortem results.

"Inspector... This is the lad Will Cooksley who discovered the body, and this is his sister Harriet, whose shawl the deceased was wearing when she was found." Greedy turned to the pair. "Will and Harriet, this is Inspector Word. He would like a *word* with you. Hahaha!"

The Inspector fixed Greedy with an irritated expression.

"Sword! My name is LeSword! Got it?"

"Oh quite right sir, yes sir, I mean, sorry Les." Greedy immediately tried to offload the blame onto Will. "Cooksley!" he boomed. "Pay attention... This is Inspector Sword. Les Sword. Have you got that?"

"I've got it Mr Greedy. And he is very important. That is right isn't it?"

"Right, yes, good... very important... yes..."

LeSword looked as if he'd walked into the beyond-hope ward at the Bedlam Hospital. All his preconceptions of what the outlying reaches of the countryside were like, and especially the behaviour of its dimwitted inhabitants, were becoming fulfilled. He decided to clear the matter up, once and for all, even though it could easily turn out to be a waste of time.

"My name is Claude. Claude...Le...Sword." He enunciated his full name slowly and deliberately, carefully separating the two syllables of his surname so that there could be no confusion.

Greedy couldn't help himself. He tried not to, but his face cracked and he had to put his hand over his mouth while his eyes filled with tears of mirth on hearing the Inspector had a name which rhymed. *What impish parents he must have had?,* Greedy thought to himself as he fought to stifle the convulsions of jollity which rippled unstoppably throughout his body.

"What's the matter Greedy? What is it that fills you with such joy? Go on – please share the cause of your merriment with the rest of us."

Greedy choked. "I can't sir," he spluttered.

Will turned his head away to avoid eye contact while Harriet held her pinafore up to her face.

LeSword felt like he was the butt of some secret joke hatched by sniggering pupils about their teacher at school. "Greedy!" he shouted. "Tell me what is so funny or I shall have you demoted!"

"I don't think you can do that Mr LeSword." Harriet lowered her apron and smiled at the Inspector as he turned to find out why she had said that. "You see, PC Greedy is a PC sir, and I don't think you can get lower than that, so I don't think you can demote him."

Greedy harrumphed at the suggestion, while LeSword went red in the face, his eyes popping in defiance. "I can make him the station bobby's boot polisher if I want to!" Then, realising he couldn't, he decided to calm down. "All right, enough of this pantomime. Let us proceed to the interrogation." He turned to Will. "*You* boy. You found the body, yes?"

"Yes sir."

"Next to a wall? Halfway up the hill?"

"Yes sir, on the left side as you go up the hill, just round the second bend."

The Inspector moved in close; Will felt his warm and fusty breath envelop his face.

"Did you kill her, Cooksley? It would be a lot easier for this investigation and for me personally if you could just say you did, as then I can get straight back to London and escape this place which appears to be populated wholly with loons."

"No, I did not kill her sir."

LeSword knew the boy was lying.

"Are you sure? In my experience it is almost always the person who finds the body who did the deed!"

"I am certain sir. I would know if I had killed her sir."

"Mmmmmm..."

Oh no, not another one, thought Will. *Perhaps all policemen do it!*

"In my experience," continued LeSword, "When a young lady is killed, it is almost always the spurned lover who carries out the deed." He pushed his face even closer up to Will's so their noses were almost touching. "Are *you* the spurned lover?"

"Well..." Will looked across at his sister. Knowing that he had already confessed his desire for Florrie, he felt unable to lie about it in front of Harriet... He also wanted to escape the hot breath which was stifling him. After taking several gulps of fresher air, he turned back face to face with his accuser. "I liked her sir. I liked her a lot..."

The glint of the eagle's eye lit up the Inspector's pupils and he stood back a little to deliver his judgement.

"Liked her, eh?... Liked her! That makes it very likely that you were *spurned* then, eh? That you were the spurned lover, yes?" He pushed his face right back into Will's, eye to eye, breath to breath, moustache to smooth pre-bewhiskered lip. "Were you spurned, boy?" LeSword curled his tongue around the S of spurned to give it more emphasis, and a satellite of spittle winged its way across the narrow void, looped upwards and glued itself to the end of Will's nose. Slowly and with menace he repeated, "Are *you* the spurned lover?"

Will gulped. LeSword was like a rapier in his face-to-face interviewing technique.

"I can't have been spurned Mr Sword..."

"Aaaaaggghhh!" The Inspector jumped back and stood up straight, waving his arms in despair. "LeSword! My name is LeSword! Why can't you imbeciles just call me by my right name which is LeSword! And that goes for you as well Greedy! Especially you!"

"Yes sir." Greedy sounded downhearted. He had imagined that having an Inspector visit Porlock would be an interesting and uplifting experience. And now he was being told off! How unfair was that!

LeSword turned his attention back to Will. "Now, pray continue with your untruthful response to my question, you little worm. What were you just saying?"

"I said I can't have been spurned sir because I never even spoke to her, let alone asked her to walk out with me." Will's head fell, downcast in sadness. "I was too in awe of her you see sir... I felt unworthy."

"He's too young for that sort of thing anyway," interjected Harriet.

"Be quiet Miss!" LeSword was not in the mood for interruptions and fixed her with a steely stare. "I am interrogating *this* suspect. We shall come to *you* later!"

Harriet looked sheepish, and felt slightly queasy at the prospect of being on the receiving end of the long arm of the law, which in this case was the rasping bladelike tongue of the LeSword.

"It's *always* the spurned lover... And I am certain that *you* are the spurned lover! And I shall prove it..." LeSword reached over to a shelf on Greedy's desk and took a piece of paper from it. He then gathered a pen and handed both objects to Will. "Right boy... Draw on this piece of paper a picture of thirteen steps rising to a setting sun and a moon and some dots in a large circle at the top."

Will took up the pen, placed the paper on the desk and scribbled down the picture as requested. LeSword snatched it up and snorted with delight – now he knew he was on to something. He reached into his pocket and took out the note which Greedy had handed to him earlier on his arrival, then placed them next to each other on the counter top, flashing his eyes between them, from one to the other, like a darting lizard honing in on its prey.

"Your drawing looks remarkably like the one on this note here which PC Greedy told me was found on the young lady's body!" he declared exultantly. "Did you draw the picture on that original note as well?"

"No sir."

"But it looks almost identical! How do you account for that?"

"I thought that's what you wanted... I saw the original note yesterday and I assumed you wanted me to copy it."

LeSword's eyes rose in astonishment.

"You'd already seen the note, had you? How did that come about? Did you find it on the young lady's person?"

"No – I didn't rummage through her clothes. That would be quite improper."

"Then how did you come to see the note?"

"Mr Greedy showed it to me."

LeSword spun like a tossed tuppenny piece to confront Greedy.

"Greedy! Is it customary to show a suspect a vital piece of evidence?"

Greedy had had enough of being told off by now... He decided it was time to stand up to the overblown overrated self-inflated meddler who had landed on his patch... He took a deep breath and delivered his rebuttal. "I showed it to him because I needed to know if he was the one who drew it, just the same as you are doing now... Are you telling me that what I did was not correct police procedure, sir!"

LeSword blinked, giving pause to consider Greedy's response.

"Oh... I see..." The Inspector sounded more contrite now. "Quite proper, Greedy... Well done..."

He turned his attention back to Will. "Right, where were we? Ah yes... In my experience," continued LeSword, "When a young lady is killed, it is almost always the step-father, or the uncle, who performed the dreadful deed... Did the young lady in question have a step-father, or an uncle?"

"Yes," broke in Harriet.

LeSword moved swiftly to delve into this new line of his enquiry. "Well, which was it... The step-father? Or the uncle? More than one uncle perhaps?"

"Both," said Harriet. "They are both one and the same person, Florrie's mother's brother-in-law. She was lonely when Florrie's father died, so Horace who is her father's brother and therefore uncle also took over as her father figure, that making him her step-father."

"Aha! This is most interesting. Have you brought this man in for questioning, Greedy?"

"No sir, I haven't sir."

"And why is that?"

"Because Horace Nichols is a friend of mine sir. We're both in the bowls club together."

"Really Greedy, I am very surprised at your attitude..." LeSword tutted his displeasure. "I am sure it must have occurred to you that this man is the prime suspect, did it not? Step-father, uncle, proximity to the victim? It all reeks of *lust* Greedy, do you not think? In my experience, lust and foul deeds go hand in hand in our line of work. This case has lust and foul deeds written all over it!"

Oh dear, Greedy was being told off again and he didn't know how to defend himself. "Shall I bring Horace in for questioning sir?"

"Yes, please do. I'm sure he will crack under a little gentle interrogation."

Greedy had a little internal chuckle to himself. *The Inspector doesn't know Horace*, he thought.

"Right!" LeSword looked pleased with himself. "Now you young lady... What is this about the deceased wearing your shawl? What are we to make of that? Did you lend it to her?"

"No sir I didn't, but my mother did... Florrie had left hers somewhere and mislaid it. Mother lent her one of my old ones."

"I see. Well I don't think there is anything we need to concern ourselves with there, eh Greedy? It just remains to consider what we need to do regarding our suspects. We don't want anyone absconding. For that reason, I am arresting you, William Cooksley, in the name of the King... Anything you say may be taken down and used in evidence against you... Do you understand?"

Will had thought this might be coming and remained emotionless, but Harriet gave a little shriek of protest.

"No Mr LeSword! My brother hasn't done anything wrong! Why do you need to arrest him?"

"Oh don't worry yourself Miss Harriet, it is merely a matter of routine. Despite your brother being the one who discovered the body, and despite him also being, in my view, the spurned lover, if he is truly not guilty of any crime then he has nothing to fear from the benevolent and reliable course of the law. Isn't that so Greedy?"

"Oh, er... yes sir... Quite so..."

"And also my many years experience of arresting the wrong man and learning from my mistakes. You'll be gratified to know only one of them was hanged."

He looked around to confirm that he had put everyone's mind to rest on the matter of a possible miscarriage of justice.

"Right... Lock him in the cell Greedy, then go and bring in Horace Nichols... We need to have a word with him. Step-father *and* uncle... Mmmmmm."

Harriet grabbed her brother's arm and looked nervously at him.

"Don't worry Hattie," Will said as the large bunch of keys jangled when Greedy took them off the hook. "I shall be perfectly fine... You go now and..." Will winked at her. "...remember what to do." He then turned and walked into the cell. The door clanged shut behind him and the key turned noisily in the lock, giving off a metal-on-metal echoing sound as the bolt snapped shut. "It's Sunday morning!" shouted Will, banging his fists on the barred window. "How can I attend church service when you've locked me in here! Let me out! In the name of the Lord, let me out I tell you!"

Greedy looked at LeSword. "Come on sir – he's not going to run away is he... At least let him go to church on the Lord's day."

"Certainly not." LeSword was implacable. "We can't have suspects running around on the loose. Now where shall we find this uncle/step-father then, eh Greedy?"

"He will be in church too sir."

"Well come on then... Let's run him in."

"I'm sorry sir, I am not going into a packed church on a Sunday and dragging out one of my friends and neighbours in plain view of everyone in the village. And that's that!"

"You will take a direct order from your superior Greedy!"

"Not that particular order sir. Any other order, but not that one!"

"Let me go to church!" The cell door rattled again as Will continued to shout for his freedom.

"Keep the racket down!" shouted LeSword.

Harriet, who had slipped out of the front door a few seconds earlier while the others were arguing and making a racket, put one finger from each of her hands in her mouth and blew a tremendous whistle which resounded along Lowerbourne and into the Porlock's main street.

"What on Earth was that?" LeSword queried, as if Greedy should know the answer.

"I've no idea sir – I'll take a look."

Greedy opened the door to his police house and wished he hadn't. The instant he did, Scamper burst into the room with a horde of screaming Scamps hollering and whooping behind him.

"My word!" LeSword found himself shouting, wishing he were anywhere else other than this ghastly little village in North Somerset. "What is this place like? Get rid of these awful children Greedy!"

He was wasting his breath. Scamper gave the Inspector an evil glare, squatted himself fair and square in the middle of the police reception area and delivered a rather smelly and pungent deposit onto Greedy's polished linoleum.

"No!" screamed Greedy. "You Scamps! Get that dog out of here. Oh my poor floor! My lovely shiny floor!"

"Euccchhhhh!" cried the Inspector. I'm not staying here with that smell. Clear it up Greedy while I wait for you outside."

The Inspector left while Greedy went off behind his desk to fetch the mop. This was their chance... Greedy had not yet pocketed the keys and they were still lying on the counter top where he had left them. Betsy grabbed them and handed them to Herbie so he could unlock the cell door, while Arthur followed Greedy to keep him busy out the back.

"I... I... I'll help you Mr Greedy. Scamper *is* a naughty boy, isn't he?"

Greedy saw the little companion grinning at him. "Yes Arthur, extremely naughty. Here... Greedy put his hand back in the cleaning cupboard and pulled out a bucket. "You take this to the village pump and fill it for me while I get some cloths."

Arthur took the bucket, accidentally dropped it with a huge *clang*, then trod in it, getting his foot stuck on purpose.

"I... I... I'm stuck Mr Greedy!"

"Oh Arthur, for goodness sake." Greedy took the bucket and gave it a pull, and Arthur's foot popped free.

Meanwhile, Herbie had turned the key in the lock and allowed Will to escape. He then re-locked the door, replaced the keys on the counter and Will and The Scamps all disappeared out of the front door, leaving Arthur behind, but that didn't matter because he was a tough Scamp and knew how the plan was meant to unfold... and it was unfolding perfectly. As they rushed out, they saw LeSword outside, waiting for Greedy. Will ducked down and lost himself among the others who smothered him tightly with their bodies as concealment, not that LeSword was in any state to detect an escaping prisoner as he shied away from the leaping Scamper who charged over to him and began to cock his leg against the Inspectorial trousers.

"Gerrroffffff!" Cried LeSword in panic, leaping up in the air while trying to shoo the excitable hound, kicking him away with his foot.

"Woof woof!" went Scamper, who now had the Inspector at his mercy. The perfectly polished police regulation shoe was in the air for only the fewest fleeting seconds, but time enough for the acrobatic dog to sink his teeth into the leather and tug hard enough to dislodge and remove it from the policeman's foot. With a "Woooooof Arraaawwwwllll" of success, Scamper scampered off with the Scotland Yard boot in his mouth, leaving the distraught LeSword shouting obscenities, all entirely wasted on a pooch whose only thought was that he had the prize and was not letting go. Only Herbie *really* knew how the policeman must have felt at that moment!

"Greedy! Greedy! Do something!" roared the Inspector who turned round to see if anyone was coming to rescue him from the open door of the police house. "Greedy! Greeeeeedyyyyyy!" LeSword hobbled back inside to find the PC. Seeing that the cell door was open, LeSword angrily charged across to investigate, forgetting that Scamper had left his malodorous present. As he crossed the room before storming into the cell to see if Will was still there, he had the misfortune to tread upon something soft and squidgy with his unbooted foot, whereupon he experienced a sinking squashy gooey slipping feeling which permeated his sock, a type of feeling with which almost everyone in the world is surely familiar, and which no one ever wishes to repeat. When he reached the barred iron door and pushed it wide open, what he actually saw made him even more testy – for the two occupants were laughing together, whilst one of them was just in the process of saying, "I... I... I spy... With m... m... my little eye... Something beginning with..." Arthur looked around for an object and saw the angry bootless LeSword. "S" (which he said as "sss" and not "ess").

Greedy looked around. "Cell! – No, wait – that begins with 'C'... Mmmmmm... Ceiling! – Oh, no – same again... Mmmmmm..." Greedy noticed the Inspector, then looked down at the floor. "SOCK!" Greedy cried out in jubilation, knowing that he must be right.

"Y... Y... Ye-e-e-e-s-s!" congratulated Arthur.

Greedy looked up at the Inspector's outraged face, and soon realised their game was about to come to an end, and he would miss his turn.

The Inspector's cheeks and forehead were purple. Greedy was very sad. Arthur grinned.

***

Meanwhile, outside in the street, Scamper was busy chewing up LeSword's shoe – he hadn't tasted anything so good since the giant humbug! Will found Harriet hiding around the corner in the main street.

"Come Watson, to church!" he chimed.

"Aren't we too late for morning service?" Harriet wondered if they should go. "The rector might not welcome us barging in halfway through.

"We'll sneak in surreptitiously at the back using our utmost stealth. We must get to church, a) to find the missing clue which I am sure lies there and b) to warn Horace that the indefatigable Inspector is after him."

"Very well. But the warden may frown at our late arrival, and mother won't be pleased."

"Mother loves you Hattie. She shows it by being concerned, which she exhibits mostly as displeasure. It is practically a mother's full time occupation."

"Yes, and I am always the butt of it."

"Not always... She finds me most objectionable on regular occasions. And you should hear what she says about father when his back is turned."

"Yes, and that's the difference isn't it... He doesn't actually have to take any notice as he is quite oblivious. But me.. It's 'Hattie do this...' 'Hattie do that...' 'Hattie wash this shirt...' 'Hattie clean the floor...' 'Hattie go and get some milk...' 'Hattie can you...' "

"Really Watson," he cut her off in mid flow. "I shall have to re-cast you as Cinderella if you carry on this way. You wait till you get husband... It'll be worse for you then!"

"I think you'll find Cinderella married a prince!"

"Yes. And what are princes like? Overbearing... Self-centred... Conceited... Feckless... Effete... Panjandrums!..."

"Panjandrums... Panjandrums? Really? Where did you learn that? And what does it mean?"

"Oh, I was in the reading room yesterday and I was looking up *periwinkles* for my research into seashells and I happened to notice as I thumbed through the P's and happened to notice what a lovely word panjandrum was: *panjandrum* – someone who's all *show* and no *do*."

"My prince shall be strong and gallant and beneficent."

"And what is beneficent pray?"

"Kind to others, especially those less fortunate."

"Well you better make sure of that, or you can tell him that Porlock Holmes will be on his case, for I shall not have my Dr Watson's sterling steadfast character and wellbeing undermined by any husband he might happen to pick up."

"Thank you Holmes. I am truly touched by your concern for my future happiness."

"Quite right Watson... And now, to church! Come on you Scamps!" he cupped his hands around his mouth to form a megaphone to address the children and shouted, "And remember... Quiet as church mice..."

***

Meanwhile, back in Greedy's police house, things had moved on.

"P... P... Pooo-ey!" said Arthur as he removed the Inspector's soiled sock.

LeSword was sitting on the low wooden plank which was what stood for a bed in the police cell, his legs crossed so that the bare foot dangled in mid air, while Arthur carefully tidied him up.

"You see?" said Greedy haughtily, "I told you Arthur would help you if you asked him nicely. You do see that now, don't you? So you won't shout at him again, will you? Or something else will happen to you that you don't want."

Telling off his superior like a naughty child gave Greedy the most intense pleasure. In fact, he hadn't enjoyed himself so much in years. The Inspector turned to Greedy and gave him a snide look. Arthur held up the sad object that was the befouled sock for the Inspector's inspection.

"Thank you Arthur," LeSword said unconvincingly. "Please can you take these handcuffs off me now?"

"N... N... No," said Arthur in his musical little voice.

Greedy burbled in the background with deep and lusty laughter.

"Greedy! What do you think you're doing siding with a child against your superior. Your miserable village and its unruly urchins have made me a laughing stock! You unlock these handcuffs at once, or else!"

"I'd best not sir," Greedy stammered between giant hiccoughs of mirth. "For if I do, it may make Arthur most displeased."

"May make him most displeased...! I am the one who's most displeased!" LeSword turned back to the child and cried out in shock at the vision before him, for the putrid sock was dangled just inches from his nose. Holding it was a child with the look of an angel, but the grin of Satan. That grin... That permanent unworldly grin, that look of joy pinned on the face of a tiny blond Beelzebub. LeSword had the horrific thought that this might be the vision emblazoned on his retinas at the moment of his death.

"I... I... I'll go and wash this for you now Mr Spector." LeSword just looked, his mouth agape. "At the pump." said Arthur chirpily.

There was a ghostly silence... Greedy nudged LeSword on the shoulder.

"Oh, er... yes... thank you Arthur, that would be splendid." LeSword on receiving Greedy's signal tried his hardest now to be nice. "And do you think you could possibly rescue my shoe from that horrific mutt of yours while you are at it?"

"A-hem..." Greedy coughed as another sign of caution to the Inspector. Arthur looked as if he was about to cry for a moment, then fixed the poor detective with a withering blue-eyed stare.

"Sorry, I meant, please could you ask your lovely dog for my shoe back – that would be very kind. If you would consider doing that for a silly old policeman like me. Thank you."

Greedy couldn't believe what he was hearing. He would savour this moment for ever! What yarns he could tell for years to come, down at the Royal Oak... and just think of all the free pints that credulous bicycling tourists, moorland ramblers and amateur huntsmen would gratefully ply him with. In Greedy's own little dream world, today was already shaping up very nicely from what had been an ignominious and unpromising beginning.

"S... S... Sock!" said Arthur joyfully, jumping up to take his leave. "Then Sh... Sh... Shoooooooooooe!"

"And... handcuffs?" begged LeSword, tentatively holding up his manacled wrists for the little chap to see.

"N... N... No," said Arthur, and bounded out into the street.

"Arrrrggghhhhhhhh!" roared the Inspector in anguish and frustration now that Arthur was out of earshot. "This is not funny, Greedy. Not at all funny! I shall be taking steps to sort this place out, Greedy, mark my words! There will be changes round here!"

"Now, I don't think you will do that sir, will you." Greedy replied in a manner that indicated the Inspector's proposed threat would be most unwise.

"I certainly shall! I am already planning to have this whole division overhauled and retrained and put under proper control and..."

"They'll want to know why."

"What?"

"The Somerset Constabulary. They'll want to know why some outsider is trying to interfere in their affairs. And I have a suspicion, that you're not going to give the reason."

"What are you saying, Greedy?"

"I'm saying, sir, that if you attempt to interfere in the organisation of our Somerset policing, and you do not give your true reason for that interference, then I am afraid, the true reason will have to come out. And that would not be good for your... *reputation...* would it sir?"

"Are you threatening me? I don't like being threatened, Greedy."

"No sir, and you don't like being handcuffed either, but I can't do anything about either of those problems until Arthur gets back. He's a good lad, very thorough for his age... Your sock will return almost unblemished I am sure, and ready for immediate wear."

"But what about my shoe? I shall have to buy some more boots, but I can't go into the village limping on one foot can I? Have you got any spare boots Greedy?"

"What size do you take sir?"

"Nine."

"I am size fifteen sir. You're welcome to try them on."

"Greedy, you irritate me more by the minute."

"Don't fear sir, we have a very good cobbler in the village. He is most attentive and can work almost miracles with careworn footwear. Anyway, I must be getting to church. Will you be joining me? Or staying here?"

Greedy positively glowed inside as he delivered his question.

LeSword gave him the most contemptuous look that he could muster, and said nothing.

Greedy picked up his helmet and sauntered off to prayer.

TWENTY TWO

The Church of St Dubricius

My love she never was, now cannot be...
But I so loved her like a seed that grows
into a multitude that would feed me,
more than the fairest farm-maid ever sows.

And what is there to choose between a life
that shoots green leaf-fronds up unto the Lord?
And one which is a girl, please be my wife...
But no... her life this world could not afford.

Am I thus cheated by her death? Or she?
Her life she'll never know, but I'm left out.
A hole in my heart where her heart should be,
a breathless heartless hole riddled with doubt.

Fair Florrie I will do this thing for you,
for in this church there sits the barest clue.

The giant iron latch on the church door presented a challenge. How not to make it clang?

"I'll do it," said Harriet. "It needs a gentle woman's touch, that's all."

"Not a gentle*man*'s then?"

"Very funny." She turned the large ring with her gloved hand, carefully as can be. Slowly the catch lifted and the door became free to move. She pushed it slowly open, but cringed when it creaked on its hinges, making most of the back row of the congregation turn round to see who was entering the house of God.

There are 18 differences to spot in the two pictures of the interior of St Dubricius' Church on the following page, plus one rather difficult one to make 19.

Will and Harriet embarrassedly tiptoed across the flagstone floor followed by all The Scamps, except Arthur who was laundering the Inspector's sock, and Scamper who was still outside playing with LeSword's boot. The rector was in mid-flow, paying tribute to Florrie, lamenting her sad and untimely end.

"Look at all the beautiful flowers," whispered Will. "Florrie would have loved them."

"She can see them, never fear," assured Harriet. I expect John's spent all night presenting them so immaculately as a fitting tribute to his beloved friend."

Will studied all the bunches, festoons, garlands, sprays and bouquets meticulously while John's father the rector continued his eulogy."

At the front of the church, seated closest to the altar, they could see Mabel, Florrie's mother, with Horace Nichols sitting by her side, his arm around her waist. Will knew that the police might turn up at any moment to arrest both Horace and himself, but first he desperately needed to talk with the rector and, even more vitally, to his son. He hurriedly scanned the packed congregation but couldn't see John anywhere among them, not helped by the fact they were all facing away so he could only see the backs of their heads.

Claaaaaannnnnnggggg...

The vicar looked up and proceedings came to a halt at the sound of the monstrous latch on the church door being clumsily lifted. Everyone turned around and stared in anticipation, as the door was thrust brutally open and in walked a large policeman. Greedy slammed the door behind him then quickly saw how full the church was and hastily took of his helmet. He bowed his head in acknowledgement of the shame caused by his rather brash entrance before spotting Will and shuffling over to his side to join him. Will shuddered.

He looked up at the large policeman and spoke in as loud a whisper as he dared. "Not yet, Mr Greedy I beg you... We are close to the solution to this mysterious case... I just need a few minutes at the end of the service and then you can take me back to the cells."

Greedy responded in his best whisper, albeit still too loud for the occasion, saying "Don't worry young Will... You can have your minutes... And I shall have a word with Horace that I've been ordered to bring him in."

"What if the Inspector should arrive? He may cause a disturbance and provoke consternation among the villagers. You never know what might happen if an outsider disrupts an occasion such as this..."

"I am pleased to be able to tell you that we should be free from interference for a short while lad... the Inspector is a bit tied up."

"Sssshhhh you two!" scolded Harriet. "People are looking at you!"

"There, that told you!" whispered Will, and Greedy softly chuckled.

The service reached its conclusion and the noisy exit of the people was more muted than usual as people stayed behind to commiserate with one another. With sad music floating in the sacred grief-filled air, Greedy slowly walked to the front to speak to his friend Horace and with Mabel too. Will wondered how difficult a conversation that was going to be. He and Harriet made their way to where the rector was standing, in the midst of a huddle of parishioners, all eager to convey their gratitude and express their shock and disbelief. When finally the way cleared for the pair to engage the priest in conversation, Harriet affirmed what a fine tribute he had given dear Florrie and how much it meant to everyone, especially the girl's mother. But what Will needed to know was *where was John*? He nudged Hattie gently with his elbow so she would get to the point.

"Oh, and did your son John arrange all the beautiful floral displays?" she finally asked.

"Yes, yes he did... It took him most of yesterday and all last night. He was so besotted with the girl, it quite broke his heart. After he finished the decorations he took himself straight to bed as he could not face the light of day. I must go and see him now for he is quite inconsolable and I fear for what he might do."

"Oh no! I hope and pray he does not become sick, or worse, do himself harm!"

"Yes... that is what I also am worried about, and that is what must be avoided, but he took it very badly." The rector took his time to reflect on his grief before continuing. "There is a strange thing though that has been puzzling me, and I probably shouldn't say this..." He paused again while the pair gazed up in expectation.

"Pray, please do!"

"He seemed most agitated, even before the time that you found her, Will. It was as if he knew..."

"Really reverend?" Will's mind was focused in now on finding out the sequence of events. "Please may I ask you reverend something very important, that may help with finding out what happened here?"

"Yes of course."

"In the afternoon or early evening of the day it happened, which would be the day before yesterday, did you see John at all? Did he say anything to you, or did you see him talking to anyone else?"

"Day before yesterday... I'm trying to think... I came into the church in the late afternoon and... yes I remember John being here. Dressed in religious robes he was, for he is studying to follow in my footsteps. And then I remember someone came into the church and talked to him briefly then went out again."

"Really? Do you know who it was?"

"No, I couldn't see, I was right up this end of the church and John and his acquaintance were by the door. But then, and this is most odd... About ten minutes later, this same person came back again, talked to John and then left, just as he had done only a short while before!"

"That is most interesting, reverend... And so, if you didn't see the person's face clearly, did you perchance see what they were wearing?"

"Oh yes, it was a coachman. There is no mistaking that. Even though it was extremely dark and dingy in here, I could make out the uniform."

"And did John tell you what passed between them during those two meetings?"

"No, and I didn't pry... We men of the cloth get asked all sorts of things you wouldn't believe by all sorts of people. That is our job – to comfort and indulge, especially people's fears and insecurities. And talking of comforting people, I really must go and see John and try to give him fortitude in his time of hopelessness, when nothing seems worth living for. So if you don't mind, young Miss Harriet, Will, I shall take my leave."

The pair watched the poor man as he made his way to the exit and the sanctuary of the rectory where his son was lying moping from a broken heart.

"Oh goodness, I do hope John will be all right," lamented Harriet. "He is such a nice boy."

"Yes," said Will. "And he's practising to be a vicar... Note that carefully Watson..."

"Right you two!" The booming deep voice could only come from one source. "I'm afraid we have to go back and see the Inspector now, or I shall get the sharp end of his tongue again. Horace here has agreed to come along as well, although what good that'll do only the Lord himself and the great detective from Scotland Yard will be able to tell us."

"Aren't they the same thing?" Will offered up the question cheekily and Greedy chuckled.

As they walked along the nave, The Scamps were playing up and down the rows of pews.

"You Scamps," said Will, in his best commanding manner.

They all snapped to attention and looked at him.

"Take a look around the church carefully for me while I'm gone, and see if you can find any clues. Especially furry ones!"

The Return to the Cell

"I may have to lock you up again," said Greedy gloomily. "It depends what mood the Inspector is in when we get back. He was in a particularly irritable one when I left."

"Well I can't really be surprised, can I?" said Will, his tone indicating he was fairly unconcerned. "After all, I did escape from his clutches so he's not going to be exactly pleased with me. But I think we now have all the clues we need to make the final, ultimate and magnificent deduction which will solve this mystery."

"Really?" Greedy sounded surprised and positively in awe.

"Yes," continued Will, "I think we are *this* close." And he held up a hand with the tips of finger and thumb only a small distance apart indicating a substantial degree of closeness.

"Well I hope you're right. And whether you are or not, I hope you can convince the Inspector or else he will carry on trying to pin the blame on anyone he happens to meet."

"Be fair Mr Greedy! You tried to pin it on me too."

"Well it's standard police work, isn't it? The person who finds the body, or one of the family, or the lover? How do I know that it wasn't you?"

"True. But I hope my investigations have not been for nothing and that when I have explained the sequence of events as I understand them, then I shall be exonerated."

"You'll pin a crime on anyone you can, ain't that right, Greedy?" Horace spoke, spelling out his unflattering judgement of his fellow bowls partner in blunt terms. "And I'm a-ready to speak to this 'ere Inspector an' see if he tries to pin it on me!"

As they turned into Lowerbourne they saw Scamper licking carefully at a drainpipe which must, one assumes, be a popular spot for all the other dogs in the district who had already left their calling cards there. Scamper turned when he heard them and licked his lips.

"Erk," said Harriet, not wishing to be the next in line to be slurped by that particular tongue.

They walked in through the front door which was open, but there was no one to be seen. The cell door was slightly ajar. From inside they could hear the Inspector's voice, as if he was talking to someone. They strained their ears before entering to try and discern what the conversation was about, and were amazed as they heard LeSword very quietly and patiently saying "...something beginning with... 'K'."

Greedy pushed at the door so it was wide enough to see in.

"Ah! There you are Greedy... Have you re-captured the prisoner?"

"Yes sir," said Greedy, indicating Will.

"And have you brought in the other suspect for questioning?"

"Yes sir," said Greedy, pointing out Horace.

"Good."

K... K... Keys!" said Arthur, confidently rattling the large bunch of keys which he held in his little hand.

"Yes," said the Inspector dolefully. "Keys... Now please will you use the keys Arthur to unlock these handcuffs that you have put me in?

"We've... We've... We've already had 'keys'," said Arthur, grinning.

"Yes, I know we've already had 'keys' Arthur. We've had 'keys' a lot of times haven't we? And that is because I would really like you to use them to unlock me... Please?"

"S... S... So it doesn't count!" said Arthur.

Greedy thought he had better intervene.

"Is it all right if we let the Inspector go now Arthur? Come on now, give me the keys. I shall need them to lock up my police station later and I can't do it without my keys, can I? And the Inspector needs to get on and do his job."

Arthur thought about it, then grinned and handed Greedy the keys.

LeSword looked on in amazement.

"Why couldn't you have done that before? He just handed them straight to you?"

Greedy fiddled with the bunch, found the little key which fitted the handcuffs and unlocked them. The Inspector rubbed his sore wrists.

"He was teaching you a lesson," said Greedy. "He has no hard feelings."

LeSword looked like he was going to burst. "No hard feelings? No hard feelings! I should be the one with hard feelings!"

"Well I don't recommend it, sir. It won't do you any good and you won't feel any better for having them, and judging by the colour of your face you may burst a blood vessel."

"Yes Mr LeSword," said Harriet. "We should all be calm and nice to one another. Shouldn't we Arthur?"

Arthur beamed at her in agreement. Scamper rushed through the door and everyone jumped in surprise. LeSword was sitting with his back against the wall at one end of the low bed. Scamper leapt up and gave the Inspector a big kiss, then proceeded to lick him all over his face as he screamed for the over-friendly dog to get off.

While they all laughed at the sight, especially in the knowledge of where the dog's tongue had so recently been, Horace decided he wanted to get his meeting with the Inspector over with.

"I 'ear you want a word with me." Horace offered his cooperation, laced with a side-dish of menace.

"I do..." spluttered LeSword from beneath a cannonade of licks, "But first, I need to get this dog off me, aaaggghhhh!"

"G... G... Good boy, Scamper, kissy kissy..." said Arthur cheekily.

"No, not a good boy... Not a good boy at all... And you ate my shoe! Bad boy bad boy... Greedy! Do something!"

"Right sir." Greedy smacked his lips. Tea anyone? I'll put the kettle on... Do you take sugar Les?"

"No Greedy, no!"

"Very well. No sugar for the Inspector. How many sugars for all the rest of you as likes it?"

"Four," said Horace, and he walked over to where LeSword lay, grabbed Scamper by the collar and pulled him onto the stone floor. He looked down at the somewhat slimy sleuth. "I thought you wanted a word with me? I came 'ere straight from church at my greatest inconvenience, and all you're a-doin' is playing with the dog."

I do wish to talk to you Mr Nichols, and thank you for coming at such short notice. But first I need to lock up my prisoner." LeSword looked towards Will. "And where are those lawless rambunctious children?

Running amok in the village I'll be bound! They should be locked up too! Do they not know that organising a jail-break carries a penalty of lifelong incarceration?"

"They are quite useful when you get to know them," said Will with admirable calm. "I would not have been able to solve this case without them."

LeSword tutted loudly. "What do you mean, solve this case? I have been brought in specially to solve this case, and no one is going to solve it before I do. *LeSword of the Yard, no case too hard...* That's my motto. Now Cooksley, you get in this cell while I interrogate Mr Nichols."

Having set the kettle heating on the stove, Greedy returned and could see that the situation was about to go badly. "Mr Sword, sir... Why don't we just listen to Will first, hear what he has to say. That way you may not have to talk to Horace here, and that would be better for everyone."

"It'll be better for 'im!" warned Horace, indicating the flustered Inspector.

"Why should I listen to a stable boy?" LeSword asked petulantly. "Unless..." LeSword's brain cells were whirring now... "Unless he is about to confess... Yes! And about time too! Is that it boy? Do you want to admit now to your foul crime?"

Will held his composure and spoke slowly, without waver, just as his hero Holmes would himself do. "No sir. But if you give me a piece of paper and a pencil, I shall write down the name of the person who did it."

"Really?" LeSword seemed less irritated now as the boy's confidence was apparent from the way he spoke. "Why can't you just tell me who did it, and then we can arrest them?"

"Because at the moment, we have no proof sir. I shall write down the name, and then, with yours and Mr Greedy's assistance, we shall set a trap to catch the culprit, and then you can look at what I wrote on the paper and see if I am right."

LeSword looked around at all the assembled people. "This is a game. How do I know you are not just saying all this to save yourself from a night in a humble cell?"

"You won't sir. Not until we set the trap. But if you will let me speak now, I shall tell you all the clues and names and circumstances which I and my partner Watson here have uncovered, and then you can see if you come to the same conclusion as do I. For you only arrived just a few hours ago Mr Sword, and I'm sure it will be most useful for you and your investigation to be apprised of all the details we have gathered."

"Aaaaaggghhhh! Le-Sword! My name is Le-Sword! When will you two call me by my rightful name?"

"Yes, er sorry Les... I mean, Claude..."

"Yes, er sorry Sir-Sword... I mean Le-..."

Greedy and Will both spoke over one another.

"Oh I give up..." LeSword looked to the Gods before continuing. "Right then lad. Here is a piece of paper from my notebook and a pencil."

He handed them to Will who scribbled down a name, then folded the paper up multiple times so it could not be read without unravelling it all.

"You must put this somewhere safe, out of the way, where you will not be tempted to read it."

"Give it here lad – I'll put it in my safe. It'll be safe there – haha!" Greedy winked. "Come on then lad... Tell the Inspector and me all what you know." Greedy looked across at his friend, Florrie's uncle. "Did you want to be off Horace? Or did you want to stay and hear what the boy has got to say?"

"I'll hear him out. If he knows what's 'appened, we might come to find peace a little more easy, her brothers an' Mabel an' me."

"Right lad. I'll finish making the tea, then when I get back you can tell us all what you know and see if we can make head or tail of it." And Greedy pottered off to his stove.

"Watson and I have been working hard on this case for two days now sir."

"Watson?" LeSword looked baffled.

"Yes, my partner here is my sister Harriet, but she is also my Dr Watson."

"So I suppose that means you are Sherlock Holmes then does it lad?" LeSword had a fit of the chuckles at the thought.

"Well actually not quite sir. I am *Porlock* Holmes. Sir George named me that. You know Sir George I expect... he lives in London the same as you do most of the time, but he also has a holiday home high up on the hill overlooking the sea in Lynton across the moor from here."

"Hahaha... London is a large place my dear boy... I don't know everyone who lives there. In fact I couldn't know even a tiny fraction of all Londoners... Millions of them there are, all hurrying and scurrying, and a lot of them up to no good... those ones are my particular interest!"

"Yes I understand, and Sherlock Holmes lives there too. At 221B Baker Street. I expect you must know him."

"I know of him, that much is true, but I have never actually called on his services! Ah, Greedy is back with our tea. Now you must tell us what you know."

"Here's your tea sir."

"Thank you Greedy."

LeSword raised the mug to his mouth and took a swig.

"Thhhssplerrrrrrpppppp...!" he spluttered, shooting a fine spray of tea-mist all over himself and most of Greedy too. "It's got no sugar in it!"

"Yes, that's right sir. Very good detective work. I can see now why you are so highly regarded at Scotland Yard. I'll fetch you a lump."

"Two, Greedy, two!"

TWENTY FOUR

The Puzzle – 4

Will took a sup from the once white, but now brown and tea-stained, enamel mug that Greedy presented to him, then began his exposition of the clues. He tried carefully to think of the order in which to present all the information so that it could be most easily understood by his audience.

"Inspector LeSword, I think it would be best if you were to ask me all the things that you would need to know, in the order you would wish to know them, for you to be able to solve a case such as this."

LeSword looked impressed with the idea, enjoying being the one to direct proceedings.

"Very well... Firstly I would, if I had been here at the time, examine the body and see if anything obvious stood out, in which case the whole matter could be immediately wrapped up without further investigation. Of course I wasn't here when the girl was found, or removed from the scene, so I have only the information given to me by PC Greedy and the doctor's post mortem. And that indicates that she could have died by accident, and yet if she had befallen such a fate, surely someone would have seen her if, for example, she fell from the *Lorna Doone* coach. As an accident is unlikely therefore, I would need to know, firstly, who were her friends and acquaintances, who were the people she spent time with, family members, lovers, where she worked and who she worked with. We'll start with those."

He looked at Will keenly, waiting to be enlightened.

"Right. Firstly, Florrie had no enemies. In fact quite the opposite, for everyone who spoke of her seemed enchanted by her. She had many friends, one of which was my sister Harriet here, although I am not sure how many of them really knew her as she was a private person and didn't indulge in village tittle-tattle the way that some of the girls in the village do. But Harriet tells me that her best friend was the rector's son John. They decorated the church together, arranging the floral displays to make it look and smell wonderful for the Sunday services. John was the only person in whom she confided, but he is unfortunately lying on his sick-bed at this moment, stricken with inconsolable grief at thc loss of his dear friend."

Horace nodded his head in agreement. "They were always together when she wasn't up at the big house. More often together than sweethearts I'd o' said."

"You mean they weren't sweethearts?" asked the Inspector keenly.

"Oh no, not no way. They never argued, nor stopped laughing and smiling when they were together, so they couldn't o' been sweethearts!" Horace bellowed with laughter at the thought.

"Secondly," continued Will, "Her family. Horace Nichols, Florrie's uncle, is here with us and he can tell you that they were all very close, that is himself, Florrie's mother Mabel and Florrie's two brothers.

"Thirdly, she worked as a maid at Ashley Combe House which is the large estate just to the west of here, running from the hills and down to the sea. It is inhabited by Sir Cosmo Drake-Harrington and his son Rufus. My sister told me that Rufus was infatuated with Florrie and proclaimed undying love to her whenever he got her alone, which was a frequent occurrence because she was working within his father's walls and therefore had no place to hide. This created a problem for Florrie, as you can imagine, and she had to enlist the help of the gamekeeper who came to her rescue on more than one occasion, and even had to threaten his master's son with a beating if he did not leave the poor girl alone. I imagine Inspector that you would consider this an important fact in the case, as I do myself."

"It could be most vital, indeed. Do continue."

"The groom is called Frederick. He is a dashing young man and although more gallant than the lascivious Rufus, I imagine it perfectly possible, even likely, that he could have fallen for Florrie too, as it seems so many others instantly fell under her spell, including myself."

Horace harrumphed. "You? You're only a child boy. What would Florrie want with you?"

"Yes, quite so Mr Nichols. All I am trying to convey to the Inspector is that Florrie was possessed of rare beauty and her attraction seemed to have no bounds. Is that not so Hattie?"

"Yes, I suppose you could say she turned heads wherever she went." Harriet answered with a modicum of envy in her voice.

"It's always the spurned lover..." LeSword repeated his favourite dictum, his overarching theory as to what motivates the practitioners of murderous crime.

"So," continued Will, "I think that is the sum of what we know about Florrie, her friends, family and workplace life Mr LeSword... What would your next question be?"

"The next thing I would try to find out is what she was doing before the time of her death, and who she had been with, or was still with during that fateful time."

"Very good... I shall tell you what I and my colleague here..." Will glanced over to his sister in acknowledgment, "...have discovered about Florrie's movements in the time leading up to her death.

"When I discovered Florrie, cold and motionless on that slope, she appeared at first glance unscathed, and I thought at the time she looked as if she could have been dressed for her own wedding, so perfect were her clothes and hair, and everything else about her in every way. Since I raised the alarm, and Florrie was taken away to the doctor's mortuary, I and my partner here have conducted research on several items that we found on the spot where Florrie lay."

"I don't know of any items found," said Greedy tersely. "Why didn't you bring these things to me?"

"That is what I am doing now Mr Greedy, for this is the first opportunity I have had since we received the results of the tests."

Greedy seemed unimpressed... perhaps he was worried he might get another telling off from the bigwig Inspector.

"And from those results, we have deduced that Florrie really was going to her own wedding."

"You haven't told me any of this!" Greedy definitely sounded miffed.

"Quiet Greedy!" snapped the Inspector without taking his eyes off Will. "Who then..." he continued, "...was the young lady's intended? Have you managed to *deduce* that, tenderfoot detective Porlock Holmes?"

"Yesterday, the local village children told me about a ship they had seen in Porlock bay. They said it was a pirate ship, but we all know what children are like, inventing the most fanciful and exciting explanations for everything so they can act them out in their games. Naturally I was dubious, so I asked them to walk around the headland towards Ashley Combe and see what they could find out. What they came back and told me, and showed me too in the form of drawings they made, indicated most clearly that a fire had been lit upon the First Rocks which guided the ship, whatever ship it might be, into the shallow bay which lay before Gore Point. We must note at this point that the grounds of Ashley Combe are riddled with tunnels, used by tradesmen sixty years ago or more and which have since become little used – the children of the village have all played in them, myself included, having fun while avoiding the attentions of the gamekeeper and his miserable dog. The Scamps, as the current crop of village children are known, went into the tunnels and found the smugglers' booty lying there, rum and brandy and port wine in casks, along with evidence of pirates' clothing, along with a gentleman's coat and top hat. Remember now that Florrie worked at the big house and so would have been seen by these ruffians as she carried on her duties, as well as when she walked to and from work. She might easily have fallen prey to their rugged charms, and indeed the children found there, among the empty bottles and other evidence of roistering and revelry, a shawl left behind which, we deduce, probably belonged to Florrie, the reason for that deduction being that she later asked our mother, Hattie's and mine, if she could borrow one of Hattie's shawls as she had mislaid her own. Her reasons for borrowing the shawl turned out to be twofold, the first being to substitute for her own, but the second, by happenstance, giving her an item of clothing which was borrowed. *Something old, something new, something borrowed, something blue.* She was wearing brand new earrings, that much is in the doctor's report on the post mortem examination. And I found, after her body had been removed, a silver charm with a small blue stone set into it... Watson, please be so kind as to show the Inspector and Mr Greedy."

Harriet took the charm from her pinafore and passed it to LeSword. Meanwhile, Will carried on with his presentation.

"Something old? Well that could have been any part of her underclothing or jewellery, could it not?. And so onto the identity of her intended... Who was she to marry? Well that brings us to the note which you have already seen... The note found by Dr Kingslake on her person... The note depicting the steps and the sunset and the stone circle."

"Stone circle?" queried LeSword.

"Yes. We believe that the ring of thirteen dots on the note are the thirteen stones of the stone circle which lies up the hill just past

Whitstones. And we deduce that that was the place where Florrie was to be wed. The thirteen steps depicted on the note represent the ones at the foot of the Lime Way – I counted them as I passed by later in the day. It is a path around the back of the hill with an easier grade than the main road. And, I'm sure you will be keen to know, the person she was to wed..."

Will paused for effect. He could sense LeSword's hairspring anticipation laced with frustration.

"...was one of the pirates she had met at Ashley Combe, a handsome buccaneering devil no doubt who had immediately rendered her love-struck!"

"How do you know she was to marry a pirate?"

"Well we know she had been fraternising with the smugglers from the presence of her shawl amongst their contraband, and we also have the note, which has many singular characteristics which enable us to deduce the type of person who would have been its author.

"One... it has no writing on it, just a crudely drawn picture.

"Two... a picture which was, judging by its unrefined strokes and harshness of the crayon, almost certainly drawn by a male hand.

"Three... the time of the liaison is specified on the note by the position of the sun and moon, and not expressed using a clock or as numerals pinpointing the hour.

"What do our learned policeman friends here make of that?"

"Someone who hadn't learned his alphabet at school," suggested Greedy.

"Yes, I would say that was so. Do you think maybe the person who wrote the note had actually ever been to school?"

"Aha!" burst in LeSword. "A pirate would never have been to school most likely, and so, the note was the wedding invitation from a pirate to his prospective bride."

"Yes... Good... Are we all agreed on the author of the note then?"

"Yes, I think so..." LeSword gave some thought to what he had been hearing, then bade Will to continue.

"And there is one more piece of evidence which I believe clinches the identity of her intended husband... when my colleague and I visited the stone circle, which we shall tell you about in detail shortly,

Watson noticed a pirate earring which had been dropped on the ground, beneath one of the stones."

"Fascinating! Well done Watson!" enthused LeSword, writing the fact down in his notes. "Please carry on with your explanation."

"So, I shall assume that your next question might be, 'who else other than Florrie was around on the hill at that time?' "

"Good question," said LeSword with keen interest.

"There were four others whom we know of who were present while Florrie was still alive, three of whom we can identify. Also there was probably another who I shall mention, one who goes that way each evening at about that time, but is elusive as he keeps himself to himself. Of course, there could be others who we don't know about, and in fact we can prove that at least one other was present later, after Florrie's death; we shall come to that in a moment. But for now, I shall tell you the ones who were definitely there as follows:

"One… Francis the road mender. It is his job to flatten down the surface shale on the hill where it has been ripped up by the horses and carriage wheels during the day. We know he was there because he stopped us and told us about it, but he didn't tell Mr Greedy because he was scared he might be blamed.

"Two… A pirate. Francis spotted Miss Florrie and wondered what she was doing out on the hill on her own, so he began to follow her up the Lime Way. At a spot about where the path forks off to Hawkcombe to the left and continues up onto the moor on the right, he saw on that side, above them, almost at the top, was a pirate, fierce-looking so Francis said, and I can imagine that seeing the large figure of a brigand such as that in the gloom at that time of the day would be a most terrifying sight, for Francis is slight of build and timid by nature. I can assure everyone present here now that he is dreadfully ashamed of himself for what he did next, for as he watched Florrie climb further towards this rapscallion, the vagabond gave him such a fearful look of hatred and wrath that he turned tail and ran back down, fearing for his own safety.

"Three… The priest. As Francis descended in dread, when he reached the thirteen steps leading down into the road he saw a parson wearing church vestments coming up."

"To preside at the wedding," said LeSword, nodding his head.

"Yes sir, I assume that is so. And…

"Four… A smartly dressed gentleman wearing a top hat and a frock coat who Francis saw accompanying the priest."

"The toff from the house then." LeSword paused for Will to continue, but there was only silence, and he wondered why the boy had not concurred with his judgement. "Who else then? You said there may have been one other on the hill at around that time." LeSword was eager tow know all the details so he could take credit for working out the identity of the assassin.

Will tried to reassure him. "This is where we are merely surmising what might have taken place, and therefore I cannot call it strictly a *deduction*, that being something which is drawn from indisputable facts. There is a very good probability that walking up the hill at that time of day was a man, a small furtive creature, much disfigured with a pronounced stoop, who lives in the shadows and speaks not a word, but growls if surprised by other humankind in an animal-like way, such as might be heard from a startled dog or bear."

"Bear? My word Cooksley, are you sure you have not now lost your sense of reality and branched out into fiction? I have been listening thus far assuming you were presenting me with the facts of the case, and now you would have me believe that there is some half-man half-animal bear-like deformed monster on the loose growling at everyone who passes by. Do you know of this creature Greedy? For if he exists, I am sure you cannot have failed to notice him!"

"No sir I do not. I fear that our young detective here is playing games now and taking us for simpletons."

"Please," cut in Harriet. "Will has made it sound like something you would read in a *penny dreadful*, but in essence what he says is true. The man of whom he speaks is actually a poor creature, scared beyond his wits to meet others, and therefore capable only of lurking in the verges and gutters as Will says, trying to avoid human contact. We met him by chance, and he let out a fearful pathetic sound which my brother chooses to call a bear's growl, but is more like the mewling noise made by a distressed cat. The reason Mr Greedy does not know of him is quite simply because he does so resolutely conduct himself with the utmost stealth."

"Who is this creature then? Do you have any idea?" LeSword was curious to find out now that his doubts had been put to rest by a more reliable source in the form of the unimpeachable Miss Harriet.

"He was, up until a few days ago, the master of a private madhouse whose sole inmate was released upon his retirement."

"Yes! The lunatic!" Greedy piped up, obviously greatly enthralled by the rousing thought of the mad-woman set loose on the moors. "What happened to the last patient in the asylum, eh? The witch?" He turned to LeSword. "We were issued with this notice, you see Les?..."

LeSword grimaced while Greedy pointed to the poster on the police station wall.

"She was the last patient in the asylum, released on the twelfth of this month, just a few days ago!"

"We visited her," said Harriet. "Her name is Betty."

Greedy's eyebrows raised while his eyes glinted bright. "You did? How did you know where to find her? I am surprised... Especially at you Miss Harriet... Were you not afraid?"

"Terrified! But Will thought it would be a good idea to find out if the old lady knew anything. Our mother knew where she might be. She was acquainted with her many years ago, around the time I was born, and she told me that the lady was of strange habits and used to go up onto the moor, to the stone circle to be precise, because she felt comfortable there, away from the teasing and tormenting of the village-folk. And that is where we met her, and her ex-gaoler too, the poor scared creature. He has no friends, and because Betty is the only person he has been close to for the past sixteen years, he seeks her out each day and brings her her supper, just as he used to when he was her custodian. She says that he will talk to no other being on Earth except her."

"And did she tell you anything interesting?" Greedy was itching to know.

"She said that she had been talking to Florrie just prior to our arrival."

"Really Miss? How can that be? Was the poor dear girl not dead already? LeSword's astuteness pinpointed the discrepancy in a flash.

"Yes. Will had found her that same morning. She was already with the angels."

"That means... my word! She really is a lunatic Greedy! We should bring her in!" Then LeSword became quietly reflective before musing. "Although, I have interviewed lunatics before by the score. You don't get much sense out of them."

"Mmmmmm... Greedy mumbled lugubriously. If you look at the poster on the wall sir, it says she was *Detained for Witchcraft.* I imagine she would find no problem regaling gullible souls with tales directly communicated from the recently departed. Maybe you should interview her, find out if that is the case... So young Holmes and Watson... what did she tell you about Florrie? What did she say the departed girl told her? Did the poor young lady reveal her killer?"

"Unfortunately not. What Betty told us was that Florrie had three people who wanted to marry her: A rich man, a poor coachman, and a brigand."

"Ha!" LeSword was onto the possibilities in a flash. "The brigand is the pirate! The rich man is this Rufus character who was shamelessly pursuing her. And the coachman..." He looked directly at Will... "Was *YOU*, was it not boy? You admitted you liked her... Liked her a *LOT*, as I recall. *You* are the coachman... *You* are the spurned lover..."

"Unfortunately not sir... I wished it were me, and said as much to the witch at the time. But Betty replied it was someone else, which grieved me to think about, but she didn't know who. I have a feeling it might have been the guard Walter who works on the *Lorna Doone* coach."

LeSword's eyes flashed like a glinting bayonet.

"I can tell from the way you say his name that you don't like him, do you Cooksley?"

"He is bumptious, sir."

"I am right then, just as I said... You don't like him."

"Your mind is as keen as you say it is sir."

LeSword added a few more lines to the scribbles he had been making in his notebook while Will had been talking. He then flicked back through the pages, as if searching for something of interest. He stopped somewhat nearer the beginning of his minutes.

"What about the young lady's missing shoe? Tell us about that please, and how you came to find it."

"Well sir, obviously I noticed Florrie had one shoe missing when I found her, and as it was a vital piece of evidence I knew that Mr Greedy would be keen to find it, so myself and my dearest colleague Watson here along with her friend Clara undertook to carry out that search with the hope of bringing the shoe to the attention of the police."

"And how did you manage to find it? Pure luck was it? Or was it where you had left it?"

The barbed comment was slid home like a clasp-knife to the heart, but Will ignored its devious intent.

"I did have a slice of luck as it happens. We had been searching for quite a while, an hour or more, when I chanced to spy a sixpence dropped by the side of the road. I happened then to remember the rhyme...

"*Something old, something new, something borrowed, something blue... AND...*"

"AND!" butted in LeSword in an eager state of excitement: "*a silver sixpence in her shoe*!"

"Yes, yes yes Mr Sword! You have it exactly... I thought that the chances were, if I had found the sixpence that had been in her shoe, then the shoe could not be far away. We spent a good deal of time wasted searching on the inside of the hill... But then I realised, to dispose of the shoe, a better hiding place would be the tree covered Cunnigar Plantation on the opposite side of the road. A mere few minutes searching around that spot, and there it was!"

"Good... Very good... I can see you've been putting a lot of thought into this. You have the makings of a detective. Albeit of the beginner class."

"Why thank you sir."

"Not at all. Always a pleasure to recognise a talent on the road to approaching my own."

Harriet sighed. "Please don't praise him too highly Mr LeSword... It goes to his head and makes him insufferable to live with. You should know that it was actually my friend Clara who found the shoe."

"Was it? Ah... in that case I shall make a note of that." LeSword jotted it down in his notebook. "Now Cooksley... Or, should I say, young Master Holmes, what else do you have to tell me?"

"I have to tell you of the other things I found after Florrie had been taken away from the spot where I discovered her, sir."

"You found things at the spot?" He paused before launching an outburst. "Greedy!" The Inspector rounded on the poor PC. "Where were *you* when the body was removed? Did you not inspect the scene for clues?"

"Mmmmmm..." mumbled the befuddled policeman.

Will's immediate thought was that he had better ride to the village bobby's rescue, even if only to save his own skin as well. "Mr Greedy went off with the corpse sir, so I was left alone at the scene. Mr Greedy personally asked me to have a look around for anything that might shed light on the circumstances of Florrie's death. Is that not right Mr Greedy."

Greedy looked up from his deflated posture, suddenly surprised and delighted at having been thrown a lifeline.

"Why yes! That's right Mr Sword... I asked young Will to find anything that could be taken as evidence and bring it to me."

"Goooood..." LeSword drew the word out slow and long, as if he was suspicious. "And what did he bring you?"

Will cut in quickly. "Oh, of course the charm with the blue stone, but other than that all I found was rubbish, sir. I showed Mr Greedy an old snail shell, and a cigarette butt, which on the face of it, either of which could have come from anywhere."

"Yes," said Greedy. "Just some old junk. Nothing of importance."

"*Until......*"

Will spoke just the one word and was gratified to see the two policemen instantly spring to attention, waiting carefully to listen to what he was about to say.

"*Until* I realised that the shell was a strange type that I had not seen before around here. And the cigarette end – that had a strange aromatic smell and was not of the coarse variety of tobacco smoked by the locals. So I went to the reading room and looked up pictures of shells and where they came from. And my dear friend Watson and I took the cigarette to Mr Wiles the tobacconist to see if we could gain from his expert opinion on its origin."

"You didn't tell me this?" Greedy seemed concerned that he might get in trouble again with the Inspector.

"No, I haven't Mr Greedy for we have only just received the results of our investigations, and I have not had time to put you in the picture up until now, this being my first opportunity to do so, which is quite fortuitous as the Inspector is now present to hear what we have discovered."

"Tell us... Tell us!" LeSword was impatient to hear."

"The shell is most unusual. Would you like to show Mr Greedy and the Inspector Watson?"

"Euuugghh. Do I have to touch it again?"

"No, just give them the hanky which the items are wrapped up in."

Harriet took the handkerchief from her pinafore and passed them to the policemen. The Inspector carefully unfolded it and looked at the contents."

"Yes... it is unusual," he observed. "I would have said it is some foreign thing brought here from distant climes attached to a ship."

"Very good Mr Sword!" Will declared with all sincerity. "I can see why you are such a legend at Scotland Yard!"

LeSword looked up and smiled at him. "Not a legend quite yet, dear boy. I still have a few murderers and n'er-do-wells to entertain at His Majesty's Pleasure before I retire... So, if as I take it my hunch is correct, then in which particular part of the world did this little shell start its life?"

"The Caribbean sir. The shells are used as good luck charms. The pirate will have sailed from the Caribbean with the Jamaican rum found in the casks in the tunnels. He left the shell with Florrie's body as his tribute to his bride-to-be who tragically never was to be."

"Good..." And the cigarette tobacco? Was it identifiable?"

"Why yes... With great good fortune Mr Wiles was able to say that it is prepared especially for the house at Ashley Combe."

"Which means our friend Rufus was also present at the spot where Florrie met her end."

"Yes." Will paused. "And one other for sure."

"One other? Do tell us... This is becoming more like a detective case I can get my teeth into by the minute!"

"Florrie carried a bear with her."

"Oh not the bear again!" Greedy groaned. "Would this be the teddy bear? Or the one that *growls* like a bear?"

"The teddy bear... She called him Jack... She would never go anywhere without him," interjected Harriet.

"What's a teddy bear?" LeSword furrowed his brow; he was not up to the mark with the latest trends in bear-naming.

"It's a toy bear... Made from cloth... Stuffed... With kapok I would imagine." Harriet tried to explain to the confused policemen.

LeSword nodded, indicating his understanding of the make-up of this new "teddy bear" phenomenon. "How is this relevant?"

"When Francis the road mender watched Florrie climb the Lime Way toward her assignation, he recalled that she had the bear with her," continued Will.

"I see," remarked LeSword, wondering where this was going.

"But when I found Florrie the following morning, her bear, from which remember she was inseparable, was missing."

"I see... That is most interesting... I presume you looked for it?"

"We spent a long time looking for it, didn't we Watson?"

"A...ges!" said Harriet, stringing out the word with feeling.

"So someone must have taken it." LeSword continued his train of thought.

"Precisely. And as of this morning, I know who took it."

"You do? Capital! Go on then... who was it?"

At precisely that moment, the door flung open and a rousing Scamp chorus greeted their ears while the police station was invaded for a second time that day.

"We've got the furry thing you wanted!" shouted Betsy at the top of her voice.

"We hope it's what you wanted anyway," said Herbie excitedly. We had to send Charlie climbing up to get it."

"Yes and he fell off and he would have died only he landed in the font," said Dougie.

"Yes and luckily he can swim," said Fanny, as if it was all in a Scamp's normal day.

They paused for breath.

"Well, do you want it then?" asked Betsy, proffering the teddy bear.

"I'll take it please," said the Inspector, looking closely at the object as it was presented to him. "It's a scruffy thing isn't it..."

"The bear was mingled in amongst the floral tributes in St Dubricius' church," Will continued with his story. "John the rector's son always does the flower arranging so he must have put it there. He and Florrie used to dress the church together, so it makes sense that he would display her bear in pride of place."

"That means he must have taken the bear from the spot on the hillside. Or even from her hand!" LeSword was on to something.

"I believe so, yes."

"So this lad John, the reverend's son, was at the scene, as was the pirate, and Rufus who is son the of baronet from the big house."

"Yes, but not necessarily all at the same time."

"Quite so. So this John is the extra person you mentioned whom we could prove was there?"

"Yes."

The Inspector wrote some more notes, then looked up and thought for a second.

"Have you anything else for us to go on?"

"Oh yes, we certainly have. This case has a most singular feature, that being the trail of swapped and discarded clothing which we have uncovered in our enquiries."

"Clothing? We already have the shawl left in the pirate den, along with the top hat and coat. What else have you found out?"

Will turned to The Scamps and spoke to them as a group. "Would you do me a great favour please and go Mr Wiles's shop and ask him for the bundle I left with him when I visited earlier. The Inspector here will give you each tuppence if you get back her quick as you can!"

LeSword's jaw dropped as The Scamps whooped and flew out of the building like a screeching flock of gulls. Will carried on where he had left off.

"The stables at Ashley Combe have horseman's clothing, for hunting mainly but looking much like the clothes that would be worn by a coachman. The Scamps discovered a coachman's outfit and hunting horn removed from the stables and replaced with some ordinary clothes. Then, when The Scamps investigated the shop in town run by Mrs Agnes which sells a miscellany of clothing items too wide in variety for description, they found a coachman's horn on the counter which Mrs Agnes had not seen before and she had no idea where it came from. A pirate costume which had been on a peg on the wall of the shop was missing, and in its place was a horseman's outfit."

"Was it the same one as went missing from the stables?"

"We don't know, but it is very possible that it was."

"Interesting... Is that the last of the clothing chase?"

"No sir, it is not. I had a hunch that whoever had taken the pirate costume had climbed up the hill on the evening of Florrie's wedding.

Therefore, I and my trusted colleague Watson here went to the top and searched among the undergrowth for any evidence of pirate visitation which may have been lost or discarded."

"That was a leap in the dark, wasn't it? I don't see why you should expect to find anything."

"The reasoning was that whoever dressed as a pirate would have to, at some point, change back into something less conspicuous, and happily my prediction was confirmed as Watson here, who has the keen eyesight of a bird of prey, spotted a pirate headdress in the bushes. And we also found a pistol."

"Good Lord!"

"But there's more..." Will turned to look at the door and happily it burst open just at that moment, the noisiness of children filling the room once more as Betsy thrust the pirate artefacts into the detective's hand.

"So what do you make of that, Mr Inspector?"

"Good good Lord!... These are bloodstains!!!"

LeSword looked carefully at the vivid marks, obviously relishing the task, now that he had some real gore to work with. "So the pirate took a beating about the head! Someone must have been brave to do such a thing."

"Or, more likely, that someone was hiding, and jumped the pirate from behind. He never even saw his attacker."

"Yes. Never knew he was there, and never knew what had happened, for as soon as the blow had been dealt he was out cold." LeSword seemed to be assembling everything slowly in the correct order in his detective's brain.

"Most interesting," he eventually muttered to himself. "I thought this case could turn out to be quite tedious and not deserving of my powers of detection... But actually it is, as I said, most interesting..."

He looked down to where six pairs of hands were thrust in his direction, waiting to receive their tuppences.

TWENTY FIVE

The Trap is Hatched

"So now you know as much as I do about the facts and circumstances of this case."

"Yes. And you have written down, on a scrap of paper, the name of the person whom you think was responsible for the death of Florrie Nichols." LeSword spoke gravely, while turning over all the evidence in his head.

"Yes, I have."

"But what happens now?" LeSword seemed perplexed. "Unless we are to look at the name you have noted down, how are we to proceed? Is this to be a guessing game with you as the quizmaster and us as contestants, throwing out suggestions as to the identity of the culprit until you tell which one of us is correct... correct in your opinion, that is?"

"What a good idea!" Will said mischievously. "We should all have a turn at guessing, using the evidence! Why don't you and Mr Greedy each take a page from your notebook and write down who you think was the author of Florrie's misfortune?"

"Capital idea! As a master detective with somewhat of a reputation at Scotland Yard, I shall rise to the challenge." LeSword took out his notebook and ripped out two more pages. "Come on Greedy. Write down who you think is the villain of this piece."

The two of them each took up a pencil, then paused while they weighed up the possible malefactors, deciding which one was the most likely.

"So, going back to what I said, how should we proceed in order to find the truth of the matter?" said LeSword as he scribbled down a name on his bit of paper.

"Do you not remember sir? I said that we should set a trap! That way, I predict that the one with the guilty conscience will walk into it and we shall then see if any of us have identified the right person."

"And how is this trap to be set, pray?"

"A trap requires a bait. And in our trap, the bait will be Florrie's missing shoe."

"But that is here in our possession already."

"Yes, but only *we* know that... And here is a most important fact: only *I* know exactly where it came to rest after it was flung. Now, 'So what?' you might say, 'It could have landed anywhere.' And that is true... But, it didn't land just anywhere, or at least, not anywhere you would expect, and that is the thing which makes our trap more likely to work: the shoe was not thrown onto the middle of the hill on the same side that Florrie was discovered... It was thrown into Cunnigar Plantation on the opposite side of the road. That confused me at first. When Watson and I searched for the missing shoe, we spent all our initial endeavours looking on the wrong side. Even when I found the sixpence, I still continued to look on that same side where I had found Florrie. It simply didn't occur to me to look on the other side until I suddenly had the thought, where would the culprit throw the shoe where no one would find it?"

"I see!" LeSword's keen mind was now working along the same lines as Will's. "We replace the shoe where it was found and we let the village know that it is still missing and that they should go and search for it!"

"Yes, precisely. And we need to offer a small reward. The only problem is, how can the miscreant be made to believe that if we find the shoe we shall know his identity?"

LeSword's face lit up. "I think I can help you there!" He suddenly became animated with excitement at the thrill of the chase, hissing through his nostrils. "The guilty person will believe that the shoe remains where he threw it. He will therefore know that he was the last person to touch it. Have you heard of *fingerprinting* young Will?"

"I know that I have fingerprints sir. We all do."

"Yes... Precisely... We all have fingerprints, and no two people have the same ones. They are all different! Scientists have been studying fingerprints for some time now, and have proved beyond doubt that they can be used to identify any person who has touched an object, simply by comparing the finger marks that they have left behind with the actual ones on the tips of their fingers. What is more, Scotland Yard have recently opened a whole new department especially devoted to this new breakthrough: the Metropolitan Police Fingerprint Bureau. It was set up by Edward Henry, Assistant Commissioner, in

1901 and we are gradually adding the fingerprints of all the most notable felons in the country to our records."

"Gosh! How fantastic!"

"Yes. I believe it is exactly as you say, fantastic." LeSword paused to ponder the magnificence of the prospect of locking up many more of his most cunning lowlifes, hoodlums and blackguards. "So," he continued, "This is what we'll do to bait our little trap… We'll put up bill-posters around the village saying that one of Miss Florrie's shoes is missing, and requesting the help of the populace in finding it. We shall inform them that by employing the latest of modern detection devices, called *fingerprinting*, we will be able to track down and reveal the identity of the last person who touched the shoe. Hopefully the perpetrator will read our notice and be so afeared to his bones that he will at once return to the spot where he disposed of the shoe, search it out from its resting place and see that it is wiped clean!"

"Yes, that sounds like a masterful plan, Mr Sword. What do you think Watson?"

"What if someone else finds it? Someone who is not the culprit?"

"Of course you are right Miss Harriet, we must ensure no one else other than the guilty party finds it first." LeSword cupped his chin in his hand for a while and pondered, before turning to Will. "You said that it was unlikely anyone could find it by chance, did you not young lad?"

"It is unlikely sir, as it was not in an obvious place. But just to be sure, might we put an instruction on the poster saying that the area to be searched is that to the east of the road, where Florrie was found?"

"Yes. Good idea. That is what we shall do… Greedy?"

"Oh, er yes sir?"

"Do you have the means for printing up two dozen posters to be displayed around the village?"

"Er, yes sir – Mrs Willis at the Post Office can quickly turn her hand to most things in that line of work."

"Good. I shall draw up some words… Right… We shall need to replace the shoe of course, but first we must decide how we can keep the area under surveillance for as long as it takes for the suspect to appear."

“Mmmmmm... The person we are looking for will probably use the cover of darkness for fear of being caught.” Greedy was trying to think of all the possibilities. “We cannot carry lanterns, for their light would give us away.”

“We'll just have to hope there's a moon,” LeSword suggested optimistically.

“The cover of darkness would be good for the seeker wishing to remain unseen, but it will make the actual finding of the shoe much more difficult, if not impossible.” Will was putting himself in the position of the person searching, which was easy to do as he had been the one who had first located it. “I don't think that I could have found the shoe had it been dark. If I were this person, I would wait until a goodly number of searchers were already out looking and I would mingle with them so as not to draw attention. Then, when everyone was engrossed in their own work, I would quickly steal across the road and up the bank. I would thus be in the correct place with enough time to find the shoe and carry it away. In my opinion that would only be possible before nightfall.”

“Good. I hope you are right...” LeSword was enthused by the plan as he could imagine it coming together.

“So where shall we hide out where we cannot be spotted?” Greedy asked, “Bearing in mind we can easily be spotted in daylight.”

“I'm afraid there is only one suitable place!” Will teased the village bobby playfully, and pointed to the cell ceiling.

“On the roof?” the PC queried nervously.

“No... Up a tree...”

TWENTY SIX

The Trap is Set

POLICE NOTICE

YOUR HELP URGENTLY NEEDED...

...to find the MISSING SHOE belonging to Miss Florence Nichols, sadly departed, which was lost on or near Porlock Hill between the Lynmouth road and the Lime Way. Remarkable BREAKTHROUGHS in the new scientific technique of FINGERPRINTING will enable the police WITHOUT FAIL to identify the last person who touched the lost shoe and bring such person to justice.

REWARD: 10/- for the finder of the missing shoe

IMPORTANT: IF FOUND DO NOT TOUCH THE SHOE FOR FEAR OF TRANSFERRING YOUR OWN FINGERPRINTS UPON IT

By Order of Somerset Constabulary .v. MCMIV

Greedy collected the printed-up notices from Mrs Willis at the Post Office and stuck them up on fences and lampposts around the village.

Meanwhile, Will was replacing the shoe approximately where he had found it in the scrub and leaf litter, before he and LeSword lithely climbed a tall tree on the Cunnigar Plantation where they could survey the scene below. “We shall need sandwiches and a drink,” the Inspector had said. “We may be in for a long vigil!” So that is what they had, in a bag hanging from around Will’s shoulders. LeSword had let Greedy off the effort of tree climbing – the Inspector needed this to be a nimble operation and decided that he and Will fitted the bill (pardoning the pun!).

Harriet meanwhile had some organising to do. “Right you Scamps… Attention!” Harriet called The Scamps to order on parade. “This is a very important job. We shall be going up the hill and your job is to watch all the people who are searching for Florrie’s missing shoe.

“Will we get ten bob if we find it?” asked Dougie.

“I can’t promise that, but I’m sure you will get a small reward for helping. All right?”

“With ten bob I could buy a bicycle,” said Charlie longingly.

“And I could buy a pony,” said Betsy, thinking about riding through the woods.

“And I could buy a motor car,” said Dougie.

“No you couldn’t… Motor cars are much more than ten bob. I reckon Sir George paid at least a pound for his!” said Charlie.

“I… I… I’m a motor car!” enthused Arthur. “Churgle Churgle Splut Pop Boooom! Bluk Bluk…” And he held the pretend steering wheel and steered round all the others making a car noise.

“I could buy one of those giant humbugs,” said Herbie, reminiscing about the one he missed out on because the other Scamps were so horrible. “And with the change, I’d buy another one and eat that one too… While you lot all watch me!”

“If I had ten shillings,” said Fanny in a posh manner, “I would start a school and teach…”

They all waited, expecting her to finish and say what she would teach. But she didn’t.”

“Well? What would you teach?” asked Betsy, knowing she probably didn’t want to know the answer.

“I’d teach how to be clever,” said Fanny, continuing her act of trying to sound superior. “I’d start with fairly clever, then I’d turn them into smart, then brilliant, then virtuoso.”

“*Oh so* what?” queried Charlie who was the same age as Fanny. “*Oh so* stuck-up?”

Fanny gave him a dismissive glare. “I hang around with you, so I can’t be stuck-up can I?”

"Oh goodness stop this children!" Harriet had had enough of The Scamps' constant bickering. "Line up again. Come on... In a straight line... Atten... shun!

"Now... What was I just saying to you?"

"Watch the people searching for the missing shoe," said Fanny without looking up.

"Yes, that's right. And you can look for it too. But make sure you keep a good lookout, and if you see anyone cross the road and climb the bank the other side, make a loud sound like a bird."

"What sort of bird?" said Herbie, wondering if he could manage to do any sort of bird at all.

"I can do a cockerel!" said Dougie. "We keep chickens, and the cockerel calls to the hens and then he..."

"Yes yes, we know what he does!" said Betsy, heading him off.

"What does he do?" asked Charlie who was interested to know.

"He... He... He..."

"Yes, that's right Arthur. He tells them it's time to wake up." said Harriet quickly.

"No, he jumps on them," said Dougie, gleefully.

"And... And... And..."

"Enough! All I asked is 'can we make a sound like a bird?', and now we're talking about the bad habits of cockerels. Anyway, it's going to be evening when we're searching, so we need to sound like an evening bird. Any ideas?"

"Owl," said Fanny.

"Good, yes... Owl. Who knows how to hoot like an owl?"

"T... T... T-wit... T... T... T-woooooooooooooooooo!"

"Very good Arthur."

Arthur beamed. "And... And... And the cock goes C... C... Cock-Dee-Doo... Doo... Doodle... Doooooooooooooooooooo!"

"Very good Arthur."

"And... then he jumps on the chickens... Splooooooffff!"

And Arthur leapt onto some imaginary hens clustered around his feet and laughed as he lay on the ground, imaginary squashed chickens flying everywhere.

“Oh this really isn’t going very well,” groaned Harriet. “Can we practise a more simple call. Maybe a dove? Are you ready?”

“Coo Coo C Coo Coo Coooooo!” they all shouted at once and the noise was deafening.

“Right. Stop! Please can you just do one call one at a time like this: Coooooo Coooooo... Have you got that? It needs to sound like a real dove telling his friends that it’s bed-time. Do you understand?”

“I... I... I don’t like bed-time!”

“No Arthur. No one likes bed-time. But you’ll be able to stay up later tonight looking for the shoe. How’s that?”

Arthur grinned.

“Right, come along then. Now we all know what we are meant to be doing, we can get on with the job. Get in single file, then we shall march to the top of the hill – like the Grand Old Duke of York.”

So they set off, in quite an orderly fashion for Scamps, and Harriet was impressed. She had quite a little battalion with its dog mascot all marching to carry out their duty for king and country, and also for Florrie Nichols.

When they arrived at the spot just below where Florrie had been found, there were already half a dozen people grubbing through the undergrowth looking for the shoe, and this was only half an hour or so after Greedy had put up the notices asking people to join the search. Of course, Harriet felt slightly uncomfortable, knowing that they had no chance of finding it, and that the ten shillings reward would elude everyone that day. She brought her little procession to a halt.

“Right, face the front... Atten-shun! Squad... Dismissed! Now, spread out, and keep an eye out for anyone nipping over that wall on the other side, remember?”

“Yes Miss Harriet!” they all shouted and rushed off into the fields, yipping and howling.

More volunteer searchers were arriving all the time, and soon the scrubby landscape was dotted with figures, poking and prodding with broom handles, trowels, even cutlery while many were using their bare hands. Multiple dogs had also been enlisted, their owners hoping that sensitive noses might be attuned to footwear and thus put to good purpose. One hour, two hours they laboured, while Scamps ran about shrieking and generally enjoying themselves as the light began to fade and the evening set in. LeSword and Will, up their tree, knew that when the light disappeared altogether, it would be difficult to see anyone on the ground from where they were perched. That was tricky, and tricky too was the aching in their bones, increasing by the minute as the air became colder and there was no ability to move to keep warm, while the stiffness of their joints and muscles could only get worse. It was getting darker by the minute. Then there came a sound...

T-wit... T-wooooooooooooooooo...

"My word, it's an owl," LeSword observed on hearing the call.

"Sssshhh... Keep a good look out. That owl is a signal."

Cock-Dee-Doodle-Doooooooooooooooooo...

"What?" Exclaimed LeSword, unable to believe what he was hearing and equally unable to keep quiet. A cock crowing at this time of the day?"

Coooooo... Coooooo...

"And now a dove I do believe! How most extraordinary!"

"Oh dear," whispered Will. "I asked Watson to teach The Scamps one bird call and now we've got a whole aviary out there! Watch carefully LeSword, for our target may be at hand."

"I am watching... And listening too."

They both watched and listened.

"I can't see anyone." LeSword was becoming impatient, and his back was killing him.

"Give time sir, give time... It is not easy to find. The suspect will only know the rough area where he disposed of the shoe."

T-wit... T-wooooooooooooooooo...

"There's that owl again by Jove!"

Cawwwwk Cawwwwk Cawwwwk...

"And now a crow!"

Cook-oo Cook-oo...

"You don't often hear a cuckoo at this time in the evening – I must report this to the British Ornithologists' Union – they will be most perplexed, as I am, I am sure."

"What's going on?" whispered Will. "Are there now two people this side hunting for Florrie's shoe? Or have The Scamps got carried away in their excitement?"

Then they both heard a rustle from somewhere on the ground beneath them. LeSword and Will strained their ears and eyes in the gloom, and watched for any sign of any movement of the thorny branches of scrub which might give away a visitor. Then they heard low snorting grumbly sound, soft yet persistent, evenly spaced, like a heartbeat, but rasping, as if from congested lungs. Then some twigs crackled.

We're in! thought Will. LeSword must have felt the same. Even their own breathing sounded too loud, now that all their senses were tuned to what was happening in the vicinity of the shoe. The grunting gradually became louder, meaning closer, as the hunter closed in on his quarry, not realising that he himself too was the quarry in this game, with two animals of prey, waiting to pounce from above! Grunting turned to snorting. *He's like a pig hunting for truffles!* thought Will, wondering what LeSword must be thinking but not daring to ask.

A low dark shadow shape appeared, bent over, eyes to the ground. This is it! The shape was very small. Small for a man anyway. Will became suddenly anxious that this might indeed be a pig, or some other creature, maybe a badger, and that it might carry the shoe away and all their hard work and planning would have been for nothing, thwarted by nature. But then, when the form neared the shoe, two arms with hands reached out, brushing the leaves aside, assuring their owner that this was the thing that he desired. Carefully, the lifeform picked up the shoe by the laces, obviously having noted not to touch, and as it stood up, Will caught sight of a bag into which the being placed the shoe, then looked around. At this moment Will recognised who it was and cursed, letting out his feeling with a groan of despair.

"Not who you were expecting then?" whispered LeSword. "Let's go get him!"

"No, wait!" said Will firmly. "That's Eddie, the hunchback gaoler. I'm afraid my plan has gone most terribly wrong. Eddie must have found the shoe by the side of the road on the same evening when it went missing; it must have been lying there just as he was on his way up to the stone circle to take Betty her supper. He must have found the shoe and tossed it into the spinney here."

"Yes, well doesn't that mark him out as the murderer? Come on, we must apprehend him at once."

"Eddie wouldn't even go near Florrie, let alone do her harm. And it couldn't have been Eddie because he took care not to wipe off the fingerprints. The culprit would wipe the shoe clean. No, this is a fearful error on my part. I shall never be like Sherlock Holmes."

"Stop feeling sorry for yourself. We all make mistakes... Even I have made one or two." LeSword thought about it for a second. "Well, perhaps *one* anyway. We need to get down and at least talk to him, either to confirm or disprove your deduction."

Will's mind was still in a state of depressed whirling when there was a louder crashing sound from below, with more disturbance than before of the undergrowth and leaf litter.

"GIVE ME THAT SHOE!" came a threatening voice.

"Now!" urged Will and poked LeSword in the shoulder to galvanise him. He shinned down the trunk of the tree in two seconds, jumping to the ground from the first bough, leaving the older Inspector to make his own way more sedately. As he landed, Will was aware of what sounded like a scuffle going on and headed straight for the source of the disturbance. After pushing between some bushes he spied two bodies writing on the ground, with Eddie growling and screaming in fear while another had hold of his bag and was attempting to wrench it from its strap. Will piled straight into the mêlée, belly-flopping on top of the bag thief and pinning him to the ground.

"Mr Sword!" he screamed, "Here, NOW!"

In a couple of moments, LeSword had arrived on the scene. "Look what I have!" he announced cheerfully, a flash of silver in the dim light showing he grasped something shiny and metallic. "Hold him there!" instructed LeSword while he gathered the suspect's arms. The handcuffs snapped tight. Will got up and LeSword rolled his prisoner over so he could see his face. Will already knew who it was – he had recognised the voice.

"Who is this?" asked the Inspector.

"This... is Walter Collins."

LeSword looked into his eyes, briefly enjoying the moment that every good copper lives for. He then turned to check on poor Eddie.

He had gone.

"What about the shoe? He's got the flaming shoe! Greedy! Greedyyyyy! Stop him!"

"He won't hear you," said Will. "I'll chase after him, I know where he's going."

Will started to run as best he could through the brush and thicket beneath the tree cover, and it was hard going. But he was stopped in his tracks by a strange sight which even in the gloom he could make out as a very small chap indeed. And it was clutching a shoe.

"Arthur! How did you get here?"

"I... I... I found it!" trilled Arthur, smiling with success and happiness all over his face.

"Where did you find it?"

"The man threw it away."

"Oh thank goodness – well done Arthur... Come on... We need to take it to Mr Sword... He's just arresting the prisoner..."

"P... P... Prisoner!" Arthur was overjoyed at the thought, and held out his hands to rattle some imaginary bars.

Will took one of the lad's little hands in his own and the pair of them made their way carefully to where LeSword was just arranging Collins for the march to the police house. Arthur saw the Inspector holding tight onto the manacled captive. The scene was like an illustrated story from an adventure comic, and the little fellow was a part of it.

"M... M... My handcuffs!" he chortled, pointing at Collins' wrists.

LeSword gave him a dirty look. Then grinned despite himself. He just couldn't help it. "Did you get it back?" he asked hopefully.

"Arthur found the shoe," said Will.

Arthur held it up for the Inspector's approval.

"T... T... Ten shillings!" Arthur beamed up at the grumpy old policeman.

LeSword put his hand in his pocket and took out his wallet... He knew when he was beaten.

TWENTY SEVEN

The Solution

Back at the police station, LeSword ushered his prisoner through the door.

"Book him in Greedy. And when you've finished, I'll take his fingerprints."

"I didn't kill her Mr Greedy... It was an accident, honest!... She fell."

"Yes yes... We've heard it all before lad..." LeSword sounded unimpressed. "Book him, then lock him up. I'll interrogate him later."

"Right you are sir," Greedy acknowledged, taking out his pencil. "Name?"

"You know my name Mr Greedy."

Greedy looked up and gave Collins his ultimate derisive stare. "Name?" he repeated, even more loudly.

"Walter Collins."

"Speak up lad, I can't hear you!"

"Walter Collins."

"Wal-ter-col-lins." Greedy repeated what the prisoner had said syllable by syllable as he wrote it down.

"Address?"

While this was going on, Will and Harriet knocked on the front door and walked in.

"Aha!" greeted the Inspector as he clocked their entrance. "Well done to you both! Sterling work! And now that the suspect is safely behind bars, I feel it is time to reveal our predictions which we wrote down, as to who the culprit might be... Fetch the names we wrote down, Greedy."

"Right you are sir."

"Oh... This is exciting, is it not young Holmes?"

"Yes sir, exceedingly. Watson and I cannot wait, can we Hattie?"

"I don't know," said Harriet despondently. "You haven't even told me whose name you wrote, but I suspect, judging from your eagerness and delight, that you have deduced the correct one, and the Inspector too by his similar self-satisfied expression."

"I am very sorry Watson, but Sherlock Holmes never divulges his solutions to his bosom friend until the very end of the conundrum. You should have written a name down yourself."

"I don't recall being asked."

"Well for that, I apologise, and I promise that when we take on our next mysterious happening, you shall be included in our little diversion."

"Yes, yes – quite right," blustered LeSword, hoping to placate the demure and steadfast young lady. "It was thoughtless of us... Thoughtless..."

Harriet chuckled, and with a hint of sarcasm thrown in she delivered her view on the matter: "It is the way of the world, for being a woman in this world, one's views are almost never sought, and then most often ignored."

LeSword looked disquieted somewhat, thinking that he might here, in the sleepiest of villages, be in the presence of one of the new exponents of feminine rebellion that was brewing among the predominantly well-to-do metropolitan populace who were demanding *Votes for Women.*

"Yes well right," he said, wringing his hands and wishing something would turn up to change the subject. Which it did, in the shape of Greedy with the three scraps of paper.

"Open yours up then Greedy. Let us hear who you chose for the gallows!"

"Mmmmmm..." Greedy reverted to his usual response as he looked at the three scraps in his hand. "Sir. These three pages were all torn from your notebook sir... And then folded up the same sir. So I have no idea which one belongs to which one of us, sir."

"That doesn't matter Mr Greedy!" Will chirped up, as if he had the answer. "Inspector LeSword is able to deduce which is which by the method of fingerprinting, thus pinpointing which of us touched which piece or paper last... Is that not right sir?"

LeSword was taken aback. "I, er, don't think you quite understand... It, er, requires specialist equipment which I don't happen to keep on my person... The analysis of the fingerprints can only be carried out at Scotland Yard."

"What shall we do?" said Greedy wistfully.

"Look," said Harriet, riding to the rescue, "You all know what you wrote – you just have to tell the others. You can't cheat, for the answers are written down when we open them in your own handwriting."

"Capital!" said LeSword. "Who did you choose Holmes?"

"Walter Collins of course," said Will with a smidgen of smugness.

"And how did you come to know that?"

"I shall tell you if you wish, but it is quite a lengthy explanation."

"We shall be most interested to hear that. How about you Greedy? Who did you have marked down as the murderer?"

"I have Eddie, the deformed wild man that growls sir."

"Mr Greedy, you were so close, for Eddie was the first to find the location of the shoe... Well, actually second I suppose if you count the fact that Miss Clara and I first found it the day before. What about you Mr Sword?"

"*Le*Sword!" The Inspector corrected him for the umpteenth time, irritated that he was still having trouble with the locals calling his name incorrectly. "I would rather like to hear your story of what happened first, if you don't mind young Holmes. Then I shall tell you all the name which I wrote down, and the reason I did so."

"Right." Will looked at the assembled people, all eager to hear what he had to say. *This would be just like Holmes' summing up at the end of a case*, he thought.

"Ahem..." He cleared his throat. "You know of all the clues which Watson and myself gathered, along with The Scamps, over the period since Florrie's passing. You also know which persons we believe to have been present at various times on the hill that evening. We shall now gather these elements together and try to shed light on what took place on that sad day.

"Florrie's misfortune was to be possessed of many of the entrancing attributes which most people crave, for she was not only beautiful, but attractive in almost every other way as well, especially in her manner and openhearted character, her calm temperament, and her utter selflessness. These are all characteristics to be admired, but in combination they marked her out for more attention than perhaps any young lady should be expected to be able to cope with. They made her the candle around which so many moths fluttered in the hope of being the one most favoured, the one to find a path to her heart, and thence to dance along it.

"Thus, she was pursued relentlessly by the master's son up at the house where she worked. I imagine that when first they met, she was flattered by his advances, for they used a sweethearts' cipher to send messages to each other, even though I am sure they were never sweethearts, for soon young Master Rufus' amorous intentions became more and more pressing, more and more assertive, more and more coercive, and thus from Florrie's side more and more unrequited. She had to stop his behaviour as it was making her work at the house not only difficult, but filled with the dread of being caught alone in a room when he might enter at any time. She needed a solution... she told him she was to be married.

"At this point, I don't know the exact order of events. It may be that Rufus proposed to Florrie before she indicated her intention to wed, or maybe it was afterwards in response to that news. Either way, Rufus proposed, and Florrie replied with a note, written in the code which they had used when they first met. This note was to have a most devastating effect on the bewitched and infatuated Rufus. We have the note here."

The policemen looked on spellbound as Harriet took the scrap from her pinafore pocket.

"What does it say?" asked LeSword with uncontained excitement.

Harriet handed it to him. He looked at it and shook his head, then waited for an answer.

"I shall tell you what it says in a minute when we come to it."

The Inspector looked crestfallen, while Greedy mumbled something sounding remarkably like "Mmmmmm..."

"I... I... I..."

"Sssshhhh!" Don't tell them Arthur. You can tell them when we get to it, I promise."

LeSword was bewildered. "You know what this says?" said he, holding the piece of postcard in front of the tiny boy.

Arthur grinned his biggest grin. "I... I... I read it!" he said with glee.

"Good Lord!" observed LeSword. "A singularly remarkable child."

"You used the word 'singularly'," chirped Will with the hint of a thrill in his voice. "I deduce that you must have been reading from the works of Dr Watson!"

"Well yes, of course I have read much about the exploits of Holmes and Watson. Any professional detective such as myself takes great interest in such things... Anyway, pray continue."

"Very good... You are aware of the tunnels, and the brandy and rum barrels, and the lost shawl, and the discarded coat and hat. Remember that The Scamps went to the stables at Ashley Combe where they found a most interesting clue: a horseman's clothes along with hunting horn had been removed from their rightful place, and expensive toff's clothes such as the Lord's son would wear were left in their place. Now, when The Scamps visited the shop in the village, they found the horseman's clothes left behind, and a pirate costume taken in their stead. Listen, as this is the part you have been most looking forward to... The note you hold in your hand with the message written in code was found in the pocket of the horseman's clothes which were left in the shop. And the message on the note, when deciphered reads..." Will paused while he searched out the little lad. "Arthur... Please tell us now what the message says..."

Arthur looked very pleased, then recited, "It... It... It says: *Dear Mister, I cannot marry you because I'm going to marry the ugly coachman.* And at the end it says: *Very sorry, from Miss Florrie.*"

Harriet laughed. "Well done Arthur, that's roughly what it says."

They all chuckled until finally LeSword spoke. "Can you tell us what the exact wording is please Miss Harriet, if Arthur doesn't mind?"

Arthur grinned.

"It says, *My dear sir, I am very sorry but I cannot marry you for I am to wed the coachman this day. Florrie.*"

Will continued. "When Rufus read this note he was devastated, so much so that he lost his mind, as people do when they are ridiculously and hopelessly in love. His only thought was that he could get Florrie to change her mind, that there still might be hope that she would choose him instead over this upstart coachman. Thus, with his brain befuddled by this all-consuming passion, he made off to the stables and dressed himself as a coachman, with a hunting horn a suitable substitute for the gay post horn of the carriage guard. Suitably garbed, now he had to find out where and when the wedding was to take place. So where better to enquire than at the church of Saint Dubricius?"

"So Rufus was the coachman who was seen by the rector talking to John his son?" LeSword's question indicated that he was following the chain of events admirably.

"I believe he was, yes... He goes into the church with the intention of asking the rector, but the first person he sees is John who is wearing clerical costume, so he asks him if he knows about the wedding. Of course, we now come on to who is actually officiating at this wedding. It is no accident that John is dressed for the occasion. His father would never dream of carrying out a wedding ceremony to a pirate in a stone circle way up on the moor. John is Florrie's companion, bosom friend and confidant, and he will do anything for the darling girl, so he has agreed to preside at the wedding. Poor Rufus is dealt a second blow when he learns that the bridegroom is not to be a coachman, but instead one of the pirates! Quickly, he heads back outside and into Mrs Agnes' shop where he swaps his horseman's clothes and hunting horn for the pirate getup, taking a fake pistol too just for good measure."

"Ha!" cried LeSword. "You have it wrong! The rector said that the coachman returned and spoke to John for a second time. He therefore could not have changed into the pirate costume at that point!"

"That is true Mr LeSword if we take it that the second visit to the church was Rufus still dressed as a coachman. But remember it was very dark and gloomy in the church, and one coachman looks very much like another. I believe that the second visit was by the actual coachman, the coachman who Florrie said in the note that she was to marry... In fact, the very coachman you have locked in your police cell at this very moment."

"Good Lord! So what was he doing at the church?"

"He was doing the exact same thing as Rufus had done before him: he wished to know where and when was the wedding."

"How would he have known that Florrie was to be married?"

"Because, the coachman also had proposed to Florrie and, unless I am gravely mistaken, he too will have received a note similar to the one which she had given to Master Rufus."

"Really? That is a remarkable thing that both should receive notes. Why should that be?"

"Put yourself in her position. Florrie has already lost her heart to the pirate, and can think of nothing and no one else. In essence, all three are love-stricken in the extreme, Florrie, Rufus, Collins... and the pirate too I shouldn't wonder. If you want to see whether I am right, why don't you ask Walter Collins for the note?"

LeSword jumped up and crossed to the cell door. "Greedy, pass me the key please."

Greedy picked up the bunch and sorted through all the keys until he found the right one, then handed it to the Inspector. LeSword turned the key in the lock.

"Collins! Hand me the note!"

Walter looked up miserably from his crouched sitting position on the wooden bunk.

"What note?"

"The note that Miss Florrie gave you. Come on, we know you received it."

"I tore it up."

"Then what did you with the pieces?"

Walter sighed, pushed his hand into his pocket and brought it out again clenched. He then threw the contents into the air where they spread out and fluttered down onto the cell floor like confetti... like the confetti that Florrie never got to see on her wedding day.

"Oh, how are we going to piece together this lot?" LeSword started to pick up the pieces where they fell, gathering them as best he could.

"I... I... I like puzzles," said Arthur, helping find all the pieces.

"Good!" said LeSword. "Very good Arthur. If you put them all together in the right places I shall buy you a giant gobstopper."

"J... J... GIAAAAANNNNNT!" chanted Arthur in delight, pounding his feet in a slow stomping manner as he imagined a giant would do. He then set to work on assembling the tiny scraps.

"Go on then young Holmes... What happened next?"

"The coachman rushed from the church straight to the top of the hill. He found a hiding place from where he could watch anyone else who would arrive, and waited."

"Surely the coachman would have met Rufus dressed as a pirate on the way?"

"No. Rufus was still at the emporium getting changed into his new costume: Mrs Agnes didn't attend to the shop at once and did some odd jobs before going through to the front and noticing the clothes had been swapped. Once he had accomplished the switch, he did indeed climb the Lime Way to where, unbeknownst to him, the coachman was lurking. Next to arrive was dear Florrie, followed half way along the path if you remember by Francis. Francis watched Florrie climb, and also spotted the fearsome pirate at the top of the hill. Florrie also saw the pirate and, in the darkness, thought it must be her beloved. We can only guess what happened at this point, but it is likely that she sped up the hill, her heart a-flutter into the arms of her intended, but of course when she was close enough to see his face, she will have known who it was and stopped in fear and disbelief. It is at this point that the coachman appears from the bushes. He sees Florrie and, in a fit of violent jealousy, smites the pirate a vicious blow over the head with a blunt weapon. The blood pours from the wound and onto the Rufus' pirate clothes as he slumps to the ground unconscious. Now Florrie is terrified. She cannot believe what is happening, and she sees the hatred in Walter Collins' eyes. She rushes into the road which the Lime Way path joins at this point. Walter, his blood now up, gives chase. The poor girl tries to get away, but her clothing is unsuited to speed and she loses her shoe. Walter catches her up, she now disabled and hobbling through the loss of her footwear. He grabs her and she screams and fights to get away. He pushes her into the hollow at the side of the road and she lands, unfortunately dashing her head against the rough stone wall as she falls.

"All is silent. Walter now loses all of his aggression, instantly replaced by the fear and regret of what he has done. He is praying that Florrie is all right and is only temporarily concussed. He kneels down beside her. As he takes her wrist to feel her pulse he is quavering with fear. If there is no heartbeat, his world is over, only the depths of hell await him. He holds and feels, listens, hopes, each tick of his own heartbeat irritating him by its noise masking the silence of her warm and tender frame. There is no sound. A pulse? There is none. It is the end.

"Without any conscious thought, he runs back up the hill to where the shoe is and flings it across the road to the right, and as he does so he is seen by Eddie, making his way to the stone circle. Walter then runs, runs and runs away, hurtling away, as if that will mean that nothing happened. It may all have been merely a bad dream. In the morning he may wake up and none of it will ever have happened.

"When Francis descends the hill to the road, the priest he sees is not the rector, it is the rector's son John, dressed in the clothes of a reverend. Accompanied by the gentleman in top hat and frock coat, they arrive at the top of the hill to find the pirate lying there, conscious by now and groaning from the pain of his head wound. The 'gentleman' is actually the pirate bridegroom. He does not wish to walk around the village in pirate garb, so he is wearing clothes which he has most likely helped himself to from the big house. These are the clothes which, if you remember, were found by The Scamps in the pirates' lair, along with the casks and bottles and Florrie's shawl in the tunnels at Ashley Combe. That is where the pirate bridegroom discarded them when he later changed back into his more accustomed attire.

"The pair tend to Rufus and bring him round, asking him what happened. He tells them about Florrie and how she ran away just as he was knocked down by his unknown assailant. John and the pirate call to her, but there is no answer. They set off to search for her and after a time, we have no way of knowing how long, they find her where she lies, her face to the wall. Distraught, the pirate leaves a lucky charm shell which he carries. John gathers her stuffed toy teddy bear and takes it with him. At some point, Rufus has recovered sufficiently and joins them. Having lit a cigarette and smoked most of it, he drops it on the ground near where Florrie lies. What should they do? The pirate cannot go to the police because, as a pirate, he will always be blamed. Rufus cannot become involved in a scandal such as this, especially as there are people who know about his lust for Florrie and his less-than-gentlemanly pursuit of her through every room in the big house. That leaves poor John. He is torn. His heart is ripped apart. He clutches the bear and hugs it to his chest. He knows his father will be furious when he finds out the circumstances. He takes to his sick bed to think about the consequences and what he should do next. He decorates the church for Florrie's requiem and places her bear among the flowers, then returns to his purgatory of indecision, the bedchamber where he still lies now."

"You see! I was right," trumpeted LeSword. "It was the spurned lover who did it! Remember what I said? It is *always* the spurned lover..."

"I... I... I finished!" piped Arthur in his high excited voice."

"Hoorah!" cheered LeSword, barely able to contain his euphoria. "Well done Arthur... Please may we see?"

"Wait Mr LeSword! Don't go blowing the pieces all over the place with your big boots," warned Harriet, as she could see Arthur's work about to be ruined before they had time to read it.

"Yes. Quite right. I shall tread carefully... Well? What does it say? I can't make head or tail of it."

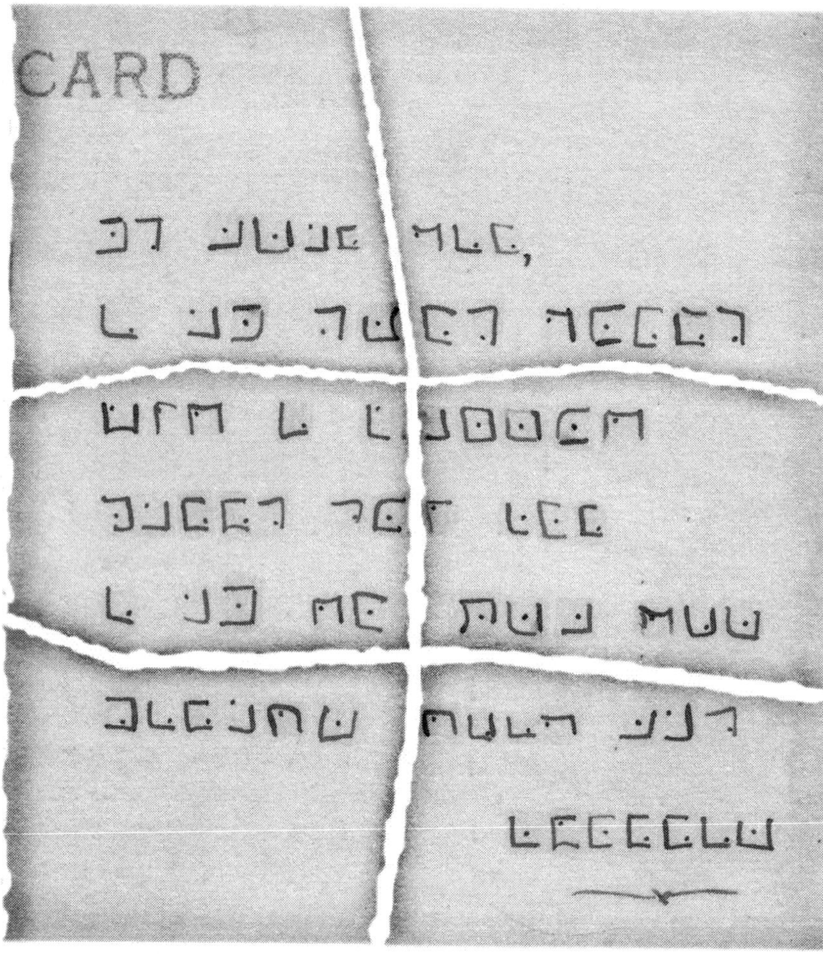

"We'll compare it with the one we already have," said Harriet calmly. She took the note they found in the shop and held it next to the one Arthur had assembled on the floor. "You see... This is the other half of the same postcard. There's only one word which is different. The rest is exactly the same."

"Well, what is it?"

"Er, I didn't learn the code," said Will sadly. "Did you Hattie?"

"No. The Scamps translated it in the shop – Mrs Agnes told them how to do it."

"W... W... Which word?" said Arthur.

"That one," said Harriet, pointing to the part which had different symbols. Arthur studied. Everyone watched, not daring to breathe. It was the most strange sensation, as if they were all mentally willing him on, but without wishing to put him off his train of thought with the slightest sound, not even a breath. Arthur studied, and counted on his fingers. As he raised each one, he mouthed a letter: *a... b... c...* (he said them as they would sound at the beginning of *apple*, and *boat*, and *cat...*) He continued until he got to *p...* then shouted out: "*p* for *pirate!*"

Then he started work on the next letter, holding up fingers and mouthing once more.

Will and Harriet exchanged glances and smiles. "I don't think he needs to bother with the rest, does he?" whispered Will.

"No," she whispered back, "But we must let him carry on."

LeSword and Greedy gently laughed too.

"*i*" announced Arthur, "for *idiot!*" and he descended into hoots of mirth. "I... I... I'm an idiot! Hahahaha!"

Harriet was shocked. "Who told you that Arthur?"

"*He* did!" roared Arthur, laughing his head off and pointing at LeSword.

The Inspector went red in the face and looked mightily embarrassed. "I, er, I... well, er... It was an accident... Arthur asked me if he could see what the handcuffs looked like when I was wearing them, so I let him put them on me, and then he wouldn't take them off again. And I couldn't get the key off him because I was wearing handcuffs!"

At this point, Greedy let out the most enormous burst of belly-wrenching merriment that was most likely ever heard in Porlock's police house.

"But we've made up and we're friends now, aren't we Arthur." LeSword looked fondly at the child, although he was still a little unsure. Children made him uneasy.

"*r*" declared Arthur joyously, "for *rabbit!*" and he did bunny-hops around the police station with his cheeks puffed out. "I... I... I like my carrot," he chanted, pulling his piece of carrot out of his pocket and munching it.

"Dear little fellow," said LeSword, trying to redeem himself.

"*a* for *anchor!*"

They waited while Arthur finished the last two letters.

"*t* for *tiger! - roooooaaaaaaarrrrrrr*"

"*e* for *elephant!*" and he held out his arm in front of his face like a trunk and trumpeted.

"Well done Arthur. Do you know what word that spells?" asked Harriet.

Arthur studied for a while before looking up and shaking his head.

"I... I... I forgot!"

"It spells *pirate* – so the message reads: *My dear sir, I am very sorry but I cannot marry you for I am to wed the pirate this day. Florrie.*"

"So there we have it," said Will. "I think that puts this case to bed, does it not Mr Sword? What name did you have written down on your piece of paper?"

"Let's have a look shall we?" The Inspector spoke with great smugness. "And by the way, the name's *Le*-Sword... *Le*... You hear? It has a *Le* on the front. Unfold the notes and read them out please, Greedy."

"Yes sir." Greedy unfolded the first one. "Walter Collins." And then the second. "Eddie... That one's mine..." And finally the third. "Collins the coachman."

"You see... Inspector LeSword shall win the reward! What say you young Holmes?"

"I say 'Well done sir!' – a marvel considering how short a time you had to study the case – what was your method sir?"

LeSword laughed. "It was simple. I only used one clue to hit upon the right fellow!"

"One clue? But that is impossible, surely? It must have been a very lucky guess."

"I used a skill which you have not yet learnt, my young detective. But you will pick up all the wrinkles of this job in time, I have no doubt. In this instance, I simply relied on the fact that you had already done all the work for me. When you listed all the suspects for me during your excellent presentation of the facts as you had discovered them, I watched the expressions on your face change with each one you described. You had a particular distaste for this Walter character which I noted without even having to try hard. I immediately knew that he was the one you'd decided upon, and I followed your example to the letter and wrote him down! What do you think to that?"

"Genius!"

"Quite so. I do like to think I exhibit a smattering of brilliance every now and again. As I think I mentioned before, I only have one great failure to my name, and that was a long long time ago."

"It must have been a great failure if you still think about it now? What happened pray?"

"It was the greatest failure in the history of the Metropolitan Police! I was a young bobby at the time. It was before dawn on the last day of August in 1888 and I was on my beat near Buck's Row in Whitechapel... I missed catching him 'in the act' by just seconds."

"Who?" asked Harriet, desperate to know.

"Why, *Jack the Ripper* of course. Mind you, if I *had* caught him then there would have been no mystery to tease us until this day. In fact, the name *Jack the Ripper* wouldn't exist at all, for that pithy and highly descriptive epithet was coined a month later when he had committed three more murders. Poor Abberline... He never got over it... He was the Inspector with the encyclopaedic knowledge of the east end of London... He wasn't meant to fail. I was only a green recruit... But it still rankles."

"No sir... I think you are right about the mystery. If you had caught him, it would have been just another solved case. But because you missed him by those few seconds, thousands of people have now pored over the facts and written about him. Perhaps our own case here in our little village will be written about one day. And you shall be the hero."

"Thank you, that is most kind. And you and Watson and even old Greedy here. Just look at him! Hahahaha!"

Greedy looked up and licked his pencil, wondering what all the self-congratulation was about.

"And Arthur! And all the other Scamps too!" cried Harriet.

"Yes... And Arthur." LeSword turned around to look at the little chap who was on the floor a minute ago, but had now disappeared.

"Arthur? Arthur! Oh where is he?"

"Oh gracious," thundered Greedy in shock. "The cell's unlocked! he must have opened it!"

"He's very good with keys isn't he!" cried LeSword as they all rushed to the door and peered inside. Arthur and Walter were sat next to each other on the bench.

"I... I... I spy... With M... M... My little eye... Something beginning with..." Arthur looked at everyone now standing there staring at him. "C!"

"Cell," said Walter despondently.

Arthur shook his head. "Th... Th... That begins with 's'."

"Clink," said Walter.

Arthur shook his head.

"Copper," said Walter.

Arthur shook his head.

"Cuffs," said Walter, looking down at his handcuffed wrists.

Arthur shook his head.

"Conspiracy!" said Walter, looking daggers at LeSword.

Arthur shook his head.

"Oh I give up," said Walter.

Arthur beamed. "C... C... Cu... Constable Greedy!" He delivered the answer to his I-spy delightedly, smiling at his favourite policeman.

Greedy chortled loudly. "Come on Arthur... You can't stay in here. This is where the naughty boys go."

"I... I... I'm a naughty boy!" said Arthur, looking very pleased to be such a thing.

"No you're not naughty Arthur," Harriet assured him. "Come on out here with us."

"I... I... *am* naughty," Arthur reiterated proudly. "*He said so...*" And Arthur pointed once more at LeSword.

The poor detective looked sheepish at having become the accused, as it were. "Come on Arthur, we're friends now, right? Come here and we'll go and get that giant gobstopper I promised, shall we?"

Arthur leapt up and jumped into the Inspector's arms. LeSword carried him through to the front while Greedy locked the cell door behind them.

LeSword sat on Greedy's chair with Arthur on his lap.

"Now... Miss Harriet and Master Will... Is there anything you would like from me for your most able assistance in solving this case? I shall get a big pat on the back when I return to Scotland Yard, I can tell you. What sort of 'pat' would you like?"

"Oh sir, yes, well actually there is something I would like sir, if the chance ever comes along."

"Go on then lad, tell me what chance that might be..."

"Myself and my sister Watson here, now we are proper detectives, we should like to be able to continue to practise our skills and methods of deduction, just like Sherlock Holmes and Dr Watson."

"Right." LeSword sounded sceptical.

"So if you ever have another crime which you are finding a little tricky to solve, even for someone with your great powers of investigation, then if the real Sherlock Holmes isn't too busy, perhaps you could possibly, if you don't mind and you need a little assistance, then you could call us in to help you?"

"Hahahahahaha!" LeSword started guffawing loudly, and his belly heaved up and down while his face became redder and redder as he started to choke with merriment. Then, in any of the tiny gaps between chortles that he could muster, he managed to insert a few words, "The real... hahahahaha, real Sherlock... hahahahaha, real Sherlock Holmes... hahahahaha, isn't too busy... hahahahaha. Oh, that's... hahahahaha, that's a good one... hahahahaha, real Sherlock Holmes, hahahahaha. I'll just pop round to Baker Street and get him... hahahahaha."

Harriet looked relieved that someone would finally back her up. "I told him Mr LeSword. I told him over and over and over I told him... I told him Sherlock Holmes is just a story and he won't believe me!"

"Oh I'm afraid that's right Master Will. Sherlock Holmes is just a character in a story. He's never solved a crime in his life, because he's never been alive! Hahahahaha."

Will looked up at the Inspector's large and avuncular face grinning down at him. And the young Porlock Holmes replied.

"I don't believe you."

None of them knew what to say. Arthur, who was still sitting on the Inspector's lap, broke the silence.

"I... I... I've..."

"Yes Arthur?" asked LeSword, interested in what the little chap was about to say.

"*Weeeeeed* myself!" Arthur squealed, laughing uproariously.

LeSword looked surprised at first. Then his expression changed into one of recognition, followed by sadness. He'd had a very up and down day. This was one of the downs.

She lives within me even though she's gone.
I wonder what she feels now? Does she know
the life she would have lived, had it been long?
Her happy children born and seen them grow?

I wish they could have been mine, mine and hers
But no, for little pirates they would be –
with cutlasses, not skates or pea-shooters,
and ropes and sails as they set off to sea.

And here I'm left, bereft, upon this shore...
What do I do now? Ride a horse aloft
unto that place where hope became forlorn
and every day I must pass that same spot?

Dear Florrie... Dearest girl... my treasure be
upon a map no pirate took from me.

The Return to the Soil

At the end of Florrie's funeral service, the coffin was brought out of the church and placed on the dray, a pony at its head for the journey up Parson's street, the lane beside the churchyard which leads to the cemetery at Hawkcombe. As is the custom in 1904, all the children of the village assembled behind the dray to accompany the coffin on its last journey, a display of new life following old, the living travelling along their own life's road in the footsteps of the departed...

At the graveside, the rector addressed the mourners, lamenting the waste of a life so young and full of promise. Then, from the assembled gathering, a strange lady of untidy, even it could be said, unkempt appearance, passed him a note... and from the note, the priest began to read...

Inside the back cover of this book, you will find a number and a code corresponding to a letter. Your number tells you how far into the note your letter appears and your code tells you what that letter is... Log on to the "thirteen steps mystery" forum at www.porlockholmes.com and add your letter with its corresponding number. When enough are added, what is written on the note which the priest reads out will be revealed.

Notes

1 Lord Wentworth, real name Ralph Gordon Noel King-Milbanke, 2nd Earl of Lovelace, inherited Ashley Combe and the Earldom on the death of his father William King in December 1893. His mother was Ada Byron, daughter of Lord Byron, who married William in 1835 and hence became Ada King until William was created the 1st Earl of Lovelace in 1838, after which she was known as Countess Lovelace, or just Ada Lovelace. She is credited with being the first person to write an algorithm for a calculating engine, the forerunner of what we now know as a computer. She died in 1852 at the age of 36. The tunnels around Ashley Combe were created by William so that Ada could enjoy her privacy.

Ralph died in 1906, but his second wife, Mary Caroline Stuart-Wortley, the Countess Lovelace, lived until April 1941 when she was one month short of her 94th birthday. She often spent time at the house after the death of her husband and was a well-known figure in the village.

Sir Cosmo Drake-Harrington is just a made up character for the story.

2 George Newnes was born in Matlock Bath in 1851 and made his fortune publishing *Tit-Bits*, the gossip magazine of its day. Ten years later he published *The Strand* magazine which is where almost all of the Sherlock Holmes stories first appeared in print. Newnes had a house built on top of Hollerday Hill in Lynton and was a great benefactor for the area.

3 Sir George Newnes financed the construction of two railways: the Lynton and Lynmouth Cliff Railway which is funicular, powered by the weight of water and runs to this day, and the Lynton and Barnstaple Railway which was powered by steam engines and closed in 1935.

4 Threepenny bits (pronounced "thruppenny bit" or "thruppence") were silver in those days and there were eighty to the pound, but you would be able to buy more with a thruppenny bit in 1904 than you could with two pounds now.

5 Arthur Conan Doyle, Scottish medical doctor and author of the Sherlock Holmes stories.

6 Sidney Paget illustrated all of the Sherlock Holmes stories in *The Strand* magazine.

7 On the cliff railway, the passenger compartment of either of the two carriages can be detached, leaving a flat truck which can be used to convey large objects up or down the cliff.

8 In 1835 Ada Byron married William King-Noel, becoming Lady King and subsequently Countess of Lovelace. She is nowadays almost always referred to as Ada Lovelace and, apart from her well known exploits with Charles Babbage and his elementary "computer", what is even more remarkable is that at the age of twelve she experimented with how she might be able to fly, built wings out of various materials, and wrote a book on the subject, illustrating her various designs. She even considered how steam power might be used to propel her through the air.

9 As it happens, it took just one hundred and ten years for this to come to pass.

The "spot-the-differences" and other picture clues

Greedy's Police House

Cell, Helmet, Umbrella, Rat, Candle, Handcuffs
First letters spell CHURCH

Car on Hill Differences

1 Flying bird missing
2 Left arm missing from George
3 Sixpence coin on the side of the road behind the car (clue)
4 Back pocket missing from Arthur's trousers
5 Mirror missing from car
6 Leg missing from dog at rear
7 Nose missing from dog at front
8 Tail missing from second dog
9 Door handle missing on car
10 George's eyebrow missing
11 Spoke missing on front right wheel
12 Hat appears on Sir George
13 Charlie's trouser leg dripping
14 Front left wheel missing on car
15 Tongue added to second dog
16 Jerrycan added in car
17 Radiator cap flying off
18 Lots of sparks and smoke

Beach Differences

1 Seagull missing top right
2 Flag on boat top centre/right
3 Fisherman's net changes to rod
4 Fisherman missing from boat
5 Shell missing top right of upturned boat
6 New shell by front of upturned boat
7 Anchor by upturned boat
8 Fisherman's boots missing
9 Curly end of shell missing by front fisherman
10 New shell beneath front fisherman
11 Starfish missing one leg
12 Spots missing from shell at bottom left
13 Starfish missing
14 Stripes missing from shell left corner
15 Fisherman's stick missing (by lagoon)

16 Fisherman's line missing (in lagoon)
17 New fisherman in lagoon
18 Pirate ship has sailed away (clue)

First Rocks Differences

1 Seagull on left rock eye missing
2 Seagull on rock leg missing
3 Flying seagull wing missing
4 Boat foresail missing
5 Seagulls in distance top right missing
6 Flying seagull beneath boat missing
7 Seagull on right rock missing
8 Bottle below centre rock turned round
9 Seagull appears below centre rock
10 Brazier giving off smoke (clue)
11 Brazier has coal in it
12 Loop missing from end of rope
13 Small crab beneath rope missing
14 Right fluke missing from anchor
15 Rock missing near large crab (middle)
16 Tip of foot missing from large crab (middle)
17 Feather lying on beach
18 Eye missing from large crab (bottom right)
19 Limpet shell missing (bottom centre)
20 "Port" missing from label on bottle (bottom left)

Tunnels Differences

1 Slot in ceiling grating missing
2 One hanging lantern missing
3 One hanging lantern fallen on floor
4 Pirate hat missing from chest bottom right
5 Pistol moved from bottom middle to bottom left
6 Pirate's spyglass (telescope) turned round
7 Florrie's shawl draped over barrel (clue)
8 Tankards on left barrels scattered on floor
9 Goblets on barrels scattered on floor
10 Rear barrel tipped over
11 Pirate money-bag at the back missing
12 Bottles missing from crates and scattered on floor
13 Pirate headscarf missing from floor and hung on wall
14 Pirate headscarf skull and cross-swords missing
15 Pirate hook tipped over
16 Pirate flag moved from wall to crate
17 One sword missing from wall
18 Chain necklace missing from treasure chest
19 One rat missing
20 One rat moved

Stable Differences

1 Horseshoe turned upside down
2 Rung of ladder missing
3 One horse's bit missing from wall
4 Part of stirrup on wall missing
5 Head halter missing from horse
6 Bolt missing from stable door
7 Coach horn replaced by lantern (clue)
8 Coachman's hat and goggles replaced by top hat (clue)
9 Coachman's coat replaced by frock coat (clue)
10 Coachman's whip replaced by walking cane (clue)
11 Riding boots replaced by gentleman's boots (clue)
12 Wooden bucket replaced by metal bucket
13 One stud missing from saddle stand
14 Fishing hook missing
15 Horse's comb missing (bottom left)

Shop Differences

1 Face added to woman's head in picture frame
2 Buttons missing from belt and bodice on dress in middle of rack
3 Pocket and handkerchief missing from coat on rack
4 Right coat on rack missing completely
5 F-hole (the "s" shape bit) missing from violin
6 Pirate costume taken and replaced by coachman's coat (clue)
7 Pirate hat taken and replaced by coachman's hat and goggles (clue)
8 Bottle, pirate hook and teapot replaced by coach horn (clue)
9 Bottle moved to bottom shelf on the right
10 Teapot moved to middle shelf, left of centre
11 Hand missing from face of carriage clock on middle shelf
12 Pistol taken from middle shelf (clue)
13 Fastening button missing from bag, middle shelf far right
14 Keyhole missing from wooden box next to baby carriage
15 Coachman's whip leant against shelves (clue)

Picture of horses ascending hill, 13 steps on the left.

Picture of Betty and stones – pirate earring beneath stone on right

Lime Way Path Differences

1 Eye missing from top bird in tree
2 Twig missing above top bird in tree
3 Tail missing from left bird in tree
4 Distant flying bird above left bird missing
5 New bark pattern on twigs in tree
6 Distant flying bird at top of picture missing
7 Twig missing above right hand flying bird
8 Wing feathers changed on right hand flying bird

9 Vertical slat missing from bench
10 Bird missing from twig in front of bench
11 Nails missing from arms and sides of bench
12 Pistol hidden in undergrowth (clue)
13 Pirate headdress hidden in undergrowth (clue)
14 Far left rabbit in undergrowth missing
15 Paw missing from front centre rabbit
16 Whiskers missing from front centre rabbit
17 Tail missing from front right rabbit
18 Rabbit underneath bench missing
19 Rabbit behind two front rabbits missing
20 Leaves missing from branch above front right rabbit

Church Differences

1 New ceiling lantern top right
2 Pattern added to central ceiling lantern
3 Missing part of cross added on far right wall
4 Border added to panel below cross on right
5 Hinge added on arched wooden door to right of altar
6 Pattern added around arched wooden door to right of altar
7 Flower display placed to right of altar
8 Flower head added to bunch of flowers left of altar
9 Centre hanging flag panel added to front of altar
10 Candlestick placed on altar
11 Two legs added to lectern in front of altar
12 Border added to rug beneath lectern
13 Drawing of saint added to wall frieze behind altar
14 Border added to central panel behind altar
15 Heart added to central cross on altar
14 Teddy bear sitting amongst flowers centre right (clue)
15 Candle placed in candlestick far right
16 Pattern added to centres of flowers front right
17 Hymn book placed on bench front left
18 Leaves added above hymn book
19 (Really difficult one!) Extra pattern added to decoration on back of choir bench right centre

About the author

After a youth spent riding motorcycles much too fast and therefore not imagining he would reach the age of 30, all too soon Jonathan Mountfort became 60 and realised he didn't have a pension, so he wrote this book. By buying it, you have helped him purchase a mug of ale from The Ship Inn or The Castle Hotel or the Royal Oak in Porlock and also encouraged him, through your kindness, to take the time to write another one. Now that you know who all the characters are and what they get up to, hopefully you can't wait!

If you like this book, please tell your friends about it – if they would like a copy then search for "thirteen steps mystery" on Amazon, or track one down from various stockists in Porlock and the surrounding villages. Thank you.

Look out for the next books in the Porlock Holmes series:

Lynmouth – the Mystery of the Arm in the Lobster Pot

Lynton – the Mystery of the Body Bound for Barnstaple

Ilfracombe – the Mystery of the Tunnels Beaches Bathing Beauty

The Scamps – Aide Memoire for readers:

Betsy 7

Herbie 7

Charlie 6

Dougie 5

Fanny 5

Arthur 3

47883238R00157

Printed in Poland
by Amazon Fulfillment
Poland Sp. z o.o., Wrocław